PRAISE FOR *A THOUSAND SHALL FALL*

"*A Thousand Shall Fall* is an intriguing tale of romance in the midst of a country divided. I've long enjoyed Andrea's work and this book was no exception. I look forward to reading book two."
—Tracie Peterson, best-selling author of over one hundred novels, including the Brides of Seattle series and the Heirs of Montana series

"Lovers of Civil War sagas will delight in this historically rich tale. Boeshaar's research shines, making *A Thousand Shall Fall* a sparkling story that leaps from the pages and into the reader's heart."
—Jocelyn Green, award-winning author of the Heroines Behind the Lines Civil War series

"Andrea Boeshaar writes the kind of books I love. They always go to the top of my to-be-read pile. Her settings are authentic, her characters leap off the pages into my heart, and her story lines are interesting. The spiritual threads are not preachy, but show how characters can react to the conflicts of life in a way that leads them to the heart of God."
—Lena Nelson Dooley, award-winning author of *8 Weddings and a Miracle* and *A Texas Christmas*

"Andrea Boeshaar writes compelling Christian historical romance that is a joy to read. She is one of my favorite go-to authors, with a voice so lovely, the spirit of the Lord is clearly felt in her stories."
—Carrie Fancett Pagels, author of *Lilacs for Juliana* and *Return to Shirley Plantation*

"Andrea Boeshaar does it again. With beautiful description and historical detail, *A Thousand Shall Fall* portrays the gamut of emotions from a turbulent time in our great nation's history. With a story of war, heartache, betrayal, and love, Boeshaar captured my attention from the first page."
—Kimberley Woodhouse, best-selling and award-winning author of *Beyond the Silence* and *All Things Hidden*

TOO DEEP *for* WORDS

A Civil War Novel

Shenandoah Valley Saga

ANDREA BOESHAAR

Kregel
Publications

ISBN 978-0-8254-4419-7

Printed in the United States of America
17 18 19 20 21 22 23 24 25 26 / 5 4 3 2 1

This story is dedicated to all United States veterans,
from the Revolutionary War on up through the
generations to today's heroes and heroines.
Thank you for your service to our country—
Let freedom ring!

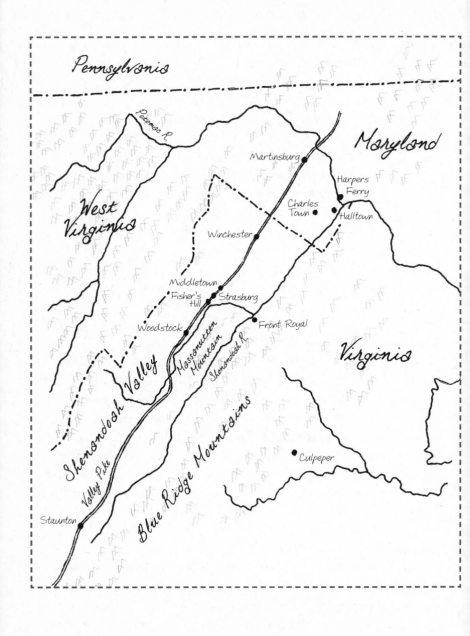

Author's Note

Although the Shenandoah Valley Saga is fictional, much research has gone into this series.

The Shenandoah Valley

Being a Wisconsin native, I had much to learn about Virginia state history during the time of the Civil War. One of the more interesting facts is that because the southern part of the Shenandoah Valley has a higher elevation than the northern part, the Shenandoah River runs northeast and empties into the Potomac. As a result, when one is traveling north on the Valley Pike, from Woodstock to Winchester, for example, one is going *down* the Valley. Traveling south, from Winchester to Staunton, is considered going *up* the Valley. It's opposite the traditional concept of "down south" and "up north."

Whiskey, Cigars, and Pipes

You'll notice that my male characters, even those who are Christians, indulge in a swallow or two of whiskey from time to time, and smoke cigars. In fact, the Union army sent cases or kegs of whiskey to its troops to keep the men's morale up so they would continue fighting. Furthermore, history shows that whiskey was widely used by Union and Confederate troops alike for medicinal purposes, and the occasional brandy and a good cigar were socially acceptable for men. For example, about a decade after America's Civil War,

Charles Spurgeon is reported to have said, "Well, dear friends, you know that some men can do to the glory of God what to other men would be sin. And notwithstanding . . . I intend to smoke a good cigar to the glory of God before I go to bed to-night." While I don't personally condone the practices, I felt it was important that my story be as historically accurate as possible—but without scandalizing my readers.

History Versus Reality

All the dated news reports are authentic from newspapers and telegraphs of that time period. Most have been taken from the Library of Congress's *Chronicling America*. While I did much research, I used my literary license and took great liberties with several prominent historical figures, like General Philip Sheridan and President Abraham Lincoln. I superimposed my characters into Winchester's and Richmond's respective histories, along with Aunt Ruth's home and the Kents' former plantation, Greenwater, and their smaller home, Little Greenwater. Even so, I respected factual accounts and did not diminish either Winchester's or Richmond's significance during the Civil War.

While the first book in my series, *A Thousand Shall Fall*, emphasized the Union, *Too Deep for Words* explores the Confederate side of the war. The state of Virginia, specifically the Shenandoah Valley, was torn in two. It had residents who were both loyalists, for the Union, and secessionists, committed to the Confederacy.

President Lincoln's First Mandated Thanksgiving Day

Abraham Lincoln was the first president to call for an official day of thanksgiving in an 1863 proclamation, which stated in part, "Set apart and observe the last Thursday of November next as a day of thanksgiving." The curator of the Abraham Lincoln Presidential Library and Museum stated that historians are not sure how exactly President Lincoln spent his Thanksgiving Day in 1864. The curator's note to me stated, "We have mainly negative evidence that they rested and gave thanks that day." Therefore, I fictionalized the evening Executive Mansion event. The White House was not yet officially known as the White House at that time.

Lieutenant Colonel John Mosby

According to the colonel's memoir, he actually did suffer a foot injury prior to the Cedar Creek battle and was knocked off his horse by his opponent. However, Mosby's memoir is sketchy as to where he went next, so I embellished the details.

Likewise the Spirit helps us in our weakness;
for we do not know how to pray as we ought,
but the Spirit himself intercedes for us
with sighs too deep for words.
Romans 8:26 (RSV)

TOO DEEP
for
WORDS

CHAPTER 1

October 6, 1864

"Well, I'll be hanged. The Yankee Cavalry is ridin' into Woodstock."

Margaret Jean Bell paused in midstroke and dropped the rag she'd been using to clean the sticky bar. She looked toward the entrance of the Wayfarers Inn where a raggedy-dressed old man stood staring out to the street. "More Yankees in town?"

"That's what I jest said, girl." The old man swayed slightly and kneaded his bristly jaw. "Judging by the black smoke over yonder, them blue-bellies is burning ever'thing in sight too!"

Margaret clutched her midsection. Questions tumbled through her mind. Would one of the Yankee soldiers recognize her and, if so, did he have an inkling of her trickery?

Instinct screamed, *run!* Her breath came and went in quick repetitions, as if she'd already cantered a mile up Main Street.

Breathe. Breathe.

Her lightheadedness slowly abated. Logic soon returned.

Wasn't she accustomed to soldiers, Yanks and Rebs alike? She was, sure as the sun set in the west. She'd learned men were men, bluecoats or gray, and she held her own in their presence, even when they turned violent. Should one of the soldiers insist on getting his money back for services that were promised but never rendered, Margaret would simply tell the truth: Mr. Veyschmidt had snatched her ill-gotten gains. Therefore she was unable to provide him with a refund. Afterward, she'd accept the beating likely to come.

All the louts who frequented the Wayfarers Inn were the same, dark and volatile.

Oh, God, get me out of this place!

Her mind turned to Carrie Ann. How lucky her oldest sister was to escape by marrying a blue-belly. Her younger sister, Sarah Jane, managed to get away by running off with a peddler, except she got herself killed in the process.

Mama too was gone now. Died at the end of September. Now Margaret alone dealt with the temperamental, tyrannical innkeeper who enjoyed reminding her of the debt she owed. And insisted on gold coins for payment no less. He paid her nothing for the daily chores, nothing for serving plates of food and ale to customers. She often worked until the wee hours of the morning when every other eighteen-year-old young lady was fast asleep. And each week the sum she owed grew larger, not smaller. Margaret, in all the rest of her life, could never repay him.

Yes, death was preferable to this wretched existence.

She set down two bottles of Mr. Veyschmidt's backroom concoction, which he called *ale*, on the bar. Then she waited. Soldiers, both Reb and Yank, usually had a powerful thirst when they walked in. They may be on opposite sides of the war, but their behavior was no different.

The portly innkeeper stared out the window and nervously chewed a fingernail. Margaret clenched her jaw. *The swine.* What a blessing it would be if the man got shot dead by a Yankee bullet.

Within minutes, a tall, bearded, blue-clad officer strode over the threshold. His spurs chinked against the plank floorboards and his accoutrements jangled with each step he took. He squinted as his eyes surveyed the room. The gold trim ornamenting his uniform bespoke an upper rank.

Odd. Men of his caliber didn't usually wander into the Wayfarers Inn.

Two additional Yanks followed him. They made such an ominous threesome that the few remaining men loitering about in the saloon scattered like roaches after a match strike.

The first officer made his way to the bar. He removed his wide-brimmed hat and a flicker of familiarity cinched Margaret's gut. Had this man visited the Wayfarers Inn before?

"Care for a drink?" Her question nearly stuck in her suddenly dry mouth. "The innkeeper says it's on the house." She poured a glass of ale and pushed it toward him.

"I said no such thing," Veyschmidt growled. His beady, wide-set eyes sized up the large officer and his comrades. He reconsidered, just as Margaret expected him to. "Well, all right. But only one's free."

"No, thanks. I'm looking for Miss Margaret Bell."

Her heart stumbled over its next beat.

"That's her." Mr. Veyschmidt pointed a thick finger. "Right there, she stands."

No help or hope of protection from him—as usual.

Margaret set her hands on her hips. "Listen, mister, I don't give refunds, so—"

"Are you Miss Bell?"

She nodded and lifted her chin, fully expecting an explosion of pain from his fist connecting with her face. If he was like all the others, she'd swindled him. She prayed he'd knock her senseless. Maybe she'd never regain consciousness.

"My wife would like two jugs of the innkeeper's ale."

Margaret's tension eased and she released an audible sigh of relief.

"She claims the ale aids in the healing of wounds. In fact, I'm living proof it does." The Yankee's mustache twitched with a small smile. "She also insists the stuff is a marvelous metal polisher. Wonder of wonders." He pierced Veyschmidt with a saber-sharp stare.

"Metal polisher?" Margaret tipped her head. The only person who touted Mr. Veyschmidt's ale as good for anything other than sheer inebriation was . . .

Margaret sucked in a breath. Surely this wasn't her oldest sister's Yankee husband?

She considered the officer again. Not a chance. This man was large and handsome with a head of thick blond hair and neatly trimmed whiskers. His rank and demeanor suggested he was too refined for a poor, skinny, pie-in-the-sky dreamer like Carrie Ann. More likely a customer heard of the ale's supposed benefits and spread the word. Medicine was scarce, what with wounded men pouring into towns up and down the Valley, so every sort of home remedy was in high demand.

Margaret fetched two stoneware jugs and set them on the bar. The officer slapped a couple of bills into Veyschmidt's wide, outstretched palm. Next the colonel retrieved an envelope from his coat's inner breast pocket and extended it in Margaret's direction.

"May I speak with you in private, Miss Bell?"

Before a single utterance passed her lips, Mr. Veyschmidt stepped in front of her as if she'd suddenly become a precious commodity. "Afraid not, Mister. You want *a private appointment*, shall we say, then you'll have to pay for it like everyone else."

The blond officer's expression hardened. "I suggest you shut your mouth and get out of my way."

Veyschmidt eyed the man, snorted, but relented. "Make it quick," he muttered to Margaret. "And you owe me every coin you get out of him."

She squeezed her eyes shut. If hating a man was indeed the same as murder like the reverend preached, then she was guilty a thousand times over.

The colonel moved several steps away from Mr. Veyschmidt. Margaret forced panic down and fingered the small vial of potion in her pocket. It was her only source of protection.

"Allow me to introduce myself, Miss Bell. I'm Colonel Peyton Collier, Cavalry Division of the Army of the Shenandoah."

Collier. So this was indeed Carrie's husband. How had her sister snagged such a fine gentleman?

"I understand you're my brother-in-law."

"Yes, that's correct."

"Well, well . . ." Veyschmidt stepped out from behind the bar and puffed out his barrel-like chest. "What a coincidence. Your, eh, wife, left quite a large tab here what needs to be paid."

Colonel Collier's face reddened and his eyes narrowed to angry slits. "Spare me more of your lies. My wife owes you nothing." Anger blazed in his gaze as he defended Carrie Ann. "Destroying your inn would be within my orders, but it's because of my wife's request to leave this place intact for her family's sake that I hesitate." He glanced at Margaret before peering down at Veyschmidt again. "I am well aware of your abuse of the Bell sisters and their mother over the past two years. They came to you in need, but week after week you overcharged them for room and board despite their hard work. In short, you enslaved them. Worse, you left my wife and her family unprotected and vulnerable to every kind of evil." The shake of his head was slight. "You are a despicable worm in my estimation and had it been up to me—"

"Please, sir . . ." Mr. Veyschmidt's voice sounded shaky and his beady eyes grew round.

Margaret tucked her chin to hide her amusement. She liked her new brother-in-law already.

"It would give me great pleasure," he added, "to watch this sorry place go up in flames."

Mr. Veyschmidt wisely held his tongue, although he chewed his thick lower lip and worked his hands anxiously. Margaret knew why.

"Pardon the interruption, sir," one of the other Yankees said. He stood even taller and had even broader shoulders than the colonel. He too had removed his hat and an abundance of shaggy brown hair framed his face. "This establishment has most likely been a Rebel meeting place and gave sustenance to the enemy. I suspect Rebels are recovering in rooms upstairs as we speak."

"No, no. Ain't no soldiers here," Mr. Veyschmidt insisted. "I refused all the wounded. Don't want the mess, the blood and all." He waved a meaty hand and shuddered.

The colonel's eyes met Margaret's and she gave a slight nod. Confederate soldiers had met here only days ago. Several injured lay in rooms upstairs as the major suspected.

"Gather your men and search the premises, Major Johnston."

"Yes, sir."

Within minutes, a small army of Yankees crowded into the Wayfarers Inn. Mr. Veyschmidt grew increasingly anxious as the soldiers dispersed to search. He fell to his knees in a pathetic, theatrical display.

"Please don't burn my inn," he begged. "This business is all I have left of my dearly departed mother who worked her fingers to the bone to make this a respectable place for one to lay his weary head."

Margaret rolled her eyes and barely kept from snorting aloud. What lies! And respectable? How utterly laughable.

"Miss Bell?" The colonel's brown eyes fixed on her. "I am allowed to show mercy where it's warranted. What do you think I should do?"

"Me? You're asking me?"

"Don't bother with the girl," Veyschmidt groused. "She's nothing. Customers often complain about her poor service. She's brazen and rude."

"Quiet, you scoundrel!" The colonel turned back to Margaret. "Miss Bell?"

"I have no place to go." Despite her best efforts, her bottom lip quivered. It wasn't the answer she longed to give.

"It's my belief that my wife will want you and your mother to live with us in Winchester. She's been worried about you. But given the fact I'm a Yankee, your mother most likely will not accept my invitation."

"Mama's dead," Margaret blurted, "and I doubt my sister will want me living with her now that she's married."

A scene from the past clouded her mind. They were girls and on the farm and she and Carrie were quarreling. As usual, Carrie was demanding that Margaret complete some menial chore and Margaret was refusing to obey. They were only nine months apart in age. Margaret thought she and Carrie should be equals, but Carrie was determined to hang on to her eldest daughter status which included being the boss when their parents weren't anywhere in sight.

The memory faded and the harsh reality of Margaret's surroundings pressed in on her. Things had changed. She missed Carrie's bravery. What's more, she hadn't begun to fathom just how much Carrie had protected her and Sarah Jane until she herself bore the brunt of drunken patrons' groping and Veyschmidt's beatings.

Remembering the bruise on her cheek, Margaret finger-combed strands of hair onto one side of her face.

"Please accept my condolences—on your mother's passing and your younger sister's also."

The colonel's deep voice recaptured Margaret's attention. He sounded sincere. He reached across the scuffed wooden bar and pressed the sealed envelope into Margaret's hand.

She inspected it, impressed by the expensive parchment. She couldn't read well, hardly at all, but she recognized her own name penned across the front of the envelope in Carrie Ann's neat handwriting.

She closed her eyes. To her left, Mr. Veyschmidt's pleas for mercy grated on her nerves.

"Carrie addressed this letter to you personally because she guessed your mother would refuse to read the missive. She didn't suppose that your mother would ever forgive her for Sarah Jane's death."

"Carrie was almost right." Margaret traced each letter with her fingertip. "You see, I received the telegram about Carrie Ann's marriage and about Sarah Jane's death, but Mama had passed on by the time the news arrived."

"You've survived quite an ordeal, Miss Bell. I urge you to come to Winchester. You can safely travel with a group of freed slaves and German Baptists called Dunkers who are following the army down the Valley. Because of the war, they've been forced to leave their homes for one reason or another." The colonel walked around the bar. Standing directly in front of Margaret, he tapped the envelope in her hand. "Besides, you'll be doing me a huge favor." Mischief glimmered in his eyes. "My wife will be quite miffed at me if I allow you to remain here." His gaze darkened as it fell over Mr. Veyschmidt, who pleaded for the soldiers to spare his establishment. "In fact, miffed is putting it mildly."

This cavalryman was afraid of Carrie's wrath? Surely not.

The colonel's features softened as he regarded Margaret again. "Carrie volunteers at an orphanage. If I were a betting man, I'd say that she will want you to help out there too. Many hands make light work."

"Oh, I would. I love children." Margaret's mind whirred with new possibilities.

"Sounds like you'll do very well in Winchester then."

One of his officers interrupted them. Margaret stepped back. The colonel appeared quite confident as he spoke with the other man, but not in an arrogant way. He scanned the dark interior of the inn with an unspoken authority. Margaret got the feeling he wasn't a man to argue with . . .

So how did he manage Carrie and her sharp tongue? The idea that this man even married Carrie was most curious.

Margaret couldn't wait to find out the answers to her many questions.

The colonel's troops finished their search and he conversed with them in undertones. Minutes later, they filed out of the inn, and he refocused his attention on Margaret. "I'm afraid I must have your decision now, Miss Bell."

She only needed one glimpse of Mr. Veyschmidt, whose beefy hands were now clasped as if in prayer—the same hands that shamelessly groped and beat Margaret and her sisters, each to varying degrees. And Mama too. He'd killed Mama the same as if he'd strangled the life right out of her.

Oh, how Margaret despised the man!

"I accept your invitation, Colonel. Thank you." She tasted sweet freedom in the air. "But please, I beseech you"—now it was her turn to beg—"light your Yankee torches and burn this den of iniquity down to the devil where it belongs!"

October 11, 1864

Dispatch:
STRASBURG, Va. Midnight, Oct. 9. 1864

Lieutenant General U.S. Grant, City Point:

In coming back to this point I was not followed up until late yesterday, when a large force of cavalry appeared in my rear.

I then halted my command to offer battle by attacking the enemy. I became satisfied that it was only all the rebel cavalry of the valley, commanded by Rosser [CSA] and directed Torbert [USA] to attack at daylight this morning, and finish this "Saviour of the Valley" [aka Rosser].

The attack was handsomely made. Custer, commanding 3d cavalry division, charged on the back road, and Merritt, commanding the 1st cavalry division, on the Strasburg pike. Merritt captured five pieces of artillery; Custer captured six pieces of artillery, with caissons, battery forge, etc. The two divisions captured forty-seven wagons, ambulances, etc. Among the wagons captured are the headquarters wagons of Rosser, Lomax, Wickham, and Col. Pollard [CSA].

The number of prisoners will be about 330.

P. H. Sheridan, Major General

Chapter 2

October 14, 1864

Such sad musings—and on a night when the sky appeared so magnificent too. Brilliant stars gleamed like diamonds on ebony velvet. Seemed a shame to waste a show of God's splendor on useless tears.

Carrie Ann Collier opened her bedroom window a little wider and poked her head out to get a better view of the glimmering heavens. The autumn breeze had a nip to it, but she ignored it to imagine Sarah Jane walking in God's majestic kingdom. True, the girl had tried Carrie's patience plenty of times, but she didn't deserve to suffer at the hands of a low-life peddler.

Would things have been different if Carrie kept a closer eye on her youngest sister?

But when? How? Carrie had been trying to keep Papa's newspaper alive and keep up with her chores at the Wayfarers Inn too.

And then one day Sarah Jane was gone; she'd run away.

If only Carrie had found her sister sooner . . .

Her eyes filled with a new onset of moist regret, but then the pounding of hooves sounded an alert before they even rode into the yard. Her heartbeat quickened—

And then she caught sight of them. Several blue-backed horsemen. *Union horsemen.*

She blinked and one particularly gallant officer came into view. He looked up at the window. Carrie's heart somersaulted.

He's home!

She closed the window and rushed to the basin where she splashed water on her face. It wouldn't do for Peyton to suspect that she'd been crying. She'd read somewhere that the most important duty of an army officer's wife was keeping up her husband's spirits so when he faced his adversaries on the battlefield, he wasn't distracted by troubles at home. It was a duty Carrie welcomed, even relished.

After quickly brushing her hair, Carrie hastily tied back her mass of auburn curls with a pretty gold ribbon, and then she headed for the door. From the corner of her eye, she caught sight of the dying embers in the hearth beckoning for attention. Peyton had been sleeping outside in the elements and would welcome a warm bedroom.

She tossed more kindling in and banked the fire, satisfied when its flames licked upward.

And now to greet her husband. . .

Carrie dashed from their bed chamber and headed for the steps. About halfway down, she met Peyton, who was taking the stairs two at a time.

"Welcome home, darling." In her excitement, she missed the next step.

Peyton caught her, his eyes wide. "Oh, the calamity that could have just occurred."

Before an apology could leave her tongue, he had drawn her closer and pressed his lips to hers. Carrie closed her eyes, enjoying the warmth of his embrace that sent a shiver down her arms.

He pulled back gently and helped her regain her footing. "You needn't throw yourself into my arms every time I come home, Mrs. Collier."

She tipped her head and batted her lashes. "No?"

He chuckled. "No."

"Then I'll reserve it for special occasions."

"You do that."

"Colonel, sir, where would you like your gear?"

With an impatient huff, Peyton turned on their stair and gave parting instructions to the enlisted man. Then his aide, Major Vernon Johnston, appeared.

"Sorry about that, sir. The men know they aren't supposed to enter the house."

"It's all right . . . *this time*." Taking Carrie's hand, he led her the rest of the way up. "New enlisted man in my regiment," he whispered. "Vern will straighten him out."

They reached the upstairs hallway where Vern's wife Meredith met them in her satin night wrapper. Her soft brown hair hung in waves to her hips. A blush stole across her face, illuminated by the lamp she held.

"Nice to see you, Colonel. I hope you're returning my husband unscathed."

"I am, Mrs. Johnston. And your husband will be up shortly."

Carrie heard the smile in his voice above the feigned formalities. Major Vern Johnston was Peyton's closest friend, and Meredith had become like a sister to Carrie.

"And now if you'll excuse us . . ."

"Of course. Welcome home, Peyton."

They continued to their quarters, comprised of a sitting room, a bedroom, and an alcove for dressing, fronted by a wooden screen for added privacy. Once inside the door, Carrie pivoted and peered up into Peyton's face.

"I'm so happy to see you."

"I should hope so. We haven't been married long enough for you to have grown bored with me."

"Oh, Peyton, don't tease."

Smiling, he stepped farther into the room where he tugged off his leather gauntlets. "No sense of humor tonight, my sweet?"

"I worry about you when you're away."

"I worry about you too." He tossed the pair of gold sheathes followed by his blue slouch hat onto a nearby chair.

"I'm perfectly safe here in Winchester, so you have no need to fret."

"Are you saying I should leave all that nonsense, the worrying and fretting, to you?"

"Yes."

Peyton chuckled lightly and raked his fingers over his dark blond hair.

Carrie's exasperation mounted. "Have you no idea how much I miss you when you're gone?"

Peyton's brows drew inward. "Was I gone that long?"

"Eight days." They'd only been married fourteen days, total.

How did the other soldiers' wives manage without seeing their husbands for months—even years? Carrie had been spoiled by Peyton's close proximity. As a colonel in General Sheridan's Army of the Shenandoah, his business kept him in the Valley.

"Missed me, you say?"

"Yes, I say."

Swooping her off her feet, Peyton spun her around. "You'd better miss me!" He smothered her giggle with a fervent kiss that made Carrie ache with desire, but all too soon he set her feet back on the carpet. "Unfortunately, I'm not home for long."

"What?" Disappointment quickly replaced longing. "But why?" It was a foolish question.

"General Merritt's entire cavalry division has been assigned to accompany General Sheridan on a mission." He unfastened the front of his shell jacket. "We leave tomorrow."

"Tomorrow? But—" She swallowed her complaint. She'd married a Union cavalryman and his duty reigned supreme. For now, anyway. "What sort of mission?"

"Nothing you'd find interesting, my little journalist." He shrugged out of his jacket.

Carrie sent him a look of mild reproof while he unbuttoned his shirt. "I wasn't asking as a journalist, but as your wife."

Peyton lifted the corners of his mouth. "Oh, yes, I have a wife, don't I?

She slapped his arm and he didn't say more. Obviously, he wouldn't expound on his mission, and perhaps it was better she didn't know details. "Well, at least we have a little time to spend together."

His features softened. No doubt he appreciated her understanding, even if it didn't come from her heart. If she had her way, he would resign his command and the two of them would travel to England. Carrie stifled a sigh. She would have to wait until the war ended for her honeymoon.

"Speaking of journalism, Peyton, the newspapers reported skirmishes up the Valley and in surrounding areas. Each time I prayed God would protect you." *And that you would keep your promise to spare Valley residents and their homes.*

"God heard those petitions, my love." He removed his suspenders, and then gathered her in his arms once more. His lips found hers in the sweetest of kisses. "Carrie," he whispered against her cheek, "if I should fall—"

"Peyton! I won't hear of it." But even as the words rolled off her tongue, she spied the silver chain he wore around his neck and the cross that dangled from it. Inscribed on the pendent were his name, army, and regiment.

"Yes, that's what you said last time I broached the subject, and the time before that. We need to have this discussion, Carrie." He placed his hands on her upper arms. "Did you at least hear what I told you to do if . . . if the worst should happen?"

She clamped her mouth shut, unwilling to have this particular conversation. However, the iron determination shining in Peyton's golden-brown eyes cracked her resolve. "Yes, I heard you. I contact Mr. Finch, your solicitor."

"Correct, and he'll handle all the rest."

She understood.

"And don't wear black when I'm gone. I'll be in heaven, walking the streets of gold."

"Stop it, Peyton. What's wrong with you tonight?"

He cupped her chin. "You're too young for widow's weeds and too pretty to wear black. Besides the color is utterly depressing."

"Widow's weeds?" She slapped his hand away. "Why are you tormenting me? I don't find it amusing in the least."

"I'm sorry, my dearest. I'm afraid I've seen my share of despondent wives lately. Widows in black, looking so lost and forlorn. I've offered to help them, but I'm a Northern Invader—their enemy, and the cause of their suffering." He held Carrie close. Nestled against him, she felt safe, protected, and cherished. She heard his heartbeat, strong and steady. "I need to rest assured that you, Aunt Ruth, and Tabitha will be all right when I'm gone." He planted a kiss on top of her head.

"When you're gone?" Carrie stepped back and stared up at him. Two could play this morbid game. "Why, you're much too ornery to die in battle." She arched a brow. "Besides, you survived the injuries you sustained at Gettysburg." The fact guaranteed nothing, but it sparked a hope in Carrie's soul that maybe God wasn't through using Peyton here on earth.

"All right." He pushed out a smile that appeared born out of sheer acquiescence and nothing more, and pressed a kiss on her forehead. "Always remember, my sweet Carrie Ann, that I love you with all my heart."

"And I will always love you, Peyton." Her fingertips found the cross-shaped pendant that rested against the soft matting of chest hair. "May we talk of better things now?"

"We may." The upturned corners of his mouth became a full-fledged smile. "However, I fear I reek. My apologies. Tabitha is filling the tub."

"At this late hour?" Carrie gave a wag of her head, although the odor emanating from Peyton's body was rather . . . ripe. "I'm sure she had something to say about that."

"She suggested it actually . . . right after she scolded me about tramping through her kitchen with my spurs on." Peyton's golden-brown eyes twinkled. "I know better, but my mind was on other things."

Warmth crept into Carrie's face.

"But apparently Tabitha's sense of smell is as keen as anyone's. She's heating water for Vern also, except one of us will be using the smaller tub, so I plan to get downstairs first."

"What about your men?"

"They will have to use the bathhouse in town. Tabitha's good graces have their limits."

"Indeed." Carrie imagined the freed black woman's reaction to Peyton and Vern, traipsing in after dark. Nonetheless, Tabitha was as much a Collier as Carrie, and she took pride in caring for her family in addition to her housekeeping and cooking. She wasn't shy about letting everyone know of her efforts. But in spite of Tabitha's craggy disposition, Carrie had come to care deeply for the older woman—almost as much as she cared for Peyton's mischievous spinster aunt, Ruth Collier.

"I trust Tabitha isn't giving you too much guff."

"No more than I can handle."

"Aunt Ruth has been behaving?"

"Of course. That is—as far as I know."

Peyton groaned. "I hate to think what that means."

"It means I do have a sense of humor tonight."

"Ahh . . ." He chuckled.

"Seriously, everything here is as fine as spring rain, Peyton. If not, I would say so."

"I trust you would." He dropped onto the settee. "Any financial business I need to be aware of?"

"None."

"Excellent. I have an appointment to see Mr. Finch tomorrow morning. Afterward, I'll rejoin my regiment."

"That means I'll only have you here with me for a few hours tonight."

"I'm afraid so, although . . ."

"Yes?" Carrie perked up.

"A photographer set up his tent just outside town. How about if you and I get our photographs taken after my appointment?"

"That sounds delightful. I've never had my photograph taken."

"Ah, well, then, it's about time." He smiled. "And I have another surprise for you."

"Oh?" Perhaps he'd inform her that he wouldn't be gone long.

"My troops and I made it to Woodstock and I personally handed your letter to Margaret."

"And?" Carrie wondered over the reaction of her sister—or stepsister, if her childhood friend Joshua Blevens had been correct. They'd made a pact as children never to lie to one another, and certainly Joshua wouldn't lie about something like her mother and sister Margaret not being blood kin. "What was Margaret's response?"

"She's coming for an extended visit."

"Here?" Wide-eyed, Carrie shook her head. "No. Please tell me you're joking." She clenched her jaw. Margaret never shared the responsibilities that weighed heavily on Carrie's shoulders. She added to them. With the wicked innkeeper's blessing, Margaret became a shameless hussy and would only bring scandal to the Colliers' doorstep. "I don't want her here."

"I had no idea you felt that way." Peyton's forehead creased and his eyebrows drew inward. "I was certain of quite the opposite. I assumed you would insist she come. She's alone and has nowhere to go."

"The Wayfarers Inn is her home."

"Not any longer. It burned to the ground at your sister's request, and in keeping with my orders."

"It's gone?" A rush of emotions flooded Carrie's being. Relief that she'd never see the likes of that place again, vindication that now Mr. Veyschmidt was homeless and as vulnerable as Carrie, her sisters, and mother had been two years ago. However, what rose to a greater level was the trepidation over her stepsister's impending visit. Mama, of course, wouldn't deign to visit a Yankee's home. "You said Margaret is alone . . . of course my stepmother, being a loyal Confederate, wouldn't step foot into our home."

"I'm so sorry . . ." Peyton's expression softened. "Your mother is dead."

"Dead?" She spun toward the hearth, her eyes burning with sudden, unshed tears. Despite the abuse and threats Mama delivered, along with Joshua's news, grief tore at her heart.

Carrie found her voice. "I guess I'm not surprised Mama died, given her poor health."

"Your sister said she passed before ever learning of Sarah Jane's tragic fate."

So the news hadn't killed Mama as Carrie feared. She was grateful Peyton didn't push the subject. He knew about her painful past.

Hearing his grunt, she glanced over her shoulder. Peyton struggled to remove his knee-high leather boots. Carrie crossed the room and bent to help him.

"I suppose Margaret convinced you that we owe her more than the dress I lost that day after I left Woodstock."

"I invited her to come, Carrie. I decided she'd be safe enough following the army north, down the Valley."

Carrie gave a last tug on his boot and it slid off. "When will she arrive?"

"To be honest, I thought she'd be here by now."

"Perhaps she enjoys being a camp follower." Carrie had spent time in a Union camp, particularly traveling in its rear with ambulances, medical personnel, and followers who'd attached themselves to the army. Some were necessary, even vital to the army, like the sutlers who provided services from blacksmithing to saddling and shoemaking. Others, like the Dunkers, were abolitionists and followed the army north to escape Confederate persecution.

And others offered services that were unmentionable in good company.

"Margaret may have already found her new home." Carrie set Peyton's boots near the door. She turned to face him and placed her hands on her hips.

Peyton unfastened the cufflinks on his shirt. Carrie's cheeks warmed at his probing perusal. "I'm shocked by your heartless reaction. I anticipated the opposite. You're kind and giving to others. I admire your volunteer work at the orphanage. I assumed you'd insist upon caring for your sister."

"Why would I?"

"Because she's family and next to God's firm foundation, a person's family provides love and stability."

"My family was never stable. You know that. What's more, Margaret is no relation to me."

"So says Blevens." Peyton collapsed against the back of the settee, opposite the hearth. "And I thought we discussed this already."

Carrie lifted one shoulder. It was true. They'd talked about the matter in great length, but she couldn't seem to shake the doubt.

"You cannot trust the word of a spy. I suspect Blevens dropped that lie in an effort to manipulate you and nothing more."

"Joshua wouldn't lie to me." The words were out before Carrie thought better of them.

Peyton arched one brow. "You still defend him?"

Carrie glanced away. She couldn't stand to see the disappointment in Peyton's eyes, yet she believed what she said was true. "I do not defend Joshua or his despicable actions here on our wedding night. But he did keep his promise to me when he located Sarah Jane."

Peyton muttered something under his breath and Carrie wished she'd never spoken Joshua's name tonight. He had nearly torn apart her relationship with Peyton. Once her most trusted friend, Joshua now sought to divide and destroy based solely on political principles—and he'd nearly accomplished his goal earlier this month. As it was, his deception caused sixteen-year-old Tommy to be shot during an act of heroics. Carrie and Peyton had both been fond of the boy, but now Peyton wanted revenge. He had vowed to kill Joshua if their paths crossed again. And Joshua would like nothing more than to meet the challenge. He viewed all Yankees as traitors and invaders—Carrie included. Truly, Joshua was the enemy.

Even so, he was most likely right about her family. It made sense. Carrie never fit in. As a girl she had often followed Papa to his newspaper office to escape Mama's demeaning rants. The newspaper office had been her refuge while growing up on the farm. She could still recall the pungent smell of the ink as Papa ran off his two-sided newspaper copies.

"Carrie, give your sister a chance." Peyton's deep voice cut through her thoughts. "I believed you would be pleased that I got her out of the Wayfarers

Inn. You'll find that she's changed a lot in the past couple of months. She's no longer that flirty, naïve girl. After you left, Margaret fell under Veyschmidt's tyrannical thumb. Things got worse for her, and it seemed to me that she has learned some valuable life lessons as a result."

Valuable life lessons, indeed. Carrie turned toward the hearth. Did Margaret blame her for the abuse she'd suffered at Mr. Veyschmidt's hand? Carrie winced. She could still feel the explosion in her cheek when Veyschmidt's fist met her face.

"You've changed for the better, Carrie. Why can't Margaret have changed for the better too?"

Carrie didn't have a reply.

"On a more pleasant subject, I managed to purchase a couple of jugs of Veyschmidt's ale before torching his establishment." Peyton's tone held a note of amusement. Clearly, he wanted to lighten the tension between them.

She forced a smile. Not only did Mr. Veyschmidt's ale have healing properties but it also shined silver, which would be favorable news to Tabitha. "Thank you, Peyton."

He sent her a devilish but utterly charming wink and Carrie's stormy mood dissipated. "No, my wife doesn't require expensive gifts upon my return. She wants home-brewed ale, guaranteed to rot a man's gut right through."

A little laugh popped out of her mouth. "Forgive me for having a poor attitude about my sister's visit."

"Forgiven . . . and forgotten." Peyton took hold of Carrie's wrist and tugged until she landed on his knee. "Did I tell you that I missed you?"

"Yes, I believe you did." She slipped her arms around his corded neck. She could count on one hand the days she'd spent with Peyton since their wedding. "But I'm getting tired of sharing you with the Union army."

"It won't be for much longer." He lay her down against the cushioned settee. He brushed several tresses off her cheek and then touched his lips to hers.

"Peyton?"

"Hmm . . ." He sounded distracted as his lips trailed to her neck then her collarbone.

"About that bath . . ."

He brought his head up sharply. "That bad, eh?"

She replied with a weak smile. While months ago, she probably smelled worse than he did at this moment, she'd quickly become acclimated to more pleasing aromas.

With a growl, Peyton stood and collected clean clothes. "I'll be back," he said with husky promise.

"I'll be waiting."

Carrie smiled as he left, although it soon faded from her lips. Thoughts of her sister's arrival plagued her anew. God had blessed her with a new life here with Peyton, Tabitha, and Aunt Ruth. Meredith too.

Yes, Carrie belonged here. She had a new home with a new family. She married a prince of a man—a man she loved beyond reason. Her life was a fairy tale come true. She hated to think of Margaret barging in—and bringing a healthy dose of reality with her.

CHAPTER 3

October 16, 1864

"This is it, ma'am."

Margaret glanced up at the two-story limestone home as the army wagon pulled to such a swift halt it nearly unseated her. She glared at the Yankee holding the reins and bit back a remark about his poor driving skills. She couldn't—and wouldn't—chance embarrassing her new brother-in-law.

"Thank you, sergeant." She climbed down off the wagon unassisted. Few Yankees possessed gentlemanly skills, particularly this one who had a penchant for spitting chew across her feet every five minutes. How grateful she was to finally arrive at her destination.

The soldier handed down her bundle of meager belongings. Margaret accepted it, careful not to make eye contact or allow her fingers to brush alongside his tobacco-stained ones. She didn't want to give him or any man the wrong impression of her character. In Winchester, she'd begin a new life—as a lady, not a hussy.

After an oblique nod of gratitude, Margaret turned toward the imposing structure. Behind her the wagon rattled its way down the road.

My, my . . . Carrie Ann's home promised an enormous improvement over the dingy, drafty Wayfarers Inn. Even so, this structure was not without its battle scars. Like many villages and cities in the Valley, Winchester bore the evidence of the destruction capable of both armies. Margaret had seen the many buildings that lay in rubble on her way through town only minutes ago. The entire wall of one home was sheared off and now the owner's painted rooms and furnishings lay exposed to the world and vulnerable to the elements.

Margaret knew the feeling.

She climbed the steps leading to the front door of what Colonel Collier had called Piccadilly Place. She eyed the two tall pillars that rose to the second story and supported a rectangular roof that covered the porch below. The black shutters framing the long windows were in obvious need of paint, and one hung loose. But even in its state of disrepair, Margaret easily imagined this home's prewar grandeur.

The front door opened and a finely dressed woman with auburn hair stepped onto the portico.

Carrie Ann! Margaret almost didn't recognize her. Her usually wild tresses were neatly coiffed and her too-thin frame seemed to have blossomed into womanly curves with the additional weight she'd obviously gained. No wonder that Yankee colonel married her.

"I was beginning to worry." Carrie Ann's hands twisted a hankie, and Margaret recognized the unease in her sister. "My husband stopped home on Friday and said he'd expected you days ago."

"The Yankees got pushed back up the Valley a couple of times." In all likelihood, crawling down the pike may have proven faster than following the army.

Carrie Ann smiled. "Well, at least you're here now." She stepped farther onto the porch, and Margaret's gut constricted. Her sister's smile was tight— the one reserved for the troublesome men at the inn. "We arrived home from church only minutes ago, so your timing is perfect."

Yes, of course. It was the Sabbath. Margaret had lost track of the days since leaving Woodstock.

"You've changed." The words slipped out before Margaret realized how they sounded. "For the better, of course, but in such a short time."

"I have my husband's family to credit for it."

Carrie stood only a foot or two away and Margaret picked up the faint smell of lavender. By contrast, Margaret radiated grime and sweat. She'd likely offend everyone in the house.

With her free hand, she attempted to tuck strands of hair into its hopeless braid. Perhaps she should go back to the army camp.

Carrie's eyes followed Margaret's movements and compassion seemed to slip into her expression. "How about a bath, a snack, and then a long nap before dinner tonight?"

Relief washed over Margaret. "You read my thoughts. I'd like that very much."

Carrie swept into the house. A delectable aroma greeted Margaret in the entrance hall.

"Do I smell fried chicken?" Much to her chagrin, Margaret's stomach grumbled loud enough for her sister to hear. But she couldn't help it. When had she last eaten a decent meal? Not since Carrie Ann left Woodstock, that's for sure. Mr. Veyschmidt had monitored Margaret's every morsel as the price of foodstuff grew higher in the South each day. Eating a chicken dinner on a Sunday afternoon was, indeed, a mere memory and a wish.

"Your sense of smell is correct, and Tabitha makes the best fried chicken I've ever tasted. But we'll postpone dinner until after you're settled."

"I hate to impose."

"No imposition. As I mentioned, we've been expecting you." Carrie behaved like a wealthy, schooled woman. How had she become such a fine lady in so short a time? Of course, she did read newspapers and all those books about highfalutin heiresses . . .

Margaret ran her tongue over her bottom lip as she took in the fine paintings on the wall before turning back to her sister. At Carrie's pinched smile, Margaret snapped her mouth closed.

"We have a lot to discuss, don't we?"

Margaret gave a nod. "Yes . . . a lot."

"But first things first." She turned to the tall, slender woman with a head of expertly styled silver hair. "I'd like to present my husband's aunt, Miss Ruth Collier."

The woman came forward and took Margaret's hand and held it between her smooth, cool palms. "Call me Aunt Ruth. We are, after all, related now."

"Very well . . . *Aunt Ruth.*" The words tasted strange on Margaret's tongue.

"And you can call me Tabitha," said a dark-faced woman coming into view. She matched Aunt Ruth's height and slender build. "I'm the one who runs this here house." She perched her hands on her waist and her dark eyes settled on Carrie. "I suppose this girl's wantin' a bath."

"Yes, ma'am, she does."

Had Carrie just called a Negress "ma'am"? Her sister surely must be a Yankee now.

"And I suppose she wants to eat afterwards."

"Correct again, Tabitha."

"Then dinner'll be late today. I can't do everything, you know?"

"We're more than happy to wait," Aunt Ruth said.

"And I'll help," Carrie offered.

"No, you won't. I ain't so old that I can't heat water and fill a tub." With a huff, Tabitha marched down a long corridor.

Carrie Ann and Aunt Ruth exchanged glances and smiles.

"Oh, don't mind her." Aunt Ruth regarded Margaret, her hazel eyes dancing in a mix of apology and amusement. "Tabitha's bark is worse than her bite, as the adage goes."

Another woman, one with soft-brown curls framing her oval face, descended the stairs.

"Meredith." Carrie Ann spoke the name with a warmth in her tone that made Margaret envious. "I hope we didn't disturb your rest."

"Not at all. I hoped our husbands had returned."

"Wishful thinking, my dear." Aunt Ruth met her at the foot of the steps and guided her toward Margaret. "Mrs. Meredith Johnston, meet Carrie Ann's sister, Miss Margaret Bell."

"A pleasure, Miss Bell."

"Mrs. Johnston." Margaret wondered if the woman was any relation to Confederate General Joseph Johnston. In this crazy war, a man's political and moral views often trumped the well-being of blood relatives.

"Meredith's husband, Major Vernon Johnston, is Peyton's friend and camp aide."

Something clicked. "I believe I may have met him. Is he a bearded, burly fellow?"

"That's my Vern." Adoration stuck to each syllable.

"He was one of the Yankees with Colonel Collier who rescued me from the Wayfarers Inn." Margaret had relished watching the place go up in flames. "I never dreamed I'd be grateful to the Yankees, but I am."

Carrie gestured to the stairs. "Come, Margaret. I'll show you to your room."

Aunt Ruth took a step back. "I look forward to getting further acquainted with you, Miss Bell."

Mrs. Johnston echoed the sentiment.

Margaret replied with a polite bob of her head and followed her sister.

"Later I'll show you around the rest of the house."

"There's more?"

"The parlor, the music room, Peyton's study, which doubles as the men's smoking room if we have dinner guests. And then my favorite room, the library."

"Yes, of course you'd like the library." Carrie had always had a penchant for books. "How did you get so lucky?"

Her sister paused on the steps and turned to peer at her. Sunlight filtered through a stained-glass window. "I prefer to think of it as blessed and not luck at all."

"So what did you have to do to get this . . . *blessed*?"

"I fell in love." Margaret again fell into step behind Carrie Ann.

The polished mahogany of the ornately carved railing gleamed, as did the dark plank floor of the corridor at the top.

"That's it? You didn't do anything at all?"

"I didn't have to." Carrie Ann paused at a closed door. Her hand curled around the ornate knob. "God took care of the details."

—◌ ◌—

"Rider's coming in!"

Lieutenant Colonel Elijah Kent heard the warning make its way up through the ranks. He tightened his horse's cinch then turned when he heard his name.

A horseman riding under a white flag of truce reined in his mount several feet away. "Message for Lieutenant Colonel Elijah Kent."

"I am he. What is it?" Eli strode toward the rider. His patience waned as he'd gotten little sleep since their devastating loss last month. General Jubal Early ordered his cavalry to harass the Yankees—and so they had, but with small measure of success. Even so, Confederate horsemen had taken some hard whacks of late.

"Sir"—the messenger saluted—"I had the pleasure of serving under your command in '62."

Eli returned the gesture. "The pleasure was mine, as I don't recall you caused me any problems."

"No, sir." The courier removed his riding gloves, revealing a withered hand. "I've got an urgent message for you from Winchester." He dug into his satchel with his functional hand and removed a thick packet of documents. "They look important, sir."

"Follow me." Eli led the other man away from prying eyes. Who in Winchester would contact him? As far as he knew, the Union controlled the lower Shenandoah Valley—and most of the upper Valley now too. But that would soon change, now that the "Savior of the Valley," Tom Rosser, manned the cavalry division.

A safe distance from his men, Eli stopped and faced the messenger.

"It's from a lawyer, sir," the rider offered before Eli asked. "Mr. Horatio Finch."

Bewildered, Eli took the envelope and opened it. He dismissed the message-bearer.

"No, sir. That is, I was asked to stay and get your reply. I'm to wait for it, then report back to Mr. Finch. If I fail, I won't get paid."

"I see." Eli opened the first letter and read, *SURRENDER, REB!* He smirked. A number of times during this long war, his faithful friend and best enemy, Peyton Collier, a Yankee colonel, had demanded his immediate and unconditional surrender. Likewise, Eli had demanded Peyton's.

"You may tell the attorney that I refuse this, um, offer." He handed back the half sheet of paper and read the more formal letter. Penned neatly and with a somber tone, Peyton requested that Eli become the executor of his estate, should some unseen adversity befall him.

My beloved wife, Carrie Ann, inherits everything I own. She has promised to care for Aunt Ruth and Tabitha. However, Carrie possesses a heart of gold and I fear my absence from this world will leave her vulnerable to smooth-talking swindlers. Unfortunately, Aunt Ruth is equally susceptible.

Eli had to agree. He'd spent much time at the Colliers' home, typically using it as his headquarters as a means to protect the women of the household. He and Peyton had promised each other at the start of this war that they would guard each other's family members whenever their armies enabled them to do so. The Union army hadn't invaded Richmond yet, nor would it if Eli could help it. But the Confederate army had possessed the Shenandoah Valley for years, until Sheridan's bloody escapades stole it from them. The Yankee invaders outgunned and outnumbered Confederate forces, but the Confederates possessed more tenacity and knew the Virginia topography. Most men in General Jubal Early's Army of the Valley grew up in these parts.

Then, again, so did many Yankees. Like Peyt.

Kneading his stubbly jaw, Eli read on. The letter described national and international laws under which married women were allowed to inherit and own property . . . *lest there be any doubt as to whom I bequeath my estate which includes Piccadilly Place.*

Smoke from a nearby campfire stung his eyes. Eli turned his back to it. He'd known that Peyt's father inherited the manor on Piccadilly Street in Winchester. It had been handed down from Peyt's grandfather. Evidently, the house included Peyton's spry aunt and opinionated, freed black housekeeper.

The letter continued. In the event of Peyton's untimely death, the church was to receive ten percent of the monies and Eli, upon acceptance of the responsibility as executor, would also receive ten percent. In the meantime, Eli would receive a handsome monthly salary.

He blew out a long, slow whistle. Peyt sure knew how to bait a man. He was offering Eli a small fortune—and presented it to him when Eli's family had nothing left. Greenwater, the Kents' ancestral home, was gone. After Father perished from a long, drawn-out illness, Mother ran out of the funds necessary to keep it up and pay both the hired hands and the taxes. She'd been forced to sell.

A soldier on horseback walked his weary mount past Eli. He respectfully saluted and Eli did likewise. Despite his war-hardened exterior, his chest constricted at the mournful memories. Father's death was no surprise. But when he learned that his younger brother Isaiah had died of some kind of swamp fever that he'd contracted in Tennessee, sorrow became a worse enemy than the Yankees.

And then the loss of Greenwater. Now Mother and Eli's younger sister Laurabeth rented a small apartment above an apothecary in Richmond. But with the money Peyton offered, Eli would possess the funds to change his family's situation.

Would it be treasonous if he accepted such an offer *from the enemy*?

Looking up from the letter, he regarded the rider. "I suppose I have no time to either consider this offer or to confer with my own attorney."

"I reckon not, sir." The messenger shifted his stance, behaving a mite uncomfortable. His pockmarked face implied old shrapnel wounds. The man was fortunate not to have lost both eyes. "Mr. Finch wants your answer today."

Eli expelled a sigh, weighing his options. Was it possible to smuggle such a large amount to his family without arousing suspicion in Richmond, should he accept Peyton's offer? His portion of Peyt's money would need to remain in a bank in the Yankee capital, for all the good it would do there for his mother, sister . . . and him.

And, of course, he had to consider Mrs. Carrie Ann Collier—young, pretty, and remarkably naïve. Her blue eyes sparkled with a mix of intelligence and innocence, but her russet curls, usually spilling from their pins, hinted at her spunk. The mere memory of her fighting a losing battle with two Confederate officers over a horse tempted Eli to smile, although it wasn't amusing at the time. She'd nearly gotten herself killed—or worse. By God's grace Eli had intervened in time to rescue her.

Yes, Mrs. Collier needed protection. But did she require *his* protection? And if not Eli's, then whose? What if Eli died before Peyton? Surely Peyt had a backup plan. Then again, knowing Peyt, he might not. The man typically got what he wanted.

Treetops dropped an array of colored leaves and from the distance came the wild honking of agitated geese. The birds obviously didn't want to be the main course tonight. Little did they know they'd save Southerners from starving.

Eli watched the nervous courier begin to pace. He very likely had a family of his own to feed, so getting paid today was foremost on the man's mind. But Eli knew what he had to do. He had known Peyton Collier since his boyhood, which was largely spent at the military academy. During off months, Peyton would visit Greenwater and, likewise, Eli would stay for a time at Piccadilly Place. They were as close as any two brothers—that is, until the war came and Peyt chose to fight for keeping states in the Union while Eli felt strongly about states' rights and opposed the heavy hand of the Federal government.

So, months ago, Eli had been stunned when Aunt Ruth announced that her beloved nephew had found faith on the Gettysburg battlefield. Eli was further shocked to learn Peyton married Carrie Ann. Married!

At first Eli didn't believe it. Peyton Braxton Collier was the quintessential ladies' man. Carrie didn't seem Peyt's type. Soon, however, Eli glimpsed in her what Peyton surely saw—and it caused Eli much envy.

"Sir?"

Eli shook off his musings. "Yes, I accept the responsibility and, if you'll excuse me momentarily, I'll sign the enclosed documents."

"Yes, sir." The messenger's entire bearing seemed to relax. "Thank you, sir."

Walking to the officers' quarters where he'd surely find an available pen, Eli considered the worst of consequences. If Peyton fell before the war was over, God forbid, and Eli assumed his duties to Peyt's family, what would his commanding officer think about it?

Nothing. Eli would be honest with General Tom Rosser now, before rumors circulated. Surely Tom, more than anyone, would understand. While a fierce warrior in battle, the Savior of the Valley had a soft spot for particular matters of the heart. And as Eli's father used to say, duty to family and friends must always trump political and financial position.

And so it shall.

The scent of rain hung heavily in the air as Eli raised his head toward the heavens. No doubt the Almighty had both the Collier and the Kent women in mind when He designed this monetary provision. Bless Peyton for still considering Eli a friend worthy of such trust and position. Though they had chosen different sides of this conflict, Eli never held it against Peyton personally. He suspected a similar respect existed between Generals Tom Rosser and his old West Point roommate, George "Autie" Custer. Indeed, at first this war seemed like a grand jousting tournament. It soon became apparent, however, that war was no game.

Pen in hand, Eli scratched his name across numerous documents. *May God give Peyton a long and happy life.* He strode back to the awaiting courier.

"Thank you, sir." The former soldier tucked the papers into his saddlebag.

They saluted each other. Then Eli watched him mount up and ride out of camp against a backdrop of gathering storm clouds.

CHAPTER 4

Margaret made her way down the stairs, her petticoat and skirt rustling with each step. How odd to wear crinoline and a corset that actually fit. Her scalp and skin still tingled from the scrubbing that woman named Tabitha had given her. Throughout Margaret's bath, the older Negro woman muttered something about "no lice sharing her house while she was alive."

Margaret hadn't been aware the parasite had nested in her hair, although she knew it ran rampant around army camps. Tabitha assured her that she knew how to kill the louse, and proceeded to do so before Margaret soaked in the tub. She feared she'd lose her God-given glory under Tabitha's capable fingers and the strong-smelling soap. But her brunet tresses seemed to be intact.

And this new frock, a deep rose and brown plaid calico day dress—Margaret hadn't worn such finery in all her born days. Tabitha said it and all her other new clothes were gifts from Carrie Ann.

Reaching the first floor, Margaret followed the sound of the voices. Within seconds, she stood at the parlor doors.

"I hope I'm not interrupting." Margaret took a half step forward.

"Not at all." Carrie Ann stood. "Please, come in."

Margaret entered the room and noted the polite smiles on the other two women. She remembered Aunt Ruth's name, but not the other guest's. Her mind spun trying to grasp the name from her memory, but it was lost in the overwhelming swirl of her arrival.

"My, but you look lovely." A certain light entered Carrie Ann's blue eyes. "Wouldn't you agree, Aunt Ruth and Mrs. Johnston?"

The tension lifted from Margaret's shoulders. Leave it to Carrie Ann to sense her lapse in memory.

"Oh, please, your sister must call me Meredith." The third woman's smile grew wider. "And I agree, Miss Bell. You're lovely."

"Please, call me Margaret." When had she ever been called *Miss Bell*?

"Of course. We're all family here." Aunt Ruth shifted on the settee. "And that color is perfect for you, as is the dress." She turned to Carrie Ann. "Your judgment was correct, my dear girl."

The corners of Carrie's mouth lifted, but it wasn't quite a smile. She must have something heavy on her mind.

Margaret studied the laces of her new black ankle boots. She peeked at her older sister. "I'm indebted to you, Carrie Ann. I've never owned such a fine gown—and all the clothes. I'm in awe of them. Your gifts are more than generous. Thank you." One thing about Carrie Ann . . . she'd always shared. Margaret hadn't realized it until Carrie left Woodstock. All her growing up years, she'd expected Carrie to share. While Margaret and Sarah Jane both had only thought of themselves and their own needs.

How selfish they had been. How wrong Margaret was about her older sister!

"Since dinner will be a bit delayed"—Aunt Ruth's gaze fell over Carrie—"perhaps you'd like to show your sister around our home and get reacquainted in the process."

"What a good idea." Carrie gave Margaret a smile, but it didn't brighten her blue eyes. In fact, there was a harshness in her tone that Margaret felt responsible for.

A log in the blazing hearth split with a decisive *crack*. Margaret jumped back, earning unwanted attention. She cursed her frayed nerves. Why couldn't she be more like Carrie, calm and collected? Dressing and behaving like a lady wasn't as easy as she'd imagined.

Her sister strode forward, looking regal in her dark blue gown with its lacy ivory cuffs and collar. Had she always stepped so lightly with her head held high?

"Follow me please, Margaret."

Margaret dipped her head to Aunt Ruth and Meredith in silent but polite parting before trailing Carrie out of the parlor.

They crossed the foyer. Large oil paintings hung on papered walls as if the Collier ancestors offered guests their personal greetings.

Piccadilly Place, as the home had been dubbed, seemed like an immense castle compared to the Wayfarers Inn. Envy nipped at Margaret like an annoying little pooch on her heels. But she successfully shooed it away. She didn't begrudge her sister a single bit of good fortune. Carrie Ann had obviously married well.

"This is my favorite room in the house," Carrie Ann said once they stood in the library.

Taking in the collection of books, Margaret gave a nod. "I can see why."

"Aunt Ruth told me that every shelf was filled with books until soldiers from both the Confederate and Union armies helped themselves to the volumes." Carrie Ann eyed one of the sparser bookcases. "Evidently, troops from General Jackson's army used Aunt Ruth's books to fuel their campfires." She shook her head. "Disgraceful."

"So you're a Yankee now that you married one?"

Carrie swung around to face her. "I'm still an independent thinker, Margaret, just like always."

"Does your husband know that?"

"Yes, as a matter of fact, he does." Two pink spots appeared on her cheeks and spread across her face. Margaret recognized her sister's annoyance. "Peyton encourages me. He enjoys a good banter."

"He does?" What man wanted to fight on the battlefield and then come home and argue politics with his wife? None Margaret knew. Then again, she'd known only louts. "Still, the colonel must have won you over to his side."

Carrie shrugged lightly. "I suppose he has. I'm more of a Yankee than a Rebel. It's like Papa always said, I possess both the blessing and the curse of seeing both sides of a coin at the same time."

Margaret smiled. "Yes, I remember Papa saying that." She took a step toward Carrie. "Even so, the colonel doesn't seem like a man who abides challenges. I heard the way he spoke to his enlisted men. Firm, unyielding, yet he wasn't mean-spirited about it." Margaret considered her sister thoughtfully. "Do you mind me asking . . . do you two get along?"

"Perfectly." Carrie's happy expression, her blue eyes shining bright, said she wasn't fibbing.

And Margaret wasn't at all surprised that it took a Union colonel to tame Carrie.

"Your husband looked familiar to me." Margaret started meandering around the bookshelves as she spoke. Her midsection filled with sickening flutters, but she needed the truth. Had the colonel been one of the miscreants who paid for her services but got potioned instead? "Did he ever come into the Wayfarers Inn any time before rescuing me?"

"As a matter of fact, he did."

Margaret's shoulders curled forward as the air left her lungs.

"It was the April before Gettysburg. A handful of Yankees came in for food and drink."

In '63—long before Sarah Jane ran away and Carrie went after her. Margaret nearly collapsed with relief.

"I'd made snapping turtle in a pot that day."

"Your favorite." Margaret mustered a shaky smile. "I marvel at your good memory."

"And I yours." Carrie's lips twitched in obvious amusement. "You may recall that one of those men was injured and I sutured his forearm against Mr. Veyschmidt's order not to give medical aid to the Yankees. I defied him, as always, and that man I helped was Peyton. Then, last August when I stumbled into a skirmish trying to find our little sister, it was his turn to help me."

"And the colonel remembered you?"

"He did."

"So, he and his men never stayed the night at the Wayfarers Inn?"

"Not to my knowledge."

Margaret exhaled. The tension left her body. The colonel hadn't been a customer . . .

"The night I left Woodstock, I was wearing that deserter's uniform, hoping to slip past the Union pickets." Carrie Ann shook her head. "I didn't make it. A fight broke out near Front Royal and I got into the middle of it."

"I figured something like that happened. I feared you were dead. Sarah Jane too. Then, after Mama died, I was on my own . . . and scared to death, condemned to live out my days at the Wayfarers Inn."

The tightness in Carrie's expression melted away. She rushed toward Margaret and put hands on her shoulders. "No, not condemned. Not any longer." Her arms slowly returned to her sides. "You're here now. You're safe." She looked away. "But this brings me to another matter: our . . . past life, at the Wayfarers Inn."

"Doesn't Aunt Ruth know?"

"She's aware. I don't hide the fact or lie about it. I was a serving-girl out of necessity. We needed room and board after our farm went up in flames. Mr. Veyschmidt allowed us to stay at his establishment but then enslaved us." With a sigh, Carrie Ann approached the padded settee and sat. "It always hurt that none of our friends in Woodstock took us in."

"Can you blame them?" Margaret walked around the settee, then dropped into the seat beside Carrie. "Mama was unhinged."

"I know . . . and I was the cause."

"No, Carrie. Mama was her own cause. She always hated the farm— ever since she was a girl, growing up there. She fancied herself in a home in town. She always said she deserved it." Margaret took in the sights of the spacious library. "She would have loved a house like this one, but of course Papa couldn't afford it. That fact made Mama so angry and bitter that she took it out on everyone else, you in particular because you're so much like him." She folded her hands on her lap, emulating Carrie. "The reverend told me at Mama's burial that anger and bitterness can worm its way into a person's mind." A state Margaret hoped not to inherit. Not another soul attended the burial, not even out of regard for Margaret. Then again, she wasn't what Woodstock folks considered respectable.

Margaret stared at her entwined fingers. "Things got worse after Sarah Jane and you left." Margaret wished she could forget Mama's sickness and the hateful things she spewed. She forgave Mama, but it wasn't the same as forgetting.

"Peyton told me. I'm sorry I left you there." Carrie's voice was feather-soft. "But I couldn't get back up the Valley."

"But why would you not leave me at the Wayfarers Inn? I liked to flirt. I will freely admit it. Men seemed amused by it, and gave me a few extra coins, though Mr. Veyschmidt always took them from me. But after you left to find Sarah Jane, he tried to—" The words stuck in her throat while tears burned.

"Oh, dear God . . ." Carrie placed her hand over her heart. "Did he . . . violate you?"

"Almost. Several times, in fact. But no. I successfully fought him off and then the last time I swore I'd kill him. I think he believed me. But I paid a price for rejecting him. When Mama's sickness got worse, Mr. Veyschmidt raised the cost of room and board. Of course there was no way I could pay the debt. After Mama died, the reverend himself buried her in a corner of the church's cemetery. No one else would. Folks said it would bring them bad luck and they'd be cursed too."

"What hogwash." Carrie rolled her eyes. "What about Joshua's parents? Didn't they come?"

Margaret shook her head.

"Hardly shocking. If they couldn't see fit to help us in our time of need, why would they attend Mama's burial?"

Hearing the edge in Carrie's voice, Margaret reached for her hand and gave it a gentle squeeze. "It had nothing to do with us."

"It had everything to do with us. Mrs. Blevens was like a second mother— maybe even like the mother ours wasn't."

"Mama was the cause. The Blevenses liked Papa and us girls, but they had conflicts with Mama over the years. Don't you remember how she screamed at them one night about some slight offense and then she threatened to burn down their horse stables?"

"What? I don't remember that."

Margaret wasn't surprised. "You always had your nose in a book."

Carrie stared off toward the bank of windows and moaned. "I blamed the Blevenses for a long time for not helping us after Papa left and the farm burned."

"If Mama had gone to the grave sooner, they might have come to our rescue."

Neither of them spoke for a long while. Carrie picked at several minuscule pieces of lint, and Margaret sensed her sister's pain went as deep as the blue of her skirt.

"Carrie, the Blevenses figured we were all right. We had a roof over our head and were learning to work hard. The Blevenses hadn't a clue about how it really was. We never told them. Mr. Blevens wasn't a patron."

"The place had a reputation."

"Maybe they thought we were nestled upstairs and safe enough away from the drinking and rowdiness."

"I don't believe it. They knew."

The mantle clock chimed and Margaret counted off the seconds as they ticked by.

At last, Carrie lifted her gaze. Tears glistened in her eyes. "I tried to find Sarah Jane. Honest, I did. The fact is Joshua finally located her. She'd been severely beaten. By the time I reached the establishment in Martinsburg at which Joshua had arranged for Sarah to stay and be cared for, she was dead."

"Your husband told me while we watched the Wayfarers Inn go up in flames." Margaret dabbed the corners of her eyes with unsteady fingertips. "It wasn't your fault, Carrie. Sarah Jane has a mind of her own, and she chose to run off with some no-account peddler."

"I know. Peyton helped me see that truth." Carrie released a heavy sigh.

"He's a good man."

"Yes, he is." Carrie's eyes sparkled at the mention of her husband.

"And I suppose we ought to feel indebted to Joshua for finding Sarah Jane." Margaret resisted the urge to shudder. Next to Veyschmidt, he was another man she needed to forgive.

"I'm afraid Joshua is no longer my friend—not since I fell in love with Peyton."

"Good, because he's no friend of mine either." Margaret stared at the shiny wooden floor. Shame seemed to burst up from the deepest part of her soul. Joshua, once a friend, had become her foe . . . and one of her unfortunate customers. He had guessed that she'd potioned him and vowed to get even.

"Joshua showed up here on my wedding night," Carrie said. "He and his accomplice had notions of robbing us. Things turned ugly and I—I killed a man in this very room."

Margaret placed her hand over her heart. "You?"

Carrie replied with a nod. "I'm not proud of it, but I had no other choice."

Margaret listened as her sister retold the story. Clearly, Carrie had shot the second Rebel spy in self-defense. Amazingly, it was Joshua who had provided the pistol. He couldn't exactly kill his own comrade. Still . . .

"Forgive me if I don't find Joshua honorable." Margaret eked out the words through the anger that threatened to choke her. "The war has changed him."

"It's changed everyone." A slow smile inched its way across Carrie Ann's face. "My husband changed for the better. He's a Christian man ever since Gettysburg. He's honorable, and—" Her expression glowed. "He's kind, noble, and every bit a gentleman."

"I can't argue." Margaret reached for Carrie Ann's hand. "But I don't want to return to that life even if it's a respectable establishment."

Doubt pinched Carrie's delicate features.

"That life is not for me. I've learned my lesson. Flirting isn't harmless. It leads men to believe falsehoods about a girl, except I'm not that kind of girl. I swear it."

Carrie Ann stared at her skirt again.

"Please, believe me."

When Carrie refused to look her in the eye, fear and regret spiraled down inside her. She glanced at the windows and could see the tips of evergreen bushes outside. Beyond shrubbery, a willow bowed majestically to a gust of autumn wind.

Margaret's heart ached. Carrie's disappointment in her was equally stirring and it laid the branches of Margaret's soul bare. She had to tell Carrie the truth.

"Do you remember that old mountain woman we used to call 'the witch'?"

"Yes." A hint of amusement laced Carrie's voice. "I remember we used to see her walking past the farm on her way to the trading post. Papa said her last name was—"

"Quagg," Margaret finished for her. "Mrs. Quagg. What you might not know is that some folks say she's a medicine woman too. I happened by her shack up on that first ridge of the Massanutten shortly after you and Sarah Jane left. I was attempting to run away. Mr. Veyschmidt accosted me and called me horrible names. He told me what he expected me to do to earn my keep as well as all the money he claimed I owed him."

"Oh, Margaret . . . we worked so hard for him, and decently too."

"Veyschmidt wasn't referring to cooking, cleaning, laundering, and straightening guest rooms."

A muscle worked in Carrie Ann's cheek. "That lowlife!"

"You weren't there to defend me like you'd been before. You put yourself in harm's way to protect Sarah Jane and me. But you'd gone after her and hadn't returned. It had been days. I was certain you'd got yourself killed, just like Papa."

"We have no proof that Papa is dead."

Margaret sighed, refusing to be sidetracked. Carrie Ann never did accept bad news until it was proved beyond all reason. "The day I ran away, I took off at dawn. About midday, I realized I had nowhere to go. I got lost and disoriented in the woods. That's when I stumbled on Mrs. Quagg's place." The homey little hovel, set deep in the heart of the forest, came to mind. "How she lives in that place all alone, I can't imagine. But she does. And she makes potions."

Carrie Ann blinked. "Potions?"

"That's what she calls them. Some say she makes medicine better than what the apothecaries sell." Margaret took note of the interest now shining in Carrie Ann's eyes. "She said I should return to the Wayfarers Inn for Mama's sake, but she gave me sleeping potion. A drop or two in a man's ale, and in five minutes he's out cold. Best of all, he doesn't remember much in the morning."

"You drugged your . . . customers?" Carrie Ann's brow furrowed. "And took their money, I presume?"

"I didn't take it. They paid Veyschmidt to spend time with me. I didn't get a nickel." Her fists clenched, Margaret tried to gauge her sister's reaction. It seemed to be a mix of pity and amusement. "I had to protect myself. What else was I to do?" Her anger melded into fear. "But now I'm terrified that I'll come face-to-face with these men. They might have figured out what I did, and demand their money back. After all, they considered me a . . . a prostitute."

"Did anyone else know about your potion?"

"Only Mrs. Quagg and . . . Joshua."

"We can't count on him to keep his mouth shut."

"Agreed." Margaret nibbled the inside of her bottom lip, wondering what Carrie would do next. "You won't make me return to that sort of employment, will you? Your husband promised you'd find me a respectable position."

"Yes, of course, I will." Carrie patted Margaret's knee before standing and pacing. She tapped her forefinger against her lips.

Margaret breathed easier. Carrie always had a plan. And if she wasn't mistaken, one brewed in her sister's mind this very minute.

"And you don't have to fear recourse from men who might recognize you. If confronted, we'll be honest. We were forced into a life of service under Veyschmidt's tyranny. You did what you had to do to survive." Carrie Ann sat down again. "My husband will see that anyone claiming repayment from you is dealt with and I'm equally confident that Mr. Finch, the Collier family's attorney, will help." She gathered Margaret's hand in both of her smaller ones, and gave it a squeeze.

Margaret couldn't stem the tears this time. They obscured her vision and tickled her cheeks. "My big sister always protects me."

Carrie Ann handed her a sweetly scented hankie.

"I always considered you bossy. But now I know you only tried to spare me from evildoers—and you did. I'm grateful."

"There, there . . . that's what an older sister is for."

Margaret set her head on Carrie Ann's shoulder. Though smaller in stature than she, Carrie was the bulwark Margaret needed. She wasn't alone in this frightening, rapidly changing world. She had family!

CHAPTER 5

"Did you tell her, Carrie Ann?"

"How could I?" Carrie glanced at Aunt Ruth before plopping down on the settee in the antechamber of the rooms that she and Peyton shared. "Margaret told me she'd been wishing upon wish that I'd return and get her out of the Wayfarers Inn. She was so sincere, in a desperate sort of way. She never wants to return to that lifestyle and, well, I am to blame for her getting into such a fix in the first place."

"Oh, dear." Aunt Ruth lowered herself gracefully into one of the armchairs, reminding Carrie that she still had much to learn of ladylike etiquette. "I hope she won't set tongues to wagging in Winchester."

"She won't. I told Margaret that you'd tutor her in a lady's proper manners and demeanor, just as you tutored me. She agreed to submit to your tutelage. That's something." Carrie recalled how rebelliously her sister—or stepsister—had behaved when it came to schooling. "Actually, it's quite a change for Margaret."

Carrie smiled, sensing Aunt Ruth would go along with her plan. Peyton mentioned how much Aunt Ruth enjoyed instructing young ladies. Perhaps she hadn't missed her calling.

The sweet scent of honeysuckle breezed in through an open window. "Margaret is not as well read as I am, so you may have to begin with the basics. At least I had imagined a life like Jane Austen's *Emma* because I'd read the book so many times."

"Not every young lady is blessed with an imagination, and I do love

52

exercising our inner creativity." Aunt Ruth's hazel eyes sparked with enthusiasm. "I am not put off by the challenge of educating your sister."

"I didn't think you would be."

Frown lines creased the older woman's forehead. "But you told me she's not your kin, my dear, so you're not obligated to her. Would you rather find her respectable employment and be done with it—and her?"

Carrie worked her lower lip between her teeth as she gave the idea thought. "No, I think not. I will defer to my husband on this matter. He's certain Joshua lied to me so he could use the information against me at some future time. And even if Peyton is wrong, I've considered Margaret my sister all my life and she's the only one I have left. She is my sister, my kin."

Her last several words caused a lump to form in her throat. Carrie harbored so many regrets. She didn't want to neglect Margaret and add to the heap of anguish pressing in on her.

"I think you're being very wise." Aunt Ruth's strong, authoritative voice cut through Carrie's muse. "If Margaret is willing, she will be an apt student."

Aunt Ruth's praise warmed Carrie's heart. "I'm so glad you think so."

"I do, but you need your beauty rest." Aunt Ruth stood. "Peyton won't like to see dark shadows under his wife's pretty blue eyes."

Carrie smiled. "No, ma'am."

"He does dote on you. Tabitha and I find it richly amusing. I can't think of anyone more deserving of my nephew's affection."

"Thank you." How blessed Carrie was that Peyton's aunt took an immediate liking to her.

Aunt Ruth strode to the door. "Margaret and I will begin reading lessons tomorrow right after breakfast."

Was that excitement in her tone? Certainly sounded like it. Carrie swallowed a giggle. "Good night, Aunt Ruth."

"Good night, dearheart."

⸙

From the summit of Massanutten Mountain, Eli eyed enemy forces below through field glasses. His view was so clear on this perfect autumn Monday that he could make out the piping on the Yankees' blue coats.

"What do you think, Eli?"

He glanced at the officer under whom he served in the Eleventh Virginia Cavalry, and then stared out across the Valley again. "I think General Gordon came up with a bold plan, but one that borders on the impossible." Lowering his arm, Eli turned to Colonel Oliver Funsten, a friend as well as his commander. "I have doubts about marching an entire Army of the Valley down a pig trail in the middle of the night between the face of Massanutten and the Shenandoah River. And all without the Union army getting wind of our movement?" Eli shook his head. "I don't think it can be done."

"General Rosser thinks the plan is brilliant."

"I suppose he would." Eli was well aware of Tom Rosser's proven record. Rosser was a seasoned veteran, well-liked by his men, including Eli, and a feared opponent, particularly when it came to hand-to-hand combat.

"I believe it might work, Eli."

"Do you?"

Funsten inclined his head and ran his hand down his hedgy beard. "We'll surround the enemy's exposed left flank and then attack before the Billy Yanks can even say 'morning coffee.' And of course the cavalry will lead the way. Finally, we will prove our division's worth to General Early."

"Perhaps so." But it was more wish than reality. Every Confederate horseman knew that General Jubal Early had little to no respect for his cavalry, let alone for Tom Rosser. Early considered Rosser weak and seldom used his horsemen in a victorious way, unlike General Phil Sheridan who cherished his cavalrymen.

Admittedly, that was only one of the many things the Yanks did better. It was they who won the last victory in Winchester, and they who devastated the Valley. What the Yankees didn't set fire to, they stole. While the burnings had slowed, even stopped over the last two weeks, much of the Shenandoah lay in an uninhabitable waste, which was why the Army of the Valley needed to either retreat up the Valley or attack the Northern Invaders. Subsisting here any longer was impossible. If it weren't for the Valley residents' generosity, man and beast alike would starve to death—which, of course, was the Federals' plan.

"I appreciate your candid assessment." Funsten gave Eli a friendly whack between the shoulder blades. "Now let's us Virginians go find some supper before heading back to camp. If we hurry, we might be able to catch an hour or two of sleep."

Eli followed Funsten down the summit to where they'd left their horses.

Mounting up, he and his commander rode southwest to Woodstock. If Eli recalled correctly, Peyt's wife hailed from that town. He hadn't had much opportunity to converse with her during his occupation of Piccadilly Place, but they'd spoken enough to become friends. Eli wished he'd met the spitfire before Peyton. But there was no mistaking Carrie's love for her husband. If ever a woman had stars in her eyes, it was she. Even more appealing to Peyt than her spunk was likely the fact Carrie loved him, and not his fortune. That's all Peyt ever wanted . . .

Eli and Funsten slowed their mounts as they entered town. Woodstock showed obvious signs of the Union cavalry's last visit. Buildings torched and charred, some standing like burned-out stone skeletons while others were heaps of rubble. Odd gaps between buildings along the main thoroughfare bore the Union's standard signature. Although the hotel still stood.

Eli dismounted and tied the reins to the hitching post, while his stomach rumbled like thunder at the thought of a tasty meal. He assessed his meager consumption of the last two days: an ear of corn, a biscuit, and two slices of bacon. Well, he would eat heartily tonight. If General Early wasn't persuaded otherwise and the army followed through with Gordon's daring plan, this meal could be his last.

CHAPTER 6

October 18, 1864

"Miss Carrie, soldiers is comin'!" Ten-year-old Gavin skidded to a halt at the doorway of Miss Rebekah Kercheval's parlor-turned-nursery for dozens of parentless children. In fact, her entire house had been overrun by orphans, but Rebekah didn't mind. She welcomed each and every child.

Carrie stood and hitched the baby she was holding onto her hip. "Blue or gray, Gavin?" She held her breath, praying it was the former.

"Yankees, ma'am." The boy wiped his nose on his shirt sleeve. "I think one of 'em is your husband."

Carrie's alarm turned to happiness. The sentiment was reflected in Meredith's gleeful expression. Peyton was safe. Major Vernon Johnston would likely be with Peyton. Their brigade hadn't been sent to Petersburg and ambushed along the way, as was the rumor flying around town.

"Aren't you supposed to be out picking the last of the fall vegetables, young man?" Rebekah gave the boy a frown. "Or don't you want to eat?"

"Yes, ma'am. That is, I do want to eat."

Rebekah put her hands on her round, ample hips. "Then go help the rest of the children in the garden. Thanks to Miss Carrie and Miss Collier, dinner will be ready at six o'clock sharp."

"Smells real good too." The boy's smile was all the thanks Carrie needed.

"Now go!" Rebekah pointed in the direction of the back door.

Gavin turned and ran out of the house.

Carrie smiled. "Gavin's a good boy."

"He's spirited." Rebekah expelled a sigh. "And he and Jeffry James Olson eat ten times more than the other children. I honestly can't say what I'd have done if you didn't bring that smoked ham for us."

"It's our pleasure." Carrie meant every word. They did a good work here. Meredith held a newborn while Margaret bounced a little one on her knee. Aunt Ruth was upstairs changing bed sheets, and Tabitha worked over the stove. "We ladies of Piccadilly Place enjoy helping with the children."

"Indeed we do," Margaret echoed.

Carrie wrapped the blanket more tightly around the infant she held and headed for the door. Sunshine spilled over the red bricks of the porch beneath a cloudless sky. In the road, harnesses jangled and horses snorted as the Union cavalry paraded past the orphanage. Carrie spotted Peyton almost immediately. A thrill shot through her when their eyes met. He tipped his slouch hat most charmingly, and Carrie's cheeks warmed.

"No wonder you fell in love with that man," Margaret's voice whispered close to Carrie's ear. "Maybe someday I'll find my hero—that is, if all of them don't all kill each other first."

"Hear, hear, sister!" Rebekah exclaimed from directly behind Carrie. "The Good Book says God hates violence."

"Well, yes, that's true," Meredith chimed in. "However, David was a warrior and a man after God's own heart. The Almighty expects us to fight for righteousness."

"Let's go inside before we catch a chill." Carrie didn't want the two ladies to begin debating anew. Rebekah held to her pacifist Quaker beliefs while Meredith defended her husband's involvement in the War of the Rebellion. Each lady knew her Scripture passages and used her sword of the Spirit effectively. But neither won the controversy. It mirrored the national conflict.

Even if the war ended today, hundreds of thousands of men on both sides had lost their lives. Families had been torn asunder and left homeless. Carrie held the baby in her arms closer. Children became orphans and as food was scarce now in the Valley, particularly for Confederates, few were willing to take on another mouth to feed. Victory wouldn't be sweet, no matter which side claimed it.

When there was no more to see, they walked back inside the house. Carrie felt a tug on her skirt. She glanced down at the three-year-old, towheaded girl. "What's wrong, Georgia?"

The child buried her head in Carrie's dress.

"She's scared," five-year-old Galena said. She was frequently her younger sister's voice. Both girls were the last of Gavin's kin.

"What's to be afraid of?" Carrie led the children into the former parlor and set the baby into one of the many donated wooden cradles. The bedrooms upstairs were filled and the number of children grew daily. Sometimes newborn babies were set at the front door without introduction or explanation, just . . . abandoned. It broke Carrie's heart.

Sitting near the hearth, she pulled Georgia onto her lap. The girl snuggled in, but Carrie still had room enough for Galena. "Tell me why you're scared."

"The soldiers—" Georgia rested her head against Carrie's shoulder.

"The Union army will keep the orphanage safe so those lawless deserters and Mosby's Raiders don't come and steal your foodstuff again."

Galena shook her head. "No, Miss Carrie. If Yankees are comin' here, they'll break the furniture and burn down the house. We heard Jeffry James say so."

"Hmm . . ." Rebekah was right. The boy was trouble. Only twelve years old, and he'd already been caught stealing. He sassed a Union guard who gave him a licking and returned him to the orphanage. But the incident did little to put the fear of God or man into Jeffry James Olson. If they weren't separated soon, Gavin would be influenced by the older boy's bad behavior. The signs were already on display. "Rest assured, girls. The soldiers who passed by were my husband's brigade and they're good men." She really didn't know that as fact, but she knew enough of them to speak for their character. "You have nothing to fear."

"Yankees do that, Miss Carrie. They burn homes and barns and everything."

"Sometimes they do, yes, but we can't be afraid. We must be brave. Besides, my husband, Colonel Collier, will not allow the orphanage to burn down." She looked at Meredith, who gently set the infant in her arms into another nearby cradle. "Major Johnston won't let that happen either."

"That's right, girls." Meredith gave a nod.

"Will you stay with us tonight, Miss Carrie?" Galena's hazel eyes beseeched her. "Then me and Georgia won't be scared no more."

Carrie's heart tore in two at the girl's request. "I'm afraid that's impossible tonight. Colonel Collier will want to see me and—"

"And Miss Carrie wants to see him too." Margaret's blue-green eyes glimmered with sassiness. "I suspect Miss Meredith will want to visit with her husband also."

"You are correct, Miss Margaret." Meredith removed the ivory apron she'd been wearing and sent a smile at Carrie. "I'll fetch Aunt Ruth and Tabitha. We had best be on our way home."

Carrie replied with a nod and watched her go. How she cherished Meredith's friendship, even though they had only known each other a couple of weeks. Meredith and Vern had stood as witnesses at Carrie and Peyton's wedding ceremony. Days later, Carrie learned that Meredith's return to the parsonage was impossible as it was now occupied by another minister. When Vern had left the pulpit, convinced that God wanted him to minister in the Union army, no one imagined the war would last so long. The church elders finally decided they needed to replace him. Meredith had every intention of traveling to St. Louis to stay with her sister until the war's end, but it only seemed logical for her to stay with them as Vern served as Peyton's camp aide and their regiment would likely remain in the area indefinitely. So, with Peyton's approval, Carrie and Aunt Ruth made the invitation. Meredith accepted.

Galena leaned against Carrie's arm. "Who will stay with us?"

"I will." Margaret crossed the room and peeled little Georgia's fingers from Carrie's dress. The little one kicked and fussed, but Margaret managed to calm and comfort her.

The sight filled Carrie with gladness. She'd never known her sister to be such a natural with children. "You've got a gift with these orphans, Margaret."

"My time is well spent here at Repairers of the Breach, and far better spent here than"—she stared at the tops of her boots—"than at my last place of employment, if it can be called such."

Hardly. After hearing all Margaret had endured for the past year, especially during the last few months, Carrie was only too glad to take her in. Peyton had been correct. Margaret had definitely undergone a change of heart. She now appreciated everything given to her.

"You're really staying with us, Miss Margaret?"

"Yes, sweetie."

"Goodie!" The little girl slid from Carrie's lap and ran from the room, most likely to taunt her brother and Jeffry James with the truth and this latest good news.

"I'm in desperate need of another pair of hands at nighttime, so I'm indebted to you, Miss Margaret." Rebekah lifted a squalling toddler into her plump arms. A hulking figure of a woman, Rebekah Kercheval had a heart as large as her constitution was hearty.

"I'm happy to help."

Carrie smiled. "I'm proud of you," she whispered to her sister.

Margaret's expression turned misty. "Those words mean a lot to me."

After a parting hug, Carrie hurried to the conveyance. God willing, they'd get home before the men. Already Tabitha groused about feeding hungry troops.

Carrie sighed happily. Peyton would be home and they could spend the night in each other's company.

The war suddenly seemed very far away.

⸙

"So after General Sheridan was informed of that intercepted wigwag message about Longstreet's division joining up with Early's army," Vern Johnston said, "we were ordered to abandon our cavalry raid on the Virginia Central Railroad and backtrack to Middletown to reinforce Wright's troops."

Carrie had become so engrossed in the dinner conversation that evening that she forgot to eat.

"Yes, except it was a ruse." Peyton dabbed the corners of his mouth with his napkin. "Sheridan's instincts were correct and Colonel Edwards, Winchester's Provost Marshal, confirmed that all's been quiet in town with the Rebs and Mosby's Raiders. Early's army has been sufficiently demoralized in the Shenandoah Valley."

Carrie wasn't so sure. "Take care that you don't underestimate the tenacity of Confederate forces. Why, I read somewhere that the Rebels have an advantage in Virginia because they know the lay of the land. They also stand to lose more than their Union counterparts so they are fierce combatants."

"Let me assure you, madam, that we are well aware of that fact." Sarcasm dripped from his tone, causing Carrie unease. The last thing she wanted to do was anger her husband when they had precious little time together. He set his arm on the top of Carrie's chair. "But I shall heed your warning all the same."

So he'd been teasing her. She should have guessed. Carrie pushed a potato around on her plate. There was still so much she didn't know about Peyton. "Forgive my impertinence?"

"My darling, your impertinence is part of your charm."

This time she knew he was kidding and rewarded him with a huff. "Very funny."

He smiled, revealing even, white teeth, and beneath the flickering tapers, she glimpsed her own reflection in his brandy-colored eyes. How easy it was to get lost in their depths. Every rational thought took flight. All that mattered was that her handsome, courageous husband arrived home unscathed. What a blessing that he'd managed to obtain a twenty-four-hour leave.

Peyton moved closer, his face now inches from hers. "Others are present at this dinner table, my sweet," he whispered.

Carrie straightened and her face flamed. She glanced around at family and guests alike. How rude to embarrass them.

Vern continued speaking as if nothing out of the ordinary had occurred. "We've been camped along Cedar Creek in Middletown the last few days, enjoying the pleasant autumn weather." He pointed his fork at his good friend and commanding officer. "Except Peyton, that fortunate rascal, was invited to reside inside Belle Grove, the Union's headquarters, along with several generals."

"Vern . . ." An unmistakable warning edged Peyton's voice.

"Oh, come on, Peyt. You must tell the ladies the good news."

"Yes, of course, you must!" Aunt Ruth clasped her hands together. "What is it?"

"Nothing definite." Peyton's reply sounded tight. No doubt Vern would get a talking-to later. "I may be getting a promotion soon."

Gasps of surprise and pleasure filled the dining room, Carrie's included.

"That's wonderful, Peyton." In her estimation, no one deserved it more.

"As I said, it's not for certain. I must prove myself worthy of such a title as brigadier general in the regular army."

"Peyton would outrank Autie Custer," Vern said, sounding proud. "Custer is merely a brevet brigadier general."

"And what does that mean, exactly?" Meredith sat beside her husband.

"It means Custer's title is temporary and he commands a volunteer brigade."

"An extremely respected and relied-upon volunteer brigade," Peyton added.

"A matter of opinion." Vern chortled. He was certainly in jovial spirits tonight, no doubt because he'd been granted leave also.

"Which brings me to a bit of unpleasant news." Peyton eyed Carrie before continuing. "Vern and I are expected at Phil Sheridan's Winchester headquarters later for a celebration of sorts."

"We only plan to make an appearance and then we'll be home." Vern evidently noticed, as Carrie did, the frown lines creasing Meredith's forehead. "That's a promise."

"Of course." Meredith's reply was as crisp as the night breeze, and Carrie shared her friend's disappointment.

"Aren't wives invited?" With a wee bit of hope, she glanced at Peyton before taking a sip from her water goblet.

"No, unfortunately, they're not. But as Vern said, we will only make an appearance and then come straight home."

Meredith pushed back her chair and stood. "Vern, may I speak to you before you go?" Carrie was no more pleased about this party than Meredith was, but she knew that she'd never talk Peyton out of going. The Union army took precedence—but only for now. "Excuse us, won't you all? It won't take but a minute or two."

An awkward silence swirled in the wake of the departing couple.

"It's been a long day." Aunt Ruth stifled a yawn. "I'm exhausted. I forgot how caring for children can wear a body out."

"I find caring for children to be exhilarating." Carrie dared a peek at Peyton. "Maybe one day Piccadilly Place will be filled with Collier children."

"Heaven help us." Aunt Ruth churned out a dramatic sigh, but Carrie knew she hoped to be a great aunt in the future.

Peyton said nothing, but took her hand and held it under the table. She wove her fingers between his calloused ones.

"It was quite the display of Union cavalrymen when you passed by the orphanage earlier," Carrie said. "The boys were particularly impressed."

"Impressed enough to behave in town, I hope." Peyton arched a brow. "Several of those urchins have been causing trouble for the scant few merchants left in Winchester."

"Rebekah Kercheval is aware of the naughtiness and is trying hard to correct it."

"Good."

"Meredith has fallen in love with the sweetest infant," Aunt Ruth said, her eyes glimmering. "She hopes to discuss the possibility of adopting him with Vern tonight. Perhaps she's broaching the subject now."

"Adoption? Hmm . . ." After a few moments' thought, Peyton slid his napkin off his lap and placed it on the table. "Then I'll be sure to get Vern home at a reasonable hour." He gently squeezed Carrie's hand before releasing it and standing. Leaning over her chair, he placed a kiss on her forehead.

"I'll stay up and wait for you," she promised.

"I'll not keep you waiting long." He sent her a bold wink before giving Aunt Ruth's cheek an affectionate peck.

Vern reentered the room. "Meredith has a headache. She's retiring for the night." The sound of her footfalls against the wooden stairs just beyond the dining room seemed to punctuate his statement.

The men left the room, and Carrie took a few bites of her now-cold dinner. Minutes later, sounds of horses' hooves pounding against the macadamized road out front signaled their departure.

Carrie missed Peyton already.

CHAPTER 7

Midnight came and went—and took the last of Carrie's patience with it. She slapped closed the book she'd been attempting to read and roused herself from the settee. Crossing the bedroom suite's sitting room, she stoked the dying embers in the hearth. What could be keeping Peyton and Vern? If they'd been ordered elsewhere, surely Peyton would have sent word.

Or would he assume that she'd eventually figure it out?

A hard knock sounded, startling Carrie from her thoughts. Before she could move to open the door, Meredith rushed in.

"Come quickly."

"What is it?"

Meredith's expression hardened. "It's our husbands."

Grabbing her night wrapper, Carrie hurried downstairs behind Meredith, who paused in the foyer.

"Listen."

Carrie stood still, straining to hear . . . why, it was singing. Drunken singing! And the male duo massacred "Yankee Doodle."

"Our husbands have returned." Meredith's voice was as tight as a drum.

"Peyton? And Vern?" Carrie could scarcely believe it. She listened more closely. Yes, it sounded like them.

"They're drunk!"

"No. It can't be possible." The words *drunk*, *Peyton*, and *Vern* didn't go together at all. Carrie had never seen either one of them inebriated. "But at least they're happy drunks." She regretted her words at once. There was nothing positive about a drunkard. Carrie learned that at the Wayfarers Inn. Even if a husband didn't go home and beat his wife, there were consequences.

"I expected better of my husband." Meredith's words sounded constricted by emotion. "He is a man of the cloth. He knows right from wrong."

"They both do."

Meredith replied with an angry grunt and yanked open the front door just as the men pushed it open from their side. They tripped and fell into the reception hall then lay on the tile floor, laughing.

Carrie assisted Peyton to his feet while Meredith helped Vern to a standing position.

"I'm disappointed in you, Vern."

"I am also disappointed." Carrie got a whiff of her husband's cigar breath. But why did his frock coat smell of cheap perfume?

Movement at the top of the stairs snagged Carrie's attention. Aunt Ruth glared down at Peyton while the moonlight streamed in through the stained-glass window behind her. She looked like an avenging angel.

Peyton had the gall to salute her.

After a disapproving wag of her head, Aunt Ruth strode back to her bed-chamber.

Peyton laughed, but stopped when his gaze fell on Carrie. His brow creased with a heavy frown that was quite pronounced even beneath the foyer's dim light.

"I'm sorry, my sweet." He slung his arm around her shoulders. "Vern and I indulged in a glass of champagne and Phil wouldn't allow it to remain empty. It would have been rude of us not to finish it."

"That's true." Vern swayed slightly forward, but upon glimpsing Meredith's scowl, he pulled his shoulders back.

"Up to bed with you," she ordered as sternly as any general, Union or Confederate.

Carrie walked Peyton as far as the balustrade before she turned to make sure the front door had been shut and bolted for the night. She gasped at the sight of two women standing at the threshold.

"Didn't mean to scare you, ma'am," the female on the left said. "Are you Mrs. Collier?"

"Yes."

"You're younger than we imagined," the other said, nudging her companion.

"We wanted to make sure your husband and his friend got home all right."

"How very kind of you." Carrie's heart dropped to her toes. Had Peyton been unfaithful in his drunken state?

"Both fellas were real gentlemen," the woman on the left said as if reading her mind. A pearl comb held one side of her dark hair away from her painted face. "That's why we followed them home. We wanted to make sure they didn't fall off their horses and end up in an alley somewhere without their billfolds come morning."

"How very considerate." Carrie's heart gradually resumed its normal pace. "I'm glad to hear the colonel and his aide minded their manners."

"Oh, yes, ma'am. They both seem like decent sorts." The dark-haired woman smiled. "You're real nice too. Little Phil said you would be."

Carrie moved a step back. "Little Phil?"

"The Yankee general."

"Of course." Carrie had met the commanding officer twice and both times the conversation was short. General Sheridan, while shorter than most men, made an impressive military figure. She didn't know anyone who would dare call him *Little Phil*.

"He said you wouldn't think badly of us if we showed up at your door to see those fellas safe inside."

"Thank you both. Very much." Carrie folded her arms. "However, I can't say how safe my husband is now that he's home." She pushed out a smile.

The ladies cackled.

"Good night, and thanks again for your kindness." Should she tip them? Carrie pressed her lips together in momentary thought. Better to err on the side of generosity.

She bade the ladies to wait a minute more while she fished several coins from Peyton's coat pocket. He muttered something, but didn't protest. Carrie placed two coins in each woman's palm. They thanked her and departed.

Carrie leaned her head against the door before turning the lock. Now, what to do about Peyton . . .

Anger and disappointment lodged painfully in her chest. She'd endured enough abuse and shenanigans from inebriated men to last a lifetime. Peyton said he was a changed man, a Christian man. He said he didn't partake in strong drink anymore. Carrie had believed him. She didn't want a drunkard for a husband.

Oh, Lord, how do I handle this situation? Carrie stared up at the moon through the window, wishing God would print the answer on its surface.

She recalled her wedding vows and her later promise never to leave Peyton. Ever. Seemed she'd gotten the reply she sought.

The foyer stood empty now. Clearly Peyton managed to drag himself upstairs on his own. She decided not to say a word to him tonight. Experience had taught her never to argue or discuss matters of importance with a drunken man. The chances were great that he wouldn't remember their conversation when sober. Yes, silence was the best approach.

Carrie trudged up the stairs. Inside their bedroom, she found her beloved collapsed on the settee and snoring like an oncoming locomotive.

He's only human, she reminded herself. *I am as sinful as he is.*

Carrie removed his jacket and tugged off his boots. She placed a pillow beneath his head. Then she removed her wrapper and crawled into bed. She quelled the urge to sob. How differently she'd planned this evening with Peyton. Instead, she was forced to listen to his noisy, drunken snores while she occupied the bed—alone.

Dear God, please don't let drunkenness become a habit. Please work in Peyton's heart and deliver him from what I know to be evil. Carrie's growing apprehension leaked from her eyes and soaked her pillowcase.

Sleep would be a long time coming.

─◦◦─

At the head of their brigade, Eli followed closely behind General Rosser as they quietly picked their way across the narrow trail with nothing but a bright moon and a prayer to guide their path. The dark face of Massanutten on one side and the swift-moving Shenandoah River on the other left no room for error, especially when the goal was not to alert the Yankees.

Reaching the bottom of the mountain, they walked their horses as silently as possible down a gravel lane, heading for Minebank Ford. It seemed to Eli that both man and mount sensed the gravity of this undertaking.

Eli knew the plan: Cross Cedar Creek and engage the Union cavalry. With General Rosser leading them onward, they formed a line on the west side of the bank. A chilly predawn mist rose up, effectively cloaking them. Every man had the Union pickets in their sights.

Eli's muscles twitched in anticipation beneath his gray wool jacket. He was glad for the bit of warmth his uniform provided on this cold, autumn morning. He checked his pistol and unsheathed his saber. He then glanced in the direction of the horse artillery. This cavalry division could not allow another disaster, such as was the rout at Tom's Brook. The Virginia Cavalry had been demoralized in that contest; Rosser's troops had been humiliated by Custer's horsemen. But, in minutes, the tide would turn. The Army of the Valley would again be victorious. This time the Yanks would be the ones surrendering or running for their lives.

Eli breathed deeply of the damp air. He was ready. Now he awaited the signal to attack.

Within minutes, he heard the crack of carbines to the east. Upstream, flames lit cannon fuses. A bone-jarring explosion, followed by another, then another, split the silent dawn.

With a Rebel yell of his own, Eli crossed the creek, leading the troops into battle. He fired his musket, as did others around him. When Eli reached the Yankee pickets, they dropped their weapons and surrendered. He left the prisoners to enlisted men.

Now to press on to the Yankee camp.

Pandemonium broke out as men making their coffee and breakfast were surprised and quickly overtaken. Some Yanks surrendered without much of a fight, but it didn't take long for the enemy to regroup and begin firing back.

Bullets whizzed past Eli's head. One grazed his cheek. The air was suddenly alive with ten thousand bees. Fog and artillery smoke blotted out the sun that popped up over the eastern mountains.

The battle for the Shenandoah Valley had begun.

―∞ ∞―

"Carrie. Carrie, wake up. I have to leave."

"What?" Her eyes fluttered open. Judging from the pale shafts of light escaping through the heavily draped windows, it wasn't much past dawn. "I only just fell asleep." She pulled her damp pillow over her head.

Peyton removed it almost as quickly. "Carrie, this is important. I can't leave without speaking to you."

She opened one eye and peeked at him. He'd pulled on his dark blue shell jacket, complete with accoutrements. "Are you still drunk?" It was the only question on her mind at the moment.

A shadow crept across his face. Remorse filled his gaze. "I'm sorry for my behavior last night."

He sounded sincere, but weren't they all after they sobered up? Carrie had heard such sentiments before—sorry they'd struck her even though she'd mouthed off, sorry for cursing, sorry for behaving unseemly—and she wouldn't tell their wives, would she? After all, they'd apologized.

A pity the same words passed over her husband's tongue now. Carrie wasn't ready to immediately forgive and forget.

"Will this be a regular event? If so, I would like to prepare myself."

"No. Definitely not." Peyton captured her hand in both of his. The shake of his head was so slight, she almost missed it. "I left drunkenness behind me when I came to faith in Christ."

"So you said."

"My actions last night were the result of my poor choices." He exhaled. "War is a hellish thing, so victories taste all the more sweet. The temptation to be merry was more than I could resist. I know that doesn't absolve me of my sin, but at least it's an explanation."

"And the women?"

He frowned. "What women?"

Carrie informed him of the two females who followed him home last night.

"They attended Phil's party, but neither Vern nor I acted inappropriately where they're concerned."

Carrie pulled her hand free and sat up. "And what exactly is appropriate behavior for a drunken man? I've seen plenty of them, and none of their behavior can be called 'appropriate.'"

"Allow me to rephrase. The worst things Vern and I did last night were consume too much champagne and sing at the top of our lungs all the way home, disturbing the neighborhood. Neither of us touched those women. And don't think I don't remember due to inebriation. Despite the champagne I consumed, I recall everything, including the fact that I've disappointed you."

Carrie stared at the quilt covering her lap and folded its finished edges. "Have I lost your trust?"

Had he? Carrie's eyes burned with unshed tears. "Not completely."

"Then there's hope for my redemption in your eyes."

"There's always hope."

A hard knock sounded at the door. "Colonel?" The deep male voice belonged to Vern Johnston. "We must leave at once."

Carrie glanced up. "Where are you going?" The deep creases on his forehead and the hard set to his gaze sent an arrow of alarm through her.

"We received reports of cannonading east of the turnpike and south of town. My regiment has been ordered to investigate."

Before a protest tumbled from her tongue, Peyton's hands cupped her face. His lips brushed against hers. She tugged on his wool coat and their kiss deepened until another hard knock resounded.

"Colonel?"

"I'm coming."

Carrie released him.

"I love you, my sweet. I love you more than words can ever express."

She opened her mouth to speak but raw, deep, and excruciating emotion barred the words she longed to say—perhaps even ought to say.

He stood and walked around the bed. His spurs and weaponry clattered with his every step. He pulled on his gauntlets and lifted his slouch hat. "I suspect it's merely Crook's troops, probing the enemy, and if I'm correct, I should be home for breakfast." He strode to the door. "Please tell Tabitha to have a pot of good strong coffee waiting. I have a drum pounding in my head." He snorted. "It's well-deserved, I realize." He pulled open the door. "We'll talk more when I return."

Carrie inched herself back beneath the bedcovers and rolled onto her right side, her back to the door. Peyton's words weren't empty. She was confident of that much. But would the drunken behavior be repeated?

Peyton closed the door behind him. His footsteps marked his way down the carpetless hallway, leading to the main part of the second floor. Outside men's shouts to mount up drowned Peyton's footfalls on the stairs. Minutes later, horses' hooves shook the ground like thunder.

Peyton was gone.

The Soldiers' Journal

FRIENDLY PICKETS: We have often remarked that when the belligerent troops are lying near one another for any length of time they become quite communicative and friendly. They forget that they are enemies, and a kind of chivalric honor and courtesy are strictly observed during their self-appointed truce. If they are compelled to fire during the existence of this self-constituted armistice, they fire the first volley in the air, so as to give the others time to get back.

The following incident, which happened a week or two ago in front of the Fourteenth Corps of Sherman's army, fully illustrates how sensitive they are on such occasions of their honor:—

Our works are pretty close to the enemy's and the pickets nearly meet in the center. There was no firing along the lines, and it occurred to the poor fellows on both sides that it would be pleasant to get up out of their rifle pits, stretch their cramped limbs, and have a little friendly intercourse with their neighbors. So a sort of ventriloquism conversation ensued from the pits, and all preliminaries being satisfactorily arranged, a regular truce was agreed upon. They jumped up, shook off the dirt, and met in so friendly a way that one would have thought they were the best and most loving neighbors in the world.

Trade was carried on in a small scale, escapes and adventures recounted, and home friends and scenes warmly discussed. In the midst of the thing, the Rebels in the rear called out to their comrades, "Boys, come back, the Major is coming." Now it happened that the Major was an old, rusty crusty customer, and had no hand in the truce at all; so when he came up he was in a fume, and called out, "———— you, come back here; and why the h———— don't you fire?" The men came back, but refused to fire on our fellows until they had got to their pits, which set the Major in such a boiling rage that he snatched a gun and popped at one of our men, slightly wounding him.

A regular cry of indignation at such a violation of faith was raised by his men, and five of them actually walked out of his lines into ours vowing that they could not, in justice to their honor, serve any longer in an army where honorable treaties were so grossly violated. Their comrades refused to interfere, and evidently deeply sympathized with their offended dignity. Our boys received them warmly; even the wounded man joined in the welcome.

Chapter 8

October 19, 1864

Eli rode behind Confederate lines to catch a few minutes of much-needed reprieve. He peeled off his hat and wiped the perspiration out of his eyes and off his forehead with the sleeve of his sweat-dampened coat. A breeze kicked up like a blessing from heaven. Removing one gauntlet, he used his fingers to rake back his sopping hair before replacing his hat and then his glove.

He'd been fighting for hours. The predawn mist had now lifted, revealing the morning's carnage across the field. He'd heard a report that General Kershaw's division had successfully overtaken Union General Thoburn's troops, and General Gordon's three divisions struck the Yankee campsite east of the Valley Pike with favorable results. Altogether, thirteen hundred prisoners and twenty cannon had been seized. From Eli's vantage point, it appeared this conflict would end well for the Confederate Army of the Valley, but it was far too early to claim the victory. While they'd routed hundreds of Federals, there were hundreds more to defeat.

He maneuvered his horse toward Confederate artillerymen. He reached for his canteen and rinsed the dirt and ash from his mouth. He tasted sweet victory. The Valley would again be theirs.

Reaching the line of cannon, he turned and saw the horsemen of Custer's, Wright's, and Merritt's cavalry, all seasoned veterans like himself, but there were more of them. The tide of the battle had turned. Eli's heart raced. They were now severely outmanned and outgunned. He directed the artillery toward the eddies of bluecoats marching toward Rebel foot soldiers. Then he urged his mount back into the fight, a challenging one to be sure.

Eli swung his saber and cut down one enemy fighter and, with his pistol in his left hand, shot two more.

In the distance, Confederate cannon pounded familiar reverberations through Eli's being. The air buzzed with bullets and carbines cracked all around. Smoke filled the air. Finally, the Union line broke.

Cheering came up somewhere behind him, spurring Eli onward. He clashed swords and defeated one opponent after another. His body pulsed with an unearthly kinetic force. He'd see this battle through and, God willing, he'd live to tell about it.

"Surrender, Reb!"

Eli would know that voice anywhere. He almost grinned when Peyton Collier appeared out of the dense fog of war and opposed him from astride his black charger. His bearded face was covered with soot and ash.

"I said surrender!"

"Never!" Eli ducked and barely missed being shot through the head. "You surrender, Yank! We've whipped you already."

"That's about to change."

For an instant, it was almost fun to clash sabers with his friend—always a friend. They parried one, two, three times. Eli brought his saber up once again, but simultaneously spurred his horse forward. A blue-belly charged him with his musket leveled at Eli's midsection. Eli made the strike first, his blade coming down on the Yankee's head before the enemy could run him through with his bayonet. The other man's lifeless body dropped to the blood-soaked ground.

Peyton evidently made a similar move, as Eli was still in one piece.

"Until we meet again, Reb!"

"I look forward to it, Yank!" Eli's voice was drowned out by the cacophony of gunfire and cannonading. He glanced over his shoulder and glimpsed Peyton fighting his way onward, flanked by two mounted cavalrymen. They soon disappeared into the smoky haze.

A shell whistled overhead. Dangerously close. Too close. Eli jerked on the reins, spurring his horse into a canter to escape the shell's impact zone. All the while, he evaded a bayonet on the left, and parried a blade on the right.

Seconds later, an explosion sent dirt, grass, and bodies flying into the air. The blast wave hurled Eli off his mount. Weightlessness enveloped him, before he slammed into something bone-breaking hard.

A tree.

His breath left his lungs as he landed on his back, but he gave in to his trained instinct to tuck and roll to avoid getting trampled. His body came to a sudden stop between two gray-clad corpses. When he was finally able to suck in air, it was only to choke on the thick smoke settling around him. His fallen comrades had likely saved his life by cushioning his fall.

And now he would suffocate.

Eli struggled to his feet, but failed time after time. *Breathe. Breathe.* His mount lay motionless several feet away. The horse had been a good one. Obedient. Loyal . . .

Breathe. Breathe.

He stopped trying to rise and instead managed to move by crawling on his belly over the debris of the battlefield. His breathing eased by increments, but then the sickeningly sweet smell of blood filled his nostrils and now he had to fight the instinct to hold his breath. Still, he clawed and scratched, his gray coat turning crimson, making for a thick clump of trees where the smoke thinned.

Keep breathing. Breathe.

Liquid fire now raged inside his leg. Reaching the base of an oak, he gulped fresher air and mentally recited his name, rank, and division, followed by the alphabet and the names of his family members—forcing himself to focus. With a clearer head, he moved his hand down his booted leg, praying to God his limb wasn't fractured. Such an injury would almost guarantee an amputation.

Eli found the place where shrapnel had sliced through his boot and lodged in his calf. He looked back toward where he'd fallen. Smoke from the explosion and gunfire rolled off the battlefield, revealing the carnage. Blue-coated forms of men, or what was left of men, littered the ground.

Peyton.

"Collier!" Eli's voice sounded muffled in his own head. And it was no match for the din of the battle. A moment's panic pierced his gut. He scanned the field. Peyt was nowhere in sight. Had he escaped the blast too?

Something sharp pressed against his jugular. Without moving his head, Eli shifted his gaze to his right. A sooty-faced Yankee stood beside him. He was breathless—and young. His mouth moved, but Eli couldn't hear him. The blast had stolen his hearing. "I can't hear you," he said, or at least he thought he said it. The Yankee hollered into his ear. This time Eli made out the words. "Surrender or die."

A week ago, Eli might have selected death over defeat, except for the agreement he'd signed only days ago. Given the choice, Eli was honor-bound to choose life.

Eli slowly lifted his arms. "I surrender."

—◌◌—

Margaret hurried down the streets of Winchester, clutching the infant in her arms closer to her breast. Gavin ran ahead because he knew his way around town, while his younger sisters clung to the skirt of Margaret's frock. Poor Rebekah's hands were full at the orphans' home, what with her usual volunteers now tending to wounded soldiers from this morning's battle. Margaret knew she had to help somehow, and offered to take these four children to Piccadilly Place. Aunt Ruth owned a cow and goat and could provide the necessary milk to keep this precious baby alive. He was the infant Meredith had come to adore and wanted to adopt. And Tabitha's pantry was filled with food to feed the other three urchins. Margaret couldn't leave the siblings behind and was certain the other ladies wouldn't mind.

Dozens of Yankees ran down the street, some on horseback but even more stumbling behind the fleeing band. Their clothes were torn and dirty, and their stares vacant as if they'd witnessed horrors that would haunt them forever.

Margaret quickened her pace; surely the ladies at Piccadilly Place would want details. About a block later, she'd worked up the gumption to make her way to the curb. She hailed an approaching Yankee horseman. As he neared, she glimpsed the bars on his arm and guessed he was an officer. He seemed bent on catching up to the routing Yankees up ahead.

"Please, sir, tell me what's happening."

"The Army of the Shenandoah is lost, ma'am. Wrecked by a surprise attack at dawn." His black horse pranced nervously as he spoke. The soldier's gaze sharpened. "It's probably good news to you secesh girls."

"You're mistaken, sir. I do not subscribe to that movement or any other. Never have." Not even in Woodstock.

"My suggestion, ma'am, is that you get your little ones home. Lock your doors and draw the draperies. The Rebels'll likely be marching into town before long. Now if you'll excuse me, I must apprehend those deserters." He nodded up the street. "Maybe if they'd stayed and fought like men, we wouldn't have lost the Valley."

She wrapped the baby's blanket tighter around him. "Can you tell me of any news about my brother-in-law, Colonel Peyton Collier? I believe he's a cavalryman."

The officer thought a moment, but then shook his head. "Sorry, ma'am, but my guess is he's in Middletown somewhere."

"Thank you anyway." Margaret backed away from the snorting charger.

"Anytime, ma'am." The Yankee seemed more agreeable after Margaret's mention of her relation to the colonel. After tipping his forage cap, the soldier spurred his horse up the street.

"C'mon, Miss Margaret!" Up ahead, Gavin waved his arms, urging her down the block.

"Coming."

"We gotta get to the Colliers' right quick," Gavin called again. "I hear cannonading a ways off. Might be coming closer."

Margaret caught the boy's anxious tone and stepped livelier, but not so fast that the little girls couldn't keep up.

At last they reached the Colliers' limestone home. The ladies must have seen them coming up the walk because they rushed out to meet her. Meredith took the infant from Margaret's aching arms.

"I hope you don't mind that I brought the children home with me," Margaret said. "Rebekah didn't have any help today."

"Of course, we don't mind." Aunt Ruth smiled at the small upturned faces.

"The baby needs to be fed. Someone made off with Rebekah's cow in the middle of the night."

"Good heavens! What is this world coming to?" Aunt Ruth led them into the house.

In the parlor, Meredith sat and cuddled the infant. "I talked to Vern last night and he was agreeable. You're going to be ours little one." She smiled at the baby. "I already thought of a name for you. McClellan Vernon Johnston. Little Mac, for short and named for the man who might be president next month, General George McClellan." She glanced at Margaret. "He was one of Vern's favorite commanders."

Margaret wasn't familiar with the man, but had heard that, if elected president, he vowed to compromise with the Confederates in order to end this horrid war.

The little girls clung to Margaret's skirt. Gavin already stood in the foyer, babbling about the cannonading he heard.

"We heard it too, but we're safe here." The calm in Aunt Ruth's voice had a soothing effect on both the children and Margaret.

Carrie Ann turned to her. "Were you able to discover what's happening?"

"Yes, actually." Margaret waited for Aunt Ruth to close the door and rejoin them before continuing. "A Yankee officer paused in his pursuit of Union deserters to tell me the Army of the Shenandoah got wrecked. Confederates will be marching into town soon."

"Oh, mercy!" Aunt Ruth put her right hand over her heart. "Tabitha, did you hear? Winchester is again under Confederate rule."

"I ain't deaf yet, Miss Ruth. I heard every word." The free Negro housekeeper lit a lamp. "We'd best hurry if we think to hide the valuables before those Rebs occupy our home again."

"Indeed." Aunt Ruth placed her hands on her hips and eyed Gavin. "You look like a strong boy. Will you help us?" She tipped her head. "I think a slice of pie might be adequate payment for your service."

"Oh, yes, ma'am!" His grin stretched from one ear to the other.

"I can help too," Galena offered.

"Good. Then come along." Like a grandmotherly goose and her goslings, Aunt Ruth strode into the parlor with the children in tow. Meredith took the fussing infant to the kitchen to feed him.

Carrie Ann scooped little Georgia into her arms. "Were you able to ask about Peyton?" The dimple appeared above her sister's eyebrow, indicating her concern.

"I inquired, but the soldier didn't know of his whereabouts."

Carrie Ann's shoulders drooped ever so slightly. "I'm so worried about Peyton. He said he'd be home by breakfast and now it's mid morning and we're hearing the worst." She stepped closer. "Margaret, did he really say the Army of the Shenandoah got wrecked?"

"He did." She felt an urge to embrace Carrie Ann and console her, but hesitated, unsure if her sister would appreciate the gesture.

"Come ladies," Aunt Ruth said, "we have much to do and it'll keep our minds occupied until we get further word about the present state of affairs. Grab something of value and follow me."

Margaret strode behind Carrie Ann as they made their way into the parlor. Aunt Ruth pointed Carrie to a large vase and instructed Margaret to gather the silver candlesticks. Each of the children took some knickknacks and framed photographs. With their arms full, they hurried to the library and carefully set the items on the polished wood floor. They made trip after trip. Once everything of value had been collected, Tabitha took the children into the kitchen for pie and milk.

"I don't want the children to know about the cellar unless the need arises." Aunt Ruth's hazel gaze found its way to Margaret. "And now, my dear, you must swear upon your soul that you will never reveal to anyone the secret room that I'm about to show you."

"I won't. I promise." Margaret meant it. She would never betray the Colliers. They took her in only days ago. They fed her, clothed her, and made her feel like she was truly part of a loving family.

"I will vouch for my sister." Carrie stood with her shoulders back and her chin held high.

Upon hearing the pledge, Aunt Ruth slid a large section of bookcase to one side.

"There's a secret cellar below the house," Aunt Ruth informed them. "Anything we don't want the Rebels to steal, we must hide—including ourselves, which was nearly the case a month ago."

Aunt Ruth held the panel aside, while Carrie Ann and Margaret, valuables in one hand and lamps in the other, found their way down then back up the narrow, creaking stairwell.

How many trips the two of them made, Margaret lost count. However, since Tabitha suffered with poor circulation in her legs and was in the kitchen hiding foodstuff, Meredith was occupied with the children, and Aunt Ruth was the lookout, the responsibility fell on Carrie's and Margaret's shoulders. But they were young and strong, especially so from completing the numerous daily chores that Mr. Veyschmidt had heaped on them.

At last the library floor lay as bare as many of the bookshelves. Aunt Ruth slid the panel closed.

"I've never seen such a thing or such a room as your secret cellar." Margaret lifted the corners of her mouth sassily and glanced at Carrie. "I've only heard about them in my older sister's bedtime tales."

Creases on Carrie's forehead told Margaret that her attempt at humor was useless. Her older sister could not rid herself of worrying over the colonel for even a moment. It was doubtful she even heard Aunt Ruth's explanation about the secret cellar.

"My father, Pappy, was an officer during the Revolutionary War. He knew he had to hide everything of value or pay a large tariff, which was out of the question, so he had the secret cellar built the same time as the house."

Aunt Ruth seemed to stand a little taller when she talked of her father.

"Pappy once told me that he and my grandmother were forced to hide in the secret cellar for days while the British ravaged their home." Her gaze circled the room. "It took years to repair the damage."

Tabitha entered the library. "I've been keeping those young'uns busy in the kitchen." She wagged her head. "That boy eats as much as two grown men."

"He's a growing lad," Carrie said.

Strains of music outside breezed into the room. Margaret hurried to the window, Aunt Ruth on her heels. A band marched down the street, playing "Lorena."

Did that mean the Rebels won the fight? Was the Shenandoah still the "Valley of Humiliation" for the Yankees?

Aunt Ruth slammed the window closed and pulled the draperies. "Don't listen to those off-key fools. Why, that band seems to play to each boom of cannon fire. They're likely to get themselves blown to kingdom come if they don't take shelter at once."

Margaret sensed the older woman's distress and saw it plainly on Carrie

Ann's face. She longed to comfort them, but words refused to form in her mouth.

Tabitha placed her hands on her hips. "Y'all may as well eat a hearty meal. No telling if we'll eat as good once the Rebels occupy our home. No doubt they'll turn us into personal maids, unless Colonel Kent is in charge. That man's the only Reb I care to see in this house."

"Dear me . . . this may be worse than I first presumed. Perhaps we should each pack a small valise." Aunt Ruth's fingers fluttered over her lacy ivory collar. "We may have to make an escape and temporarily vacate Piccadilly Place. The emphasis, of course, being on the word *temporarily*. But if the Confederates regain their hold on Winchester, loyalists will suffer. Mark my words."

"It's happened before," Tabitha added.

"Very well. But in the meantime—" Carrie Ann linked arms with Aunt Ruth while looking at Tabitha. "We'll eat our meal in the dining room . . . And, Tabitha, please set two extra places at the table in case the news Margaret heard is hogwash from a deserter. The band striking up those Confederate tunes most likely doesn't know any others." She lifted her head high as if hope itself held it there. "I have a feeling that Peyton and Vern will arrive home soon."

Margaret hoped so—for Carrie Ann's sake.

CHAPTER 9

With the setting sun on her face, Carrie stood on the back covered porch and admired the view. Soon the construction of the barn and stables would be completed. A crew made up largely of Quakers, men with whom Rebekah Kercheval was acquainted from her church, had been hired to do the building. The incessant hammering of weeks ago had lessened enough that it could largely be ignored.

However, all hammers were silent today. No doubt the workmen needed to be home protecting their families and property.

Carrie hugged her shawl more closely around her shoulders. The temperature fell as fast as the sun set—and still no word from Peyton. She didn't expect an important officer like him to pause in the midst of battle and dispatch a message to her. She'd have to wait. Trust in the Lord. Surely Peyton would come home soon.

Smoky clouds tinged with sulfur still scented the air and tickled her nostrils. Thankfully, the Confederate bands had quit their annoying grandstanding about mid afternoon when more gunfire and heavy artillery was heard in the distance. Another rout ensued afterwards, but this time, Rebel troops ran down the streets of Winchester. It was a scene eerily reminiscent of the battle exactly one month ago.

The battle noises had dissipated now. But which army was victorious? And Peyton . . . would he come home at last?

She whirled around and entered the house. Why was she so worried?

God was in control. But Carrie hated the way she and Peyton had parted this morning. It wasn't the way she wished to send her husband off to battle. No kindness or words of love.

"Yankees are coming!" Gavin tore into the hallway. "Yankees!"

The little girls screamed in terror.

Carrie caught the boy by the arm. "Stop it. You're scaring your sisters."

"Yankees." He pointed toward the front door.

Carrie shook her head at him. "Gavin, we are Yankees in this house. You are safe."

"Oh, yeah . . ." His features relaxed.

Carrie made her way to the entrance while Meredith, Margaret, and Aunt Ruth calmed the girls. Tabitha beat her to the door.

"I'm still the housekeeper of Piccadilly Place," she huffed.

"And a fine one you are at that." Despite her agreeable retort, Carrie skirted around the older woman and reached the doorknob ahead of her.

"Humph!" Tabitha folded her arms over her slender frame.

Carrie fully expected to see Peyton on the porch and his cavalrymen coming up behind him. Instead an officer whom she'd not seen before occupied the doorframe. He doffed his slouch hat, revealing a shiny bald head.

"Ma'am. I'm Major Donald Tucker and I intend to use your home for a Union hospital." His eyes took in Tabitha, still standing beside her.

Carrie shook her head. "I regret to inform you, sir, that neither you nor anyone else will use my family's home without our permission." Clearly, the man didn't realize the Colliers were loyalists. "My husband is Colonel Peyton Collier, cavalry division under General Wesley Merritt."

Deep lines formed across Major Tucker's forehead. He backed up a couple of paces and glanced around the porch. "I could have sworn I was here last month." Tiny crinkles appeared around his eyes as he stared into the evening sunshine, toward the empty lot next door. The property was littered with the charred remains of their former neighbors' home.

"You most likely occupied the Monteagues' house. It burned on the night of October first." Carrie would never forget it—her wedding night. "But tell me, Major, is the Army of the Shenandoah really lost?"

"No, ma'am. It was another victory for the Union. The nineteenth and sixth corps got walloped badly, but we regrouped and licked the Rebs." He inhaled, then released an audible sigh. "However, both sides took heavy casualties."

"Might you know the whereabouts or condition of my husband?"

"Afraid not, ma'am. The fighting took place over a wide swath of the Valley between here and Middletown and east as far as Massanutten."

Carrie's heart took a tumble, but she tried not to let it show. "Well, I'm confident he's in good health tonight."

"Some of the officers took up at Belle Grove. That's where Generals Custer and Sheridan decided to stay and much of the cavalry is camped on the Belle Grove property."

Sounded like a possibility.

"The fact is, ma'am, I've got two ambulances carrying our wounded on their way here along with a wagonload of injured Rebel prisoners coming up behind it. I need a spacious facility in which to operate and medically treat them. Both hospitals are filled and the Taylor Hotel is spilling over with the wounded and dying. So much so, they're lining up on the curb."

"Sounds like the last battle a month ago."

"Similar, yes." Determination shone in his dark eyes. "Most homes, churches, and schools in town are full also, so your home is needed, ma'am."

"Of course we'll accommodate you, sir." Peyton would want his family to accept the Union army's wounded. She swung the door wide open. Major Tucker muttered his thanks and hailed his staff.

"Tabitha, we've got company."

"So I heard." One brow arched, she eyed the major. "Something I don't like about him," she muttered. "Good thing we hid the silver."

Aunt Ruth rushed to the foyer, and Carrie explained the situation. "Thank God the Union army prevailed!" Aunt Ruth leaned against the balustrade—but only for a moment. Then she sprang into action. "Meredith, take the children upstairs and pull the sheets off all the beds. Tear them into bandages. Leave the quilts and pillows on the mattresses. We do need something to sleep on." She paused, deep in thought. "And there are extra blankets packed in the cedar chest at the foot of my bed."

Meredith gave a nod and collected the children.

"Please, use my bedchamber," Carrie said. "You'll be safely out of the way and you can build a fire in the hearth. The children can sleep in the anteroom."

"A generous plan. Thank you." Her friend stared at the precious bundle in her arms.

"I have an empty drawer in my wardrobe. Pad it with a quilt; it will make a suitable bassinet for now." Better, actually, than the wooden crates some of the infants slept in at the orphanage.

Once Meredith and the children were safely ensconced upstairs, Carrie attended to Aunt Ruth's instructions.

"Union wounded will go in the library," Aunt Ruth told incoming orderlies, carrying injured men who moaned and writhed on the stretchers. "Confederates in the music room."

Above the chaos, Carrie heard the chink of dishware. She hurried to the dining room where Major Tucker was clearing the table by rolling everything atop into the linen spread.

"What do you think you're doing?" She yanked the tablecloth from the man.

"I need this table to perform amputations."

"Out of the question." Aunt Ruth came up behind Carrie. "This table has been in my family for generations."

"Sorry, ma'am."

"I'll find another table you can use," Carrie put in quickly. An idea formed and she snapped her fingers. "The worktable in the kitchen."

"Oh, no, you don't." Tabitha had entered the room and now stood with hands on hips. "You're not taking my worktable."

"Tabitha, dear, be reasonable." Aunt Ruth patted the dark-skinned woman's arm. "We'll purchase a new and better worktable for you."

"I don't know . . ." She scowled at the major.

Margaret stood a ways off, watching the goings-on. A couple of soldiers were already carrying out the dining table. Aunt Ruth instructed them to set it and the matching chairs in the barn. Thankfully the roof was on the newly erected structure. A few other Union men hauled in Tabitha's table. After they set it down, Major Tucker shrugged out of his coat and wiped off the floury top with his shirt sleeves.

Carrie concentrated on the supplies she'd need. "We have the bandages . . . oh, and Tabitha, don't forget a jug of Mr. Veyschmidt's ale."

"If that doctor don't kill some men, that ale will."

"I've already proved its medicinal value. Now please be a dear and get it for me."

She shuffled toward the kitchen.

"I will assist the doctor with his surgeries," Aunt Ruth said, her eyes running over the saws and clamps that Tucker unpacked.

He overheard the offer. "Not necessary, madam. I have adequate staff."

"I insist, sir. My nephew is a cavalryman and I want to do my part for the Union army." Aunt Ruth tipped her head. "You wouldn't deny me that pleasure, would you, Doctor?"

Major Tucker glowered. "Oh, fine." He waved her into the dining room and two soldiers moved aside. "Sharpen up this saw blade, Lieutenant."

"Yes, sir." The tall, light-haired man hurried from the room.

"Who's first, sergeant?" Tucker rubbed his palms together in what appeared to be anticipation.

"I'll find out, sir." The young enlisted man with carrot-orange curls and freckles across his nose marched off.

The corners of the major's lips twitched in a way that made Carrie shudder. She'd assisted Dr. Paul-Henri LaFont with amputations during her stay at the Union camp last August, but never was LaFont pleased about performing the surgeries. Amputations were the final resort in order to save men's lives. But then why did Major Tucker seem so eager?

"Carrie Ann, dear . . ." Aunt Ruth slipped a motherly arm around her shoulders and pulled her aside. "I think it best that you and Margaret nurse the Confederate wounded in the music room. Tabitha and I will care for the Union men and I will periodically assist the doctor when necessary." Aunt Ruth leaned closer. "You've both got spunk enough to put any unruly Rebel in his place."

"Of course. Margaret and I work well together." Carrie's legs wobbled with relief. She hadn't been looking forward to witnessing the severing of limbs.

With purpose instead of dread now guiding her steps, she strode through the entrance hall. She motioned for Margaret to follow, but then had to jump onto the first stair alongside her sister as more orderlies arrived.

"Are you ready to hone your nursing skills?" Carrie hoped her glibness would ease Margaret's mind.

"Not that I had any before. Tell me what I do first."

"Well, Dr. LaFont taught me that first and foremost in dressing a wound is stemming the blood flow." Carrie tried to recall his instructions. "Next is cleaning the wound. If the patient is in horrible pain, we'll grant him a swallow or two of whiskey."

"Tabitha gave me the bottle of laudanum she keeps in the medicine cabinet." Margaret patted her apron pocket. "But I don't think she intended it for the Rebels."

"Likely not. But it's my belief that when it comes to doctoring, there is no enemy, merely wounded and needy men."

Carrie glanced over the railing and into the dining room. Major Tucker was, again, inspecting his saw's blade. He grinned and nodded to the lieutenant who had done the sharpening. Did he have to appear so delighted with what he was about to do? It grated on Carrie's taut nerves. How she wished Peyton would come home.

Tabitha entered the foyer, holding a bucket of water in one hand and a large basket of rags and bandages in the other. Somehow she also managed to clutch Veyschmidt's ale to her chest. Both Carrie and Margaret quickly relieved the older woman of her burdens.

"I've set a kettle of water on to boil and I'm on my way to see to the needs of our boys in blue."

"Thank you, Tabitha."

As the last syllable rolled off Carrie's tongue, an unearthly shriek cut through the house. Orderlies came into view, carrying a Rebel soldier toward the dining room.

"No! Don't take my leg! Don't take it!"

Bile rose in Carrie's throat as the men passed. The Rebel didn't look older than fifteen, but he'd likely seen as much hard fighting as any man.

God, please be with him.

Margaret clamped on to Carrie's arm and held it tightly until the Rebel's screams mercifully diminished behind the dining room's doors.

Carrie whispered up a prayer for strength and courage. "Come along, sister, we have work to do."

CHAPTER 10

Pain.

Eli's mind reeled from it. His head. His leg. His entire body.

Captured.

He remembered that much. Corralled like sheep about to be led to slaughter, he and the other secessionist soldiers. All day in the sun with nothing to wash the dirt out of their dry mouths.

At least his hearing returned.

Then a wagon ride to . . . to *somewhere*. Men piled on top of men, as if they weren't human. The smell of death so close that it lingered on his body.

Was he in prison, or was this hell? Weeping, wailing, and gnashing of teeth. Yes, that described his present existence. If he wasn't already a believer and confident in his faith, he'd convert this second.

Water! He required a sip, a gulp—a bucketful. Had Yankee doctors removed his leg? *Please, Lord, no!* Could he move his toes? Perhaps. Or did he suffer from phantom pains?

Another explosion of pain burst, radiating from his leg. His head bounced like a ball on a hard surface. He heard his own agonized groans. Then, blessed darkness.

From the distance, a woman called his name. Mother? Laurabeth? No. The woman addressed him formally.

"Colonel Kent, can you hear me?"

Her voice sounded familiar. She knew his name.

Cool fingers touched his face, his forehead. Liquid wetted his lips. Water. *Thank you, Jesus* . . .

"Slow down." Her voice was feather-soft. So sweet her breath across his cheek. "Just sip. You can have as much as you want."

Fresh water, not muddy river water. Eli forced his eyelids open. A room. Familiar. He'd been here before.

The angel of mercy placed a pillow behind his head. Eli rolled his head to the right. Pretty blue eyes stared back at him.

"You'll be pleased to know I gave those orderlies a good tongue-lashing for dropping you and the others on the floor like they did. How shameful."

Carrie Ann Collier.

His dry, cracked lips moved upward. He was not the occupier this time; he was the prisoner.

She leaned forward. "Here, swallow this." She spooned a bitter-tasting substance into his mouth. Before Eli gagged, she urged him to drink another swallow of water. "It's laudanum." She whispered the word and pressed her forefinger to her full, pink lips before glancing over her shoulder. "I can't let those Union soldiers know. They warned us not to give aid to the enemy." She let go of an exasperated sigh. "I wish Peyton would come home. He'd straighten these men out."

Oh, Lord . . . she hadn't heard the news.

Numerous times this afternoon, Eli had inquired about Peyton. Quite often his request for information got him jabbed with bayonets from men in blue who would have been more than happy to run him through. The October sun blazed down on him and the other prisoners, creating a powerful thirst that rivaled his pain. But he wasn't gut shot, so he and his fellow prisoners were corralled like cattle, except given no water to quench their thirst. Before he lost all strength, despite a comrade's attempt at tying a tourniquet around his leg, a Yankee finally told him what Eli feared. Peyton was dead.

Eli closed his eyes. "I wish it had been I who'd died on that battlefield this morning."

"Why would you say such a thing?" Carrie pressed a cool cloth across his forehead. "You're alive. Be glad for that, although you're quite a bloody mess."

"My leg . . ." *Oh, God, was it still attached to his body?*

It seemed to take forever before she replied. "Judging from what's leaking out of your boot, you've lost a lot of blood. I'd wager your leg is broken too."

So his limb was still attached. A blessed relief. "Don't let them amputate."

"For now, the only thing getting cut off is your boot, but I'll wait until your pain subsides."

"Do what you must." He managed to open his eyes once more and reached for her hand. "But promise me you won't let them amputate."

Her eyes dodged his pleading stare. "I can't promise any such thing, especially if it'll save your life."

Eli closed his eyes as the laudanum set to work. "What use will living be if I lose my leg and waste away in a Federal prison camp?"

"You'll be alive. Isn't that enough?"

Eli opened his mouth to argue.

"I wouldn't care if Peyton came home without a limb. I'd love him just the same and I'd rejoice that at least he'd returned to me."

Eli winced. *Peyton's widow.* But, perhaps, the terrible news he'd heard this afternoon was false. Perhaps the enlisted man bearing the news hadn't correctly heard Peyton's name. But what if it were true?

He squeezed his eyes shut. It might be said that Peyton fell indirectly by Eli's hand. He'd crossed swords with Peyton this morning. They had been fighting against each other, though neither could actually kill the other.

A knot lodged in his throat. He'd ordered the cannon to blast into oncoming Yankees. True, he'd had no idea that Peyton would ride right into it. But would that matter to the Collier ladies? All they might need to hear is that Peyton was dead.

Eli's heart twisted. They'd hate him forever.

⸺ ❧ ⸺

"Carrie Ann, why are these men's jackets and shirts ripped wide open?"

Wringing out a rag, Carrie glanced up at Margaret. "Ripped open on the battlefield, I presume, to make sure these men weren't gut shot."

"And if they were?" Margaret's brow furrowed.

"They would have been left to die." Carrie placed the cloth across Colonel Kent's forehead. He seemed to be resting easier now. "Peyton was left on the Gettysburg battlefield after he was severely injured by a saber's slash. I've seen the scars. Amazingly, Peyton survived, thanks to Majors Johnston and LaFont who didn't give up on him, but, of course, the glory goes to God Almighty."

Margaret knelt beside a wounded soldier who moaned and rolled his head from side to side in agony. She clutched the dry rag in her hands as she stared at him.

"Margaret." Carrie caught her sister's attention and pointed to her apron pocket. *The laudanum.*

Within seconds, Margaret's blue-green eyes registered understanding. She glanced around to make sure she wouldn't be seen by Federal soldiers before administering the drug. She followed the spoonful with a ladle of water. In minutes, the Rebel soldier quieted. Margaret then dipped the rag in the bucket and placed it over the man's forehead.

On her knees, Carrie sat back and regarded Colonel Kent's knee-high black leather boot. The left, when compared to the right, looked twice the size.

"I believe I broke my leg when I was thrown off my horse," he murmured. "Afterward, or perhaps simultaneously, I took shrapnel from the same shell that killed . . ." He pressed his lips together. Dark whiskers shadowed his strong jaw. "It killed a lot of men."

"Then the Almighty's angels were with you today, Colonel."

"A matter of perspective, Mrs. Collier."

She ignored the retort. The man should be glad he was alive and that his limbs were still connected to his body, unlike the poor soul who lay two men down the queue. That Rebel's arm dangled by one stubborn piece of sinew, the rest had been severed on the battlefield. He bled profusely despite Carrie's and Margaret's efforts, but the Union medical staff seemed in no hurry to give him aid. Carrie guessed the injured man would be dead within the hour.

"Margaret—Margaret . . . will you help me cut off the colonel's boot?"

"Of course." She wiped her hands on her apron and scooted over to Colonel Kent's left side. "Carrie Ann, I never did see sights like these before."

She noted her younger sister's peaked complexion. "Would you rather help Meredith upstairs with the children?"

"No. My place is here, helping these men." Her chin lifted in stubborn determination. Yes, the fortitude had always been there, but her younger sister had finally turned that strength to something other than herself. The change was most welcome.

"All right, then. Ready?" Carrie gripped the sharpest knife that Tabitha claimed to own and began to cut the leather. Once she'd slit it open to the ankle, Margaret carefully pulled the shoe portion off his foot. The stench that rushed out and quickly permeated the music room turned Carrie's stomach. She grabbed the offensive item and ran to the window. She managed to lift the sash with one hand and toss out the blood-filled boot with the other. Behind her, sounds of retching told Carrie that she wasn't the only one sickened by the smell of moldering flesh and blood.

It was apparent that the colonel had bled into his boot for the past twelve hours with no medical attention, save for a nearly ineffective tourniquet. Why hadn't he received better care? That boot should have been the first thing to come off.

Months ago, when Carrie followed the Union camp, she'd watched and assisted Dr. LaFont—the same man who had saved Peyton's life. The good doctor didn't consider the color of an injured man's uniform. Instead he attended to the most severely wounded first.

Not so with Major Tucker.

"I'm sorry. I vomited in the water bucket." Margaret ran her sleeve across her lips. "I'll go wash it out and refill it from the well."

Carrie sympathized. The sickeningly sweet smell of blood, urine, and humanity was enough to try anyone's gag reflex. For that reason, she'd left the window open in spite of the evening's growing coolness.

Carrie knelt beside the colonel and examined his injured left leg. An unnatural bend appeared several inches below his knee, and a large bruise spread upward. It was broken, no doubt. Upon closer inspection, she saw an entrance wound, but no exit wound, which indicated that a foreign object was still lodged inside the colonel's leg. As long as it could be removed and the bone hadn't been destroyed, as was the case with most minié ball injuries, the break could likely be repaired without amputation.

Movement at the doorway seized Carrie's attention. Aunt Ruth walked into the music room, carrying a lantern. Her eyes fixed on Carrie's patient, then recognition dawned.

She hurried forward. "Oh, dear . . . is that Eli Kent?"

"Yes."

Aunt Ruth hunkered beside him and placed her hand on his forehead. "No fever. That's good."

"I'm no doctor, of course, but I think he'll be able to keep his leg." Carrie smiled. "He'll be a debonair Southern gentleman again in no time."

Aunt Ruth's lips lifted briefly at the corners of her mouth. "I doubt Major Tucker will arrive at the same diagnosis." She hugged herself.

Carrie noted her ashen face. Aunt Ruth was accustomed to seeing the horrors of war. She had been a nurse in the western territories during the Spanish American War in '46. "You don't look well. What's wrong?"

"That man—Tucker—he is a butcher. A butcher!"

Carrie sucked in a breath and glanced around to be sure that no Union soldiers hovered near. "Why do you say so?" she asked, keeping her voice low.

Aunt Ruth leaned into Carrie. "He amputated the wrong leg on a young Confederate soldier," she whispered. "After realizing his mistake—and I use that word *mistake* loosely—that horrid man proceeded to take off the injured one." Tears glistened in Aunt Ruth's eyes. "That boy can't be more than seventeen years old, and now I doubt he'll live to see the dawn."

Carrie thought the Rebel looked awfully young. With heavy heart, she glanced toward the pickets at the door. They were occupied, murmuring among themselves.

"Worse, Tucker is completely nonchalant about the matter." Aunt Ruth sniffed and produced her hankie.

"Perhaps we should send a courier with a message to Belle Grove, begging for a qualified surgeon."

"And how do you think you'll accomplish that?" Aunt Ruth inclined her head toward the many Union troops traipsing through the house. "These soldiers don't want to risk Tucker's wrath. They will never allow you to hire a courier and send a message."

"We have to try. Besides, we're not prisoners."

"True, but Tucker has imposed a curfew on us of nine o'clock. He said the orders came from his higher-ups."

"Speak louder please, ladies." Colonel Kent's raspy voice held an odd note of amusement. "I cannot hear you when you whisper." Immediately his features contorted with pain.

"I know what you're attempting, Eli, but don't try to be brave on our accounts." Aunt Ruth inspected his leg and Eli let out a yowl. Aunt Ruth pushed herself to a standing position.

Carrie stood also.

The older woman shook her head. "I fear Tucker, that sorry excuse for a medical doctor, will insist upon amputation."

"Then we must request a replacement."

"No!" This time Colonel Kent heard even their whispers. "I prefer death to amputation!" His dark eyes locked on Carrie. "You promised."

She hunkered at his side. "I swear I will do everything in my power to see that you keep your limb—and your life." In truth, it was hard to imagine the handsome colonel enjoying life as a cripple.

Aunt Ruth gave a nod of silent affirmation, and the corners of the colonel's mouth twitched upward as he drifted off.

Margaret entered the room, with a sloshing bucket of fresh water. Carrie and Aunt Ruth moved outside of Colonel Kent's earshot.

"We must stop Major Tucker." Carrie wasn't afraid to try sneaking out of the house if that was their only option.

Margaret set down the bucket and crossed the room. She stood beside Carrie and listened to the volleying of ideas, most of which were impractical to say the least.

"I brought along a bottle of Mrs. Quagg's sleeping potion. Maybe we could offer Major Tucker a glass of whiskey or cup of coffee as a show of our gratitude." Margaret winked.

Carrie perked up as possibilities flooded her mind. She clasped Aunt Ruth's hands then quickly and quietly informed her about Mrs. Quagg's potion.

"You don't say . . ." Aunt Ruth's eyes widened.

"A few drops of potion," Margaret whispered, "and I promise he'll be sound asleep in no time. He'll stay asleep while Carrie Ann writes her request for another surgeon and hires a courier."

Carrie exchanged glances with Aunt Ruth. "It sounds possible, don't you agree?"

"Indeed." A spark of respect entered Aunt Ruth's gaze as she regarded Margaret. "It's certainly worth a try—as long as we won't kill him."

"Oh, no, ma'am. We won't." Margaret beamed. "I've used the potion plenty of times and I ain't killed nobody yet. I'll go fetch it."

Within minutes, Margaret produced her vial of liquid lethargy and the ladies agreed on a plan of action. Since the children slept, Meredith would be free to assist in caring for the wounded. Tabitha was already doing her utmost for the Union men, both wounded and able-bodied alike. The latter had the poor woman rushing to and from her kitchen, bringing them food and making and serving coffee.

So it was no curiosity when she produced a glass of whiskey for Major Tucker, the officer in charge.

From where she knelt, caring for the dying amputee, Carrie felt no remorse for her part in the scheme. What's more, most of the guards were aware that Tucker enjoyed slaughtering enemy combatants. She was confident they wouldn't stop her from sending a missive to Belle Grove.

Within the hour, everything fell into place. Major Tucker slept soundly in a chair in the parlor. His snores filled the room. Aunt Ruth discovered a sympathetic guard outside the house and convinced him to find a courier willing to take a message to Belle Grove.

With those details taken care of and the wounded being tended to, Carrie strode to the well-room and washed up before making her way to Peyton's study. She unlocked the door and entered, then sat behind his desk. Peyton had invited her to enter his office any time she felt the need. He'd shown her where his important papers were kept locked in a wall safe, located behind a shelf of books. She'd committed the combination to memory. Thankfully, Major Tucker and his men didn't insist upon occupying this room. Evidently they still held some respect for Peyton's rank.

Dipping a pen in ink, Carrie pondered to whom the letter should be addressed and decided on General Sheridan himself. Several men stated that he was at Belle Grove, Union headquarters in Middletown. In her missive, she described the details of the Collier ladies' most distressing present situation and requested Major Paul-Henri LaFont as Major Tucker's replacement. Not wanting to seem disrespectful she added that any other qualified surgeon would do. She signed the letter and then took out another sheet of stationary and wrote, this time, to Peyton.

Why, when she thought of him, did a sense of foreboding envelope her?

Perhaps it was merely the guilt she experienced for not sending him off on a better note this morning and then seeing all the wounded after today's battle.

Carrie began to write. She begged Peyton to come home, but also stated that she would abide by his decision, whatever it might be, and wrote that she understood his sworn duty to defend and protect the United States of America. Carrie worked her bottom lip between her teeth as she dipped the pen into the ink bottle.

I am so very proud of you, my darling, but the battle today was so close that I find myself worrying over your welfare. If you cannot come home, please send back word with the courier and alleviate my anxieties. Your loving wife, Mrs. Carrie Ann Collier

After signing and sealing this missive, Carrie tucked it into the envelope. She whispered up a prayer. Oh, that the words she'd penned would reach Peyton. *On the wings of Your angels, Lord.*

"Carrie Ann?"

She startled. Across the room, Margaret stood in the doorway.

"The courier has arrived."

CHAPTER 11

"Carrie Ann, a number of these men's wounds, including Eli's, cannot wait much longer for medical intervention."

At the sound of Aunt Ruth's voice, she turned from the parlor windows where she'd been watching the pinks of dawn stretch across the sky. She had hoped to see Peyton and his men on their mounts cantering down Piccadilly Street toward home. "What should we do?"

"For Eli, I believe that with your help, we can straighten his leg while Tucker finishes slumbering." She dangled a bottle from her fingertips.

"What have you got there?"

"Chloroform. I borrowed it from Major Tucker's medical bag."

"Tsk, tsk, Aunt Ruth." Carrie grinned, wishing she would have thought of it.

"But now how to get Eli to the surgical table in the dining room." Pursing her lips, Aunt Ruth regarded the guards, who stared right back. "Young man . . . yes, you there."

The Union soldier stepped into the room. "Trouble, ma'am?"

"In a manner of speaking." Aunt Ruth indicated with her hand to Eli's wounded form. "I need this man taken to the surgical table in the dining room, and I want him transported there carefully."

"What fer?" The young man stroked the peach-like blond fuzz on his jaw. "Major Tucker's sleeping."

"Exactly. Now, hurry up so we can tend to this man."

"He's a Reb, ma'am. He can wait till mornin'."

"No, he cannot. Besides, what do you care if we operate on him? Now, do as I say." Aunt Ruth sounded so authoritative that Carrie wondered if the guard would salute.

"Well, I guess there's no harm in lettin' you practice on him."

"That's the spirit."

Eli groaned.

Aunt Ruth clapped. "Get the stretcher. Hurry now."

The young Union man walked to the room's archway and whispered to his comrades, but Aunt Ruth was determined to have her way. Within minutes she had the pickets scrambling.

When she returned, she placed her hands on Carrie's shoulders. "You've seen Paul-Henri do this surgery. You've assisted him. I'm confident your attempt will be better for Eli than if we do nothing. For the remaining Rebels, we'll have to fish out the bullets or minié balls and hope for the best."

Carrie wanted to find fault in Aunt Ruth's logic, but couldn't. Instead, she lifted Veyschmidt's homemade ale and followed Aunt Ruth into the foyer.

"I'll fetch a bucket of clean water." Margaret rushed toward the well-room.

Carrie entered the dining room and willed herself not to gag. The nauseously sweet smell of blood, mingled with men's body odor, hung heavily in the room. A predawn breeze drifted in through the slightly opened window and a chill slithered down her spine.

Please, God, give me wisdom and guide my hands.

Tabitha brought in a kettle of boiling water and set it down just as the Union soldiers deposited the colonel onto the surgical table. His features twisted in agony from the none-too-gentle transport. Carrie made up her mind then and there that she couldn't—wouldn't—let him or any others die for lack for medical attention.

Aunt Ruth got right to work and sprinkled a few drops of chloroform onto one of Peyton's clean handkerchiefs. "Now, Eli, you're going to have to trust us. You simply have no other choice."

"Certainly a man is not without choices." Beads of perspiration dotted his forehead. He appeared to be considering his fate. Then Aunt Ruth moved his leg and he let out a groan. "Do what you must," he muttered breathlessly. "I trust you—more, in fact, than that Yankee quacksalver."

Carrie stroked his dark, damp hair off his forehead. "I will do my very best, Colonel. I promise."

"I know you will."

"Sleep now, Eli." Aunt Ruth dropped the handkerchief over his nose and mouth. Within moments, his body went limp and she removed the cloth. Her gaze met Carrie's. "And now, my dear girl, it's up to you to extract the foreign object from his leg."

"I'm ready."

Using a pair of tongs, Aunt Ruth pulled a knife from the steaming kettle then wrapped the handle in a cloth and presented it to Carrie. "I'll assist you." She began by unwrapping the colonel's wounded leg just as Margaret entered with an armful of bandages. Again Carrie whispered up a prayer. She inspected the oozing, swollen point of entry and doubt crept in. What if the foreign object was imbedded in the broken bone? What would Dr. LaFont do?

"Margaret, dear," Aunt Ruth instructed, "if the colonel so much as peeps, put a drop or two of this"—she handed over the chloroform—"on that handkerchief beside him, and place it across his nose and mouth."

"Yes, ma'am."

"I believe we're ready, *Dr. Collier*." Aunt Ruth's hazel eyes twinkled.

Knife in hand, Carrie summoned every ounce of her remaining courage and slit open the wound. Blood flowed out and she forced herself not to take a step backward. Instead she recalled the way Dr. LaFont would simply insert his hand into the wound and dig around until he found whatever foreign object lurked inside.

Swallowing hard, Carrie did the same, praying she'd paid close enough attention during similar surgeries. Sometimes, she'd closed her eyes, or watched the patient's face, not Dr. LaFont. Two months ago, so much blood and death had overwhelmed her that she'd shed a river of tears. Finally Peyton had become concerned and sent her here to Winchester and Aunt Ruth.

"What's it feel like inside his leg?" Margaret peered over Carrie's shoulder for a better view.

"Like the warm insides of a catfish, but I'm not thinking about it. I'm concentrating on finding that—" She gasped. "I found it!"

"I knew you would." Aunt Ruth sopped up the red bodily fluid that spilled out.

"Now to remove it without injuring something important . . ." Not that Carrie could make the distinction of which sinew beneath her fingers was important and which a man could live without.

Twice Carrie lost hold of the slippery object, but grasped it again. At last, she produced the deadly thing, a piece of shrapnel from the look of it, and dropped it into the rag Aunt Ruth held out.

"Now, if you'll hold this piece of cloth against the wound, Carrie Ann, I'll straighten his leg. There may be more bleeding afterward." She glanced at Margaret. "Perhaps you ought to give him a quick whiff of the chloroform now, just in case."

Margaret did as instructed.

"Grab hold of his leg, right above the knee, Carrie Ann. Hold it still."

Aunt Ruth pulled and pressed. Carrie grimaced. The sight was painful to watch, let alone experience. Poor Eli.

He exhaled a throaty groan. Margaret quickly reapplied the handkerchief to his lower face.

Finally Aunt Ruth pronounced the bones adequately aligned.

Carrie washed the wound with Veyschmidt's ale for good measure, and then stitched it up. When she finished, Aunt Ruth and Margaret wrapped it snugly.

"It's up to our merciful Savior now." Aunt Ruth dropped the knife into the kettle. "We have others to mend before Major Tucker awakens so we'd best hurry."

"I'll check on the injured Yankees and see if Meredith needs anything." Margaret pressed her lips together for a second. "Pardon me. I meant injured *Federals*."

"Never mind, dear." Aunt Ruth waved off the apology. "In this home *Yankee* is not a slur."

Tabitha kept water boiling and medical paraphernalia within Aunt Ruth's and Carrie's reach. Except for the young Rebel amputee, who'd perished during Colonel Kent's surgery, Carrie and Aunt Ruth were able to give aid to the other prisoners.

The mid-October sun had just popped over the magenta horizon when Carrie's strength melted away. She dropped onto one of the steps in the foyer and held her head in her hands. Margaret sat beside her, shoulder to shoulder.

Upstairs, the children were stirring, and the baby's cry reached Carrie's ears.

"I'll see to the children," Margaret said before Carrie could rise. The grandfather clock in the parlor chimed seven and minutes later horses' hooves sounded out front.

The courier. The idea of a reply from Peyton sufficiently revived Carrie. She rose and unpinned her bloodied apron.

"It's General Sheridan!" one of the pickets called.

Men scrambled to their stations—all except Major Tucker, who couldn't be roused even when an enlisted man tugged on his arm.

Carrie smiled. *Perfect.*

A guard pulled open the front door and in strode the commander of the Army of the Shenandoah.

Carrie hurried forward. "General Sheridan, sir, I didn't expect a personal reply to my missive."

"Mrs. Collier." He bowed politely. "Your missive was most distressing." His dark eyes roved around the foyer while more troops flowed into the house like a sea of blue. "However, there is another matter more pressing which I must speak with you and Miss Ruth Collier about in private. And my aide would like a private word with Mrs. Johnston. Is she still here?"

The man beside the general nodded politely, his expression stern.

Carrie felt as though she'd been socked in the stomach. Why would General Sheridan want to discuss a pressing matter unrelated to Major Tucker's behavior?

She probed the question while showing the aide into the parlor and the general into Peyton's study. Then at last she found her voice. "If you'll excuse me, sir, I'll fetch Aunt Ruth and let Meredith know your aide is waiting to speak with her."

"Of course." He seated himself in a padded leather armchair.

Carrie rushed to find Aunt Ruth. Her heart beat out an anxious rhythm. Locating the older woman, she told her of their guests. Moments later she found Meredith and suggested the parlor as a private meeting area.

"Why would the general's aide have to speak with me in private?"

"I can only guess." Carrie's stomach cramped as if she'd swallowed a peach pit. "However, I reckon we'll all know shortly."

"You're right, of course." With her head held high, Meredith headed for the parlor.

Margaret caught Carrie's elbow. "Perhaps I should take the children back to the orphans' home. They're getting antsy and the girls are frightened by all the soldiers."

"A fine idea. Thank you."

Carrie hurried back to Peyton's study. When she reached the crowded foyer, she nearly collided with Major Paul-Henri LaFont.

"Ah, Petite—I mean, *Mrs. Collier.*" He removed his hat and bowed. "You are as lovely as ever. How pretty you look in your frock and not men's trousers."

At another time she would have found the remark amusing, but all she could think of at the moment was discovering the reason for General Sheridan's visit. "If you'll excuse me, Dr. LaFont. Guests are waiting for me and I dare not detain them any longer."

"But, of course." He bowed again.

Carrie crossed the foyer and entered the study where Aunt Ruth was engaged in polite conversation with the general over the lovely October weather.

However, as soon as Carrie closed the door, the commander's placid expression vanished. "Please sit, ladies. We have much to discuss."

The general reclaimed his seat and Aunt Ruth took the matching leather armchair. Carrie selected the small side chair, moving it into the circle of three. Collecting her skirts in shaking fingers, she seated herself in proper fashion.

"First, I will address Mrs. Collier's message." General Sheridan's eyes were midnight black and he spoke from behind a thick, curling beard. "You have my word, Major Tucker will be punished for neglecting his duties."

"Sir"—Carrie clasped her hands tightly—"it goes far beyond neglect."

"She's right, General." Aunt Ruth relayed the sordid account of the young Confederate who lost both legs to amputation—when one of them was perfectly good.

"That is a disgrace!" Sheridan slammed his right fist into his left palm. "The Union army has no use for officers of such ill caliber. Why, General Ramseur was wounded yesterday and he was brought behind our lines and cared for at Belle Grove. The surgeons did everything in their power to save his life."

"Is General Ramseur dead?" At Sheridan's slight nod, Carrie's heart sank. Stephen Dodson Ramseur, "Dod" to his friends, was a hero in the Shenandoah Valley. Living in Confederate Woodstock, she had heard all the tales of his daring. "What a shame." She caught Aunt Ruth's troubled regard. "But it's good to know that the Union doctors treated a Confederate general to the best of their abilities. We cannot say the same about Major Tucker."

"He will suffer the consequences of his actions. Believe me." The general's additional promise was enough for Carrie. An ounce of tension left her shoulders. "And now some hard news, I'm afraid." Sheridan's dark eyes rested on Carrie and she held her breath. "Mrs. Collier, your husband and his men were heroes during yesterday's battle. They bought the Union army time to regroup from what began as a devastating rout. Once we re-formed our lines, we had little trouble overpowering the enemy."

"And Peyton?" Carrie whispered, fearing the worst. Her eyes clouded with unshed tears.

"He's missing, Mrs. Collier, and presumed dead."

"Missing?"

A little cry escaped Aunt Ruth. She brought her hand to her mouth.

Carrie shot to her feet. "But why is he presumed dead if he's only missing? Maybe Peyton is on the battlefield and in need of medical care—like what happened to him at Gettysburg."

The general slowly rose to his full height which wasn't much taller than Carrie. "Mrs. Collier, soldiers have a way of keeping track of each other, especially during battle. The rear cavalrymen in your husband's regiment reported that those troops fighting alongside your husband yesterday perished during heavy artillery fire. Your husband's body hasn't been found and, to be honest, it may never be found. Artillery shells are designed to do two things: dismember and destroy."

"But then how am I to believe that my husband is dead?" Carrie's mind couldn't absorb it all, even though it was exactly what she'd feared yesterday when Peyton hadn't returned. "He said it was a small uprising and that he'd be home by breakfast."

Aunt Ruth rose and drew near. She placed one arm around Carrie's waist. "Thank you, General Sheridan." The anguish in her voice only vexed Carrie all the more.

"No!" She resisted stamping her foot. "He's not dead."

"Carrie Ann . . ."

Ignoring the warning in Aunt Ruth's voice, she glowered at the army commander and clenched her fists at her sides. "Perhaps if my husband had come home sober and at a decent hour the night before last, the entire outcome would be different this morning."

"Carrie Ann, please . . ."

General Sheridan held up a hand, forestalling Aunt Ruth's pleas. "I'm sorry, Mrs. Collier. Truly. I knew your husband well and he was an asset to the cavalry. He had gumption and dash. He will be sorely missed."

"But he's not dead. He can't be. He's . . . *missing*. You said so yourself."

The general's chest expanded with his large intake of air, but no reply was forthcoming. Carrie folded her arms while the man collected his hat and paused only long enough to grasp Aunt Ruth's hand in a momentary show of condolence. Then he left the room, closing the door behind him.

Aunt Ruth dissolved into tears and collapsed into the leather side chair.

"He's not dead! Do you hear me, Aunt Ruth?"

Carrie's attempt at bravado was thwarted by her quivering chin and scalding tears. Peyton couldn't be dead. She needed to tell him she loved him. She needed to forgive him for overindulging, although it seemed so unimportant at this moment. She would rather have Peyton alive and drunk every day than . . . *missing and presumed dead.*

A knock sounded at the door before it opened wide. Tabitha entered and knelt beside Aunt Ruth's chair.

"Our boy's gone, Miss Ruth." Her voice was thick with emotion. "He's gone."

"No, he's not." Carrie ground out each word. "He is missing. That is not the same as . . . *gone!*"

The ladies stared at her as if she'd grown a second head.

Carrie pulled back her shoulders. "My papa used to say that a good journalist needs evidence when writing a story. It's the same in life. Right now, we have no evidence that Peyton's dead."

"Oh, Carrie Ann," Aunt Ruth said in a strangled voice. "It's not the same at all. Not at all." She let go of her tightly wound dignity and sobbed.

Carrie swatted her own tears away. She could insist upon all the evidence in the world, but that wouldn't change what, for now at least, was the truth.

Peyton was most certainly . . . *gone.*

Chapter 12

October 20, 1864

Dead.

Margaret jogged down the street not caring that her gait was an unlady-like one.

Dead. Poor Carrie and Meredith. They were widows now . . .

Margaret had heard the news this morning from Miss Rebekah Ker-cheval, who had learned it from soldiers marching past the Repairers of the Breach. Rebekah habitually inquired about everyone she knew, Colonel Collier and Major Johnston being among them.

Dead. The word was so final—and frightening, although just a month ago, she would have preferred death to life at the Wayfarers Inn. Now, however, she valued her life and the lives of those she held dear.

However, everything would change now. Margaret increased her strides until she ran the last block to Piccadilly Place. Once inside, she breathlessly pushed her way by the Yankees. One must have either guessed or recognized her as a household member, and pointed to the closed door of Colonel Collier's study. She knocked on the paneled door and a faint voice from behind it bid her enter.

She turned the knob, opened the door, and stepped in. She resisted the urge to wrinkle her nose at the waft of stale tobacco, rich leather, and the faintest hint of brandy. Stepping farther inside, Margaret glimpsed the rows of bound volumes lining shelves that occupied an entire wall. At the other end of the study stood the colonel's impressive mahogany desk. Closing the door behind her, she found the four women huddled together and sobbing.

Margaret's heart crimped. "I heard the terrible news." Tears welled in her own eyes.

Aunt Ruth came forward with arms wide open. "Oh, my dear. It's the worst news possible."

"Not the worst, Aunt Ruth." The forcefulness in Carrie's tone seemed out of place. "We have hope. We all have hope."

Margaret stepped back and regarded her sister. She knew that expression—had seen it on Carrie's face before, the stubborn tilt of her head, her lips pressed firmly together, unshed tears pooling in her eyes. She'd declared war on reality.

Carrie placed a hand on their friend's shoulder. "Meredith's faith will keep her strong. She knows Vern is in glory and in the arms of the Savior. Meanwhile our faith will keep us hanging on by a prayer until Peyton comes home."

"Comes home?" Margaret's frown melted away. Maybe there was hope after all.

"Mm-mmm . . ." From where she stood, closest to the door, Tabitha wagged her head capped with white hair.

Tiny prickles inched up Margaret's spine. Had Mama's illness struck Carrie? But no. Mama used to utter sheer nonsense when her mind took its leave. Carrie seemed to possess all of her faculties.

"My faith is a comfort to me, yes." Meredith dabbed her eyes with her lace hankie. "And I cannot say that I'm surprised by this sad news. Ever since Vern left our church's pulpit for the Union army, I have feared this very moment." She drew in a ragged breath. "Now it has come to pass."

Carrie wrapped her slender arms around Meredith's shoulders. "There, there, dear friend."

"You've lost your husband too." Meredith gently pushed Carrie away and tucked strands of hair behind Carrie's ear. She cupped Carrie's cheek. "You must face the truth bravely—as I hope to do."

Margaret held her breath.

"But bravery does not come without tears," Meredith added. "As widows, we will lean on each other."

"If I were a widow, then yes. But I'm not." Carrie straightened. "Peyton is missing, but that doesn't mean he's dead."

"Oh, Carrie Ann . . ." Aunt Ruth waved her white hankie as if in surrender. "Stop being so stubborn and accept facts. Peyton is dead. You heard what General Sheridan said."

Carrie sent Aunt Ruth an icy glare then marched out of the study.

Margaret grimaced as the door slammed in her sister's wake. The weight of the other ladies' attention pressed in on her until she felt obligated to find an explanation. "My sister is exhausted."

"We are all exhausted," Aunt Ruth muttered. "And yet, we should support each other in our grief. Carrie's foolishness only intensifies it."

Margaret swallowed. "Carrie has a hard time accepting bad news."

"To say the least!" Aunt Ruth used her fingertips to wipe the sorrow or perhaps frustration from the corners of her eyes. "My goodness, but she lashed out at General Sheridan when he took the time to deliver the news personally. Carrie should feel honored that Peyton meant enough to the general for him to favor us as he did."

"Yes, ma'am, I understand, but Carrie is only acting out because she's hurt beyond imagination. She's lost everything. Again."

That horrible January night flashed like a series of lightning strikes through Margaret's mind. Papa, gone for months. Gunfire from both the blue and the gray. Their farm in the crossfire. Flames licking across the roof, first the house and then the barn. The smoldering ruins later that left them cold, afraid, and homeless. Sarah Jane was crying. Margaret whined. And Mama was out of her mind and babbling some crazy thing.

That left Carrie Ann to figure things out. Desperate, she'd fatefully accepted Mr. Veyschmidt's offer of a place to stay. Little did Carrie know until it was too late that the evil innkeeper had been charging them an exorbitant amount of rent—a sum they were never able to repay, until Colonel Collier rescued them.

Tears burned behind Margaret's eyes as the truth of the loss took root in her heart. Would Carrie come to accept it? The man she loved was dead.

"Everyone in Woodstock says Papa is gone, but to this very day, Carrie Ann insists he's alive."

"Yes, she does, doesn't she?" Aunt Ruth's lips narrowed into a grim line.

"Ever think maybe it's us that's so cruel, Miss Ruth?" The housekeeper dried her eyes on her apron. "Miss Carrie loves our boy enough to foster false hopes is all. Is that such a sin?"

"A sin, no." Aunt Ruth released a long, slow breath. "But it's most unhealthy and before long she'll have all of us believing Peyton is alive."

Margaret knew the result of such beliefs. Like Carrie's fairy tales, they never came true.

She peered at the paneled door. "I should go to her. My sister needs me."

"Talk some sense into her . . . if you can."

Margaret acknowledged Aunt Ruth's request with a parting nod. Leaving the study, she found no sign of Carrie in the entrance hall. She checked upstairs. Nothing. Returning to the first floor, Margaret peeked in the parlor. Not there. Next, the music room, still filled with wounded Rebel troops and—

Margaret sagged against the doorframe. Across the way, Carrie conversed with a Union officer.

"Petite, you did a fine job on the Lieutenant Colonel Kent's leg," the darkly handsome man remarked with a strange accent. "I could not have done better."

Carrie Ann shrugged off the compliment, sniffed, and lifted her hankie to her nose.

"Ah, but you have heard about your husband, *oui*?" The officer set his suntanned hands on Carrie Ann's shoulders. "I only learned the bad news minutes ago myself. You must know that he died the way every soldier dreams of dying."

"Horse rubbish. No man dreams of dying."

Margaret's eyes widened at her sister's gruff response.

"Everyone dreams of dying, Petite. No one gets out of this life alive." The officer raised a brow. "We all must go at some time. It's only natural to wish for it to happen in a certain way."

The idea sent a chill down Margaret's spine. The thought of death frightened her. Even now a bedsheet covered the body of the young man who'd succumbed to Major Tucker's butchery.

So then, what happened when a soul perished? Was there really a "glory," as her sister claimed minutes ago?

Carrie Ann's chin trembled. "But why must Peyton be presumed dead? He's *missing*. Why can't he be presumed *alive*?"

"Perhaps you should ask Eli Kent that question."

Margaret turned to consider the man. He sat propped up against the wall and, while his complexion was still sickly pale, he was alive and his dark eyes even had a bit of renewed life in them.

"This war is so fickle, is it not? Men fight against their relatives and friends, brother against brother." The doctor motioned to Colonel Kent. "The lieutenant colonel and Colonel Collier and I served out West with General Sheridan. I am not ashamed to say Colonel Kent is my friend, even though he chose the wrong side to fight for and is now an enemy combatant."

"And a prisoner." The colonel's tone matched the discouragement that seemed to dull his stare. "Don't forget I'm a prisoner."

Margaret wondered how the two men kept such perversion of human nature in check when lots of folks could not stem hatred's flow. Men, women, and children despised their enemies passionately and that wouldn't soon lessen after the fighting ceased.

Carrie Ann strode slowly toward Colonel Kent. "Are you going to tell me you killed Peyton? Because if you are—"

The colonel held up his hands as if in a second surrender. He shook his head, topped with swarthy locks. His dirty shirt and jacket slid open, revealing a well-toned chest beneath a sheath of dark hair.

Margaret turned away. Her cheeks flamed.

"Ah . . . and who do we have here?"

Margaret straightened as the Yankee officer approached.

"Allow me to introduce myself. I am Major Paul-Henri LaFont, Cavalry Division Surgeon, Army of the Shenandoah." He bowed. "At your service."

"I'm Miss Margaret Jean Bell, formerly of Woodstock, Virginia. I'm Carrie Ann's sister."

"Well, well . . . I would say beauty runs in the family, yes?"

Margaret's cheeks burned with his charm, which, of course, had been the doctor's intention. But never again would she return a man's flirtations.

She pulled back her shoulders and lifted her chin. "Excuse me, sir, but I should return to the study. I must comfort my friends."

"How kind of you." The man sounded sincere. Was he?

But, perhaps there were decent men in this world—men with good hearts like Colonel Collier and Major Johnston.

Perhaps . . .

Margaret didn't wait to find out if this officer was one of them. She turned and hastened from the music room.

—⟨⟩ ⟨⟩—

"Did you kill Peyton?" The question threatened to strangle Carrie as she knelt beside the lieutenant colonel.

"We clashed sabers on the battlefield." His voice was a hoarse whisper. "But I couldn't kill Peyt, just like he couldn't kill me."

"You're enemies."

"We were friends first. When we chose opposing sides, neither Peyt nor I expected this war to last so long. A few contests on the battlefield and we Secessionists would show those Federals that we meant business—that's what we thought." His dark brown gaze roamed over his unconscious comrades. "We never imagined the thousands that would fall, some our brothers, some our friends." His eyes came to rest on Carrie. "That aptly describes yesterday's battle. When the artillery smoke cleared, Peyt was gone but I saw the carnage. I shall spare you the gory details."

"So you didn't actually see Peyton's body?" The idea fed Carrie a morsel of hope.

"I didn't need to see a body." He turned away. A heavy frown creased his brow. "The fact is, I don't believe there was a body left to be seen."

Horror gripped her while General Sheridan's words "dismember and destroy" echoed in her head. Carrie hugged herself from the chill of reality. "I saw Peyton only yesterday morning. He said he'd be back by breakfast." Tears obscured her vision. "It's impossible to imagine him never returning. Can you blame me for yearning for proof?" She choked back rising emotion.

"If I could offer you any hope at all, I would. What I suspected on the battlefield was later confirmed by a Union private." The colonel seemed to gulp back his own emotions. "Please accept my condolences."

Despite his soft words, Carrie clenched her fists in steely determination. "I don't want to accept condolences. I won't accept them!"

Colonel Kent winced as though she'd struck him. "There's something else you need to know . . ."

She wanted to run.

"Only days ago Peyton sent papers to me by way of a courier. He requested that I become executor of his estate."

"You're a liar!" Carrie whispered the words, but she wanted to scream them. Her face flamed with mounting contempt. "You are the enemy. You're intentionally trying to wound me." *Like Joshua.*

"Not true." A muscle worked in his jaw.

"Out of the many good men Peyton knew, why on earth would he choose you?" Her words met their mark. The colonel recoiled.

Good.

"Besides," she continued, her fingernails digging into her palms. "I signed a pledge to share Peyton's wealth with Aunt Ruth and Tabitha, caring for them always, and I shall. They are my family."

"This has nothing to do with that pledge."

"My husband trusted me." She ignored the niggling of doubt.

"Undoubtedly."

"Then why would he request such a favor of you?"

The colonel's features fell and his body seemed to curl into itself, whether from physical pain or Carrie's pointed words, she couldn't tell. "I suggest you speak with your husband's attorney."

"I will." She scrambled to her feet. "I'll make an appointment with him as soon as I'm convinced my husband is dead. I refuse to presume."

"As you wish." He regarded her with a stony expression. "At any rate, Mrs. Collier, I cannot make good on my promise to your husband at the present time. If you'll notice, I am a captive of the Union army. I've been informed that we'll be transferred to a prison in the next twenty-four hours."

CHAPTER 13

In spite of the noise coming in from the foyer, Eli heard Carrie's soft yet persistent sobs drifting through the music room's open window.

Please, woman, stop your bawling. His leg muscles twitched with the longing to get up and do something about it. Even growing up at Greenwater with a mother and two sisters, Eli had never known a female to cry so hard and for so long. Hadn't it been hours?

Perhaps it only seemed like it.

He should alert Aunt Ruth or Tabitha and tell them to usher Carrie into the house. And why on earth was she emptying her soul outdoors at this late hour? She'd catch her death.

Perhaps that was her plan . . . and she'd take Eli's sanity with her.

At last the young brunet he'd seen coming and going all day arrived with a tray of food.

"Are you related to Mrs. Collier?"

"Her sister." Her snipped answer made her sound quite unfriendly.

Most likely she feared him or at the very least didn't trust him. "You have my word. I'll not hurt you or anyone in this household."

"As if you're in a position to hurt a mouse." She tossed her head and threatened the pins in her chignon. "Besides, I'm not scared of you." She deposited the square, wooden tray on the floor beside him. A rich aroma of stew and the promised goodness of Tabitha's biscuits set Eli's stomach to rumbling like distant thunder.

Eli tried again. "Miss, your sister, Carrie Ann . . . she's outside. She's obviously upset."

She arched a brow and placed her hands on her hips. "Your point, sir?"

So much for a conversation. "My point, ma'am, is that you may want to bring your sister indoors then tuck her into bed with a spoonful of laudanum and a cup of hot tea."

"Mister, gunpowder won't budge my sister until she's ready to be budged."

He considered her womanly form. "Are you older than she?"

"None of your business."

Eli coughed, lest she discover he found her impertinence rather amusing—and very much like her sister's.

"You'd best fill your belly now, soldier, because we've heard reports of Rebs starving in prison camps."

Probably true.

Eli watched the shapely brunet check on his comrades. Only two of the wounded were in any condition to take some sustenance. But when one of the men touched her forearm she jerked back, sloshing his stew onto the floor. She quickly mumbled an apology and exited the room.

Minutes ticked by and Carrie's sobbing again reached Eli's ears. At last the brunet returned with Aunt Ruth and several dishcloths to sop up the spilled stew.

Eli's gaze parked on Aunt Ruth. Finally! A woman of reason.

He waved to catch her attention. "May I have a word?" He tried to sit higher up against the wall. Each time he moved, an explosion ripped through his left leg.

"Are you terribly uncomfortable, Eli?"

"Yes, but the physical pain I can manage." He inclined his head toward the open window.

"You're chilled. Of course." Aunt Ruth rushed to close it.

"Carrie is out there."

"We're aware of it."

"She ought to come inside."

Aunt Ruth released a long breath and placed her hands on her hips. As she stared down at him, Eli glimpsed her red-rimmed eyes.

"It has been a terrible day. The day I have feared coming since the war began. Of course, after Peyton survived Gettysburg, we thought our boy would retire his command. But as soon as he could ride a horse, off he went to fight again. Tabitha and I fretted anew. And now . . . our worst fears have been realized."

"I know." Eli's chest constricted.

"At least Peyton had the good sense to marry Carrie Ann."

"Who is sobbing outside the window at this moment." Eli's impatience mounted.

"And so she shall remain until she herself chooses otherwise."

Eli groaned.

"Tabitha, Meredith, Margaret, and I have not only had an emotional shock, but we've been subjected to Carrie Ann's sharp tongue."

"So you decided to leave her outside like a hound?"

"On the contrary." Aunt Ruth sounded exhausted. "It's good that Carrie Ann has come to accept facts. Better she weep now and get it out of her system. There is much that needs deciding, especially since you'll not be able to help us."

"Then you're aware of Peyton's request and my promise to your family?"

"Fully. I took the liberty of summoning Mr. Finch, our attorney, and he produced the documents in question. I must say I am surprised by Peyton's choice of executors, but not entirely, given the friendship that once existed between you and my nephew. Apparently, not even a civil war could sever that bond."

"No, it couldn't." Although Eli's helplessness would drive him mad before he reached any Yankee prison. "We'll figure something out."

Eli glanced around the room, relieved that between the din of soldiers' voices and Aunt Ruth's whispers they couldn't be overheard.

"On my honor," he said, "I thought I'd die before the agreement went into effect."

Aunt Ruth dragged over a wooden chair and sat down. "I think Peyton knew his time was at hand. He had developed an extraordinarily close relationship with the Lord. He said things to me, you see, and to Tabitha, and Carrie Ann also, instructing us what to do if he fell in battle." She blinked away the moisture gathering in her eyes. "He wanted us to be prepared, not worried or frightened."

"Oh, Aunt Ruth . . ."

Eli's war-hardened heart cracked. For the first time in years he grieved, and not only for his friends who perished in battle or his brother and father who died from illnesses. No, he grieved for the children who became orphans with a swing of his saber. He grieved for the women who became widows because he'd ordered it to be so. In truth, he'd long ago stopped thinking of the enemy as human beings. They were adversaries, bent on imposing their president's ideology—one which violated states' rights—on the South. Like General Robert E. Lee, Eli had felt obligated to defend his homeland of Virginia.

But in doing so, he'd killed his best friend. Eli squeezed his eyes closed. *God forgive me.*

"No one in this household blames you, Eli."

Aunt Ruth's perception amazed him. He forced himself to look her in the eye. "I ordered the blast that killed Peyt."

"Knowing you'd kill him?"

"Knowing I'd destroy the enemy."

"Oh, Eli." She knelt and set her hand on his shoulder. "You did your duty as Peyton did his."

"My motives suddenly don't seem as important as men's lives."

"I suspect that your motives were results of strong principles and beliefs, like Peyton's and thousands of others who willingly put their lives on the line." A tear slipped down her cheek. "I can't help thinking of what a blessing it is that Peyton died this year instead of last. Had he perished at Gettysburg, I would mourn forever. But since he placed his life in Jesus's hands, I now have the promise that I'll see my beloved nephew again."

"Tell Carrie of your peace." He inclined his head toward the window. "Perhaps it will help her cope."

"She knows." Aunt Ruth attempted to rise with the support of the chair. "My knees aren't what they used to be."

Eli held out his hand and tried to assist her, but he was little help in his weakened state.

The click of weaponry took him by surprise. A Union guard stuck his musket in Eli's face. "Give me a reason, Reb, 'cause I'd love to blow your head off."

"Good heavens!" On her feet now, Aunt Ruth staggered backward. "Put that weapon away."

"Not until you're out of danger, ma'am." The young enlisted man put himself between Aunt Ruth and Eli. "Now you go on, ma'am. Leave the room."

"Sir, you are gallant to defend and protect me, but this man is no threat. He was a family friend before the war."

"Well, ma'am, war changes folks." The soldier stared at Eli through slatted eyes. "This here's an enemy combatant."

"It's all right, Corporal. You may back away."

Eli glanced in the direction of the familiar feminine voice. Carrie stood at the doorway with swollen eyes and a blotchy complexion.

For a moment, the young man seemed to weigh his options before wisely deferring to the ladies of the house. "If you say so, ma'am."

"I do." Carrie marched forward. But as she neared, her expression softened. "Thank you, Corporal."

"Yes, ma'am." The Union guard backed away and strode from the room, looking over his shoulder as he stepped into the entryway.

"Nice of you not to berate the poor fellow," Aunt Ruth whispered to Carrie.

Eli heard the reprimand in her hushed words.

"Oh, Aunt Ruth, I'm sorry for being vicious all day. I've been so . . . angry." She clenched her jaw and stared up at the sculptured plaster ceiling. "I'm still angry."

Sorrow crashed over Eli once more. "I understand, my dear girl." Aunt Ruth embraced her then kissed her forehead. "And apology accepted."

"And, Colonel Kent." Carrie stood rigid as she addressed him.

He raised his chin.

"I must apologize to you as well. I made terrible accusations. Will you forgive me?"

"Of course. Again, you have my condolences. If it were possible for me to help you, I would."

"I know that." Fresh tears appeared on her lashes. She sniffed and studied the toes of her boots.

"How about some hot tea, my dearest?" Aunt Ruth led Carrie from the music room. "Perhaps a cup of Tabitha's nighttime elixir? A good rest is what we all need."

Eli sagged with relief at the ladies' exit. Carrie Ann was in from the cold.

Eventually she would heal and so would Aunt Ruth and Tabitha. They would take care of each other in Eli's absence.

"Since everyone is apologizing, I reckon I ought to do my part." The brunet who served him supper sauntered over. She'd been spoon-feeding broth to a wounded sergeant. "I'm sorry for my earlier behavior."

"It's quite all right, Miss Bell." Eli wondered. "It is Miss Bell, isn't it?"

"Yes. Miss Margaret Jean Bell. I'm Carrie Ann's younger sister."

"A pleasure, Miss Margaret."

She inclined her head slightly.

"If my memory serves me, your family is from Woodstock, correct?"

She paled. "Why do you ask?"

He frowned, puzzled. "Conversing, I suppose."

"Yes, we're from Woodstock. Colonel Collier rescued me from . . . from a bad situation there, and my sister has taken me in. I'm indebted to both of them . . . well, only her now that he's . . . gone." Sadness rounded her eyes. She glanced down at Eli's untouched tray of food. "Aren't you going to eat?"

"I suppose I should."

Again, a little nod. "Need help?"

"No. Thank you." At least that was one thing he could do by himself.

"Very well. I'll come back for the tray later." Miss Bell turned on her heel and left the room.

Eli swiped off the sudden perspiration on his forehead brought on by the smallest amount of exertion. He didn't feel feverish.

He raked his fingers through his damp hair. He despised feeling so helpless when, clearly, there was a great need here. Coming to the Collier ladies' aid was the least he could do . . .

Except he could do nothing.

Whatever the future held for Peyt's wife and kin, it was beyond his control. He was in no position to advise or protect.

A Union prison camp awaited him.

—◦◦◦—

Carrie awoke with a start. "Peyton?" She reached out with her left hand, only to find the other half of the bed stone cold. "Peyton?" she whispered into the darkness. Her throat constricted as disappointment settled around her. She could have sworn Peyton entered their bedroom. Wasn't that what had awakened her?

She held her breath, listening, waiting. Sadly, the only sounds now filling her ears came from dying embers in the hearth, soldiers' voices outside, and occasional nickers from their horses. No clanking of Peyton's accoutrements or rustling of his uniform being shed after a long day in the saddle.

He can't be dead. He just can't be! Wouldn't she feel some sort of finality in her soul if it were true? They'd been as close as any two human beings could be. They had shared their dreams for the future—a future beyond this dreadful war.

Tossing aside the bedcovers, Carrie stood. Her eyes felt swollen from crying herself to sleep. Why had God allowed her to meet Peyton, fall in love, and marry him, only to rip him away from her after nineteen days of marriage? It seemed like a cruel joke.

But God wasn't cruel. Tabitha told her tonight that what didn't kill them would strengthen their faith. And Carrie recalled Jesus's words about trials being for a believer's own good.

At the present, however, Carrie would prefer death over the spiritual strengthening, particularly if Peyton truly was dead.

But maybe he wasn't . . .

She sat by the window and stared into the yard. A slight breeze stirred and cooled the scalding sorrow that stained her cheeks. What would Peyton want her to do? Would he want her to give up on him?

No! At least not without clear evidence. She'd heard soldiers talk of the fog of war from so much smoke hovering above the battlefield. Even Peyton's comrades who claimed they saw him fall might be mistaken.

Eli might be mistaken. He'd been delirious when he arrived.

Carrie pressed her lips together and hugged herself as the night breeze wafted in. The idea was reasonable doubt enough for her.

She walked back to bed and crawled beneath the covers. Until God showed her in a way she could accept, she refused to believe the man she loved was gone . . .

After all, there were those who thought Peyton perished at Gettysburg, and how wrong they were about that!

CHAPTER 14

Why had she agreed to this task? She'd never been good at sewing.

"Ouch!" Margaret quickly brought her bruised forefinger to her lips and glanced around the parlor. Neither Aunt Ruth nor Tabitha even glanced her way. After all, it was the umpteenth time she'd pricked a finger. "I don't mean to complain, but these threadbare Confederate rags don't seem worthy of your buttons."

"They need a good washin' too," Tabitha grumbled.

"I agree—with you both." Aunt Ruth squared her shoulders. "However, if it appeases Carrie Ann we must do it. She's already in such despair."

Margaret couldn't ever recall pitying her older sister, but now her heart ached for her. At the same time, she wondered at the older ladies' lack of emotion. True, they wore dark frocks onto which they'd pinned aprons, but they sat here dry-eyed, sewing buttons onto Secessionist fighters' shirts—the same men who most likely killed Colonel Collier. But Carrie Ann insisted on fixing the men's shirts before they were transferred.

"Perhaps I should trade places with Meredith and watch the children. She can sew on buttons. She's likely better at it than me."

Aunt Ruth peered at her over round spectacles. "Why such problems, Margaret dear?"

"I've never been good at making stitches, even if it's simple sewing."

"What are you good at?"

The housekeeper's tone caused Margaret's face to flame. She was failing here. She couldn't even be a good guest. "I reckon I'm good at nothing."

"You're right about that." Tabitha snorted.

"Oh, honestly, Tabitha. You're not at all amusing." Aunt Ruth sent the dark-skinned woman a glare then fixed softer eyes on Margaret. "Everyone has God-given gifts. We simply haven't found yours yet."

"Maybe God forgot about me when He was passing out gifts. Carrie Ann is good at everything. She tried to teach me to read and write but it was no use. And I can't sew." She looked at Tabitha. "But I can cook a few things."

"You ain't going in my kitchen. I'm the housekeeper and cook here."

"I can carry a tray piled with plates of food and I don't usually drop it."

"You ain't doing that either—and don't go answering the front door again like you did earlier."

"I was only trying to help."

"Of course you were, dear." Aunt Ruth cleared her throat and glared at Tabitha. A softer expression returned to Margaret. "You're a guest in this house and, therefore, you're not expected to do chores."

Margaret forced a polite expression. Did that mean she couldn't stay here indefinitely? She certainly didn't want to wear out her welcome. But maybe with Colonel Collier dead, Carrie Ann wasn't welcome here either.

Better she find out sooner rather than later.

"I'm curious . . ." She looked from Aunt Ruth to Tabitha. "You don't seem grieved about the colonel's death."

"Don't seem real yet." Tabitha went back to her sewing.

Aunt Ruth let out a long, pain-filled sigh and peered at Margaret. "My nephew was a hellion so I sent him away to military school to straighten him out. Since then, he's only been home for short visits. When the war began, Tabitha and I fully expected to hear news of his death, but it didn't come. Then last year we had a close call. He was wounded at Gettysburg. Some thought he'd perished on the battlefield. But Dr. LaFont, whom you've met, sent us a message stating that, while grievously wounded, Peyton was still alive. Within an hour I was on my way to Pennsylvania."

"So maybe he's not dead after all!" A surge of hope rose up in Margaret. "Maybe Carrie is right."

"That depends on when you speak with her." Aunt Ruth kept on stitching.

She didn't even have to look at where she placed her needle. "She vacillates, sometimes believing Peyton is dead, sometimes hoping and praying he's alive. Quite distressing." Aunt Ruth removed her spectacles and dabbed the corners of her eyes. "General Sheridan would not have wasted his time coming here if a chance existed that Peyton survived the battle."

"You believe he's dead then?"

"My dear . . ." Aunt Ruth's eyes misted over. "I believe he will forever be alive—in heaven."

"Yes, ma'am." A more pleasant way to say the colonel was dead. "What happens to Carrie Ann now?" Margaret stared at the tattered shirt on her lap. "Will she have to leave?"

"Leave?" Aunt Ruth's shocked tone brought Margaret's head up quickly. "Heavens, no. We need Carrie Ann more than ever, don't we, Tabitha?"

She replied with a nod then glowered at Margaret. "So don't get any notions about traipsing off with her. Carrie Ann is a Collier now and she belongs with us."

"What about Mrs. Johnston?"

"Meredith has many decisions to make. She's welcome to stay as long as she likes."

Then it was Margaret who, alone, didn't belong. "Perhaps Rebekah Kercheval will allow me to work at the Repairers of the Breach for room and board. It seems I am good with children."

"That's because you're still a girl." Tabitha's words landed on Margaret's ears like a scolding. "You've got some growin' up to do before you can go anywhere." She nodded at the little-touched sewing on Margaret's lap. "You'll be no good to Miss Rebekah or to yourself if you ain't got a skill to get you by."

"Tabitha is right, my dear, and you did agree to my tutelage." While firm, Aunt Ruth's voice held the compassion Margaret needed.

She coughed to clear the relief lodged in her throat. "I thought everything changed now that the colonel was . . . wasn't here no more."

Aunt Ruth sighed. "Nothing has changed where you're concerned. We're family now. You belong with us."

Margaret's shoulders sagged forward. Maybe God hadn't forgotten about her after all.

She resumed her attempt to sew, holding the rag of a shirt as close to her face as its foul odor allowed. She squinted as she glided the needle in and out of the tattered, blurry buttonhole.

"Margaret dear, indulge me." Aunt Ruth held out her spectacles. "Put these on."

"Why?" Even as the question left her lips, Margaret complied. Suddenly the button on her lap shone with clarity. "Glory! I never saw such engravings on a button before."

Aunt Ruth opened a book and set it on Margaret's lap. For the first time ever, each letter of every word appeared crystal clear.

"I always wondered how folks could read when the letters were all melted into each other."

"We've made a grand discovery." Aunt Ruth clasped her hands together and smiled proudly. "You have a weakness in your eyes, Margaret. All you needed was someone to take note of it. Spectacles will solve the problem. Now you'll be able to read—and sew."

"My goodness." She regarded the words before her with and without the aid of the spectacles. The difference was, indeed, remarkable. "And here I believed Mr. Veyschmidt was right about one thing at least, calling me simpleminded."

Aunt Ruth clucked her tongue. "I highly doubt that evil innkeeper was right about anything."

"Thank you." Margaret felt so light and happy that she even smiled at the crabby housekeeper. "I can't wait to tell Carrie Ann."

"Let's surprise her." Aunt Ruth's hazel eyes twinkled. "You shall learn to read better first and then impress your sister with one of her favorite Jane Austen books as we do needlework here in front of the hearth this winter." She leaned across the way and gave Margaret's hand a gentle squeeze. "Carrie Ann will be delighted, and she will require some delight in the months to come, wouldn't you agree?"

"I would, yes."

Gloom settled over the room again.

Aunt Ruth sat back and examined the garment in her hands. "Margaret, you made a good point. These shirts are pathetic and not worthy of our buttons, so I have come up with an idea." Her lips formed a grin and a sparkle entered her eyes. "There's a trunk of Peyton's discarded articles of clothing in the attic. I say we go fetch those things and send off the Confederates with some more practical garments. After all, it's our humanitarian duty."

"If you say so." Tabitha snapped off a button without the aid of a scissors.

With spectacles still on her nose, Margaret began removing buttons. She had no fear she'd cut off a fingertip now.

Aunt Ruth collected the buttons.

Within no time, they'd completed the task. Tabitha gathered up the tattered, stinky attire and put it all in the hearth. The items weren't even worth tearing into rags or bandages. Next it was a march up to the attic where they battled cobwebs in order to get to the trunk. The colonel's former wardrobe nearly filled an entire wooden chest.

"I had planned to cut up these things and give the fabric to Rebekah," Aunt Ruth said, while eyeing a fawn-colored wool jacket. "I think I'll still do that."

"Those little ones will be needin' warm clothes." Tabitha shook out a white shirt and scrutinized it with expert eyes. "I wonder what Miss Meredith will do now that Major Johnston is gone."

"I'm sure she'll think of something. In the meantime, she'll stay with us. She's like family." Aunt Ruth inspected another garment. "We will, of course, continue to volunteer at the Repairers of the Breach. But, trust me . . . there is plenty here to keep all of us occupied."

"I'll say." Tabitha huffed.

Margaret allowed both ladies to fill her arms with clothing before they filled their own. Aunt Ruth's expression seemed a strange mix of misery and delight as she reverently ran her fingertips over a sleeve. "I remember when I gave Peyton this Davenport frock coat. He wore it at his twenty-first birthday celebration."

"He looked dashing in that shade of gray," said Tabitha. "All the young ladies practically swooned over our boy."

"They certainly did." Another sad smile on Aunt Ruth's face. "The frock coat must go to Eli." She gave a decisive nod.

The ladies began to reminisce. Margaret stood quietly by and listened to one amusing tale after another about Peyton Collier and Eli Kent, the mischievous duo. She could well imagine what kind of men they were, charming in their pursuit of females and as devoted as sandbags to their conquests. It was, however, nice to hear that the colonel had changed his ways after being wounded at Gettysburg last year.

With their arms filled with clothing, they headed back downstairs. Meredith met them at the end of the hallway, breathless.

"I've been searching everywhere for you."

Concern creased Aunt Ruth's face. "What is it, Meredith?"

She took Margaret's arm and steadied herself. "The undertaker has come to visit."

—∽ ∾—

Carrie admired Meredith's quiet courage as she sorted through the details of her husband's burial. Since she and Vern didn't have family nearby, only a sister in Missouri, Aunt Ruth offered a plot in the Collier cemetery at the far end of the property.

Meredith accepted. "I really don't know where I'd be without your support. How blessed I am that God led me to you."

"Part of God's plan." Aunt Ruth sniffed.

"But what does He want me to do in the future? I must do something with my life. I'm no longer a minister's wife."

"Don't think about that right now." Margaret hunkered beside Meredith's chair, her skirts ballooning around her. "We'll be your family."

"Indeed." Carrie stacked her hand on top of Aunt Ruth's, who still held Carrie's right hand. "We're quite the collection of people."

"Very true, my dear girl."

The undertaker cleared his throat. "And now, Mrs. Collier, let's discuss *your* husband's burial."

Carrie's light mood turned dark and heavy. She didn't want to talk about this matter—particularly because she wasn't convinced Peyton was dead.

"As there's no body, you can't very well have your husband lie in state." Mr. Listerman spoke with an air of confidence that grated on Carrie's already frayed nerves. "Allow me to suggest—"

"I suggest we wait. We may hear from Peyton soon." Carrie held her breath, sensing the reaction would not be favorable. It seemed she was the only one who believed Peyton was merely . . . missing.

As she anticipated, the room fell silent. Aunt Ruth's gaze fell on Carrie like a wet woolen blanket.

"We should make sure," Carrie said in her own defense.

Aunt Ruth placed a hand over her heart. "Not this again."

Carrie turned in her chair. "Allow Meredith to bury Vern. It only seems right, since there's a body to lie in state." She scrutinized Mr. Listerman, standing only a few feet from her. He ran his forefinger around the inside of his stiff collar as if it strangled him.

"Carrie, dear, we can do both on the same day. Peyton and Vern were quite good friends and ours is a mere memorial service."

"Actually, Miss Collier and Mrs. Collier," Listerman said, "a burial is still quite appropriate. In place of a body, mourners in your position typically fill the casket with mementos. A letter, perhaps, a photograph, garments the deceased wore."

Carrie folded her arms. She refused to part with a single item.

And speaking of . . .

"What about the identifying pendent that my husband wore? Have you or your associates found it?" She would know for sure that Peyton was gone if the undertaker located the trinket.

"No, ma'am, but we don't expect to, considering the circumstances."

The arrival of a buggy out front stole Carrie's attention. Mr. Finch, the Collier family attorney, climbed down then weaved in and out of Union troops as he made his way to the door.

Within minutes, Tabitha showed him into the study.

He had doffed his black hat.

"Thank you for coming today, Horatio," Aunt Ruth said, taking over the hospitality role, much to Carrie's relief. "Something may arise in which you can help."

"Of course. Anything."

Aunt Ruth made the introductions. Carrie already knew Horatio Finch and his wife, but neither Margaret nor Meredith had met the attorney.

"I'll make tea and bring it in," Tabitha said.

Mr. Finch sat down. "Please accept my condolences, ladies."

"Thank you." Aunt Ruth folded her hands in her lap.

Carrie dropped back into her chair.

"We were speaking of the deceased's items that might be used in place of a body," Listerman informed Mr. Finch, who gave a nod.

"And now, Mrs. Collier—" The undertaker ran his tongue over his thick bottom lip. "You must forgive my straightforwardness, but you asked about the silver trinket and chain your husband wore."

"Yes." Carrie gripped the chair's wooden arms.

"While we didn't find it, as I stated, my associate has found—remains." His eyes slid to Aunt Ruth. "We are confident we have made the correct identification."

Carrie's eyes widened, her jaw dropped slightly. "Peyton?"

"Then there's proof positive—my nephew is d-dead?" Aunt Ruth removed her hankie from her sleeve's cuff and pressed it to her eyes as if that alone would stave off the sadness trickling out.

"I'm afraid so," Mr. Listerman said with a mournful expression.

"What sort of . . . remains?" Carrie tipped her head. It sounded suspect.

"Oh, for pity's sake!" If Aunt Ruth were standing, she'd likely stamp her foot. But Carrie refused to let the matter go. "I want—no, I *need* to know."

The older woman churned out a weary sigh.

"Hair, fingers, a bootless foot." Apology shone on Listerman's narrow face. "I'm afraid my work is morbid business."

"To say the least." Meredith paled.

Carrie gave an unladylike snort. "There's a pile of those very things you described burning out back, compliments of Major Tucker." She turned to face Aunt Ruth. "A body part or parts thereof are hardly proof positive that Peyton is dead."

Aunt Ruth massaged her temples. "Please, dear one, let's not wade through gory details."

"How can I not?" Carrie held her arms out in a helpless gesture. "I love my husband. I am not eager to have him taken from me."

"Of course you're not." Mr. Finch's eyebrow dipped. The portly man and his wife had attended Carrie and Peyton's wedding only twenty-one days ago. "No woman wants to face the fact that her husband has been killed, especially a newly married woman. We understand."

Except Carrie refused to face it. Her heart screamed otherwise. "I want to see the remains with my own eyes."

"Oh, dearest, I do understand." Aunt Ruth fanned herself with her hankie. "However, you will never rid yourself of the ghastly sight. Isn't it better to remember Peyton as he was, a strong, handsome, courageous man who loved you deeply?"

Carrie studied her folded hands. "Perhaps."

"Let's move on, shall we?" Listerman's expression was grim at best. "Many details must be decided upon soon."

Carrie's stomach rolled. "I think we're acting too hastily. Why can't this wait until we're sure—until I'm sure—that Peyton will never return?"

"Because it's not proper." Aunt Ruth pushed her shoulders back. "News of Peyton's death is circulating. His friends and comrades will want and expect to say farewell." Her expression fell. "Besides, we all need closure."

"I don't." Carrie stood, every muscle in her body tensed. It seemed all who knew Peyton were more than happy to declare him dead and gone and move on with their lives. Couldn't they understand her life would never go on without him? Fighting to keep a glimmer of hope alive seemed futile now, but acceptance was unbearable.

Tabitha and Margaret entered the room and served tea.

"It appears the commotion in the foyer has increased." Aunt Ruth peeked around her chair. "What's happening?"

Carrie became aware of boisterous male voices filling the hallway and foyer beyond the study's doorway. She strode in that direction, intending to discover the reason.

"More Union soldiers arrived to take the wounded Rebels to prison," Tabitha announced.

Margaret whirled around and faced Carrie. "But those men aren't in any condition to travel." She looked at Aunt Ruth. "Please, you must do something. Sergeant Morris is beginning to come around after his amputation, and Captain Jefferson survived being shot through the neck, but a jostling wagon ride could cause bleeding again. He'll likely die. And what about Colonel Kent's leg? He's not ready to be moved."

"I agree." Aunt Ruth set down her teacup. "But I'm sure Paul-Henri has the situation under control."

"Excuse my interference," said Mr. Finch, "but are you speaking of Colonel Elijah Kent?"

"Yes, the very one you stated is executor of Peyton's estate." Aunt Ruth stared at her hankie. "Obviously he won't be any help to us while he's in a Union prison."

"Hmm . . ." Mr. Finch placed his teacup and saucer on the corner of Peyton's desk. "I must speak to him before he's transported. If you'll excuse me?"

"Of course."

"I'd best go too," Carrie said.

"No, dear one." Aunt Ruth stood and blocked her path. "We have funeral arrangements to make. Horatio can join in when he returns."

Carrie forced her knees to bend and sat back down. The last thing she wanted to do was plan Peyton's funeral.

"Have you given any thought to caskets?"

Carrie arched a brow. "I was under the impression that Peyton took care of these details."

"Oh, no, no. The colonel merely purchased our body retrieval plan."

"But you, sir, have found no body." Each word came through a tightly clenched jaw.

"Please forgive my niece. She's beside herself with grief."

"And understandably so." Listerman spoke to Carrie as though she were little Georgia's age.

Carrie closed her eyes.

"Now, about the casket . . ." Aunt Ruth's voice sounded miles away. "We'd like something nice, but not overdone."

"Very well."

"I'll take care of contacting the reverend."

"I already did—uh, per your nephew's wishes."

Mr. Listerman droned on asking questions and with each, Carrie's sense of disbelief mounted. Peyton's parting words replayed in her mind and tears pricked. *Always remember, my sweet Carrie Ann, that I love you with all my heart.* They seemed to be fading beyond her grasp now. What if Peyton were truly dead and she never got the chance to say she loved him with all her heart too?

But perhaps she'd imagined the past two months because she couldn't really be sitting here, planning her beloved's burial—or rebelling against it.

At least Aunt Ruth was doing a fine job without her. Slowly, Carrie forced her eyes open, stood, and strode to the study's door. Neither Listerman nor Aunt Ruth made a move to stop her.

Stepping out of the room, Carrie closed the door a bit too firmly behind her.

CHAPTER 15

Eli immediately recognized the men in blue who'd come to transport him and the other wounded Secessionists to prison—except these fellows weren't Yankees. Two belonged to his regiment and one was none other than . . . *Major Joshua Blevens*. He'd been one of the scouts who had accompanied Carrie here to Piccadilly Place last August. Eli couldn't figure out which unit he belonged to, actually, although Blevens alluded to Lieutenant Colonel Mosby on several occasions.

"What on God's fertile footstool are you doing here?" he whispered. He glanced nervously at the doorway.

"I've orders to rescue you and the others and get you over battle lines to safety." He tossed several articles of clothing to Eli.

Earlier Aunt Ruth had come in, carrying a pile of what she'd called "discarded but clean" articles of clothing. She'd easily persuaded the Union guards to allow the prisoners to make use of the donated items, and now Eli knew why.

They weren't Union soldiers; they were members of Mosby's Raiders.

"You have taken quite a risk," Eli said when Blevens neared.

"We were supposed to go to the house next door and collect you." Blevens's tone was barely audible. "But I see it's burned down, no doubt at Collier's hand."

"He's dead."

Eli didn't have to wait long for Blevens's reaction. His bright eyes immediately widened in surprise.

"Dead?"

Eli gave a nod. "Mrs. Collier is in despair. If she recognizes you, her benevolence may vanish and we'll all hang." Which might be a better option than dying in a Yankee prison camp up north.

"I have my orders, sir. I must admit I almost backed out when I learned the wounded Southerners were housed in the Colliers' place, but I'm no coward." Blevens squared his shoulders. "What's more, Carrie will never betray me. She's like my younger sister."

"Do not underestimate her, Major."

"No, sir, I won't." Blevens's assured expression belied his words.

Eli sensed trouble—bad trouble—on the horizon.

Pain shot through him when he sat. He waited for it to subside then removed his clothes and donned the new ones. His leg throbbed at the slightest movement. How would he endure a bone-jarring wagon ride?

Two of the other wounded men cried out each time they were moved. Still, the disguised Rebel soldiers worked feverishly to dress them. While Eli's pain was excruciating, the other prisoners were far more gravely injured than he. Would they survive the journey?

Eli's pulse quickened as he buttoned the cambric shirt which had a familiarity about it. Peyton's, no doubt. His former West Point pal had been taller, with broader shoulders, but his castoffs were a godsend. Eli's torn and battered uniform could no longer provide the necessary warmth he'd require as the days grew colder.

An impeccably groomed gentleman in civilian clothes strode into the room with an air of confidence that implied he held a respectable position. He came toward Eli and halted a few feet away.

"Lieutenant Colonel Elijah Kent?"

"Yes, sir?"

"I'm attorney Horatio Finch."

"The Colliers' lawyer." Eli inclined his head. "I recognize the name."

"May I speak with you?"

"Of course." Eli looked toward the doorway. "As long as the Yankees allow it."

Finch pulled over a chair and sat down. "That, in fact, is the reason I'm here. You see, I was told you're on your way to a Union prison. How very disappointing."

"That's not the word I'd choose to describe it, sir."

"Of course." Finch leaned forward. "You're the executor of Colonel Collier's estate. While you're . . . indisposed, I suggest you choose someone to stand in your place. Ruth Collier, for example."

Eli mulled it over. "No, if Peyton had wanted it, he could have named her himself. He did not."

"Mrs. Collier then? I promise to advise her on every transaction."

Eli shook his head. "She is distraught and her decisions can't be trusted right now."

The man sat back. His bushy brows slanted inward. "Then what do you propose?"

Eli was hard-pressed to think of a suitable plan at the moment. "I'll write to the Colliers as soon as I find out where I'll be. The Union army allows prisoners to send and receive letters, or so I've been told."

"I overheard someone mention Elmira Prison in New York." The attorney's expression softened. "I'm afraid it will not be pleasant there. Considering your injury, the possibility of infection is probable. Your risk of contracting disease is also great."

"I appreciate the words of encouragement," Eli retorted. On the other hand, Finch hadn't said anything that Eli didn't already know. More men died from disease than in battle or from wounds.

But Eli had no intention of going to prison. Not now that his comrades had come to ensure his escape.

"We will leave the particulars of Peyton's will in place."

"I don't think it's a good idea." A heavy frown creased Finch's forehead. "These ladies require some income on which to live and for day-to-day expenses. In addition they have a funeral to plan."

Eli took his responsibility to the Colliers seriously. "May I sign a bank form allowing the Collier ladies to receive a year's worth of income from which they can draw monthly? Hopefully, the war will end in the next twelve months."

"Yes, well . . ." Finch slapped his palms against his thighs before standing. "I heard that back in '62. Nevertheless, I will summon the banker here in Winchester and ask him to draw up the proper forms."

"Quickly." Eli emphasized the word. The commotion in the music room increased. Disguised Confederates conferring with the Yanks. "I won't be here much longer."

⁓

Carrie made her way to the well-room and drank two ladles of cold water. Her jumbled nerves seemed to calm. Next she headed for the music room. She found Margaret waiting for her just outside the doorway.

"I thought you were helping Meredith return the children to the orphanage."

Margaret shook her head. "I decided you may need my help more than Meredith." She leaned close to Carrie. "I've got a bottle of laudanum in my apron pocket. Let's give each Rebel soldier two spoonfuls."

Carrie tipped her head. "Didn't we run out of laudanum two days ago?"

"Yes, but—" Margaret's brow puckered and she dropped her gaze to the tips of her shoes. "Dr. LaFont has plenty."

Stolen? Carrie's hand flew to her throat. "And if he misses the bottle, then what?"

"I replaced it, only now the brown bottle contains whiskey."

Carrie leaned one shoulder against the wall. Her limbs felt weighted with lead. She longed for her soft bed upstairs.

Except she dare not give in to the idea. These wounded men needed her. It might be the last kind word and deed they receive before . . .

Carrie cut her thought process. She preferred to focus on life, not death.

She took Margaret's arm. "I trust you remembered a spoon."

"Yes." Her blue-green eyes twinkled.

"Then let us go be angels of mercy." Colonel Kent came to Carrie's mind. "Perhaps we'll make at least part of the Rebels' journey to prison camp tolerable."

"You read my mind, sister dear."

Armed with laudanum and good intentions, they entered the music room. The sight that greeted Carrie caused her chest to constrict. Union men assisted wounded soldiers into Peyton's old clothes.

A part of her was angry that she wasn't consulted, but the better part realized the garments had been discarded years ago. Aunt Ruth had every right to give them away, and it was for a good cause.

Soft moans came from the direction of where Colonel Kent sat. He winced with his every movement. Carrie's irritation dissolved completely as she crossed the room.

"Where's Mr. Finch?" She hunkered down beside him.

"He left to fetch some necessary documents." The colonel quickly explained the financial circumstances.

"Don't worry about us. We'll survive." Besides, it was only a matter of time until Peyton came home.

"I have no doubt. You're an intelligent woman. Nonetheless, you may want to budget wisely."

"I'll be sure to do that, Colonel."

He captured her hand. "Savor the good memories of Peyton."

Carrie jerked her hand free and the colonel ran his fingers down the lapel of his fawn-colored jacket. "I seem to recall Peyt wearing this shirt and coat. To a party of some kind." Lines appeared on his forehead and his eyes narrowed in thought. But in a blink, he refocused on her. "You can rest assured that your husband died in a blaze of glory, leading a charge. His army was victorious."

"Blaze of glory . . . what nonsense." She removed his boot and exchanged his smelly worn sock for a thick wool one. "I hate this war. It sickens me."

"I hate it too, hate the killing. Never more than at this moment."

Carrie sat back and waited. It seemed he had more to say.

But moments later he merely shrugged and gave a sorrowful wag of his head.

She was about to help the colonel get his boot on when she realized it was minus its mate. She'd cut it off in order to inspect and dress his injury.

"I'll go see if I can find a pair of boots for you, Colonel Kent." She pushed to her feet.

"Thank you. And—"

She paused.

"I am very sorry for your loss, Carrie. Please believe me."

His use of her first name startled her and yet, strangely, she liked the sound of it from his lips. It reminded her of better times. Just two months ago, they'd conversed on the portico outside the kitchen. She recalled now that he'd asked her to call him Eli and she'd given him permission to address her as Carrie. And to say Colonel Eli Kent was a typical Southern gentleman was an understatement. His subtle drawl was a tribute to the fact. However, she'd seen the soldier side of him too, a stern and shadowy side to his personality which served as a reminder that he would never tolerate the nonsense Peyton overlooked because he loved her.

And Carrie had felt loved. Cherished. She never doubted Peyton's feelings for her.

If only she could tell him that she loved him too and dispel any doubts in his mind.

Regaining her hold on her tumultuous emotions, Carrie managed a tight smile as Margaret approached. Her sister had made her way around the room, sneaking a spoonful of laudanum into patients' mouths. Now it was Colonel Kent's turn.

Amazingly enough, he refused the pain diffuser.

"I shall need a clear head." His tone left no room for argument.

Mr. Finch strode briskly into the room and handed the colonel a parchment.

Aunt Ruth called for Margaret to help her, so Carrie used the time to find boots for him. She remembered seeing an extra pair at the bottom of Peyton's wardrobe. It seemed appropriate that the colonel should have them. Peyton had named Eli Kent executor of his estate, after all, and the man did have a great need for them. He was going north to prison where it would likely be colder than here in Virginia.

She returned to the music room as Colonel Kent penned his name at the bottom of the parchment he'd been given.

"There." Mr. Finch inhaled and straightened his tie then stared at Carrie. "Now you won't have any financial worries for at least a year."

The colonel arched a swarthy brow. "What happens after a year?"

"Hopefully the war will end before we need to figure that out."

"Or, perhaps, Mr. Finch, you can find a legal way around Colonel Kent's obligations to us."

Eli frowned. "I beg your pardon?"

She faced him, her skirts swirling at her ankles. "You have much to consider, leaving for prison in a matter of moments. We'll merely be burdens to you."

"Hardly that." Crinkles at the corners of his eyes disappeared. A softer light entered his eyes. "I'll manage, Mrs. Collier. You have nothing to fear. Trust me."

"My husband obviously did—does, so I will too."

Eli opened his mouth, but before another word could pass through his lips, the blue back of a Yankee guard stepped between them.

"Time to go, Reb." The enlisted man stood over the colonel while two men in blue set down a canvas stretcher.

Carrie nestled the boots on either side of his midsection, then stepped out of the way. The men lifted the stretcher and Carrie whirled toward the room's entrance. But in her haste, she slammed into another soldier.

"Excuse me, sir." She stared up into the officer's bearded face and beheld the bluest eyes she'd ever known—the eyes of a man she'd never forget. *Joshua Blevens.*

"You!" Red hot anger rushed into her face. What in the world was he doing here? In a Yankee's uniform! Again!

"Pardon me, Miss." Warning flashed in his eyes before he skirted around her.

A scream caught in her throat and threatened to choke her. She should cry out and reveal Joshua's true identity as a Rebel spy. Then she'd request a front-row seat to watch him hang.

"Carrie Ann, we're liable to get trampled standing here." Margaret appeared and cupped her elbow. Seconds later, she sucked in a breath. "Say, isn't that—"

"There's nothing more we can do here, Margaret." The words and voice belonged to her, but Carrie felt somehow detached from the scene. She couldn't condemn Colonel Kent to prison or worse. "We must leave the Federal troops to do their work."

Federals . . . ha!

"But, isn't that man there Jo—"

"I'm sure I will swoon if I'm forced to listen to the groans of the wounded." Clutching Margaret's hand, Carrie led her to the foyer. Her heart hammered beneath her ribs. In the foyer, Carrie sagged against the far wall.

Confusion rippled Margaret's brow. "I'm sure that's—"

"You are correct, but don't mention that horrid man's name in our home."

Margaret leaned close, her eyes wide. "Is he a Yankee now?"

"No." Carrie should speak out against him, but for the life of her, she couldn't do it. Besides, what did it matter? So he and his fellow Confederate operatives would get their wounded somewhere safe—somewhere other than a Union prison, somewhere in which they might heal. Was that such a terrible crime?

They came around the corner, Colonel Kent on the stretcher. He halted the men and—poor spies that they were—they dutifully obeyed his order. Carrie set her hands on her waist. So he knew of the plot to be rescued. What a fool she'd been to trust him.

"Thank you, Miss Bell," he said to Margaret. He turned toward Carrie. "And Mrs. Collier, I'm grateful for your good care. Please pass on my sentiments to the other ladies of the house."

She looked away. Her chin trembled in outrage and sorrow. "Get out of this house. Get out now!"

A passing Union officer, one of those who'd accompanied Major Tucker, chuckled.

"What'd you expect, Reb? A farewell party? Now git!"

One after another, the wounded Rebels were taken out and stacked into ambulances. Carrie felt paralyzed. Would Peyton consider her actions treason? Hadn't her silence, her protection of Joshua, done great damage in the past? But wasn't it also true that Peyton, only days ago, named Confederate Colonel Eli Kent as executor of his estate?

It was all so confusing. Her strength gone, Carrie lowered herself onto a stair. Margaret settled beside her.

"Are you a Confederate sympathizer?" she whispered.

"No . . . not intentionally."

"You couldn't turn on him, could you?"

"To my shame." Moist regret sprang into Carrie's eyes.

Margaret leaned against her. "I would have done the same." She gave a little laugh. "I suppose I did."

"Listen to me." Carrie tugged on her hand. "If I ever see those men again, I swear I'll shoot them. I trusted them both, and they betrayed me and jeopardized the Colliers' good reputation—my husband's good name!"

"Have no fear, Carrie Ann." Margaret stared at the open front door. "I am indebted to you and this family, so I will help you pull the trigger."

CHAPTER 16

November 4, 1864

Carrie bolted upright in bed. A deep rumbling in the distance broke the silence. Another battle? Several moments later, lightning brightened the bedroom suite, and she collapsed against her pillows. No, just another early November thunderstorm.

Carrie pressed a hand to the other side of the bed. Still empty. Hard to believe weeks had passed since the Cedar Creek battle. A chaplain had presided over both Vern's and Peyton's graveside memorial services. Aunt Ruth placed a few mementos into an otherwise empty casket and it was laid to rest in a plot beside Peyton's parents and grandparents. Generals Sheridan and Custer and other important Union officers paid their respects. All the while Carrie kept her lips pressed together so the opposition inside of her didn't explode. What would Peyton say when he returned home to find his name etched on a slab of granite in the Collier cemetery? It was hardly the welcome home he deserved.

But if she said anything hopeful about Peyton's return, it plunged Meredith into a deeper sorrow. And Aunt Ruth and Tabitha would eye Carrie as if she'd come unhinged, while poor Margaret stood by, looking confused.

Surely a part of Carrie would have died with her beloved, and she didn't feel dead inside. Rather, she felt determined—just like she felt strongly she'd someday be reunited with Papa!

So Carrie had kept quiet and allowed Aunt Ruth to manage the funeral details. When it came time to part with Peyton's things, Carrie simply refused to part with anything she had left of him. Aunt Ruth didn't press her. Besides, Peyton's best military frock coat, the one he'd worn to that insufferable party the night before the Cedar Creek battle, comforted her. On particularly lonely nights, she put it on, wrapping it around herself like a cocoon. She could smell Peyton's scent on the coat, cigar stench and all. But it was something intimate of his, and Carrie treasured it.

Then, just last week, Meredith decided she needed to get on with her life. She had a sister in St. Louis, but with winter fast approaching and railroad tracks being unreliable across the country, such a journey wasn't feasible now. At Aunt Ruth's further suggestion, Meredith moved in with Rebekah Kercheval to help run the Repairers of the Breach. The orphans' home bustled with more youngsters than ever. Not surprisingly, Rebekah admitted to feeling overwhelmed, and she welcomed Meredith's assistance and companionship—even if the two disagreed on certain spiritual issues. Carrie could only imagine the debates held over tea once the children were abed.

Rebekah also welcomed Margaret's daily volunteering, although who affected whom still remained to be seen. Margaret had taken a particular interest in the Quakers, and Carrie found it a positive development. Aunt Ruth warned, however, that the Religious Society of Friends believed differently than other Christians. Quakers' faith stemmed from the idea that people were inherently good; whereas the Bible taught, "There is none righteous, no, not one." The Friends also seemed to place more value on trying to emulate the way Jesus Christ lived His life while on earth, rather than on trusting a risen Christ alone for salvation. Still, it seemed a fine line to Carrie, and Margaret was, after all, a grown woman. She claimed the Quakers believed the Bible was God's holy Word and that God revealed Himself to every individual differently. No two "revelations" or religious experiences were alike. That was certainly true, and in recent days Margaret read aloud from God's Word each morning with the aid of her new spectacles and occasional assistance from Aunt Ruth.

Best of all, hearing the Word helped more than Margaret. It soothed Carrie's soul, reminding her that heaven awaited each believer. And that followers of Christ could exercise mountain-moving faith, which, of course, she needed right now. Everyone doubted her belief that Peyton was alive . . . somewhere.

Another roll of thunder and Carrie inched deeper under the bedcovers. Heavy rain splashed against the windowpanes and pelted the roof, most likely sleet on this cold November night.

Was Peyton somewhere warm and dry?

And where was that rake, Eli Kent? His escape had compromised the Colliers' reputation—after all, Eli was the executor of Peyton's estate and he and other Rebel combatants had escaped from their home. It appeared suspicious. Carrie admitted it. Even Aunt Ruth thought so. At the time, a Union officer had come around investigating and questioning the entire household about the escape of the "enemy combatants." Of course they'd all denied participation in any escape plan. Union army officials were obviously still suspicious, though. They'd sent a spy in the form of a female to bait Carrie, telling her that if she needed Eli, he would be in Richmond. Not likely! She didn't walk into their snare. Carrie recognized a trap when she saw one.

Carrie's lips lifted as she recalled the dressing down she'd given the grubby messenger. She only hoped that General Sheridan heard of her reaction and the Colliers would no longer be considered suspect.

But now what to do about it?

The storm outside intensified. If Peyton were here, she'd snuggle up close to him. She felt so safe in his arms.

Peyton, where are you? Carrie clutched his pillow to her. For now this would have to do.

—⁂—

Eli tested his leg. Would it hold his weight?

"Easy there, Colonel. I'll fetch whatever you need."

He eyed the shadowy figure of a female whom he'd only glimpsed from beneath a dim lantern. He couldn't tell if she was pretty, young or old, as the light bouncing off the cave's walls distorted her features. The cap she wore hid her hair. Eli supposed that was the point. Dorcas, the only name she'd reveal to him, was a Confederate sympathizer who nursed wounded men, carried messages to and from Lieutenant Colonel John Mosby, among other necessary duties to the Confederacy.

"Miss Dorcas, if I don't get out of this cave for a minute or two, I'll go insane."

"If you take even one step out," she warned, "the Yankees will kill or capture you. Guaranteed. The woods is crawling with blue-backs."

"I've been in here for weeks." It seemed like years. Hidden well into a cavern that Mosby claimed was one of many beneath the Shenandoah Valley had come to make Eli feel more unsettled than safe.

"Calm down, Kent." Mosby sat off to the right, near a small campfire. Its smoke swirled high into the cavern. Giant teeth-like rock dripped from the cave's walls and seemed ready to devour both man and beast. "A few days more won't kill us. We've got food, supplies, and fresh water. And, of course, we've got Miss Dorcas."

"Sure do, Colonel Mosby." She gave a push on Eli's shoulders and he sat down hard on the solid, blanket-covered platform that served as his bed. He grimaced as pain zigzagged up his leg.

The woman was too bossy for her own good. But she had been kind enough to deliver a verbal message to Carrie, letting her know he'd soon be in Richmond and if she needed anything, he would help whatever way possible, limited as it may be. Carrie responded with some choice words, according to Dorcas.

Choice words indeed!

But how could he blame her? After what Major Blevens said had occurred on the Colliers' wedding night, Carrie had good reason to be furious. It was a miracle that Eli and the rest of the wounded Secessionists escaped Winchester without getting caught and killed. Carrie had kept their secret just as Blevens predicted. *Thank God.*

Then, after days of hiding in barns and beneath the ruins of various structures, they'd met up with Mosby's men who led them to this cavern. By then, two of Eli's comrades had perished. Eli's leg felt like a smoldering campfire, but instead of spitting sparks and ash, his wound sent pain ricocheting up through his entire body. As it happened, Mosby himself was nursing a foot injury. Days before the Cedar Creek battle, Mosby and his troops encountered some Yankees. A skirmish ensued and Mosby was knocked off his horse. His contender's mount then ran over him. Mosby couldn't even wear a boot due to his foot injury. So they teamed up, the spies who'd rescued them and Mosby's men. Their comrades led them here to this cave.

Eli sat transfixed on the lone figure at the small fire. An idea formed. "Hey, Mosby, is there any way that you know of to transfer money from a Washington Bank to Richmond?"

"Legally?"

Eli smirked. "Yes. *Legally*." He should have anticipated such a reply from his comrade. Mosby led the fearsome Forty-third Battalion Virginia Cavalry, famous for its raids and Robin Hood–like escapades. Its latest had been a train robbery in which Mosby's men captured thousands of Yankee greenbacks—"funny money," as some called it. The men then divided the money between themselves as payment for their service to the Confederacy.

"I'm acquainted with a banker in Richmond," Mosby said. "His name's Nolan Pratt. He still conducts business with the Union. He passes any pertinent financial information he learns to President Davis." Mosby stretched out on his back. "He'd assist you in the money transfer, but I suggest you request gold coinage. It's best to use it in Richmond."

"And the withdrawal wouldn't arouse suspicion?"

"How'd you mean, Kent?"

"I came into an inheritance of sorts. The deceased was a Yankee colonel. We were best friends at the military academy."

"Ah, well, rest assured. Pratt will be discreet."

"Excellent." Eli's mother and sister wouldn't starve this winter after all. Now, if he could escape this damp, dark cave before he lost his mind!

Charleston Mercury

November 8, 1864

RICHMOND, NOV. 7: "There is no military success of the enemy which can accomplish [the destruction of the Confederacy, nor] can save the enemy from the constant and exhaustive drain of blood and treasure which must continue until he shall discover that no peace is attainable unless based on the recognition of our indefeasible rights."

~President Jefferson Davis

New York Tribune

November 9, 1864

Sidebar
THE VICTORY. LINCOLN RE-ELECTED.
~
He Has Nearly All the States.
~
ALL NEW ENGLAND FOR HIM.
~
New York Close but Pretty Sure.
~
NEW JERSEY FOR McCLELLAN.

CHAPTER 17

November 9, 1864

Margaret hung up her hooded woolen cloak and unwound the soft knitted scarf from her neck. She draped it over her cloak on the brass hook. It had been a long while, if ever, since she possessed sufficiently warm outerwear. How grateful she was to have them now and to be here in Winchester with her sister and new collection of family members.

Feminine voices wafted from the dining room, so Margaret strode in that direction.

"Perfect, Tabitha. Boiled potatoes, carrots, and cabbage with our corned beef. General Sheridan is, after all, Irish."

"I'm baking apples for dessert."

Margaret salivated just hearing the menu. "Sounds delicious."

Two ladies turned their startled expressions on her.

Aunt Ruth's features relaxed and she smiled. "Oh, good. You're home." She steered Margaret toward the stairway. "You must hurry and dress for this evening. General Sheridan and two of his staff are coming to dine with us."

"Yes, ma'am." Margaret walked upstairs with wary anticipation. She could think of a dozen other things she'd rather do than keep company with a Yankee general and his officers. What kind of men would they be? If they behaved gallantly, like Colonel Collier, then dinner might be pleasant, but if they were the lowlife sorts who stumbled into the Wayfarers Inn, it might be a dreadful party.

In her bedroom, she changed into the best dress she owned, thanks to Carrie Ann. A fawn-colored frock with a neckline of ivory lace. It fit perfectly, although Margaret needed assistance buttoning up the back. She also needed to contend with her thick mop of hair.

After poking her head into the hallway to make sure it was empty, she scurried to Carrie's quarters and knocked on the door. Hearing the call to enter, Margaret turned the polished knob and let herself inside. A fire burned in the hearth, but Carrie stood near the window, gazing out into the back yard and wrapped in her husband's Yankee frock coat. She held a framed likeness of him in her arms.

Margaret's heart broke for her sister. Two photographs arrived days ago via special delivery. One depicted the colonel in a proud pose, and the other was an image of both him and Carrie together. They might have been cheerful reminders, were it not for the colonel missing and presumed dead. Alas the images sank Carrie deeper into gloom.

"Surely you don't plan to wear that to entertain your dinner guests." Margaret meant the comment in jest, hoping for her sister's smile or wisecrack.

Neither was forthcoming.

"Will you button up the back of my gown?"

Carrie snapped from her dark muse. "Of course." She set the photograph on the dressing table and reverently folded the frock coat over the chair. "Remember how excited the young men in Woodstock were when they found out Virginia had seceded from the Union? Remember how eager they were to defend Virginia's independence?"

"Yes." How dapper they had appeared in their crisp gray uniforms. But what a fool Margaret had been to admire and flirt with them unabashedly.

"Mr. Lincoln's army was just as eager to tamp down the rebellion and put Virginia back in its place within the Union. And all that . . . for what? Death and destruction."

"I cannot argue, but perhaps tonight's guests will provide us a welcome reprieve."

"You think so?"

Margaret stumbled back slightly as Carrie tugged on her dress.

"With that stunt Joshua and Colonel Kent pulled last month, I'll be lucky if I'm not arrested. I'll shame the Collier name."

TOO DEEP FOR WORDS

"Oh, nonsense. If authorities wanted to arrest you, they wouldn't come to dinner first."

"True." Her brows dipped with the weight of her frown. "However, I don't want my mere presence to remind General Sheridan and his staff of the incident."

"I don't think your *mere presence* will accomplish that."

Carrie finished fastening the gown and Margaret turned to face her. Perhaps if Carrie understood how she was needed tonight she'd snap out of her gloomy mood. "I could use some moral support tonight around those Yankees." She gently peeled the colonel's frock from her sister's shoulders and reverently hung it in his stately armoire. "Despite Aunt Ruth's lessons in etiquette, my social skills are still lacking. It's a comfort to lean on you."

"Then I suppose I owe it to you—and Peyton—to attend the dinner party."

"You owe me nothing." But at least Carrie had agreed to come downstairs now and greet guests.

Margaret selected a black gown from Carrie's wardrobe cabinet. The sequins on its bodice caught the firelight and glimmered. She laid it on Carrie's bed.

"I can't help feeling that Peyton is not dead. And anyway, I promised him I wouldn't wear black if something happened to him."

"I know. But Aunt Ruth will insist upon it."

"If Aunt Ruth had her way, I'd be head to toe in widow's weeds." Carrie studied the black gown then searched Margaret's face. "Do you think Peyton is dead? Our dinner guests do." Carrie took up the photograph of the colonel and held it to her heart. "Everyone seems to think so. Perhaps I'm wrong and this odd sense I'm experiencing is merely wishful thinking."

"Trust your instincts." Margaret closed the wardrobe doors. "I do."

"Thank you." Clinging to her husband's photograph with one hand, Carrie touched the neckline of the shimmery black gown with her other. "I needed to hear that." Moments later, her expression brightened. "I suppose I should change my gown."

"And quickly."

Carrie set the framed photograph on her dressing table once more, and then crossed the room and disappeared behind her privacy screen.

"Will you brush and style my hair before we go downstairs?" Margaret called to her. She pulled out her hairpins. "After chasing children for a couple of hours, my hair requires a bit of coif."

"Yes, I'm happy to help." Minutes later, Carrie reappeared from around the screen, the back of her dress unbuttoned. "But first, I need your help."

Margaret fastened all the tiny fabric-covered buttons.

"Everyone is moving on with their day-to-day activities." The looking glass was filled with Carrie's tearful reflection. "But my life has seemed to stop. All my plans for the future are hanging in the balance as I wait and wonder over Peyton. My hope is waning."

Margaret knew that feeling. "Papa used to say, there's always hope. However, I must admit to experiencing none from the day you left the Wayfarers Inn until the day your husband and his troops rescued me."

"Peyton was a good man—is a good man. He's the best, most honorable husband . . ." Carrie wiped her eyes with her fingertips and turned toward Margaret once more. "He promised to take me to England after the war. We planned to tour lovely stone manors and stroll through colorful gardens. He said we'd visit a castle like the kind I've only read about in novels."

Carrie and her novels. Margaret gave in to a tiny smile. "You can still travel abroad."

Arms folded, Carrie turned away.

"I'll be your traveling companion since I'm working toward becoming a spinster anyway. We'll be the two Bell sisters, touring England."

Carrie arched her brows. "Except I'm a Collier now."

"So? We can still travel together."

Carrie gave her a sidelong glance. "Perhaps we can."

Margaret blinked in surprise. "Really?" She'd only meant to cheer her, but if Carrie was serious about traveling, Margaret was happy to accompany her. "We have something to look forward to then, don't we?"

"I guess Papa was right. There is always hope."

Margaret was pleased with her success.

Carrie lifted her chin. "And now for your hair, m'lady."

Margaret giggled at her sister's theatrics and sat down at the dressing table. "Can you perform magic with my hair?"

"Hmm . . . it will be difficult, m'lady, but not impossible." Carrie winked at her in the mirror.

Margaret's smile lingered. "I shouldn't be amused by your cheekiness, except it's rather amusing."

"But in all seriousness . . ." Carrie lost her feigned accent.

"Yes?"

"I need to get away from Piccadilly Place for a while."

Margaret swung around so quickly that she nearly got the hairbrush in her face. "Carrie? You're not thinking about leaving, are you?"

"Escaping is the better word. Every room reminds me of Peyton in some way, and I need a reprieve from the sadness."

The next question stalled on Margaret's tongue, but she pushed it out. "You will take me along with you, won't you?"

———⌒⌒———

Each bite of food that Carrie ate seemed to stick in her throat. It wasn't that she disliked the meal. On the contrary. Tabitha had gone above and beyond all expectations. Clearly, the housekeeper adored General Sheridan. In her mind, he fought for the slaves' freedom. Fighting to keep the Union together was merely secondary.

But Carrie sensed General Sheridan had more than slaves' welfare on his mind tonight. He seemed as distracted as Carrie felt.

Lifting his water goblet to his lips, he took several swallows. When the general set down the glass, a flash of silver caught her eye and she noted the band he wore on his right pinky. His fingers were stubby, his hands wide. As a self-made man, Sheridan did not let his short stature diminish his ambitions. In the last few years, he'd risen steadily through the ranks. But if the general really had slaves' best interests at heart, he would have insisted Tabitha dine with them when Aunt Ruth suggested it. Tabitha refused, citing her proper place, and none of the Union men argued.

Carrie sensed the officers wanted Negroes to be free but not equal to whites. If that were so, the men were misguided. Why, the Declaration of Independence stated that all men were created equal . . .

Aunt Ruth passed the basket of biscuits to the officer on her left. More light chitchat ensued around the table. But the mantle of guilt and measure of anxiety that pressed in on Carrie nearly suffocated her. Weeks ago, she'd blamed General Sheridan for Peyton's death. She'd lashed out, and he didn't deserve that. Her behavior had been unacceptable. If Peyton was alive and discovered what she'd done, he'd be ashamed. After all, Peyton was his own man and made his own decisions. It was doubtful that Sheridan ordered Vern and Peyton to stay at the party and imbibe. Carrie needed to apologize.

And yet, letting go of her feelings seemed entwined with forgetting about Peyton. Carrie could never do that!

Then, of course, there was the matter of Peyton naming Eli Kent as executor of his estate, followed by the Confederates' escape. Carrie wasn't sure how she'd accomplish it, but she somehow had to tell General Sheridan the truth without falling out of the man's good graces.

Tabitha entered the dining room and began collecting plates and silverware that the guests had finished with.

General Sheridan leaned back in his chair. "Delicious dinner, Miss Tabitha."

"Thank you kindly, sir." Tabitha seemed suddenly lighter on her feet.

"Let's move to the music room, shall we?" Aunt Ruth scooted her chair back. The officer to her left stood and offered assistance. "Lieutenant Elroy brought his violin." She bestowed a smile on the gentleman now rising from his seat. "I'm honored by your offer to entertain us this evening."

"It's my pleasure, ma'am."

Margaret and two of the officers followed Aunt Ruth from the dining room. General Sheridan hung back, pulling a cigar from his pocket.

"I'll be along in a moment, Mrs. Collier." Sheridan lifted a match. "I have a hankering for a smoke."

"May I keep you company?"

"If you can abide my bad habit."

"I'll overlook it, sir." Carrie snatched her shawl and followed the general outside. "Peyton enjoys a good cigar now and again, and my father is never without his pipe in the evenings."

"Are you aware that you spoke about your husband in the present tense?"

"Did I?" Carrie inhaled the frosty November air. "It's difficult to accept that he's really . . . gone."

"I understand."

"And on that subject . . . General, I must apologize for my behavior the day you came to deliver the news of my husband's . . . *missing and presumed dead* status. I should not have spoken to you with such impertinence."

Sheridan replied with an amused snort. "I have heard worse things come from even the most delicate ladies, Mrs. Collier. Rest assured, I do not hold the matter against you."

"Thank you, sir."

He bit off the end of his cigar and spit it into the yard. Next he lit the rolled tobacco and its tip glowed red with each drag. Ribbons of smoke swirled up into the night.

The gloomy day had given way to a starless sky. Sheridan's stout figure would be a mere shadow but for the light streaming through the windows of the house.

"Sir, if I may bring up another matter."

"Of course."

He was being awfully gracious tonight. Then again, a tasty meal and a good cigar typically improved a man's disposition.

"Sir, I find that my family and I are in an unusual predicament."

"Oh?" Sheridan considered her. "How so?"

"Days before the Cedar Creek battle, Peyton named his West Point friend the executor of his estate, except . . ." Carrie mustered every last ounce of courage. "Except he's a Confederate officer—Lieutenant Colonel Elijah Kent."

"Eli?" Sheridan chuckled. "So he's moved up the ranks, has he?"

Was the reaction good or bad?

"I'm acquainted with Colonel Kent." A cloud of cigar smoke left the general's mouth when he spoke. "He and your husband were stationed with me at an army fort out west before the war began. From what I recall, Kent is a good man—as good as any, I suppose. He merely chose to fight on the wrong side of this conflict."

"There's more, sir."

"I thought maybe there was." He leaned one shoulder against an outer pillar and crossed one foot over the other.

Carrie chose her words with care. "Last week, we were visited by an officer conducting an investigation. The wounded Confederates who left under what we assumed were your orders, were really rescued by Rebels in disguise." Fiery indignation heated her face. How could both Joshua and Colonel Kent risk their reputations—Colonel Kent especially! "They and their wounded comrades made an escape, and . . ."

She swallowed hard and softened her voice. If General Sheridan heard an edge in her tone, he might decide she hid something from him. "Eli Kent was one of those men."

"One of the wounded Rebs who escaped from your home?"

"Yes." She pulled the shawl more tightly around herself.

"I see." The general stroked his bearded chin.

Carrie's knees threatened to buckle from both fury and fright. She held her breath, waiting for his reply.

"Did you have anything to do with the escape?"

"Absolutely not!" At least not the planning of it. "But I recognized one of the Confederates from my hometown of Woodstock." Carrie's hands tightened around her shawl. She owed Joshua nothing now, especially when her family's honor could be at stake. Any promises she made to protect her former friend were null and void. "We were childhood friends. I failed to sound the alarm when I recognized him. I suppose Major Blevens's gall stunned me." It still felt like a dream—a nightmare.

"Blevens?"

"Yes, sir. You may be acquainted with him as Major Brown, one of your scouts last August."

"The scout I trusted—and who betrayed me." Sheridan spoke in a dangerously dark voice. "I remember him well. All along he was a Confederate spy."

"That's right, sir." Carrie winced. Her crime seemed suddenly magnified. "General, I hesitate to make excuses for myself as I can't really understand my own behavior. All I can conclude is that I was distraught. I wasn't thinking clearly. If I was, I would have had the presence of mind to react differently. You see, he deceived me also."

"Did you explain this to the investigating officer?"

"No. I was too afraid and ashamed to admit it, especially in front of Aunt Ruth and Meredith."

"But now you're not . . . afraid and ashamed?"

"Yes, I still feel those things"—Carrie turned and stared out into the darkness—"but Peyton would be so disappointed in me if I didn't tell you the complete truth." Scalding tears gathered in her eyes. She blinked before turning back to Sheridan. "I'm willing to accept my punishment, but I beg you not to hold my family accountable. I didn't say a word to them either, although my sister Margaret also recognized Joshua. She, however, took my lead and stayed quiet. Later she asked if Joshua had defected from the Confederacy. A couple of months ago, I had wondered the same thing." She momentarily clenched her jaw. "Now I can say without a doubt that he hasn't."

The general drew on his cigar as if the thing strengthened him somehow. "If Blevens dares to sneak behind Union lines again, he'll be shot on sight."

"That's just the thing, sir. Joshua didn't sneak. He walked boldly into my home, knowing that he'd deceived me once when he escorted me out of camp that night last August. I sincerely questioned his loyalties, exactly as my sister had weeks ago. But Joshua is not a Union sympathizer. He ruined my wedding night and nearly tore Peyton and me apart at the onset of our marriage. Peyton said he'd kill Joshua if he ever saw him again. But Peyton wasn't home that day." A knot of sadness formed in her throat. "I wish to God he had been."

"There, there, Mrs. Collier. You've righted any wrong you committed by confessing the matter to me. As noted, I too was fooled."

"Yes, sir." Her admission had given her some peace of mind. She stared out over the darkened yard again, mustering another bout of courage. "I would hate for my husband's good name to be tarnished, should someone make the connection between Colonel Kent and us."

"Ah . . . well, I won't lie. It's a prickly situation. I can't fathom what Peyton was thinking."

Carrie wished she knew.

"However, I am confident of this, Mrs. Collier: your husband is a hero and died a hero's death."

"Your words should comfort me, sir, but they do not."

The general stood silently, puffing his fat cigar, as the seconds ticked by and violin music wafted from inside the house. Finally he turned toward her. "Men like your husband, Mrs. Collier, have been trained to die in the glory of battle. In Peyton's case, he led a valiant charge that bought my commanders the precious time they required to re-form their battle lines."

"So you've said, sir."

"Peyton knew it was perilous," Sheridan continued, "even suicidal." The general droned on, but Carrie didn't hear any more. Her mind had parked on that word, "suicidal." Why on earth would Peyton choose such an action? Surely there had been some other choice for his men and him.

A wave of nausea slammed into her. Did Peyton leave that morning thinking she didn't love him anymore, that he had nothing left to lose? She'd been stubbornly silent while the man she loved went headlong into battle. If only she could somehow do it all over again. She would forgive Peyton's celebratory drinking and tell him how much she loved him. She'd beg him to return to her unharmed. She'd plead with him not to take any risks. The glory of war and hero status wasn't worth it. Not to her.

But it was too late for all that now.

"I should go in." Unshed emotion threatened to strangle her, and she barely eked out the words. Tears caused her vision to swim.

She turned for the door, but the general caught her elbow. She blinked to rid herself of the tears and pulled the hankie from inside her sleeve to dry her eyes.

"I would like to honor your husband's service as well as his family's loyalty to the Union. I think you need to come to Washington and deliver this account of the Rebels' escape directly to Mr. Abraham Lincoln."

"The president?" Carrie sniffed, hoping the darkness sufficiently hid her traitorous emotions.

"Yes, the very one. The Union's victory at Cedar Creek all but guaranteed his reelection to a second term."

"What do you have in mind, sir?"

"I'd like to make you an offer." General Sheridan tossed his cigar stub out onto the rain-soaked side lawn. "In fact, it's the reason why I all but invited myself to dinner here tonight." He raised his arm and indicated to the doorway. "Let's step inside. I'd like to propose my idea to all of you ladies."

Carrie walked into the house ahead of the major general. Indeed he held much authority in his palm, and her confidence inched upward several notches. With it, her sadness lessened. Peyton would approve, she was sure; she'd done the right thing by telling the truth.

In the parlor, Carrie stood by the warm hearth. General Sheridan offered to get the others from the music room. Carrie nodded her thanks.

Minutes later, Aunt Ruth, Tabitha, and Margaret entered the room, and the general voiced his proposal.

"As you're likely aware, two weeks from tomorrow is the second official, nationally celebrated Day of Thanksgiving. In honor of Colonel Collier and his service, I would like to extend an invitation to all of you—"

Carrie looked at Margaret and Aunt Ruth. Both appeared interested in the offer. Even Tabitha had a gleam in her dark eyes.

"—to join me to dine with President Lincoln and his family at the Executive Mansion in Washington. "

"Oh my!" Aunt Ruth sat forward on the settee. "But how would we get there? The trains aren't running." "

"For the past month, my cavalry has been repairing the tracks from here to Washington and from Martinsburg up the Valley so trains can deliver supplies to Union forces."

"We'd ride by train, then?"

"Yes, Miss Collier. In my private railroad car."

"What about Tabitha?" Carrie blurted. Would the general allow a freed black woman to accompany them? "And Meredith Johnston?" Vern had made the ultimate sacrifice for his country.

"Miss Tabitha and Mrs. Johnston are, of course, invited." The general gave a small but gallant bow as his gaze rested on the housekeeper. "We'll stay at Willard's Hotel."

"Thank you, General," Aunt Ruth said. "But accommodations aren't necessary for us. We own a town house only blocks from the Executive Mansion."

"Then it's settled." General Sheridan rubbed his palms together. "For security purposes, I cannot reveal the exact date and time we will depart, but I can say this much: be ready to leave by the fifteenth."

"That's next week, General." Aunt Ruth gaped at the man. "There's so much to be done."

"I have every confidence you ladies will accomplish your tasks in plenty of time."

Carrie was tempted to smirk. He spoke like a man who wasn't accustomed to taking no for an answer.

"Thank you, General," Aunt Ruth said. "It's a most generous and exciting offer." Her hazel eyes danced before finding their way to Carrie, then Margaret. "Perhaps you'll both locate your father too."

Carrie hadn't considered that possibility. Was she losing hope of finding her father alive? God forbid! It had been six months since she'd received the last letter from him. The postmark indicated he was in Washington. She'd held onto the belief that he was still alive through all these past months, but now, with Peyton also absent from her life, her confidence and optimism were being stretched thin. Yes, perhaps they would learn news of their father. She looked to Margaret.

Margaret arched her brows in silent question, with a knowing little smile across her lips. Carrie discerned its meaning. Hope revived. It seemed her prayers had been answered. Her escape was imminent.

CHAPTER 18

November 22, 1864

"I hope the carriage comes soon," Tabitha groused. "We're liable to freeze to death here, waitin' on that no good Mr. Rhodes."

"Now, Tabitha . . ." Aunt Ruth looped her hand around her friend's arm. "Mr. Rhodes is dependable—most of the time, anyway, when he's not been imbibing. Besides the brisk air is good for us after being cooped up all day on the train."

Margaret shivered beneath her woolen cloak. Aunt Ruth's comment was debatable.

"Brisk? It's downright freezing!" Tabitha spoke the words Margaret had longed to say. The proud housekeeper tugged her wrap more tightly around her slender shoulders. "And when I corner that Bobby Rhodes, I'll give him what for."

"I might be inclined to do the same," Carrie stated weakly, leaning against Margaret. Poor thing . . . she hadn't felt well all afternoon.

Margaret set her arm around Carrie's shoulders, hoping to warm her.

"Miss Ruth, looky there." Tabitha pointed at Carrie. "Our girl's gonna catch her death on account of that no-good man. She's shivering cold."

"I'm all right. I think that café where we ate lunch may have made me ill."

"See, Tabitha?" Aunt Ruth lifted her chin. "Tomorrow she'll feel as good as new." The strong timbre in the older woman's voice kept Margaret at ease. "Now let's all take a deep breath and relax."

Margaret hid a smile. Aunt Ruth's sole mission today seemed to be keeping everyone appeased, although at this late afternoon hour and, standing out in the elements, temperaments were sorely tried.

Was it only this morning that they'd boarded the Winchester and Potomac Railroad car? It was Margaret's first train ride and, while slow going, she found the passenger car more comfortable than riding in a wagon over the rutted Valley Pike. When the train stopped at the station in Harper's Ferry, they ate a lunch of soup and biscuits. Then they boarded the Baltimore and Ohio Railroad car. The train went faster, but time crept by slowly.

Margaret, Carrie, Aunt Ruth, and Tabitha occupied themselves with their needlework while Sheridan and his officers played checkers or walked to the smoking car for cigars and card games. Margaret had to admit, while in the ladies' presence, the Yankees behaved respectably.

One was even rather handsome, but she didn't dare look him in the eye and give him the wrong impression. She was a proper lady now.

"A shame Meredith wouldn't come along with us." Margaret kicked at a small stone that lodged beneath her boot.

"She didn't want to leave Baby Mac and the other orphans."

Margaret didn't miss that note of respect in her sister's tone.

"Mr. Rhodes really should have been here by now." Aunt Ruth glanced up and down the street.

"Stopped at his favorite pub, no doubt." Tabitha shook her head. Forgot all about us, I'd say."

"Hush."

The banter continued a few more seconds before the ladies resigned themselves to the wait.

"Everything is so large here in Washington," Margaret murmured. She had been immediately awestruck when the train pulled into the city. Woodstock had been a thriving community before the war, but in its heyday, her hometown couldn't compare with the sights of the Union capital. Tall brick buildings reached toward the heavens and buses, pulled by teams of horses, traveled up and down the large thoroughfares solely for customers' conveniences.

After disembarking from the train, General Sheridan had bid them farewell, but not before reminding them that the Thanksgiving Day reception and dinner would begin at three o'clock sharp. "Don't be tardy," he warned. "Mrs. Lincoln frowns upon those who straggle into events after appointed times."

"We'll be prompt," Aunt Ruth assured him.

They thanked General Sheridan for sharing his comfortable train compartment. He had tugged the rim of his slouch hat then strode across the street toward the five-story structure that was the Willard Hotel.

"Welcome to the big city."

Margaret swore Aunt Ruth's teeth chattered.

"Before we arrive at the town house, there are some things you should know."

Margaret and Carrie gave Aunt Ruth their full attention as she explained the household situation.

Mr. and Mrs. Rhodes were the caretakers. More specifically, Mrs. Rhodes was the cook and housekeeper while Mr. Rhodes was the chauffeur, general handyman, butler, and valet.

"A butler?" Margaret nudged Carrie. They were almost like royalty—at least it seemed like it.

"Don't be impressed, Margaret dear. Our cozy town house is not so grand, I assure you."

"I can't wait to see it." Carrie's complexion looked more peaked than before.

Tabitha's keen eyes picked up on the same thing. "Our girl belongs in bed, Miss Ruth. Maybe we ought to consider hiring a carriage."

"Very well." A worried frown creased Aunt Ruth's forehead as she considered Carrie, who rested her head against Margaret's shoulder. "When we arrive at the town house, we'll get you to bed, Carrie. Mrs. Rhodes is aware we're coming today so I imagine she's prepared a scrumptious dinner."

Carrie moaned.

"Some soup then. That'll perk you right up."

"Not that woman's soup." Tabitha huffed. "She couldn't cook if her life depended on it. I'll make some good strong broth, Miss Carrie, while you have a bath. You'll feel better in no time."

"Oh, Tabitha, don't start that. Mrs. Rhodes is capable in the kitchen." Aunt Ruth sighed. "Be grateful that you don't have to cook for a change."

"Oh, I'll end up cooking. I always do."

After a dismissive cluck of her tongue, Aunt Ruth called their attention to their tentative schedule. Margaret hoped it would get Carrie's mind off her illness. It sounded as though Aunt Ruth had their stay in Washington planned right down to the minute.

"Therefore," she summed up, "we will get to bed early tonight and tomorrow morning, after breakfast, we'll begin shopping for new dresses for the Thanksgiving Day party. But I don't have to remind you that, as we're a family in mourning, they will be somber gowns."

Somber or not, Margaret could barely contain her excitement. She'd never gone on a shopping trip for something as extravagant as a store-bought dress. This was better than all of Carrie Ann's highfalutin make-believe stories all strung together into one because this was real!

"Here's Mr. Rhodes with the carriage now." She waved at the oncoming carriage. "See, Tabitha? He didn't forget us."

"Hmph!" Tabitha frowned at the man and sniffed as he tripped out of the buggy to assist the women.

Margaret assisted Carrie into the conveyance. Her concern for her sister grew.

"Carrie? Are you doing any better?"

"No, but I'm sure it'll pass soon."

"You're mourning your husband," Aunt Ruth said. "Physical ailments can certainly be a part of grief."

"I reckon that's right." Margaret set her gloved palm over Carrie's hand.

"I'll be fine now that we're off the train. The constant rocking to and fro and the smell that belching engine made my head foggy."

"There, there, dear . . ." Aunt Ruth reached across the coach and patted Carrie's knee.

Margaret wondered if her sister was finally admitting the colonel was dead or if she merely placated Aunt Ruth and Tabitha. They certainly believed it, and Margaret understood why. Still, she encouraged Carrie to trust her instincts. She could be correct. They were here in Washington City, after all. The same city from whence Papa's last letter came. Only last summer, the thought of riding through the city was a laughable notion. Yet, here they were.

"Contemplate finding our papa." Margaret squeezed Carrie's hand.

But even with holding on to that spark of hope, it was obvious that Carrie missed her husband. She said so many times a day. They'd only been married nineteen days and spent less than half that time in each other's presence. Nonetheless, the memories Carrie had shared with Margaret were perfectly romantic. The newlyweds had cuddled in the parlor, danced in the music room, and kissed in the library. Little wonder Carrie longed for a getaway from those persistent, painful memories at Piccadilly Place. Now she'd gotten her wish . . .

Except, Margaret supposed, there were some places of the heart that were inescapable.

───◦◦───

"Oh, Eli . . . this home is ever so much better than that apartment above the apothecary."

"I agree, Mother." Eli took in the sights of the parlor. Laurabeth dusted and added finishing touches to a small, built-in oak shelf opposite the wood-framed hearth. "We'll be very comfortable here."

"Then you're not thinking of reenlisting once your leg heals?" Her disappointment was hardly concealed.

"I'm sure there's a job for me to do somewhere within the Confederacy." He paused to admire a framed portrait of his father near the stairwell. "Although I doubt I'll be rejoining the cavalry anytime soon."

Eli had only begun putting weight on his leg. He walked, and stood, with the aid of crutches. Glancing back at Mother, he wondered if she would prefer that he reside elsewhere. "I suppose I can continue the rent on the apartment in town . . ."

"A fine idea, son." Not one of her tawny locks had come loose from their pins. Her frock contained not a single wrinkle. Even on moving day, Mother was the picture of genteel womanhood. "It's not that I don't want you here."

"I understand."

"No, I don't believe you do." She strode regally to the writing desk and retrieved an envelope. "You see, I received a letter from Pat Winslow, stating that he and his daughter Averly will be in Richmond for a visit."

"How nice." Eli hadn't seen the man in years. Pat had been one of Father's dearest friends and Eli's godfather. He made his fortune in shipping and brokering before he was knighted by a young Queen Victoria for his bravery on the high seas and preserving a most important shipment: a monkey, gifted to her by an African chieftain. His daughter, Miss Jane Averly, or simply Averly as she preferred, was Pat's only child. But she was hardly a child anymore. By his calculations, she was twenty-two or so now . . .

"Oh, Eli, I would have told Pat and Averly not to come. Richmond is so dismal at the present time. However, I didn't have the extra funds to post a reply. Of course, he and Averly will be shocked that we no longer live at Greenwater, but if you're at the apartment we'll have ample room here." Mother tipped her head. "Unless we should allow the Winslows to stay at the apartment as our guests." She tapped one slender finger against her lips, momentarily pensive. "Or Pat could stay with you and Averly can reside here with us—although that does leave us unprotected." She threw her hands in the air. "I'm so conflicted."

"First of all, you're quite safe here on the edge of town, Mother." The words came out harsher than Eli intended. "The apartment is just half a mile away. Whatever you decide is fine with me."

He needed to find a quiet place to lie down and elevate his leg. All the activity today caused his injured limb to ache to the point of irritability. He hobbled to a nearby armchair and sat. It would have to do for now.

"Mother, you are, of course, aware that food is scarce in Richmond. You may not be able to feed the Winslows."

"But, Eli, now that you have money—"

Eli wrestled with impatience. "It's not that simple. The Union's blockades have prevented goods and supplies from reaching the entire South. Store shelves are as sparse as the government's rations, and many of our soldiers are hungry and barefoot, and winter is quickly approaching."

"Are you saying we will not have a Thanksgiving Day turkey?"

"Not unless you can find one to shoot."

Mother rolled her eyes. "You were always a petulant child. It's no wonder you and Peyton Collier were such good friends at the military academy." She replaced Pat's letter in the desk. "I thank God each day that he and his aunt didn't persuade you to join the Union."

"We owe the Colliers their due respect, Mother." Eli had explained the situation in more detail than necessary. Now he regretted his decision. It wouldn't be unlike his mother to use the information as a weapon against him whenever Eli didn't cave to her wishes or share her opinions.

"Eli, I can assure you that President Davis and his cabinet are not starving. Neither is the Congress."

"Meaning?"

"Meaning . . ." She leaned close. "A gold coin or two will buy anything in this city." Straightening, she pierced him with the same bright gaze that Isaiah and Laurabeth had inherited. Eli and his eldest sister inherited their darker features from Father.

Ironically, Peyton Collier had been a better fit in this family with his golden hair, similar to Mother's in her younger days, and his keen brown eyes, similar to Father's. When Peyt had spent a holiday with them, during their West Point days, those who didn't know better often mistook him for a Kent. Peyt and Eli had taken great pleasure in fooling many an unsuspecting young lady, giving their names as Peyton Kent and Eli Collier.

"What is so amusing, Elijah James?"

"Nothing." Eli stroked his jaw and wiped the nostalgic grin off his face. But he reckoned Mother was, at least, owed a brief explanation. "When you mentioned Peyt, I recalled something funny from our youth."

"It's a wonder that young man didn't meet his Maker sooner."

"Agreed. But he evidently turned his life around. I like to think he met Jesus as Savior rather than eternal Judge."

"Of course Ruth Collier would say that ne'er-do-well nephew of hers turned his life around. The alternative is unconscionable."

"I liked Peyt," Laurabeth said, glancing over her shoulder.

"We did not invite you into this conversation, young lady." Mother's voice was razor-sharp. "Get back to work."

"Mother, don't speak to her that way. Laurabeth is not some unskilled hireling. She's your daughter."

A scowl shadowed his mother's face. "Laurabeth is my responsibility not yours."

Eli bit his tongue, debating how to be respectful, although he refused to cow to his mother's meanness, especially where his little sister was concerned.

When he'd left for the West, Laurabeth had been only ten years old. Now she was sixteen, but Mother's constant pecking at her was taking its toll. Eli had picked up on that much in the short time he'd been back.

It was on the tip of his tongue to speak his mind, but he glimpsed Laurabeth's moist eyes before she returned to her tasks.

"You will not disrespect me in my own home, Eli!"

"Mother, this is *my* home. I purchased it for you and Laurabeth, true. However, I will not allow you to domineer me or abuse Laurabeth. I have seen enough hell on the battlefield. I don't want it in my living quarters. Is that clear?"

"Quite clear." She ground out each word and her upper lip twitched with a hint of a sneer. "I merely ask that you remember your place, Elijah James. You are my son. I am not one of your enlisted men taking orders. And you are responsible for caring for Laurabeth and me, now that your father and Isaiah are gone."

Eli softened. "Point well taken, Mother." He stood, tucking a crutch beneath each arm. "I will work on taming my verbiage and tone of voice." Slowly, and with each painful step, Eli made his way to the front door. Relief at seeing the horse still hitched to the buggy emboldened him.

"Where are you going?"

He paused. "Can you ask me that question as politely as if you spoke to a distinguished officer in the Confederate army? I am one, you know."

She forced a polite expression. "May I ask where you are off to, Colonel?"

Despite the sarcasm, it was a start. "I'm off to see about continuing the rent on the apartment above the apothecary."

"Alone?" Mother was beside him in seconds, her brow furrowed. "Shouldn't you at least take our neighbor along in case of trouble, such as a broken wagon wheel?"

"We're in the city. I'm sure someone will step up to assist. Besides"—he kissed his mother's cheek—"the sooner I take care of that business, the sooner we can prepare accommodations for the Winslows."

"Bless you, Eli. And I mean that." She appeared quite sincere. "Surprisingly, I am glad you're home."

Eli lifted his brows. *Surprisingly?* He didn't bother to investigate the remark. On the whole, Mother meant well. However, life with Aunt Ruth and Tabitha, in spite of his troops' enemy occupation of their home, had been a far easier, even more pleasant existence, especially after Carrie Ann's arrival.

A pity she'd fallen in love with Peyt before they'd met.

He hobbled from the house. Would to God that he'd adjust to being home again—except nothing about returning to Richmond even remotely felt like home.

CHAPTER 19

November 23, 1864

Morning had yet to dawn when Carrie awoke on her first full day in Washington City. She'd bathed, sipped a cup of broth last night, felt better, but sleepy, so she went to bed without a full tour of her surroundings.

No time like the present.

Tossing off the bedclothes, Carrie rose and pushed her feet into her satin slippers. With her wrapper pulled around her shoulders, she tiptoed from her bedroom. In the hallway, she could just make out four closed doors and assumed them to be entrances to the bedrooms Aunt Ruth mentioned. At the end of the hall was a narrower doorway . . . *the water closet.* Carrie padded in that direction, hoping her hunch was correct.

She was.

At Piccadilly Place, each bedroom had a chamber pot surrounded by a privacy screen. Here in Washington City, however, the household shared two blue-and-white porcelain pots covered with wooden seats. One was located downstairs, primarily for guests, and this one upstairs. The waste was disposed of by using pulleys that sent it into the city's sewer system.

Carrie recalled the latrines on the farm and at the Wayfarers Inn, both rustic. This inside lavatory was far nicer—and warmer—on a chilly November morning.

With her needs now taken care of, Carrie used the pump on the side of the sink to wash her hands. Afterward, she strode downstairs and into the kitchen to see if she could start a pot of coffee or tea.

"You're up already, Mrs. Collier?" Mrs. Rhodes stumbled into the kitchen, yawned, and stretched. She wore a flopping white bonnet over her gray locks. "What be your pleasure this mornin'?"

"Perhaps some tea."

"A good choice." Smiling, she lit the stove. "I prefer tea in the mornin' like any good Brit." She chuckled. "I sure am sorry to 'ear about Peyton gettin' 'imself killed. I knew 'im since 'e was a youngster and came to stay 'ere with 'is folks."

Carrie forced back an argument. Seemed no one believed her anyway. "Will you tell me about them, Peyton's folks?" She didn't know a lot about his parents, other than the sparse details Peyton shared and those Aunt Ruth had given her. "I've got the notion that the pair was more interested in their social standing than parenting."

"That's puttin' it politely, I'd say. Mr. Rhodes an' me pitied the boy, always ignored and left behind. It's why Peyton got 'imself into such trouble. That's me own opinion, of course. At least 'is parents were forced to give 'im some attention when 'e was bad, even if it weren't pleasant." Mrs. Rhodes waddled over and sat in a chair at the table. "But Peyton was always a good boy for me an' Mr. Rhodes. Never 'ad a problem with 'im, we didn't."

"What did Peyton like to do when he was here in Washington?"

"Liked to eat mostly." Mrs. Rhodes snorted a laugh. "That boy loved me rice pudding."

"And when he got older?" Carrie sat down at the table, opposite the woman. "What did he like to do then?"

"Go out on the town, like 'is folks." Mrs. Rhodes shook her head. "And when 'is military academy friend, Mr. Elijah, come along with 'im, those two boys would raise Cain in Washington City."

"I picked up on the fact that Colonel Kent was a hellion too last August when he and his troops occupied Piccadilly Place. Peyton trusted him . . ." Sorrow fell over her. "Right up to the last decision he made about his family's needs."

"Miss Ruth told me as much. Tales of two reformed rakes . . . quite common in English society, actually. Brits love their gossip."

Carrie would have liked to argue that point as well. A colonel leading troops in the Rebellion didn't exactly sound like reformation—as far as she understood it, anyway.

Mrs. Rhodes pushed herself up to a standing position and then shuffled to the stove. Satisfied it emanated the proper amount of heat, she put the kettle on to boil. "So you know 'im, do you? Mr. Elijah?"

"We've met." And Carrie didn't think she'd ever forgive him for taking advantage of her kindness. He must have assumed her to be such a little fool. And how dare he threaten Peyton's honor and add to her grief the way he had!

An unregenerate rake to be sure. Just wait until Peyton learned of the betrayal.

And he would learn about it, wouldn't he? Carrie blinked back tears.

"Pardon me sayin' so, but you don't appear like most the females those boys brought 'ere."

"So I've been told." Carrie dabbed the corners of her eyes with her fingertips and managed a smile. "But Peyton was always respectful to me, even when he came into the Wayfarers Inn wounded the first time I met him. And he was a Christian for the last year and a half of his life."

"Miss Ruth wrote and tol' me that news. Glory hallelujah is all I can say."

"Amen."

Mrs. Rhodes snorted a laugh as she sat down again. "Well, I s'pose you an' me should discuss menus."

"Isn't it best to talk to Aunt Ruth about that?"

"She said you're the woman in charge now." Mrs. Rhodes winked. "A blessing Miss Ruth has taken a liking to you, ain't it?"

"She's done more for me than my own mother."

"An' now you're a young widda . . . what a shame."

Carrie squared her shoulders, refusing to give in to self-pity. "Before we discuss menus, there is one think I'd like to mention."

"Go ahead."

"It's about Mr. Rhodes drinking and forgetting us at the train depot yesterday."

"I am sorry 'bout that. Tabitha and Miss Ruth scolded my Bobby good. I didn't defend him. Gave up on that."

"Very well." Carrie couldn't see beating a dead horse, as the adage went. "Well, then, what do you suggest for today's menu, Mrs. Rhodes?"

"You're askin' me?" The older woman sat up a little straighter. "This is a nice change . . . a very nice change."

Carrie was pleased the woman thought so.

"It's a pleasure, workin' for you, Mrs. Collier."

Carrie was glad to have won the woman over. She stood and collected her teacup and saucer, grateful that her insides were behaving this morning. She didn't feel nauseous and her sips of tea seemed to be sitting well in her stomach. Perhaps the change in scenery was already doing her some good. "Now, Mrs. Rhodes, where might I find a newspaper?"

"Usually it's delivered by now, so you'll find it at the front door, mum."

"Thank you."

Saucer and teacup in one hand, Carrie ambled to the main entrance and pulled open the heavy paneled door. A man stood before her. She gasped and her tea sloshed over the rim of the cup.

"Beg your pardon. Didn't mean to startle you."

"No harm done." Carrie took the newspaper just as the deliveryman glanced up beneath his black knitted cap. His blue-eyed stare was one she'd known all her life.

"Papa?" She dropped her teacup and saucer. It broke to pieces on the tile floor. She heard the impact, but couldn't tear her eyes from her father's haggard countenance. He appeared unshaven, his normally auburn whiskers now grizzled after two long years. His slacked jaw and rounded eyes said he felt as dumbfounded as she at their surprise encounter.

But then he blinked, pivoted, and scurried down the walkway.

"Wait! Don't go!"

Carrie stepped over the broken porcelain, aware that she couldn't very well chase Papa down in her slippers and nightclothes. She could only watch him go. He was laden with two heavy satchels at his hips, their straps crisscrossed over his upper body. He made one delivery and then another, never even glancing in her direction.

Her vision clouded. Wasn't he glad to see her after all this time? Why wouldn't he speak to her?

She blinked, doubting her own eyes. Was that really Papa? What were the chances that in a city full of people the one person she wanted to find happened across her doorstep at the exact moment that she stepped onto the stoop? She'd call it providence.

But was it?

Her knees wobbled and she reached out to grasp something, anything, to keep her upright.

"Mrs. Collier, come inside before you catch your death out there."

A gust of wind sent a shiver through her while she watched her father's retreating back. Carrie had always looked up to him. She'd wanted to be just like him. To be an objective reporter, thinking clearly and observing carefully, always on the lookout for a story. It was Joshua who first suggested that her father wasn't the man she thought he was. That a man should take care of his family first, and that other passions should come second. She'd never thought about Papa's departure as selfish before, and she'd continued to refuse to believe it, even when she learned that he'd allowed her to believe a lie about who her mother was. But was it a lie? Doubts and questions assailed her.

The housekeeper took her elbow and guided her back into the house. "For heaven's sake . . . oh, but you dropped your teacup. Well, no matter, we'll clean this right up and pour another. Now let me take a look at you. You're as pale as a ghost, mum. Did you have a shock? Why, that no good—" Mrs. Rhodes put her hands on her hips. "Did that newspaperman say somethin' rude or vile?"

"No . . . no." Carrie pulled herself back to the present. "That newspaperman . . . that is, he . . . well, he happens to be someone I've been searching earnestly for since the end of August."

"Oh?" The housekeeper tilted her head. "Why's that? Did he steal somethin'?"

"Not that I'm aware." Carrie was still stunned. Papa—delivering newspapers and looking for all the world like a man who had fallen on hard times.

"Mr. Rhodes is acquainted with 'im. Sees 'im at the pub, he does. Goes to show what kind o' man 'e is. Goes to show what kind o' man my husband is too, God love 'im. Now come away from that door."

Carrie's heart squeezed painfully. "I'm quite sure that man is my father."

"Those are two fine birds, Jim." Eli scrutinized the wild turkeys that his father's former field hand held by the legs. They'd been killed, plucked, and cleaned.

"I reckon we should hang these over in that shed, Mista Eli. They'll keep until tomorrow out in the cold."

"Good idea."

Once the task was completed, Eli paid the freed black man. "It's fortunate that I met you in town last week."

"Yessuh." He stared at the gold coin Eli had placed in his palm. "Thank you, suh."

"You're welcome."

Jim scraped at the brown lawn with one large foot. "Suh, I ain't got the right to speak to you, I know, but I wondered if you'd consider buying me from Masta Ormsby."

"Buy you?" The question didn't make sense. "My father freed all the Negroes on his property a decade or so ago—you included."

"Yessuh, but we ain't got paperwork what says that. So soldiers rounded us up and sold us at auction. Now I belong to Masta Ormsby, but he ain't got much for me to do and . . . well, he gets real mad about it. Lifts his whip when he does."

"I see." Eli rubbed his cold-numbed fingertips across his jaw. It was galling to learn his father's good intentions had been thwarted.

"I'll work real hard for you, Mista Eli, and I don't need much room." He smiled and his even white teeth seemed to take up his entire face. "I could fashion me a lean-to off the kitchen of this house in no time."

"I won't argue the need for another man to help my mother around here."

"Yes, suh. You was always a good-hearted boy. Somethin' of a rascal, but good-hearted just the same."

"Thank you, Jim."

"Masta Ormsby'll probably be real glad to get some gold coins for me. He'll gladly let me go."

Eli considered it and gave a nod. "Would you deliver a message for me, Jim? If he's inclined, I'll meet with old man Ormsby today." He cleared his throat, wishing he hadn't just regressed fifteen years when, as a youngster, he and his friends referred to the older gent quite disrespectfully.

Jim chuckled. "Yessuh." He seemed to grow taller before Eli's eyes. "And I knows where you can buy a housekeeper and cook for Missus Kent." Another broad smile. "Masta Ormsby'll likely part with her too. He needs the money real bad. I heard his missus say she be taking their daughters to her parents' place in Louisiana ifn he don't find a way to get some money."

"I'm glad you informed me of the situation, and my mother will definitely appreciate some extra help."

"Yessuh. Her name's Emmie, and she cooks real fine. Why, she'll dress them turkeys up and surely impress your guests." The large man gave a nod toward the house. "I remember the Winslows from when they'd come visit Greenwater. Miss Averly was just a towheaded girl back then. She be all grown-up now."

"Yes, she is." Eli pushed out a polite smile. It was crystal clear to Eli, and to everyone else for that matter, that Averly had matrimony on her mind. She'd make a good wife; Eli was certain of it. She was a lovely and capable woman. But even when he allowed his thoughts to stray in that direction, a vision of Carrie Ann Collier appeared and absorbed his mind.

Eli faced big Jim Greenwater again. The man, like many slaves, had borrowed the last name from Eli's father's estate since he'd never had a surname of his own. "If you'll deliver my message, and tell Mr. Ormsby that I will be by his home at about two o'clock this afternoon, then I will sharpen my negotiation skills."

"Thank you, Mista Eli."

"However, I will free you once the matter is settled. Although I defend the sovereignty of statehood, I don't think it's morally right to own another human being. This time, the proper paperwork will be drawn up. I'm certain those were my father's wishes all along."

"I believe so too, suh. Thank you, suh."

Jim left and Eli turned his one crutch toward the house. Dr. Bates, the Kent family's longtime physician, had advised Eli to stay in bed and allow his mother and Laurabeth to pamper him after so many years of uncivilized soldier life. But Eli wasn't ready to become an invalid yet and moved to the apartment above the apothecary. He figured the less he needed to rely on crutches, the stronger his leg would become. Eli wasn't about to make anyone, least of all his mother and sister, wait on him.

Stubbornness carried a painful price, especially at the end of the day. But every day became a tad bit easier.

And he had the Collier ladies to thank for it. What's more, with the money that Peyton left, Eli could feed his family and might be able to free Jim and Emmie. Money righted a lot of wrongs in this world.

But this world was nothing like he'd ever known. War had changed everything and everyone, including Eli. His injury had knocked his pride to its lowest peg. He found himself reading the Kent family Bible instead of drawing strength from within himself or looking to a commanding officer. His strength was a fraction of what it had been. But, perhaps, that's where God wanted him—dependent on the Almighty and not a military figure or his family's reputation in Richmond.

And perhaps God wanted Eli dependent on him for patience too, particularly where Mother was concerned.

Eli's tolerance of her complaining and backbiting had vanished shortly after his arrival home. His jaw hurt from clamping down on unspoken harshness, for he'd been taught better than to purposely disrespect his mother. He could hardly blame her for clinging to the world she knew, one that didn't exist anymore. For her that time was genteel and good, one steeped in purposeful naïvety. Mother's biggest concern on any given morning was which of her many dresses she'd wear to which upcoming social event. Father fostered the fantasy. He didn't believe a proper woman should be bothered with the harsh realities of life. Unfortunately, he left her terribly unprepared to handle even day-to-day affairs, let alone the horrors this war had brought to their doorstep. Even Father couldn't have imagined it. And now Mother, like many Southerners, had difficulty believing their former lifestyles were gone forever.

Except they were.

As for Mother's matchmaking, it would have to stop. Eli wasn't about to honor some old-fashioned tradition that began generations ago. No, when it was time to marry, he would select his own bride.

And the sooner Mother and the Winslows understood that, the better.

CHAPTER 20

Chilled, Margaret stepped closer to the fire in the parlor, her gaze fixed on Papa. He seemed to have blown in with the gust of wintery air. When Carrie had said she'd seen him this morning delivering newspapers, Margaret worried her sister's grief had gotten the better of her. But here he was, standing in the Colliers' town house.

Margaret blinked. "Papa, I can't believe it's really you."

He opened his arms wide. "Don't I get a hug from my second oldest daughter?"

"Yes, of course." She went forward and dutifully embraced her father. The faint scent of strong drink brought back terrible memories and she quickly stepped back. She pulled her shawl tighter around her shoulders. Had Papa been drinking? She never remembered him to indulge that way.

"And, Carrie"—Papa turned to her—"I'm sorry about our meeting this morning. It wasn't the way that I'd hoped our reunion would be." He held his arms out to her. "A hug for your dear old Papa?"

Carrie remained in her place, her arms folded in silent protest.

"Now, Carrie Ann, don't be angry . . ."

Margaret knew her sister's emotions went far deeper than a mere show of stubbornness. "Papa, why didn't you contact us? People assumed the worst when we didn't hear from you. Mama was certain of your demise right up to the time she breathed her last."

"Breathed her last?" Battered hat in both hands, Papa ran his fingers around its brim. "You mean she's . . . dead?" His brows slanted inward. "When?"

"Beginning of October. She'd been ill for quite some time."

"You would know that," Carrie added, her voice razor sharp, "if you had given us an address where we could write to you."

"I see."

"I don't believe you do see. Not at all." Carrie punched out each syllable.

"Now, my dear girl"—Aunt Ruth hugged Carrie around her shoulders—"this is your father . . . for whom you've been searching." She gave Papa a small smile. "Carrie wrote letters and took out advertisements here in Washington. I'm surprised you never saw them or heard of her missives. She sent them to the newspapers."

"And speaking of," Carrie said, "he ran away this morning without a word. Nothing. A simple, 'I'm busy now, but I'll come by later' would have sufficed. I was questioning my sanity."

Truth be told, Margaret, Aunt Ruth, and Tabitha had all questioned Carrie Ann's sanity. Margaret winced, but quickly lowered her head so it wouldn't be noticed. She should have believed her sister. What's more, Carrie had a right to be angry—so did Margaret.

But, somehow, she wasn't . . .

"I'm sorry, Carrie." Papa's contrite expression matched his words. "I've been down on my luck, you see"—he turned to Margaret—"I planned to contact you girls as soon as I acquired respectable employment as a journalist. My work at the *Democratic Leader* is not anything I can be proud of yet. I was waiting for the day I got the chance to cover a good story and write about it—"

"And what if you never got that chance, Papa?" The weight of Carrie's question could have chinked Massanutten Mountain.

Papa's shoulders drooped.

"Would you never have contacted us? Would you have allowed us to go on assuming the worst?"

"I knew you girls were all right on the farm with your mama."

"The farm burned to the ground two years ago, Papa. Shortly after you left. We were forced to take refuge at the Wayfarers Inn where we became indentured in order to pay our room and board." Carrie's arms fell to her sides.

She clenched her fists. "We suffered abuse, Papa. And Sarah Jane ran away." Her blue eyes filled. "I went after her, but found her too late. She's dead."

"Sarah Jane?" Papa's jaw dropped and deep creases appeared on his forehead. After several seconds, he glanced up with a relieved expression. "But you did all right for yourself, Carrie Ann. And Margaret . . . just look at you. Two finer young ladies I've not seen yet in Washington City."

"No thanks to you."

"Carrie, hush." Aunt Ruth hugged her in two quick successions as if to shake off Carrie's bitterness. "One must always honor one's father."

"Some father."

Margaret blinked at her sister's outrage. Still, she couldn't blame Carrie for feeling neglected. Margaret felt it too.

"You abandoned us," Carrie continued, despite Aunt Ruth's warning to guard her tongue. "You allowed us to suffer when you should have protected us. Had you let us know where to find you, we could have sent word of our need. In fact, I tried to locate you many times over."

"She did, Papa." Margaret couldn't stand mute. Carrie had a viable claim against their father.

"I didn't think—"

"Precisely the problem, Papa. You didn't think of anyone or anything else but yourself and your journalism career. I defended you, wanted to be like you. Well, I say you deserve your hard luck."

"Carrie Ann Collier!" Aunt Ruth's hand fluttered to her throat.

"Please . . . let her speak," Papa said. "She has a right, and maybe I have been selfish. But a man has his pride. I didn't want my daughters to see me this way." Papa's blue eyes slid toward Carrie again. "After your mother and I divorced, I figured . . ."

"Divorced?" Margaret's jaw slacked open. "Mama never spoke of a *divorce*."

Carrie still hadn't changed her stance and, garbed in a black frock, her red hair appeared to flame like her constrained temper.

"I'm surprised your mother didn't mention it. She's the one who insisted and initiated the action. I was unable to give Mathilda the life she wanted— the one she deserved. I wasn't a farmer. She'd married me because she believed in my writing ability and in my dream of becoming a great journalist. She believed we'd live the life that you have now, Carrie . . ." A tentative smile touched his lips. "Why, you're the perfect image of a fine young woman in your pretty frock and with your hair pinned up. My little tomboy grew up."

Carrie rolled her eyes.

"And, Margaret that color green always complemented your brunet hair and mysterious blue-green eyes. You're the very picture of what your mother hoped to be."

His words cut right through her. "No! . . . Do not compare me to her. I refuse to live on the coattails of some man's dream and die in a saloon." The words tumbled out before Margaret realized they came from her mouth. Carrie held out her hand. With trembling legs, Margaret stepped toward her and clasped it. "Thank God for Carrie. She insisted her Yankee husband come and rescue me from that horrible Wayfarers Inn."

"Peyton was—is—a good man." Carrie gave Margaret's hand a gentle squeeze.

"Yes, he was," Aunt Ruth stated rather decisively.

"Was?" Deep creases lined Papa's forehead. "Are you a widow, Carrie?"

"Yes, I'm afraid she is," Aunt Ruth replied. "My nephew was killed last month at the Cedar Creek battle."

"I'm sorry for your loss."

"Spare me your condolences and pity." Carrie's grip tightened around Margaret's hand.

"Papa means well," she whispered.

"And the road to hell is paved with good intentions, is it not?"

"Oh my . . ." Aunt Ruth gave a tug on Carrie's elbow. "Why don't we all sit down and finish our discussion like civilized people, hmm?" She guided Margaret and Carrie toward the settee and showed Papa to an armchair near the warm, crackling hearth. "Tabitha is assisting Mrs. Rhodes in the kitchen. I'll ask one of them to bring us some tea."

She left the room. Carrie glared across the parlor at their father. Margaret sunk further into the settee. She disliked confrontation. Seemed her childhood was one battle after another. Sometimes with her sisters over chores, with Mama and her insanity, but the worst involved Mr. Veyschmidt and the drunken men who stumbled into the Wayfarers Inn.

"Speaking of Mrs. Rhodes," he said, shifting in his chair. "I heard from her husband that you're going to be spending Thanksgiving Day with the president at the Executive Mansion."

Carrie's eyes turned icy. "So that's why you came here tonight. You want to either join us at the Executive Mansion so you can get the leg up on the story or you want me to give you information about it."

"He wouldn't do that." Margaret stared at their father. *Would he?*

"Tell the truth, Papa," Carrie pressed. "Is that why you came tonight?"

"Of course not!" Papa drew his chin back and appeared quite insulted. However, his rapid blinking and the lack of conviction in his expression revealed something different. He was lying. Margaret could spot a liar across a smoky saloon, and she saw one here in her own father.

"I suppose we can't blame you, Papa, for wanting to spend the holiday with us." Margaret turned on her sweetest charm. "You've missed us, haven't you, and spending Thanksgiving Day with Mr. Lincoln himself is quite the chance of a lifetime, wouldn't you say?"

He sat back and seemed to relax. "Certainly."

"It probably would make an outstanding newspaper article, although Carrie would know better than me . . . I mean, better than I." It pleased her to have caught her own grammatical slip. "Carrie, maybe you should write the story." To Papa, she said, "Carrie kept your newspaper going in Woodstock. She wrote all the articles and then printed it on her own, including working that prickly old press of yours."

"Did you now? I'm impressed."

"You gave me the responsibility. Why are you surprised?" Carrie closed her right fist. "I'd rather hear that you're grateful."

Reaching out, Margaret took her hand. Carrie's relaxed against Margaret's palm, giving Margaret the courage to stand with her sister.

"I'm sure a story about Thanksgiving Day at the Executive Mansion would take you away from the drudgery of delivering newspapers to the glory of writing them, wouldn't it, Papa?" The quicker he confessed the better for all of them.

"It would, my dear Margaret, yes . . . but I'm sure that can't be arranged at this late hour. Thanksgiving Day is tomorrow."

Carrie and Margaret gasped in unison.

Papa stood. "I realize that I've no right to ask—"

"You dare show up here after years of avoiding your responsibilities to us." Carrie jumped to her feet, nearly pulling Margaret up with her. "And now you ask for our favor?" Tears glistened on Carrie's lashes.

Margaret blinked away the moisture gathering in her own eyes.

"You are correct—you have no right. Now, get out!" Carrie pointed to the doorway at which Aunt Ruth suddenly reappeared.

She glanced at the three of them as if sizing up the situation. "Oh, dear . . ."

"So much for civility, Aunt Ruth." Margaret pushed to her feet. "Our father has admitted that he only came here to ask a favor—one that he hopes will advance his journalism career. These past two and a half years have not changed him."

"I see." Aunt Ruth fidgeted with her neckline, a gesture that typically proved her discomfort. She turned to Papa. "And what is it that you want, Mr. Bell?"

"I had hoped . . ." He wrung his hands. "I hoped that my daughters would spend Thanksgiving Day with me, and that I might accompany you to the Executive Mansion." He faced Aunt Ruth again. "I realize it's a lot to ask, but, in all honesty, it's my last hope."

Margaret hugged Carrie's arm. She pitied Papa now. A man brought down hard, he'd turned to strong drink. But perhaps in confessing the truth he'd recall his own words—"there's always hope."

"He wants to use us," Carrie pointed out. "We mean nothing more to our father than a means to attain his own selfish goals."

"That's not true. Please believe me. I thought often of you girls. It broke my heart to sign the divorce papers before I left Woodstock. And I wrote to you girls. Didn't you receive my letters?"

"The last letter we received was last spring," Carrie said. "I read every word. You mentioned you were well and that you had completed your interviews of both officers and enlisted men in General Jackson's army. When I saw the Washington postmark on the envelope I concluded you had begun interviewing Union soldiers and you'd be home soon."

"That's partially true. In fact, I began interviews. However, your mother told me not to return, so I didn't." Remorse shone in his gaze. "That's the truth and surely it proves my intentions here today are honorable."

Carrie hurled a glance toward the ceiling. "How can it ever be honorable to abandon your daughters?"

"I didn't abandon you. I sent letters." Papa sat forward.

"We received your last post six months ago."

Margaret nodded, confirming Carrie's statement.

Papa's thick brows formed a V. "The mail is not dependable, as you must know."

"We're aware, but how would you know if we received your letters or not?" Carrie's stare remained cold and hard. "We couldn't write back because no return address was penned on the envelope. We had no way to tell you about the farm and Mama—and, speaking of"—Carrie sprang to her feet and strode toward Papa—"is Mathilda Bell my biological mother or my step-mother? Joshua thinks the latter is true."

"What?" Margaret wasn't sure she'd heard correctly. "We're not sisters?"

"Of course we are." Carrie lifted her glare from Papa long enough to slip an assuring look to Margaret. "Nothing will change that, but Papa owes it to both of us to tell us the truth."

"What are you talking about?" His lost expression matched his question.

"Is she my stepmother, Papa?" Carrie placed her hands on her waist.

"She is your mother, of course." He massaged the back of his neck. "I don't know why Joshua would say otherwise."

"I do." Carrie arched a brow and faced Margaret. "Joshua is a Confeder-ate spy and he hoped to shift my loyalties and put a wedge between Peyton and me."

"So he said we're not kin or only partially kin?" The idea was almost amusing, unless Carrie believed it. She had obviously at least entertained the notion. "You didn't turn me away. You sent your husband to come for me at the Wayfarers Inn."

"Peyton suspected Joshua was lying so I chose to believe Peyton." She turned back to Papa. "However, I needed to hear the truth from our father's lips. Papa, do you swear on your own soul that Mathilda is my mother?"

"I swear." He pushed to his feet and raised his right palm, only to quickly lower it. "But I shouldn't have to swear. You ought to believe me. I've never lied to you."

"No, but you have operated under false pretenses." Carrie's glare returned.

"Hence your visit today. You wouldn't be here except you want something." Her voice grew louder with each word. "You don't give a whit about Margaret and me!"

Papa appeared to shrink beneath the weight of Carrie's accusations. He stared at his well-worn hat. "I shouldn't have come back here. My presence has upset you. I'll take my leave." As he made his way to the parlor door, Aunt Ruth stepped into his path.

"Your daughters are hurting. Carrie loved my nephew and she's mourning the terrible loss . . . we all are. Margaret has suffered abuse at the hand of that dreadful innkeeper . . . Can you even try to imagine the pain your daughters are holding inside their hearts? I believe God brought you here at just the right time, Mr. Bell. Your daughters need you more than ever."

Margaret wiped away her unexpected tears. Carrie's trickled freely down her cheeks.

Papa took a step toward them. Then another. "Oh, my poor, darlings." His expression crumbled. "You mean the world to me. You must believe that, but . . ." He neared. "I wanted to prove your papa wasn't the man I really am—a pauper with dreams of greatness, one whose business ventures aren't profitable. I wanted you to be proud of me, not pity me." He shook his head and sighed. "I see my thinking has been all wrong. You needed me, and to my shame, I didn't have a single clue because my foolish pride held me back."

Reaching them, Papa placed his arms around both Margaret and Carrie, holding them, one to each side. Margaret heard Carrie's soft sobs above her own. Aunt Ruth was correct; they needed their papa.

Papa's cheeks were damp too. "My darlings. My poor, poor darlings . . ."

New York Times

November 24, 1864

Thanksgiving Day.

In every loyal State, from the Atlantic to the Pacific, this day will be observed as an occasion for special recognition of the national and individual mercies vouchsafed by Providence during the year soon to close. . . .

Thanksgiving Day is peculiarly a home festival. It is a day for reviving old scenes, for freshening old memories, for renewing old feelings, for strengthening old ties. Cities and villages, and the peaceful farm homes, all through the breadth of the continent, will welcome its return. The rush and wear of "the working day world" will for the time cease. The "cares that rust away the heart with gall" will give way to kindly emotions. Sorrow will put off its weeds of mourning, and find comfort in the light of loving countenances. If affliction saddens, it softens too; it may make the joy more subdued, but it does not make the gratitude less fervent . . .

CHAPTER 21

November 24, 1864

Carrie eyed herself in the mirror, certain the black gown's high, stiff neckline would chafe her chin by the evening's end. At least the bodice's draping collar hid her too-thin frame.

"I promised Peyton that I wouldn't wear black if . . . well, if the worst happened." Which she was still certain *had not!* "Besides the newspaper stated that today is a time to put off weeds of mourning and find comfort in loving countenances."

"And the same newspaper would cut you to ribbons if you didn't wear black to this auspicious event." Aunt Ruth sighed. "I'm afraid society demands it."

"Pshaw!" Carrie fidgeted with the starched material beneath her chin.

"Hold still, dear one."

Aunt Ruth finished pinning the black, straw-braid hat on Carrie's head. She had to admit, it was a millinery showpiece. The outer brim was decorated with black Chantilly lace and lavender silk flowers.

"There. You look mournfully beautiful. And, if it will make you feel better, I made the same vow to Peyton about wearing black. However I think he'd forgive us. After all, we're attending an important event in his honor."

"But why must we appease society?" Carrie whirled from the mirror and faced Aunt Ruth. "What if Peyton lies in one of this city's growing hospitals and somehow hears of his family's appearance at the Executive Mansion . . . dressed in the black he asked them not to wear?"

Aunt Ruth clucked her tongue. "Even Peyton had to give in to what was expected of him." Inspecting her reflection, Aunt Ruth adjusted her ebony hat adorned with tiny pearls.

"I still say Peyton wouldn't like it."

"Think of it this way. Peyton's commander invited us this evening, and his president, Mr. Abraham Lincoln, is hosting the gathering. By attending and dressing appropriately, we are honoring Peyton's service to his country."

Carrie considered Aunt Ruth. Black suited her. The color accentuated her lovely gray hair as did the silver and pearl broach at the center of her gown's neckline.

"You always look dignified, Aunt Ruth, and ever so appropriate."

"I should." Her hazel eyes rounded with emphasis. "I've been at it for over fifty years."

"Is your duty to the Collier name how you manage your grief?"

"Yes. Keeping my focus on duty has always been my way, although sometimes I strayed and became discouraged in my well-doing. Don't you think that at my age I have seen my share of heartbreaks and disappointments? But I am a Collier. Our women have, through the ages, been survivors—and so, my dear girl, will you." She glanced around the room as if making sure nothing had been missed. "Now, come . . . the carriage is parked out in front, waiting for us. The driver is impatient. We're not his only obligation tonight."

Carrie allowed Aunt Ruth to guide her out of her bedroom. At the foot of the stairs, they met Mrs. Rhodes. Since their arrival, she'd worn nothing but dresses, over which she habitually pinned a stiff white apron.

"Should I be waitin' up on you this evening?"

Aunt Ruth pulled on her gloves. "Yes, please. We won't be out late, but we may bring a guest or two with us when we return."

Papa. Carrie gave her Chantilly lace glove a yank. Her anger with him hadn't yet abated.

"Yes, mum." Mrs. Rhodes helped Aunt Ruth place her black fur stole around her shoulders.

Carrie draped her fine new fox fur around her own shoulders, feeling the softness against her neck. It was a luxury, to be sure. However, Aunt Ruth determined that all four ladies in the Collier entourage would have new gowns, albeit in black. She also insisted on the loveliest accessories to wear on this special occasion—and so it was. Though she missed Peyton, Carrie could, at least, be thankful today for her newfound station in life. She no longer was an abused, rebellious serving-girl at the Wayfarers Inn. Neither was Margaret.

And all thanks to Peyton . . .

They left the town house. Margaret, Tabitha, and Papa were already outside in the carriage. The temperature was mild and a delicate mist fell. She and Aunt Ruth hurried to the curb. Papa climbed from the conveyance and opened the door. He wore his recently purchased black suit, crisp white shirt, and black necktie and usurped the footman by assisting both Aunt Ruth and her into the roomy cab.

"Thank you, Charles." Aunt Ruth sat beside Tabitha and adjusted her hoops.

Next to Margaret, Carrie did the same and for several long seconds, the entire inside of the carriage seemed one huge billow of silk and taffeta.

However, Aunt Ruth's greeting to Papa hadn't gotten past Carrie's notice. "They're on a first-name basis?" she whispered to her sister.

The closing of the carriage door muted any reply. Papa wedged himself between the door and Carrie. After a slight lurch forward, they were on their way down the block to the Executive Mansion.

"Your father looks dapper tonight ladies, wouldn't you agree?"

"Oh, yes," Margaret agreed. "I've never seen him dressed better."

Carrie remained silent. She was doing her best to forgive the man, but she felt so betrayed by Papa's ambition. True, he apologized and he seemed sincere. But it wasn't enough.

And what about her childhood? Had he lied about that? Was Mama her stepmother and Margaret her stepsister as Joshua had said?

She watched him from beneath the tulle of her hat. He swayed slightly as the carriage rolled onward.

Papa had stayed and dined with them last night and, while painful at first, it ended up being a pleasant evening. Nonetheless, the aftermath of his actions hurt and it didn't disappear so quickly. In his absence in Woodstock, she'd made excuses for him. She'd built up his reputation as a journalist. She'd done her utmost to keep his two-bit newspaper alive until she'd been no longer able to obtain supplies for his broken-down, ornery press. She'd shouldered all the responsibility that should have been his all along.

And she couldn't get herself to ask him about Mama and Margaret. She feared the truth would be a setback for Margaret, just like it had cast a long shadow on Carrie's being—until Peyton and Aunt Ruth talked her around it. Margaret didn't have the same advantage as Carrie, being Peyton's wife, although Margaret had begun settling in to her new life with the Collier family and now enjoyed her work at the orphanage.

Would Papa insist Margaret stay with him in Washington now and take care of him? Would he heap on Margaret the weighty responsibilities that he'd dumped on Carrie?

Last August, Joshua had called Papa an irresponsible dreamer, and Carrie argued the point. Now, however, she was convinced that her childhood friend was correct. Her stomach lurched. On top of Peyton's status of *missing and presumed dead*, it was simply too much.

"Are you all right, Carrie?" Margaret's gloved hand covered hers.

"I think so." She took a couple of deep breaths.

"Despite this horrible war," Aunt Ruth said, "it is a day of thanksgiving. God has blessed us with so much."

"O' course, it'd be perfect if our boy was here to see this day."

"Carrie and I plan to search the hospital tomorrow."

Carrie gasped at Margaret's blunder. She wasn't supposed to tell!

Momentary silence, as heavy as lead, filled the carriage.

"We'll discuss the matter later." Aunt Ruth's crisp tone struck Carrie like the November wind.

"No need. My mind's made up." She wasn't about to be talked out of searching for Peyton. But she supposed Aunt Ruth could try . . .

Margaret whispered an apology as the carriage reached the Executive Mansion.

"If you're going to the hospital tomorrow," Papa said, "I'm happy to accompany you. I help out there now and again. I met a very talented writer there. He works as a nurse . . . Mr. Walt Whitman. Like me, he founded a newspaper. About ten years ago, he printed his own work—a volume of poems. He gave me a copy. His work is quite good."

"You would do that for me, Papa?"

"Of course!" His palm engulfed her hand.

Carrie's heart softened toward him. What would it hurt to give him another chance . . . besides this Executive Mansion opportunity? He was, after all, her beloved Papa.

Across the way, Aunt Ruth sat tight-lipped. The dimness in the carriage made her expression indiscernible. Did she disapprove—or was she glad to see Carrie overcoming her "stubbornness," as Aunt Ruth termed it last night?

"Will you just look at that!" Margaret's tone was filled with awe as she stared out the carriage window toward the presidential estate.

Carrie wondered if she deliberately changed the subject.

Margaret captured Carrie's other hand and gave it a gentle squeeze as the carriage rolled to a halt. The door swung open. "Are you ready, sister dear?"

Carrie felt a mite fortified. "Yes. I'm ready."

The footmen helped them alight from the carriage. Papa offered his arm to Aunt Ruth and they led the way up the front stairs.

"I hope black folks is welcome," Tabitha muttered. "I hate to get all dressed up only to eat in the kitchen with the hired help."

"If you are unwelcome," Carrie said, "we will all eat in the kitchen to show our solidarity."

"That don't make me feel much better."

"Well, it made me feel more like my old self to say it."

"Now you're worrying me, Miss Carrie Ann." Tabitha snorted a laugh.

On the front portico, well-dressed men in black trousers and frock coats over starched white shirts took their names, making sure they were on this evening's guest list. They were, so they were escorted into the entrance hall. President and Mrs. Lincoln stood near tall marble pillars that dwarfed even the president. Carrie noted that Mr. Lincoln appeared exactly like the drawings and photographs she'd seen of him in various newspapers. His tawny-haired wife, garbed in a muted rose velvet gown, stood at his side. She resembled a child, standing beside her tall, thin spouse.

Carrie and the others stood in the queue to greet the Lincolns. Within minutes, it was their turn. General Sheridan appeared. He'd obviously been standing off to the side, watching for them. The upper left of his Union-blue frock coat was decorated with ribbons and medals that testified to his courage and daring in various battles. Stepping forward, he made the introductions.

"Mrs. Collier's husband was killed at Cedar Creek last month," he told Mr. Lincoln. "Had he survived, Peyton Collier would have been promoted to the rank of general. He was an outstanding soldier." Sheridan's black eyes came to rest on Carrie. "It's at my insistence that Mrs. Collier and her family came tonight."

"You have my deepest sympathies, madam." President Lincoln bowed politely over her hand. "Mrs. Lincoln and I are honored to number you among our guests this evening."

"Thank you, sir." Carrie pushed out a smile. Mr. Lincoln was, perhaps, the homeliest man she'd ever met. Deep lines crisscrossed his face, but his blue eyes held a depth of sorrow so sincere that Carrie couldn't doubt it.

Introduction to Mrs. Lincoln came next, although her greeting was far less cordial than her husband's. Carrie recalled reading somewhere that Mrs. Lincoln disliked all officers' wives, but the reason why escaped her now. After receiving the woman's aloof greeting, Carrie hurried to move aside to join Margaret and Papa, who had been introduced ahead of her.

Refreshments were served and Carrie watched Papa converse with General Sheridan. She hoped he'd keep quiet about his true reason for attending tonight. Peyton said that Union commanders disliked journalists, and Carrie read somewhere that General Sherman was reported as stating, "If I had my choice I would kill every reporter in the world, but I am sure we would be getting reports from Hell before breakfast."

Here's hoping General Sheridan and Mr. Lincoln didn't share Sherman's sentiments.

Soon they were ushered into the State Dining Room. Several large round tables were covered with festive pumpkin-colored cloths. Places were neatly set with beautiful porcelain dinnerware, gleaming silverware, and crystal goblets. Within minutes, the guests were each seated in one of the Queen Anne–styled chairs. Contrary to her concerns, Tabitha had a place at General Sheridan's table, along with the rest of the Collier group.

A three-course dinner was served, the first being delicious squash soup. The entrée consisted of sliced turkey, mashed potatoes with giblet gravy, and green beans. For dessert, they indulged in generous slices of sweet potato pie. Tabitha approved of the treat, from the spiced sweet potatoes to the pie's flaky crust, saying the Executive Mansion's recipe was nearly as tasty as her own.

After the meal was finished and plates removed, an officer left his place at another table and strode across the room. He introduced himself as General

Josiah Ebbs. Within minutes he pulled up a chair beside General Sheridan and began talking about Sherman's "magnificent" march to the sea. Papa sat forward, eager for some snippet of news to report.

"I overheard President Lincoln say he's not concerned that no one has heard from Sherman since he left Atlanta." General Ebbs steepled his slender fingers. "But many of us are wondering why his army seems to have vanished."

"Knowing Sherman, he's tramping all over the Confederacy, unrestrained." General Sheridan took a swallow of brandy from the snifter which had been set in front of him. Ebbs had requested one also.

President Lincoln strolled over and pulled up a chair. He leaned forward to better hear his two generals above the din in the room.

"I'm certain Sherman is feasting well today." Ebbs gave an amused snort. "He and his men have been subsisting very well off the spoils of war."

"May I ask about the injured men?" Carrie blurted. When the men's gazes fixed on her she almost regretted not holding her tongue. But how could she? "Do we know the identity of all the patients in the Washington hospital? Do they have food enough?"

"The population at the hospital is, unfortunately, growing by the minute," the president said, his voice more solemn than ever. "As far as men's identities, I'm sure the physicians do the best they can, and I have been informed that food and supplies are satisfactory."

"As I have told Mrs. Collier," General Sheridan said, his dark eyes briefly touching down on Carrie, "men have a way of keeping track of one another."

"Yes, sir, but there is the fog of war phenomenon in which men can get separated from each other and even disoriented." Carrie knew that because Peyton had told her.

"Are you burdened for the wounded, Mrs. Collier?" the president asked.

"You might say so, yes."

"You have my deepest gratitude, madam." The president's features brightened, but he didn't actually smile.

"What is the care like for our men if they're taken prisoner?" Carrie didn't need to look at Aunt Ruth to tell she disapproved of the questioning.

"I have heard it's inferior, especially for those unfortunate enough to be held in Andersonville." The president's long, slender fingers wrapped around the water goblet in front of him. He stared into its clear depth as if it held some mystical powers. "I have had news from City Point informing me of numerous soldiers being moved from Libby's island prison—"

"Belle Isle, sir," Papa put in politely.

"Ah, yes . . . a hellish place, from what I understand." General Ebbs drained his brandy. "However, some of our men were sent to the Washington hospital from Richmond under a flag of truce. A new surgeon general, one M. L. Bell, is paroling Union troops too wounded to rejoin the fight. Our Anaconda Plan is finally working. The South is short of food . . . and medicine too."

"M. L. Bell, you say?" Papa kneaded his jaw thoughtfully. "Our relative perhaps?"

That's when she remembered Cousin Mikey and his wife, Eunice. He was a physician in Richmond—but surely he wasn't M. L. Bell, the man presently being discussed.

The flash in Papa's blue eyes said otherwise and alarm rang in Carrie's head. She glanced at Margaret, who opened her fan and gave a subtle nod. Not a word about their Rebel kin would be uttered at this table.

But how could Cousin Mikey accept such a position as overseeing the medical needs of Federal troops locked behind bars at one of the most notorious prisons in the Confederacy?

Carrie shuddered and prayed Peyton hadn't been taken there. But what if he had?

"Are you cold, my dear?" Papa set his arm across the back of her chair. "Would you like your stole?"

"No, thank you." The room was actually overly warm and perspiration tickled Carrie's nape.

After a polite incline of his head, Papa returned his attention to the men. He had to know that later she'd inquire about Cousin Mikey. Perhaps Margaret would as well. He had always been one of their favorite relatives. Carrie called to memory the image of him, a swashbuckling man with his easy laugh and zest for life. She'd known he was a medical doctor who served in the Confederate army, but over the years she'd lost track of him. It appeared that he'd worked his way up the ranks.

General Ebbs hailed the server, carrying a tray of refilled brandy glasses.

Aunt Ruth pushed back her chair and stood. "Ladies, I believe it's time for us to traverse to the parlor where we can join the other women and leave the men to their brandy and discussions of war."

Her tone left no room for argument, although, given the choice, Carrie would stay and listen to the men. However, she dutifully followed Aunt Ruth, Tabitha, and Margaret from the State Dining Room. Now she'd hear recitations of poetry or listen to aimless prattle. She sighed and cast a look at Papa. He caught her eye and smiled. Some things never changed.

Well, Carrie would just have to get the scoop from him later.

CHAPTER 22

Eli stood on the back porch and drew on his pipe for the first time in a long while. He released the smoke with a contented sigh. "Tobacco grown in the Barbados is nearly as good as Virginia tobacco."

"It's rich, wouldn't you say, Eli?"

"Perhaps." A smile hiked up one side of his mouth while Eli eyed his guest. Pat proved he was still the decent fellow that Eli remembered from his youth. He liked inserting himself into the goings-on in the political world, and since he had the money to speak his mind, he often did. But politics aside, Father had trusted Pat implicitly, so Eli figured he could too. "Don't ask me to divide my loyalties between tobaccos now. I'm a hearty Virginian."

"So you are." Pat rose and stared out over the yard. The rain had moved on and now stars dotted the inky sky. Moonlight danced off Pat's bald head. "Dinner was delicious tonight—"

"A bit sparse, I'm afraid."

"But very good. I expected worse, coming to Richmond. But why partake in a Thanksgiving feast that the Yankee president proclaimed?"

"Seemed a good time to celebrate." Eli took a moment to ponder what he was about to share and decided the news was safe with his godfather. "I inherited money from a friend of mine—a Yankee officer. He was killed last month. I contacted my banker, who was able to work out a withdrawal of some funds in the form of varying values of gold coins. The money enabled me to purchase this house for my mother and sister, and obtain a groundskeeper and a cook. If we're careful with the last of our gold coins, we'll make it through the winter months."

"Ah, yes. When I arrived, I exchanged my British currency for gold and did not have an easy time of it. Seems the bank in Richmond is about out of money, and it takes a wagonload of Confederate dollars to equal a gold coin."

"It's true." Eli was glad he made his withdrawal when he did.

"Guard your money with your life, son."

"My money is safe." Eli had buried it in a metal lockbox in the cellar. "Now tell me, what brings you to Richmond?"

"Besides visiting your family?"

Eli inclined his head.

"It's no secret: the Confederacy is dying. Six months ago, I wouldn't have believed it, but now I'm certain of it." Pat turned, folded his arms, and leaned his slender frame against one of the white pillars that towered beyond the second floor of the house. Even in his mid sixties, the man possessed the same high energy as that of younger men. "It really never had a chance. In fact, Jeff Davis himself referred to the idea of a Confederacy as a grand theory when he and I chatted back in 1860, before I left the States. I predicted that war would come, and I didn't want Averly growing up in the midst of it. The Barbados offered so much more than Richmond. We wanted for nothing there." His deep voice took on a melancholy tone. "While slave trade is illegal, the institution of slavery remains strong, so we owned—and still own—maids, valets, cooks, housekeepers, and groundskeepers. It's quite the wonderful life there."

"Then why did you leave it—and why now? The war is still unfolding and President Davis shows no intent at conciliation."

"True, Eli, but I covet a position." He began to whisper. "A position in the United States Senate after the Confederacy falls—and it will fall. Soon."

Eli sensed it also—the demise of the Confederacy. The Union victories this fall had turned The Cause into a lost cause.

"I must begin my campaign immediately, beginning with Mr. Davis and his cabinet. Then Congress. After meeting with politicians here, I'll go to Washington City and speak with Mr. Lincoln. We're old acquaintances from his days as an attorney in Springfield."

"Sounds like you've got your future all mapped out." Eli wished he could say the same for himself. His life seemed quite the opposite.

"I have my plans set, true, but I'll need help."

Eli felt the weight of Pat's stare and shook his head. "I'm a Confederate cavalryman, not a politician."

"Good, because I'm an excellent politician, but I need a cavalryman, one who has lived through battles and can speak frankly and unfettered with me about them."

"I don't think so, Pat." Eli preferred not to speak of past battles and bloodshed. None of their planning, the sneak attacks, the midnight raids—the thousands of dead souls—had made a difference. "Thanks anyway."

"I'll see that you get a pardon."

"A pardon?" Eli leaned forward, his hand resting on the porch railing. "Why would I need a pardon? I'm no criminal."

"There's a rumor circulating that Confederates who attended the military academy will be punished especially hard for their treasonous acts against the United States. If that works itself from rumor to legislation, your life will be worth nothing, Eli. You will be a man without a country for the rest of your days."

Eli strolled to the end of the portico. "I don't base decisions on rumors, Pat, although I consider them carefully."

"That's all I ask. But you should know, I obtained the information from a very good source, namely Mr. Lincoln's vice president. You see, Mr. Johnson and I occasionally correspond. He's interested in purchasing land in the Barbados and I am helping to facilitate the sale. After all, that's what brokers do, is it not?"

"Hmm . . ." Eli emptied his pipe in the damp brush on the other side of the porch. Pat Winslow certainly sounded calculating enough to become a politician. It seemed he had the connections.

"Virginia will need a man like me in office," he said, revealing his confidence. "Our state will need a man who understands the division of his homeland. One who can relate to Virginia's citizens, not just in part, but in relation to the state reentering the Union."

"I wish you the best, Pat."

Pat crossed the porch. Bending slightly, the older man came so close that Eli smelled his recent swallow of whiskey. "You are going to need someone—someone like me who can work out a deal for you. Men like Johnson want to bring the hammer of justice down on top of the heads of former West Point cadets who chose to side with the Rebellion."

Eli's teeth tightened on the stem of his pipe.

"Your mother and sister will suffer, perhaps more than they have already."

It was the dagger in Eli's heart that shattered his resistance. "So what is it, exactly, that you're proposing?"

"Employment. You will work as my lead security detail—at least that's what we will call it in public. You will attend important sessions with me and provide security for Averly and me at various political events. In private, you will act as my trusted advisor."

Eli shook his head. "It's not possible. I have not been officially discharged from the army. I've been furloughed for sixty days, after which I am to report for duty to the Army of Virginia in Petersburg."

"Fret not, son. I will have no problem convincing President Davis and his cabinet that you're unfit for duty due to your leg injury when your furlough is up. Besides, in sixty days I plan to be in Washington and I want you with me."

"Pat, with all due respect, I know of soldiers in the saddle with worse injuries than mine. General John Bell Hood is a prime example. He had one leg amputated at the hip and possesses a withered, useless arm. Yet he was recalled to duty despite having to be strapped into his saddle each day and only one hand with which to fight."

"Hood enjoys killing and his enthusiasm for it is contagious among desperate men. That's why he was called up again. General Lee wanted a killer. Truth to tell, Hood is a hothead. I met him in Texas before the war began. He was a second lieutenant then."

Eli agreed about the hothead description. He and Peyt served with General Hood in California, along with Union commander Phil Sheridan. They despised Hood, a man with pride as large as the Texas territory from which he hailed.

"By the way," Pat added, "Hood's promotion was never confirmed by the Confederate Congress. The position would have gone to another, more deserving man if the matter had worked its way up proper channels."

"I wasn't aware of that fact." Eli rubbed his stubbly chin with the backs of his fingers. Pat certainly did have his sources.

"Hood enjoys feeling powerful and he's out to win the heart of a South

Carolina belle he met here in Richmond. I believe she was visiting friends . . . a Miss Sally Buchanan Preston, if I'm remembering correctly. Hood proposed marriage, but she refused him. Her rejection, some say, pained him deeper than his physical wounds. It also made him more reckless on the battlefield. That, coupled with the fact that Hood must consume large quantities of laudanum and other such drugs in order to abide his physical infirmities, makes him unfit for duty, in my humble opinion. Hood is out of his very mind. How can he effectively lead an army?"

If in charge, Eli would have left General Joe Johnston in his place.

"Hood's service will result in catastrophe, Eli. Mark my words."

"This is all news to me, Pat."

"Of course it is. You've been at war the past three years. Your mind has been fixed on your duties. But I have been in the Barbados, reading newspapers and writing and receiving letters from friends in England and here in the States, primarily Richmond and Washington City. I have learned much from them."

"Interesting." Eli would have to find out if what his godfather said was correct. He'd made up his mind long ago not to believe hearsay, but to use it as a navigation tool of sorts. "Nonetheless, if Hood can be strapped into his saddle, surely the powers that be in the Confederacy will deem me fit enough to return to duty."

"Not necessarily. The Congress is open to suggestions, specifically mine. I've made generous monetary contributions to many of the politicians in office. I'm confident they will go along with my request. All you need to do, Eli, is accept my offer and I can proceed."

Leaving the Army of Virginia and obtaining a pardon after the war . . . the offer was tempting. But Eli couldn't accept. He was bound by his honor to the Confederacy, whether it lived or died.

"I can offer a handsome salary too, Eli. Unlike many Southerners, I did not invest all my money in the Confederacy. True, I've lost a substantial amount, but I have equally substantial funds left."

Eli didn't need Sir Patrick Winslow's money, and yet he did. Making another withdrawal from the bank in Washington wasn't feasible. The Richmond bank was already stressed. Financial ruin threatened this city's wealthiest citizens.

Pat tipped his head. "You want more?"

"I want to make sure that *you* don't want more." Particularly a match between him and Averly.

"I don't understand."

"Your daughter, Pat. While she is lovely and intelligent, it's without question that she and I are ill-suited."

"Because of your injury?" Pat guffawed. "Averly doesn't care about that. She has loved you since she was fourteen years old."

"I'm flattered. Truly. But . . ." Eli didn't know how else to deter the man but to be brutally honest. "I love someone else."

"Oh?" Pat tilted his head. "Is your mother aware of this?"

"No. We haven't had much time to converse. I moved into my quarters above the apothecary shortly before you arrived."

"I see."

"Besides, the secret is best kept to myself for now. The object of my romantic interest recently became a widow, and things are not conducive for declaring myself to her anytime soon."

"I should say not." Pat turned thoughtful for several long moments. "And you're happy to live off her money, should she agree to marry you in the future?"

"Absolutely not! Her money is hers alone. Her deceased husband, my longtime friend, has left me a generous stipend. I used a portion of it for necessities." Eli wasn't about to list them all.

"But if the funds were allocated to you, Eli, what's the trouble?"

"No, trouble, other than I will work and support my future wife and family."

"Then you must accept my employment proposal. How better to seal happiness with a Yankee's widow than to be granted a pardon from the United States government, if needed, and your own income?"

He made a good argument.

Pat held out his right hand. "Do we have a deal?"

Eli's mind conjured up Carrie Ann, sitting on the back porch at Piccadilly Place, with her hairpins threatening to come loose as she laughed at something he'd said. She'd rivaled the red-gold August sunset.

Eli also recalled her blue eyes flashing in anger when they parted last month. He'd assumed it had been a ruse to throw off the Union pickets. Was it?

Either way, without his own money, how could he ever hope to be worthy of her affection?

Sliding his palm into Pat Winslow's smaller hand, Eli gave it a firm shake. "You've got a deal."

The Jeffersonian

Stroudsburg, Monroe Country, PA

December 8, 1864

A FURIOUS BATTLE. THE ENEMY . . . REPULSED.

DISPATCH: Nashville, Nov. 30, 1864: Midnight. The enemy at 4 p.m. made a heavy attack with two Corps, but after persistent fighting he was repulsed at all points, with a loss of six thousand killed and wounded.

Our loss is known to be about five hundred.

During the battle one thousand prisoners were taken, including a Brigadier General.

The battle took place at Franklin.

—☙ ❧—

Evening Star

Washington D.C.

Wednesday, December 21, 1864

TELEGRAPHIC NEWS: THE WAR IN TENNESSEE

Nashville, Dec. 19—A courier who left Franklin yesterday, reports that the rebel force is in full retreat. . . . Franklin is reported to be full of rebel wounded, over 3,000 being left there on their retreat. Every church and public building in the town has been taken for hospitals. Our wounded occupy nearly all the churches.

Nashville, Dec. 20—The rebel army [under General John Bell Hood], from all accounts, has become utterly demoralized, and is unable to make a stand. It has scarcely any artillery. The telegraph is working to Spring Hill. Trains will run to Franklin this morning.

DETAILS OF THE BATTLE

Cincinnati, Dec. 19—During the night of the 15th, Hood withdrew both his wings from the river, contracted his lines everywhere, and was holding a strong position . . .

Our plan of battle was a continuance . . . in pressing the advantage gained on the enemy's left. At about half-past eight o'clock our batteries opened from a hundred pieces simultaneously along the [Union] line. The rebel artillery replied feebly. . . . [General John] Schofield moved on the left flank of the enemy, and before his veterans the rebels gave way like frostwork.

CHAPTER 23

December 24, 1864

Carrie finished tying the red satiny ribbon around the last Christmas gift and placed it beneath the freshly cut tree. Its piney scent filled her nose. Earlier, Margaret, Aunt Ruth, and Carrie had decorated it with lovely painted-glass bulbs. Each one had a special story and Aunt Ruth reveled in the telling. When she lit the candles on the tree's branches and the lamps in the parlor were turned down low, Mrs. Rhodes exclaimed that she'd never seen a lovelier Christmas tree. Tabitha grudgingly agreed and even craggy old Mr. Rhodes mumbled something that resembled a compliment.

"How long has it been since we decorated a Christmas tree?" Carrie studied the holiday tree, feeling truly blessed.

"I can't recall," Margaret said with an unmistakable note of awe. "Mr. Veyschmidt, that devil, refused to celebrate the Lord's birth. He wouldn't even acknowledge it. It was just another day to him and, unfortunately, to many others who straggled in for company."

"But we didn't let Veyschmidt keep us from humming Christmas songs, did we?" Carrie squared her shoulders. "I think we even spread a little Christmas joy to others who were lonely and needed it."

"That's a nice way to remember it, I suppose." Margaret stared at the Christmas tree.

"I've decided to bring to mind only the good from our past—all of it."

"I'd call that a Christmas miracle."

Carrie smiled. Like her sister, she forgave Papa, choosing to move forward with their relationship. After all, Papa was trying awfully hard to make good on his previous failings.

He'd made good on his promise and accompanied Carrie to each one of Washington City's hospitals where she'd searched for Peyton. Sadly, she didn't find him. She did, however, meet Papa's friend, Mr. Walt Whitman. He was witty and intelligent and they talked of writing—one of Carrie's favorite subjects. In no time, it seemed, Mr. Whitman convinced her of the need to write letters for the wounded soldiers who wanted word sent home but were unable to write for themselves for various reasons.

Carrie immediately set to work and, for nearly a month now, volunteered a portion of her time at one hospital or another. Margaret and Aunt Ruth frequently joined her.

But Papa could not. Now that his article about Thanksgiving Day at the Executive Mansion had been picked up by several prominent newspapers, such as the *New York Times*, he was busy with chasing story leads and writing articles. The Thanksgiving Day event had, indeed, proved just the chance he'd needed . . . and Carrie couldn't be more proud of him. What's more, she was proud of Peyton's service to his country. He deserved the honor that President Lincoln had bestowed upon him as well as other soldiers. Carrie's only wish was that Peyton had been there to receive the ribbon and medal himself.

She turned from the tree and made herself comfortable in an upholstered armchair.

"You know," Margaret began, "it was very kind of you to give Aunt Ruth, Tabitha, and me allowances so we could purchase personal items and Christmas gifts."

"It seemed the right thing to do. We all need to learn to manage finances. What better way to begin than with our own bank accounts?" Carrie lifted her teacup and saucer from off the side table.

"But, it's your inheritance, and Aunt Ruth's and Tabitha's, not mine." Margaret picked at a speck on her skirt. "I should really earn my keep if you plan to continue giving me an allowance."

"But you are earning your keep. You assist Mrs. Rhodes—"

"And get scolded from Tabitha each time I do." Margaret smiled. "I've decided Tabitha only gives such earfuls to those she truly cares about."

Carrie rolled her eyes. "You also earn your keep, so to speak, by accompanying me to the hospitals where you've been darning socks and mending soldiers' clothing."

"I'm glad you feel that way. I don't want to ever become burdensome." Something akin to relief brightened her features. "Besides, now that I have my spectacles, I'm finding sewing to be rather relaxing and enjoyable." Margaret sipped from her steaming cup.

But moments later her features fell. A frown creased her forehead.

"What is it?" Carrie set down her cup and saucer.

"Remember how we talked of being traveling companions one day?"

"Yes."

"Remember how you disguised yourself to go after Sarah Jane when she ran off?"

"Yes . . ." Carrie tipped her head, wondering where the questions were headed.

"Well . . ." Margaret scooted to the edge of the settee, enthusiasm sparkling in her teal eyes. "Papa and I recently discussed Cousin Mikey and his wife, Eunice. Evidently, poor Eunice is in failing health and Cousin Mikey is rarely home."

"Yes, I overheard Papa mention something of the sort." Carrie pulled her shawl more tightly around her. The last of the embers glowed in the hearth, but gave off very little heat. "What's that got to do with disguises and travels?"

"Let's you and me go to Richmond, Carrie."

"What? That's impossible. It's the Rebel capital and I'm a Union officer's wife."

"Not if you travel as Carrie Ann Bell, my sister, and General Michael Bell's cousin, coming for a visit to cheer his ill wife."

The idea tickled Carrie. "Papa would paddle us both and Aunt Ruth would lock us in our bedrooms for a month."

"Not if they don't know about our plans until after we're gone."

Margaret's eyes darkened with earnestness and all Carrie's amusement vanished.

"You're serious?"

"I am."

Margaret fiddled with the fringe on her shawl. "What if . . . what if you were right about the colonel being alive just like you were right about Papa? What if your husband is in Libby Prison? I have heard just awful tales about it from the wounded at the hospital."

Carrie's heart grew heavy as she stared into her teacup. They had received a letter from Cousin Mikey in response to Papa's general inquiry "for a friend." Papa feared his cousin wouldn't reply if he knew Papa asked about his son-in-law. Unfortunately, Cousin Mikey sent an ambiguous missive of his own, stating that he could neither confirm nor deny Peyton's incarceration at Libby.

"Hear me out, sister dear."

Carrie grinned. "Very well. What do you have in mind?"

"Let's pay a visit to Cousin Mikey. He's the chief medical director at Libby Prison. What better contact could we possibly have if we're searching for your husband there?"

"Do you know what that would entail? We would be found out in no time."

A little smile played across Margaret's mouth. "By the time we obtain passes from the city's provost marshal, the weather will be better. We can take the steamer to City Point. Politicians and others, including women, use that mode of transportation quite frequently. I heard a nurse brag about tending the wounds and ailments of General Grant's staff. She travels about rather freely."

"I don't know . . ." Carrie nibbled her lower lip, pondering the idea. Ironically, she wasn't the one coming up with the scheme this time.

"You want to find your husband, don't you?"

"Yes, but—"

"I've been talking with wounded soldiers and casually asking them hypothetical questions. According to those men, chances are good that the colonel was taken to Richmond if he was captured on the battlefield. If he was injured, Cousin Mikey would know about him because he'd be in the prison hospital."

Carrie longed to believe that Peyton was *alive*. The thought enabled her to rise each morning and kept her going all day without a single tear.

"Your plan has appeal. Please, go on."

"Our story will be that we're employed by a wealthy woman in Winchester who decided to winter in Washington. Having sufficient help, she gave us a few months' leave. So, we decided to visit our cousins." Margaret's eyes sparkled. "It's practically the truth."

"I don't know . . ." Carrie could think of all sorts of reasons they shouldn't attempt such a feat, the danger being first and foremost. But what if Peyton languished in Libby Prison? She'd read horror stories about that place. How could their cousin be in charge of such a filthy, rat-infested facility?

"Think of dear Cousin Eunice, ill and in need of companionship." Margaret held her hands over her heart dramatically. "I'd rush to her bedside, but I can't travel to Richmond alone."

"Why would you? We barely know the woman."

"Oh . . ." Margaret waved off the remark. "But two *unwed sisters* could travel together. Cousin Mikey will be grateful for our help. Then, while in Richmond, we might even volunteer our nursing skills, further endearing him to us." She arched her brows and grinned. "He always said we were his favorite Bell cousins. If the colonel is being held prisoner, you'd likely find him."

"Except I'm not unmarried."

"We'd have to fib about that part . . . obviously."

Carrie replied with a wide-eyed stare. "Obviously."

She stood and made her way to the mantle, decorated with fresh evergreen boughs and holly. She'd never do anything to jeopardize the Collier name, not to mention Peyton's reputation with the Union army, although Joshua and Eli nearly managed it with their escape last October.

Carrie bit down hard. Just thinking of those two men, Eli in particular, set her blood to boiling hard like Tabitha's teakettle.

"So what do you think?"

Carrie knew what answer her sister hoped for, but she wasn't prepared to give it . . . yet. "I suppose fibbing is essential, considering the circumstances." Aunt Ruth wasn't above an occasional fib. She smiled, remembering the number of tall tales they'd both fabricated in order to keep Rebel troops appeased during their occupation of Piccadilly Place.

"Carrie?" Margaret got up and strode across the room, standing close to Carrie. "We'll go to Richmond then?"

She recognized both hope and daring in Margaret's gaze. "It sounds as half-baked as any of my past follies and I'd like to think I learned and matured by enduring all the trouble I got myself into as a consequence of them."

"And you have." The corners of Margaret's mouth turned upward. "That's why I need you. You're an expert at . . . half-baked follies."

"Thank you for that." Carrie sent a glance toward the ceiling. She could well envision Peyton's scowl if he could overhear such a plot.

But if she found him, he'd be grateful . . . wouldn't he?

"Please, think it over?"

Carrie gave a nod. "I'll sleep on the idea, and I suggest you do the same."

"That's all I ask—for now."

For now? Carrie nearly choked at the tenacity in her sister's tone. "So am I to understand that you are determined to see this crazy notion through?"

"I'm committed to it, yes—for *poor Cousin Eunice.*" Margaret winked.

"You are becoming quite the imp." Carrie gave in to a little laugh. "Aunt Ruth will be so proud . . . once she forgives us."

"She will. And I'd wager she'd do the same thing if she was thirty years younger."

Carrie couldn't argue. However, she was suddenly too exhausted to strategize. "Let's talk more about this tomorrow—or perhaps the day after."

Margaret captured her right hand and gave it a firm shake. "Deal."

Carrie gaped at the manly gesture.

"Oh, mercy me!" Two scarlet buds bloomed in her younger sister's cheeks. Her hand fell to her side. "It seems Aunt Ruth has a bit more tutoring to do before I'm truly a well-mannered young lady."

—⊙ ⊙—

"This isn't exactly the perfect Christmas of years past, but it's the best Eli could muster." Mother sent him a pitiful glance from her place at the head of the dining table.

Eli sat back, refusing to be daunted by her ungratefulness. "We have more than many Southerners do on this Christmas morning." He glanced at Pat and Averly, then his sweet sister, Laurabeth. Since he'd come home, they had become allies. "Many Confederate soldiers don't even have boots."

"They're wearing their good shoes into battle? Impossible." Mother cackled over her joke.

Except Eli didn't find it amusing. "A number of our troops are barefoot and half-starved in the trenches. But look at us"—he spread his arms out wide, indicating their empty plates and the leftovers on the sideboard—"I say, let us thank the Almighty for our ample provisions, such as this generous breakfast of eggs, ham, and biscuits."

"Here! Here!" Pat raised his water goblet.

Mother appeared unimpressed. "Oh, forgive me, Eli. I miss Greenwater terribly. It was my home for decades. It's where my children were born and where your father, God rest his soul, passed from this life into the hereafter."

"I understand. It was my home too."

"Personally," Laurabeth ventured meekly, "I prefer Little Greenwater." Her fawn-colored eyes settled on Eli. "This home is ever so cozy."

"Hush, Laurabeth." Mother scowled. "No one asked for your opinion. Can't you behave more like Averly? Observe the way she sits at the table without slouching or speaking the first thing that comes to her mind."

Laurabeth retreated into herself like an exquisite tortoise into its shell.

Eli lifted his porcelain cup and gulped down a retort with his coffee. While he planned to confront his mother on her ill treatment of Laurabeth, now was not the time.

"And Isaiah . . ." Mother dabbed her eyes with her napkin then turned to Pat. "If only he would have accepted your offer to move to the Barbados. Instead he listened to his older brother"—she hurled a glare down the table at Eli—"and joined the army."

"Now, Helena, I would have fought for the Confederacy too," Pat said, "if I didn't have extenuating circumstances at the time and an impressionable young daughter to raise."

Mother had no reply and, once again, Eli held his tongue. He'd known for quite some time that she blamed him for Isaiah's death and resented Eli's absence during Father's long illness and subsequent passing. But duty had called Eli away.

"Enough of this dismal conversation." Pat rubbed his palms together. "It's Christmas Day. Let's open our gifts before we dress for church."

"Oh, yes, let's, Daddy." Averly clasped her hands and smiled.

"I think opening gifts is quite appropriate." Mother stood, followed by everyone else at the table. Like obedient ducklings, they all followed her into the parlor where a scant number of gifts lay beneath the decorated Christmas tree.

"Open mine first, Eli." Averly rushed to retrieve the small square package wrapped in brown paper and tied with string. "It's a framed daguerreotype of me."

Eli unwrapped it, sensing all eyes upon him, particularly Pat's. He examined the picture, framed in sliver. "It's a lovely likeness of you, Averly."

Her feline-like, green eyes lit up with pleasure. Despite her public display of affection and his compliment, Eli couldn't detect even the slightest pink in her cheeks. "I've imagined you carrying my picture with you at all times and knowing that I am praying for your safety."

"Thank you, Averly." He struggled momentarily to craft the best reply, one that would deflect her intentions without hurting her feelings. "But I think this daguerreotype is much too fine to be stuffed into my coat pocket." Eli strode to the pianoforte and placed the silver-framed picture on the instrument's polished top. "I believe it should be placed somewhere out in the open for all to admire."

"Oh . . . well, that's nice too." Her disappointment was palpable in the suddenly too-quiet parlor. But it couldn't be helped. Eli refused to cave to her whims—or anyone else's in this room.

"Averly, darling," Pat said, ever the diplomat, "you must have forgotten. Eli has obtained furlough from the army."

"But he's always off somewhere and wears a Confederate frock coat." She faced Eli again. "Pray, what consumes your time these days?"

"The Confederate army is desperate. Even furloughed, I'm required to do light duty. I've been given a position as one of the security details at Libby Prison." The words passed his tensed jaw. He disliked being put on the spot this way.

Pat cleared his throat. "Averly, wouldn't you say that Eli is a dedicated man to continue his service to his country when it's not required? For myself, I'm impressed."

"Yes, you're right, Daddy. Eli is a good man." She batted her lashes at him.

Eli looked away. "We have a gift for you too, Averly. Laurabeth chose it. It's from her, Mother, and me." The overemphasis on the family gift left no room for Averly's hopes and imaginings.

Smiling, Laurabeth fetched it from under the tree and presented it to their guest. While Averly unwrapped it, Eli left the room, intent on a breath of fresh air. He fished his heavy coat from the front closet and headed for the covered porch behind the house.

Stepping onto the repaired planks, Eli pulled the door shut behind him. Snow glistened on tree branches. The worst winter in recent memory, some folks said. Eli was only too glad to do something to help the flailing Confederacy, and of late, he'd rather spend his time on duty at the prison than enduring a certain simpering female and a bossy mother, although he enjoyed getting better acquainted with Laurabeth. Beneath her meek exterior lay an educated and determined young lady. She harbored dreams of becoming a doctor one day. A doctor! Tall aspirations, indeed. But how to get around Mother, that was the question to which even Eli had no answer.

Since leaving the military academy, Eli had been an officer. He'd given orders to other men. He was accustomed to taking charge and leading. However, when he stepped foot into this house—Mother's house for all intents and purposes—he was continually forced to swallow his pride, bow gracefully, and give the woman her way. After all, they had guests.

As for one of them, there was no doubt in Eli's mind that Averly was not as innocent as her father might think. No, she struck Eli as an accomplished flirt. True, he wanted a woman with tenacity, but he also prayed for a helpmeet who possessed a special sweetness that was reserved for only him.

Eli sat on the porch rail as a blast of winter air hit him. He shivered beneath his coat, thanking God that he wasn't freezing in the trenches outside of Petersburg. He prayed for the troops who were as they faced Union foes.

Quite unexpectedly, an image of Carrie Ann Collier filled his mind. Now there's a woman with just the right mix of sweetness and spice. The recollection of her pierced Eli's heart like a musket's bayonet. Carrie, kneeling over him while he lay injured in the Colliers' music room, her eyes puffy from so many tears over Peyton's death. Her broken little voice asking if Peyton named Eli executor because he hadn't trusted her. Eli had done his best to vanquish her fears, but he'd been helpless to do much else. He had hated leaving her behind. But allowing himself to be rescued was preferable in every way to wasting away in a Yankee prison.

Besides, she knew he was here in Richmond if she needed him.

His breath came out in a succession of frosty puffs. He wished he could be with Carrie now to assure her that in time everything would work out and to offer his services if she, her sister, Aunt Ruth, and Tabitha should find themselves heavily burdened.

The question was, would Carrie ever think highly enough of him to ask?

The Alexandria Gazette and Virginia Advertiser
January 23, 1865

In the speech of Mr. Orr, of Mississippi, in the Confederate Congress recently, heretofore referred to, in relation to certain charges made in the Richmond Sentinel newspaper, he said: "For the sake of argument, let it be conceded that they have proposed to send commissioners to Washington to open irregular negotiations for peace. These commissioners might be sent with no other power than to confer and consult with the authorities there on terms of an honorable peace, with instructions to report the results of such conference to the President and to this House. Such negotiations would be irregular, and yet they might, I think they would, if ratified by the treaty-making power, secure an honorable and satisfactory peace. Who but a madman would denounce these means and this result as treachery of the most infamous character? From the supposed relation of the paper to men in power, it may have been intended, in indulging in bitter denunciation, to have the effect of intimidating the advocates of an honorable, peaceful settlement of the war. If this was the design, allow me to assure you, Mr. Speaker, that a greater mistake was never made. Denunciation will be met by defiance. This movement is not in the hands of timid or time serving men. . . ."

. . .

All the Richmond papers condemn the tone of Mr. Orr's speech, and any terms of peace, except on the basis of Southern independence.

CHAPTER 24

February 11, 1865

Sitting beside her sister in the riverboat's saloon, Margaret leaned over to Carrie Ann. "I think we did the right thing by hiring Mr. Jones to be our chaperone."

Carrie looked up from her book. "He's quite the recluse. He's barely said two words to us and he appears to avoid polite conversation."

"Well, so far he's been a gentleman." Margaret glanced at the man as he stood on the steamer's deck, smoking a cheroot. If not for his references, she'd judge him to be a shady character. "From his appearance, I would have never guessed the man to be as reliable as we were told."

"We'll see, won't we?"

Margaret leaned against her sister. "He got us a ride on the mail packet boat, now didn't he?" she whispered. "And the train ride from Washington City to City Point wasn't terrible."

"No. I had expected worse."

"Indeed." Sitting beside the window, Margaret could see the packet's white flag of truce flapping in the wintery breeze as they made the last leg of their journey from City Point to Richmond.

Carrie returned to the book on her lap.

Margaret settled into her seat on the padded bench. She and Carrie were well prepared and had procured the necessary traveling passes. In fact, obtaining them had almost been the easiest part of the planning.

Since Christmastime, they had prayed about this journey in earnest, pleading with God to put a halt to their idea if He wanted them to abandon it. But, in the last two months, everything miraculously fell into place. Best of all, Carrie's spunk had returned.

They had successfully kept Aunt Ruth in the dark about their plans. By now, however, she knew they were gone. No doubt she was upset about it. Numerous times, Carrie suggested that they enlist Aunt Ruth's help, but Margaret felt certain that Aunt Ruth would squash their ideas. For that reason, their mission had to be kept secret. She hoped Aunt Ruth would forgive them, particularly her.

Margaret inhaled and the mildewy scent that seemed entrenched in the saloon tickled her nostrils. Well, whether right or wrong, it was done now. It wouldn't be long and they would be settled in Cousin Mikey's home in Richmond.

"In his last letter, Cousin Mikey mentioned that things were rather glum in Richmond," Margaret told Carrie. "I imagine so, what with the war not going in the Confederates' favor."

Carrie looked up from her book. Her lips curled upward in a distracted smile before she dove back into her novel.

Margaret surveyed the other passengers in the steamer's saloon. A young mother sat across the way. She wore widow's weeds and held an infant against her shoulder. Other women in black garb rode the steamer too, along with haggard-faced men with bandaged limbs. Their gray coats looked as faded as their spirits. Most likely, they had been deemed unfit for the Confederate army and were paroled. Maybe they were returning home. They had to be pleased about that much, at least . . .

Unless they had no homes to return to. General Sherman's troops were on the march again. Each morning Carrie read aloud from the newspapers and it was reported that Sherman's army was leaving Savannah and heading to South Carolina. He was destroying entire towns and cities. At this rate, there wouldn't be much of the South left to save.

Margaret readjusted her spectacles and focused on the small book of Quaker prayers from which she'd been reading. The Friends did not believe in taking up arms and fighting against another human being. How much better off the North and South would be, had their politicians been Quakers.

—◌◌—

"A St. Valentine's Day reception for your cousins, sir?"

Eli considered the handwritten invitation he held, then stared at the hulking frame of the chief medical director of hospitals, Lieutenant General Michael Bell. Weeks ago, the man had noticed Eli's limp when he reported to work and inquired about it and Eli's use of the crutch. After Eli described his injury and how and where it occurred, General Bell offered his medical services. It was one of the best offers Eli received in a long while as his injury seemed slow to heal. What a relief to hear from General Bell that all was well and quite normal, if not miraculous.

As the frigid January weeks became longer, rain-drenched February days, Eli and the general developed a friendly relationship. And now this invitation to meet the general's young, female cousins . . . It wasn't the first Valentine's Day invitation he'd received and it, like the others, hinted of a matchmaking scheme. Even so, Eli gave the general a polite smile and decided to use Pat and Averly as excuses. "Very nice of you to think of me, sir. But I'm afraid my family is presently host to out-of-town guests, and, therefore—"

"Bring them. The more the merrier." The general's chuckles bounced off the empty hallway of Libby Prison, dubbed Castle Thunder by unknown prison wiseacres, whose nickname for the facility stuck.

Eli resumed his walk alongside the doctor after the examination of his leg. Earlier this week, at the general's suggestion, Eli had given up his crutch and began using a walking stick to assist his gait. Now, General Bell encouraged him to put his stick in a corner and try getting along without it for short periods throughout the day. Overall, the general stated, his leg was healing nicely—thanks to Carrie Ann Collier.

But hadn't her maiden name been Bell?

Eli smiled at the irony. "I just now made the connection, although I'm aware your last name is quite common."

The general paused and his bushy brown brows arched with interest.

"The young woman who tended to my leg in Winchester—"

"A fine job she did, son."

"Yes, sir. Her maiden name was Bell. Carrie Ann Bell. I first met her last August."

His blue eyes widened. "Why that's my young cousin's name. And, yes, she and her younger sister, Margaret, found employment in Winchester as companions to a wealthy spinster. What a happy coincidence that they will have another familiar face to greet them here in Richmond."

Companions? Both of them? "Hmm . . . interesting." Eli withheld Aunt Ruth's name, unsure of what the general had been told. Obviously not the truth. He urged the nervous knot in his chest to unwind, be calm.

"When their employer decided to winter in Washington City, the girls traveled with her. They were reunited with their father there. Charles is my first and favorite cousin. So after the girls were given leave, they asked to visit me."

"Their father is accompanying them?"

"No. He found work in Washington and can't get away."

"But he let his daughters make the trip?"

"Evidently their employer hired a chaperone and they are traveling first by train and then riverboat. I'm to meet the mail packet boat on which they're arriving this afternoon. I'm sure they will be exhausted from their trip."

"I imagine so." Eli sent him a side-glance. "But tell me . . . they endangered themselves for a . . . a visit?"

"I gather it's not so perilous to be among family than to live in Yankee-controlled Winchester and Washington."

Eli stared at the tips of his black boots. A Yankee-controlled city wasn't even half the story. Carrie married a Yank!

"The poor dears. They had no choice but to accept employment from a Yankee woman after their home in Woodstock was destroyed. No doubt they've heard all sorts of abolitionist propaganda."

"Undoubtedly. Although I will say that last October Carrie fought for the well-being of the Confederate wounded, myself being counted among them. I'm convinced I would not have my leg—perhaps my life—if it weren't for her care."

"That's my girl." The general puffed out his chest.

"And when our men showed up, wearing disguises, Carrie recognized one of them, but she looked away and we were able to escape."

"Quite the heroine, eh?"

"Quite." Eli hoped his testimony would keep the little heroine out of Libby Prison, should she be found out. Authorities locked up women for lesser offenses than, say . . . *treason*. However, Carrie would have to return to Aunt Ruth at some point and without blemishing Peyton's good service to the Union.

Between thumb and forefinger, Eli kneaded his scratchy jaw. How could she have taken such chances? Then again, with men like Phil Sheridan and Michael Bell on her side, Carrie was likely safer and more protected than the average citizen—unless neither officer knew Carrie's capabilities, which was also very likely.

They continued their stroll toward the doorway, when Eli touched the commander's arm, halting him. "I beg you to keep the story of Carrie's heroism under wraps, General Bell. I would hate for your cousins to get into trouble with the Federal government when they return to Washington."

"Of course. Although I don't mind revealing to you that I plan to talk the girls out of returning."

"Sir, if my memory serves me correctly, there's a contract involved." *A marital contract.* "Carrie, for sure, will have to return to . . . *her employer.*"

The general digested his remark with thick, pursed lips. "I'm sure there's an attorney in Richmond who can find a loophole."

Eli shrugged inwardly. Carrie was, after all, a widow now. Technically, she had no ties to the Collier family—except she'd promised to take care of Aunt Ruth and Tabitha.

"I urge you to wait, sir. Speak with Carrie . . . *Miss Bell.*" Involving a lawyer would be about the worst thing that could happen.

"I see. So you're on a first-name basis with my young cousin?" The general narrowed his gaze rather suspiciously.

Eli studied the frosted glass door which led into the hospital wing's administrative quarters. How much and how little could he divulge? "We became good acquaintances when she cared for me."

"I see." General Bell broke into a boisterous chuckle and placed his large hands on Eli's shoulders. "Let's surprise her and Margaret then, shall we? It'll be our little secret until tomorrow night." The general's arms fell to his sides. "I ran into another of Carrie Ann's friends—Major Joshua Blevens of Woodstock. I remember that boy when he stood half a cornstalk high."

Eli tamped down the urge to wince. "Is he aware that the Bell sisters are visiting Richmond?"

The general inclined his head. "I saw no reason not to invite him. Major Blevens recently earned twenty days' leave. He's staying at a boarding house in town. He said he'd enjoy seeing the girls again."

Now he suppressed a groan. He would have to seek out Blevens at once and persuade him not to reveal Carrie's true identity—or notify the authorities. Blevens seemed extremely loyal to the Confederacy, and Eli didn't have trouble pumping him for information about Carrie last August.

"So, now that you know the particulars, Colonel Kent . . ."

Eli dragged his thoughts to the present. "Sir?"

"Will you attend the St. Valentine's Day reception tomorrow night?"

Eli smiled despite the lead ball of dread in his gut. "I wouldn't miss it for the world, Dr. Bell."

―‧٥ ٥‧―

"Carrie, I know that we vowed to shoot Joshua Blevens the next time we saw him, but I think tonight is not the appropriate time or place."

"What are you talking about?"

Margaret leaned closer. "The day Joshua left Piccadilly Place, disguised as a Yankee . . . remember? We vowed that we'd shoot him if he crossed our paths again. But my newfound faith commands me to peace and to love my enemies. After all, God hates violence."

"We vowed?" Thinking back, Carrie recalled the day and her anger at both Joshua and Eli for abusing the kindness of the ladies of Piccadilly Place, but she didn't recollect any vow. "If I made such a promise in anger and grief, then I repent. I never hope to shoot another human being again. Once in self-defense was enough."

"I'm glad to hear that." Relief spread across Margaret's face like Cousin Eunice's apple butter on warm biscuits this morning at breakfast. "Look who's headed our way with Cousin Mikey."

Standing near the warm hearth, Carrie followed her sister's line of vision toward the spacious parlor's entrance. Alongside their smiling cousin strode none other than Joshua Blevens.

Carrie clenched her fists. "That toad!"

"Now, Carrie Ann"—Margaret worked her hand into Carrie's—"be calm and polite. He has the power to expose us and then our journey here will be for naught."

"I suppose you do have a point." Carrie drew in a long breath. "Although there is no guarantee Joshua won't expose us. Perhaps we should revert to our plan of shooting him."

Margaret giggled at the quip, while Carrie forced herself not to seethe at the man in Confederate gray headed their way.

He stared back, a wry smile curving his mouth.

"Look who I found, ladies," Cousin Mikey gave Joshua a friendly slap between the shoulder blades. "Your childhood friend. He's here in Richmond on leave after receiving accolades for his bravery. Colonel John Mosby himself wrote the recommendation."

"Congratulations, Major Blevens." Margaret's words sounded a bit mechanical, although not unfriendly.

Carrie pushed out a polite smile.

"I'll let you all get reacquainted." Cousin Mikey glanced over his shoulder. "Mrs. Bell, my better half, is beckoning to me. More guests have arrived." After a small bow, he made his way through the rapidly filling parlor.

"What are you two doing in Richmond?" Joshua clasped his hands behind his back and leaned toward Carrie with a jeering grin. "Defecting from the Union?"

Carrie's palm itched. "How I would love to slap your face."

"Do it and see what will happen."

"I'm not that stupid."

"We're here to cheer up our Cousin Eunice," Margaret said, pulling Carrie behind herself.

"Bah! I don't believe it for a moment."

"It's true, at least in part," Margaret said. "We believe there's a certain wounded man," she stated carefully and in a whispered tone, "who might be detained in Libby Prison."

"I see." Joshua leaned closer so his face was only inches from Carrie's. "You're searching for your husband, eh?"

She lifted her chin to express her defiance. "Yes."

Margaret placed her gloved hand on his forearm. "Please don't report us, Joshua. We really are here for a good purpose with no political bearing whatsoever."

Joshua raked his gaze over Margaret. "You look a lot different than when I saw you last."

Margaret suddenly took to studying the lacy trim at the wrist of her dark blue and green plaid frock. A blush crept up her neck, staining her cheeks.

Carrie bristled. "My sister has turned her life around for the better." No doubt Joshua picked up on the stunning change that the presence of God made in Margaret's life. "She realized her mistakes, repented, and asked our Lord to forgive her. He obviously did, because he has set her on the path of righteousness."

"How very well-rehearsed, Carrie Ann."

She gave up.

"I wouldn't expect a man like you to understand, Major Blevens," Margaret said, her voice shaking.

"A man like me?" He cocked an eyebrow.

"Margaret volunteers at the Repairers of the Breach Orphanage in Winchester," Carrie added. A proud swell over her sister's accomplishments washed away a goodly amount of the emotional wounds Joshua had inflicted.

"We even purchased small Christmas gifts for the orphans and sent them to Winchester by railcar. Allow me to point out," Carrie said, her voice so tight with anger at Joshua that it threatened to strangle her, "that many of the children are Confederate orphans, but it makes no difference to us."

Joshua turned to Carrie and arched a brow. "Is that right?"

Carrie inclined her head. "So you see we're not as diabolical as you presume."

"Diabolical never entered my mind." Joshua straightened himself up to his full height of nearly six feet and folded his arms over his broad chest. "Stupid, naïve, and scheming . . . now those are the words rolling through my head."

Empty as it is. "Major Blevens, I believe that last we met you were wearing a Yankee uniform."

Joshua grinned, then bowed courteously. "Touché, Miss Carrie Ann." The deep lines at the corners of his eyes softened. "I never would have accepted the assignment if I'd known the point of rescue was the Collier home. I was under the impression our men were being held at the Monteagues' place next door. When we arrived, I was shocked to discover it had been burned to the ground. But by then, I couldn't back out." He wetted his lips. "Friend to friend, I'm real sorry about your—"

"Sister." Margaret blurted the word. "We are mourning our sister Sarah Jane. However, Cousin Mikey had planned this St. Valentine's Day party before he learned of her death."

Joshua's gaze swung to Carrie. "Sarah . . . died?"

Carrie replied with only a nod, although guilt and sorrow screamed loudly inside of her.

"Sarah looked bad off, but I was sure she'd recover."

Carrie tried to squelch the steadily rising pain.

"Mama's dead too," Margaret said.

"And, yes, Major Blevens, the woman was our mother." Carrie fixed her eyes on her black lace, fingerless gloves. Oh, how she'd love to sock Joshua in the jaw for all his lies and manipulation. She'd trusted him, and he betrayed her.

"Sarah Jane and your mother?" Joshua sounded genuinely mournful, but it didn't mean much coming from him.

Besides, how much death could this family bear? Carrie blinked back the moisture gathering in her eyes. It seemed more imperative now than ever that she find Peyton alive.

"Please believe me when I say that I'm sorry for your losses."

Joshua leaned close to Carrie again. "It's rather confusing to me that you're not wearing widow's weeds."

"It's none of your business."

He straightened. "A disguise?"

"Oh, dear . . ." Margaret set her gloved hand on the sleeve of Carrie's midnight-blue gown. "Our cousin has found someone else with whom we're acquainted."

Carrie turned toward the entryway where guests chatted with Cousin Eunice. About midway between the older woman and where they stood, Cousin Mikey and Colonel Elijah Kent were making their way over. As Eli passed, several females turned to stare. Carrie supposed he made a notable figure with his deep dark eyes and swarthy features. Locks of his raven-black hair had fallen onto his forehead, giving him a rakish look. His jaw was clean-shaven and the fabric of his gray frock coat seemed stretched to its limit across the expanse of his wide shoulders.

Carrie looked away. Even snakes could look good all dressed up. She wouldn't be fooled by his charm again. Like Joshua, Eli had betrayed her—betrayed all of the ladies of Piccadilly Place. He had put them in a precarious position with the Union army and caused them to be investigated. Why, if Peyton had foreseen such behavior he'd not have made this most untrustworthy man executor of his estate.

Carrie doused her raging indignation. Killing him with kindness would have to suffice. The lieutenant colonel had the authority to arrest both Margaret and her and charge them with spying, for which, of course, they were innocent.

However, it may not appear that way to Eli, and Joshua might very well back up those charges.

She glanced at her former friend. No doubt duty took precedence over friends and family members. Worse, Carrie had read somewhere that Confederates were not as kind to female spies as the North.

Carrie trembled slightly as Eli neared. His limp was barely noticeable, but he used a gleaming, brass-tipped walking stick for assistance. He paused to exchange pleasantries with several other guests before continuing in their direction.

Cousin Mikey reached them first. "My darlings, look who else I invited." Since their arrival, he frequently used endearments when addressing them. Not having children of his own, Cousin Mikey obviously enjoyed stepping into a fatherly role. "Colonel Kent, you remember my cousins."

"Of course. Miss Margaret." Eli gave her a charming bow that put a blush into her cheeks. "And Miss Carrie Ann." He lifted her partially gloved hand and placed a kiss on the backs of her uncovered fingers. "I owe you my life, and it is a pleasure to see you—to see you both—again."

"Likewise, Colonel." Margaret muttered the reply without eye contact.

"Well, well, what a surprise." Carrie yanked her hand away. So he thought he'd play along and perhaps kill her with the kindness that she'd planned to use as a weapon against him. Another guest hailed Cousin Mikey and he moved out of hearing.

Eli's smile vanished. "We need to talk." He glanced at Margaret, Carrie, then Joshua. "All of us need to talk."

Before she could utter a word, he took hold of Carrie's elbow and led her from the parlor. The pressure of his hand was firm yet gentle, and the warmth of his touch spread up her arm.

Carrie didn't dare balk at his command. The seriousness in his dark eyes made her heart drop.

What was he going to do with her? She was his enemy's widow. *A Yankee.* And she was here in the Confederate capital. How ignorant she'd been to assume she and Margaret wouldn't run into anyone they knew. She'd read somewhere that the majority of Confederate troops were dug into trenches outside Petersburg, guarding that city against Grant's siege. Of course some of the men would go in and out of Richmond.

The study, where men typically ended up congregating at such gatherings, stood open and empty. Eli led them inside and closed the oak and lead-pane doors. Gold muslin curtains hung over the glass, cinched in the center, making it possible for someone to peer into the room even with the doors shut. On the adjacent wall, heavy draperies of the same color lined the long windows that faced the street. A large bookcase filled the far wall, displaying numerous medical volumes. Cousin Mikey's desk and the glowing hearth occupied most of the wall closest to Carrie.

Wary, she glanced from Eli to Joshua. Both men held her fate in their hands. By their word, she and Margaret could be apprehended. Somehow she had to convince these officers that this visit to Richmond had nothing to do with politics per se. It was merely Carrie's last attempt at finding Peyton.

The question was, would they believe her?

CHAPTER 25

There were no words to describe how Eli felt at the moment, looking at Carrie as she stood in the general's study. Happy to see her again, certainly, although he was extremely concerned too. She appeared thinner than he recalled, but still quite fetching in her deep blue gown with its wide ivory-lace collar.

"You're in uniform, Colonel Kent." Carrie tipped her coppery head. "Have you returned to the Confederate cavalry?"

"No. I've been furloughed because of my leg injury which, you can see, is healing perfectly, thanks to you." A swell of affection engulfed him, followed by a niggling of unrest. "When I first heard General Bell was expecting a visit from his cousins, it didn't take long for me to discover you ladies and the general are related. I will admit to my irritation upon learning of your daring, but then I wondered if you, Mrs. Collier—I mean, *Miss Bell*, as the general is introducing you tonight—are in some sort of predicament and need my assistance."

"Trouble usually follows Carrie Ann, that's for sure." Blevens's remark earned him glares from both women.

"Please allow me to explain, Colonel." Miss Margaret took Carrie's hand. "We are on a mission for truth and perhaps even justice."

"Oh?" Eli folded his arms. "Let me guess. You're writing an article."

"Quite incorrect, sir." The corners of Carrie's pink mouth curled upward.

"We've been volunteering at the Washington City hospitals," Miss Margaret said. "Among one of our acts of kindness is writing letters for the wounded. We've heard reports that many of the captured and wounded Yankees from the Cedar Creek battle were transported to Libby Prison."

"I see . . ." Eli made the connection quickly.

"Carrie was right about our father being alive even though everyone in Woodstock, including me, thought he was dead. She could be correct about her husband still being alive."

Eli churned out a sigh. He should have guessed that Carrie would attempt to move heaven and earth to find Peyton. Alas, she never would.

"Am I to understand that firsthand accounts aren't good enough for you, *Mrs. Collier?*" He couldn't keep the edge out of his tone. "Not even Peyton's commanding officer's opinion matters?"

Carrie squared her shoulders. "General Sheridan said Peyton was missing and presumed dead. That is not exactly a definite statement." Her eyes turned an icy blue. While Eli was glad to see she had some spunk left, her unwillingness to accept Peyton's death was unsettling.

"Planning our journey has strengthened my sister's belief that the colonel is alive," Margaret added with a steady tone and assured expression.

"They're telling the truth." Blevens raked one hand through his hair. "I've known these girls all my life and this is typical of them. Neither ever had much sense."

"Joshua, you will never understand." Margaret clenched her hands at her sides. "You are a man with a heart of stone. And you're a liar. You told Carrie that she and I weren't kin. Papa said otherwise."

Carrie touched her sister's arm. "Please don't provoke him."

Blevens peered around the younger sister. "That's an odd statement coming from you, Carrie Ann. You've always enjoyed provoking me."

Carrie pressed her lips together, although Eli sensed she would enjoy giving Blevens a good dressing down.

"I appreciate your opinion, Major." Eli crossed the room, took Carrie's elbow, and guided her to a nearby armchair. "But the turn in our conversation is taking its toll on the ladies. They are mourning loved ones." He then helped Margaret to a chair.

"Take note, Joshua." Carrie's lips twitched with a smile. "This is how a true gentleman behaves."

Eli touched her shoulder. "Enough goading." Glory, but he had heard enough disparaging remarks from Mother and Averly. He almost wished he were in the trenches with his troops.

Almost. But now the truth had to be told.

"Miss Margaret," he began, "I'm afraid you have done your sister a great injustice by encouraging her, noble as it seems. Her husband is dead and the sooner she comes to terms with the truth, the better."

"But Carrie was right about Papa." Remorse washed over the younger woman's face and in that moment, Eli believed she only had Carrie's best interests at heart.

"Don't believe him, Margaret." Carrie raised a stubborn chin. "Of course Colonel Kent would say something like that. He has a monetary stake in my husband's death."

Eli drew back. He couldn't feel more wounded if he were gut shot. He stared down at the pretty young widow, now seated comfortably in the arm-chair. She put on a courageous front, but he feared she'd crumble at any moment. Anger was obviously her defense, albeit not a solid one. She needed to hear the truth—again.

Eli pulled up a chair and sat beside her. "Mrs. Collier, Carrie, I was there at Cedar Creek that day. I know what I saw because, unfortunately, I have seen it too many times before."

"You're mistaken, sir." Her gaze was as pointed as a bayonet.

"No, madam, I'm not."

A softness fell across her face. "But you survived."

"The shell didn't burst on top of me."

Carrie's chin quivered ever so slightly.

Eli stood. "Miss Margaret, Major Blevens, would you please allow me a few minutes alone with Mrs. Collier?"

"Yes, sir." Blevens unfolded his arms. Looking at Margaret, he nodded toward the door.

Margaret glanced at her sister.

"It's all right. Go with Joshua. I can hold my own with Colonel Kent."

Eli forced himself not to smirk. "Please make our excuses to the general and his wife. We'll return to the reception soon."

Once the two left the study, Eli steeled himself to break Carrie's heart for a second time.

"There's nothing you can say to make me believe that Peyton's gone," she began. "I would feel it in my soul if he were dead."

"Your mind and soul operate together, do they not? Perhaps if you allowed your mind to accept the truth—"

"You're wrong." She stood and pushed back her shoulders. "Besides, why would I believe anything you say?"

Eli arched a brow. "Excuse me?"

"You betrayed me."

Another whack to his honor. "I would never do such a thing."

Her gaze turned as frigid as the winter weather. "You of all people. The executor of my husband's estate. You played me for a perfect little fool."

"What on God's footstool are you talking about?"

"You accepted our medical care, food, and clothing. You made me think you had my best interests at heart and that you took your responsibilities as Peyton's executor seriously." She crossed the room. "You led me to believe the lines of war blurred where we Collier ladies were concerned when all the while you were planning an escape. I felt like a fool after you and Joshua and the others pulled it off." She poked her finger into Eli's chest. "What's more, you jeopardized the Colliers' good name and left me to answer to Union officials . . . including General Sheridan, himself!"

"My apologies." He captured Carrie's hand, but she pulled away from his grasp. "I knew nothing about the escape until I recognized a couple of men the morning it occurred." Eli took a step toward her, wishing he could gather her in his arms and make her believe him.

She looked away and folded her arms.

"Would you rather my men and I perished in a Yankee prison camp? Certainly you can understand why I didn't announce our rescuers." Eli watched his reasoning play across Carrie's features. "Wouldn't you have done the same, had you been in our situation, if the opportunity presented itself? I know Peyton would have acted similarly."

"Yes, perhaps."

The vulnerability that shone in her eyes wrestled his pride to the limits.

"But I needed to trust you, and you not only betrayed my trust, but your actions could have gotten us hurt or killed."

"For which I humbly apologize." Locking his hands behind his back, he turned and paced. "And were I in a Federal prison now—or dead, which is highly likely if not for the escape—I would not have been able to beg your forgiveness." He paused in front of her again. "Which I do."

No argument was forthcoming.

"In the meantime, you and your sister have put yourselves in great danger by traveling here to Richmond, not to mention the possible damage you could do to the Collier name by this folly."

"General Sheridan knows we're here . . . and he knows why."

Eli narrowed his gaze. "He allowed it?"

"Yes."

"You are spying for the Union then?"

"Of course not! I merely want to find out if my husband is being held prisoner here in Richmond."

"There are myriad other ways to find out answers while remaining safe in Washington."

"Our written requests turned up nothing. Our cousin, General Bell, could neither confirm nor deny that Peyton languishes with other prisoners in Libby Prison."

Eli resumed pacing, calculating her response and concluding she told the truth.

"We've told our cousins more truths than falsehoods for our visit."

"Leaving out, of course, that you're the widow of a Yankee officer."

"Not a widow. That is pure speculation at this point."

"Then all the more reason you shouldn't be here." Foolish, courageous woman. Were he a gambler, he'd put money on Peyton's demise, not that he found any pleasure in being correct. He didn't know whether to shake some sense into Carrie's pretty head or stand and admire her. He arched a brow. "What exactly does General Bell know?"

"Only that Margaret and I are companions to a wealthy woman from Winchester. We are mourning our youngest sister and we've come to visit our cousin and his ill wife whose disposition has been fortified enough to hostess this fine party to which I had no idea you and Joshua had been invited."

Eli forced a grin. "How nice we could surprise you then." He sent her a mild glare. Didn't she fear the consequences of her actions? Why had she taken such risks?

But hadn't she taken similar chances months ago when she'd headed down the Valley in search of her sister? And then she'd mouthed off to Major Rodingham, a man known to enjoy killing on and off the battlefield. Carrie had nearly gotten herself shot.

Eli kneaded his chin. "So now you expect Major Blevens and me to keep your secret?"

Her expression softened. Her blue eyes darkened. "Will you?"

How could he refuse her, when she stared up at him so hopeful and trusting?

But in all honesty, her ruse put Eli in a precarious situation. He had a sworn duty to his country, but he'd vowed to protect Carrie Ann Collier and her family. He had feared the two responsibilities might cross right from the start.

And now they had.

"Despite my sister's outburst, I think Joshua will keep quiet." Carrie studied her folded hands.

Eli dipped his head slightly in agreement. "He gave me his word that he'd tell no one. And you're certain that United States officials will still think highly of you, Mrs. Collier, even though you're consorting with the enemy here in Richmond?"

"I am."

Her confidence surprised him.

"I confessed everything to General Sheridan after a Union officer was sent to investigate your escape from Piccadilly Place. At the time, I feared it would be discovered that Peyton named you as executor of his estate and then it would appear that I had something to do with your getting away."

He winked. "You did."

"Only because I was exhausted and in shock." Two deep pink spots appeared on her face and her eyes turned frosty. Shoulders held back, she marched to the door.

Eli quickly jumped into her path.

"Let me pass."

"Please, forgive my teasing. I realize there's nothing amusing about what happened then as well as now." He'd simply wanted to prove a point, although he understood why she might despise him. His escape could have potentially ruined the Colliers' good standing in Winchester. "I'm sorry, Carrie. I never intended any harm to come upon you, Aunt Ruth, or Tabitha. Furthermore, I would never intentionally tarnish Peyton's good name as an officer. I was in pain and faced with the decision of a Union prison or escape. I chose escape. In all honesty, can you blame me?"

"In all honesty?" Carrie met his gaze for a long moment. "No, I cannot."

"Am I forgiven, then?"

"Oh, I suppose so." She turned toward the windows, facing the darkness beyond them. The room's lamplight danced across Carrie's red-gold hair.

"Your answer sounds quite ambiguous, Mrs. Collier."

She turned to regard him and several curls brushed against her cheek. She swatted them behind her.

Eli stepped toward her until she stood but a breath away. He touched her shoulder. "Peyton is gone, Carrie. Isn't it time you accepted it and found some peace?"

She said nothing.

"I learned from Mr. Finch that some of Peyton's own men said he'd perished at Cedar Creek, and if Sheridan deigned to deliver the bad news he was obviously certain of it."

"Men can be wrong."

Eli closed his eyes so she wouldn't glimpse his mounting frustration. In the last few months he'd grown to despise this war, brother fighting brother, friend fighting friend. Peyton had trusted him, and Eli had to admit that he'd never known a better friend than his former West Point roommate. Therefore he felt it was his duty to convince Peyt's beautiful, stubborn wife of the truth once and for all.

God give me the words . . .

"A few days ago, I took a carriage ride past Greenwater—my family's former plantation. Circumstances arose that made it necessary for my mother to leave and someone else purchased it. She's yet to recover."

Carrie's expression softened. "I'm sorry to hear it."

"The day I rode past, slaves were clearing the brush and debris that had accumulated around the house. My father paid his workers, so in one respect it was a familiar sight. And as I watched, I half expected to see my father open the front door and meet my carriage, smiling, his arms opened wide to greet me. I'd come home at last. And in one piece, no less. The vision seemed so real to me. But, in truth, Father has been dead for many months now."

Tiny droplets appeared on her lashes. She worked her lips together as if battling his words. "I was right about Papa when no one else believed he was alive." Carrie's eyes pleaded for Eli to agree.

"How many eye-witness accounts told you otherwise?"

"About Papa?" She tucked her chin. "None."

"Instinct is one thing, but wishing upon a star because you want something to be true is another."

She moved her body so she faced him full on. "You don't understand, Eli."

"Oh, I do understand."

"No, no, you don't." She stepped nearer and her wide hoop skirt brushed against his knees. "General Sheridan said that Peyton led a suicide charge and," she choked, "it's all my fault."

"Impossible." Eli reached inside his coat for his handkerchief as sadness trickled onto Carrie's cheeks. "How can it possibly be your fault?"

"I was angry with Peyton. He'd come home intoxicated from General Sheridan's party the night before. When he woke me up the morning of Cedar Creek, he apologized and said he loved me, but I was stubborn. I wanted to teach him a lesson, to show him I didn't care for drunken behavior. So I didn't respond." A little sob burst from her throat. "He left thinking that I . . . that I didn't love him anymore."

"Nonsense. It was a lovers' spat, nothing more. I'm sure Peyton knew that. He was no fool." Especially when it came to women.

"But I should have sent him off with more than my cold shoulder."

"Perhaps so." She looked so broken that Eli pulled her into an embrace. Her hair smelled like lavender.

A moment lapsed and then another. Her hands pressed into his back and she sobbed into his shoulder. Eli couldn't recall feeling more helpless and yet if it meant Carrie would accept the truth, he'd listen to her cry for as long as she had tears to shed.

"Carrie, you're wrong about Peyt." When her heart-wrenching sobs dissipated, Eli pushed her back slightly and cupped her damp, tear-stained face. "When I clashed swords with him that morning, he looked as confident as ever. Despite the fact the Federals were losing the battle at the time, he ordered me to surrender." Eli smiled, hoping she'd find even a morsel of amusement in his words. "There is no doubt in my mind that his charge was anything but suicidal. Peyt was always audacious in battle—even when we were at the military academy. He took chances, but that's why he was a favorite among his commanders."

She blinked and hope shone through her tears. "Really?"

"Really." Eli took the handkerchief from her hand and dabbed away the last of her sadness. He yearned to make her smile. "Besides, what woman wouldn't be miffed at her husband for coming home drunk?"

Carrie inhaled a ragged-sounding breath. "He told me he'd abandoned imbibing and other bad habits for his new Christian faith." She sniffed. "All things were new—or were supposed to be . . ."

"But even long-standing Christians occasionally stumble. Doesn't the Good Book say something about a righteous man falling seven times and getting back up again?"

"Does it?"

Eli gave a nod. "You'll find it in the book of Proverbs, if I'm not mistaken."

Carrie stared up at him as if he possessed all the answers of the universe. Except, he didn't. But he'd make an attempt for her sake.

"Listen, Carrie . . ." He set his palms on her slender shoulders. "Peyton knew you loved him when he went into battle that morning. He wasn't some young, inexperienced swain. And he loved you. He made a mistake the night before, yes, but it wasn't one that was unforgivable. Am I correct?"

"Yes. I would have forgiven him when he returned."

"I'm sure Peyt knew it too, that morning—and he knows it now in glory." Eli studied her tortured expression. "But, perhaps the one you need to forgive is yourself."

"Perhaps." She slipped from beneath his touch and began moving around the room, pausing occasionally to read a title on the general's bookshelf.

Eli considered the damp handkerchief in his palm. "You know, you could have contacted me instead of General Bell and saved yourself a trip to Richmond."

"I had no idea you were here."

"I sent a messenger to tell you, and I understand you had some choice words for the young woman."

Carrie's eyes grew round. "Not that strange woman who followed me to market and then stopped me on the street?"

"The very one—Miss Dorcas."

"So that was legitimate?" Wide-eyed and with a blush in her face, she strode toward him. "I thought General Sheridan was testing my loyalty to the Union." Her eyes glimmered with amusement. "By the way, General Sheridan said you were a fine man, although misguided politically."

Eli replied with a wry smile. "I'm sure he did."

They regarded one another for a long moment.

"Eli, for the first time, I don't doubt what you saw at Cedar Creek." She wetted her lips and his thoughts turned to the idea of kissing away her sorrow. "But at the same time, I have this burning desire to search Libby Prison's hospital for myself." Her head tilted. "Can you somehow understand that?"

He understood, all right. Carrie Ann Collier was as obstinate as this night was cold. "I will do what I can to help." He motioned to the door. "In the meantime, we should rejoin the reception. It is, after all, being held in your honor."

"Yes, I suppose we should."

"Would you like to freshen up?" He placed his hand on the doorknob. "If so, I'll make your excuses."

"Thank you." She touched the sleeve of his frock coat. "I mean that too, Eli, and I'm sorry I thought the worst of you. Peyton was right. You are a good friend."

Eli had trouble meeting the intensity of her stare. In truth, Peyton would knock his head off if he discovered how badly Eli longed to kiss his wife.

Except she was a widow now . . .

He gave her a dutiful little bow then opened the door. Carrie hurried up the stairs while Eli strode into the parlor. A trio of musicians began to play a waltz. The idea of holding Carrie in his arms again, not to sob but to enjoy a dance together, was difficult to shake.

General Bell sauntered over and the nutty, fruity, leathery smell of brandy followed him. "All is well, I trust." He gazed out over the waltzing guests. Blevens had somehow convinced Miss Margaret to dance with him.

Eli hiked up half a smile. "All is well, sir."

The general cleared his throat. "Is there something you'd like to speak to me about, son?"

"Excuse me?" Eli turned and faced the barrel-chested man. "Should I have something to say?"

"I peeked in on you and my young cousin some minutes ago," the general said, one hand behind his back and the other holding an empty snifter. "I discovered the two of you embracing." Storm clouds brewed in his gaze. "You weren't taking advantage of Carrie Ann, now were you?"

"Of course not, sir."

"I have heard you are a fine gentleman and from a respectable Richmond family."

"That's true, sir." Eli could hardly admit he'd been comforting Carrie while she sobbed over her fallen Yankee husband. However, he sensed his reputation was now in question. He drew in a slow breath while his mind raced toward an alibi, one that would protect his family's good name as well as Carrie's and Margaret's safety and identities.

Only one idea seemed plausible.

"Sir, if you will kindly grant your permission, and if Miss Carrie agrees, I would like nothing better than to court her properly." If nothing else, he'd have an excuse to keep an eye on her.

In a flash, General Bell's frowning countenance morphed into a victorious smile. His eyes twinkled. "You have my permission, Colonel Kent. Now, let's celebrate with some of my best brandy and Virginia tobacco, shall we?"

"I'd enjoy that, sir."

A sudden sense of doom shadowed Eli as he followed the general. He couldn't very well introduce her to his family as a Collier—Peyton's widow. Mother would be apoplectic and might report both Carrie and Margaret to the authorities. Women sat locked behind bars in Libby Prison for lesser offenses.

How, then, did he protect Carrie without lying to his mother and sister? To Pat?

Another knight's words gnawed at his conscience. *Oh what a tangled web we weave, when first we practice to deceive* . . .

Chapter 26

February 15, 1865

"Courtship!" Carrie paced the small guest bedroom she and Margaret shared. "Can you imagine what Peyton would say?"

"He would approve, of course. Especially since the ruse only adds to our safety here in Richmond." Margaret turned from the tall framed mirror. Two beds protruded into the center of the room from opposing walls. Matching multicolored Persian carpets filled the spaces near the wardrobes, and the thick burgundy draperies framing the bank of windows effectively kept the cold, damp mid-February wind at bay.

"If Peyton is dead, which I'm beginning to think he is, then I'm in mourning. We should probably return to Washington as quickly as possible."

"But you can't give up yet. Where's your faith?"

"It's been chipped away by everyone who believes Peyton is dead. Then last night it all but crumbled under Eli's sensible argument."

"Now, Carrie . . ." Margaret set her hands on her sister's upper arms. "You owe it to yourself and Aunt Ruth to at least investigate further. After all, God allowed us to get this far. Besides, it could be worse. You could be the one forced into a courtship with Joshua by our well-meaning cousin." Margaret's insides cramped at the idea, although she'd suffer through it for Carrie's sake.

"I'm so sorry, Margaret." Carrie embraced her and Margaret felt her shoulder blades through her gown's stiff material. Carrie had grown too thin. "It's just our bad luck to have an overeager cousin who desires for us to marry

Confederate officers." Carrie pulled back. "He's dead set against us returning to our *Yankee employer*. For that reason alone, we should leave Richmond."

"Not until we know for sure your husband isn't languishing in Libby Prison's hospital or locked away behind bars. Perhaps he's too sick to tell nurses his name."

The troubled pucker appeared above Carrie's eyebrows. "You're right. I have to know."

"You feel it in your soul, don't you?"

"I do, Margaret, I really do." She took a step back. "It's just that Eli made so much sense last night."

"I'm sure he did. He's a good man. I can tell, even if he did escape and cause us to be investigated. However, he apologized and, truly, I can't blame him. Can you?"

Carrie gave a wag of her head, sending a wayward curl cascading down her neck.

"Nevertheless—" Margaret tucked her sister's lock of hair back into its pin. "Colonel Kent doesn't know *everything*. Only God is omniscient."

Carrie's lips turned upward and seconds later she burst into laughter.

"What's so funny?" Margaret set her hands on her waist.

"You. The way you're arguing with me. It's like when we were girls on the farm and I told you that Mama said to gather eggs for breakfast. You would go on and on until finally I ended up doing the chore myself."

Margaret sighed. "I hated gathering eggs. Those chickens were so mean." She rubbed the backs of her hands. "They'd peck me until I bled."

Carrie sat on the bed and giggled as if she'd just heard the funniest thing ever.

"It's hardly amusing." She smiled in spite of herself.

"Chickens." Carrie fell back on the mattress, laughing. "A farm girl, afraid of chickens."

"Oh, get up." Margaret tugged on Carrie's hand, then pulled her to a sitting position. "Just look what you've done to your hair." She sighed. "Talk about doing chores over again . . ."

"Touché, sister dear."

As Margaret fastened the pins that came lose, she thanked the Almighty that they could find something about their past to laugh at. It wasn't all so terrible. In all the darkness of the past few years, Margaret had forgotten the lighter side of life.

"Did you find Joshua a good dancer?" The twinkle in Carrie's gaze was reflected in the mirror.

"Passable, I suppose, not that I'm any expert."

"You had plenty of young men falling all over themselves to dance with you when you were—"

"A shameless flirt?"

"When you were younger is what I was going to say." Carrie faced Margaret. "I'm sorry if I dragged up something that's better forgotten."

"No, you didn't drag up anything that wasn't already on my mind. The fact is I was glad for my dancing experience last night."

"I know you're even less enthusiastic about this courtship ruse than I am. Perhaps we should beg to discuss the matter with Cousin Mikey and tell him we're spoken for and that Papa approves of our intendeds."

"Oh, Carrie, you heard him last night. He doesn't want us marrying Yankees, but he'll believe that's who our 'intendeds' are because we told him we're working for a Yankee woman and our Papa is residing in Washington City, the Union capital."

Carrie winced. "True."

"Let's leave the matter alone. It's just pretend and the colonel and Joshua know it. I thank God that they're willing to play along." A wave of nausea worked its way up to her throat as she imagined Joshua Blevens paying her visits. He had paid Veyschmidt to spend the night with her and, until the potion took effect, she'd had to endure his groping and drunken, slobbering kisses. No matter how much a gentleman Joshua Blevens behaved, she'd never forget what he was to her that night—a man who wanted a prostitute.

Margaret just prayed he wouldn't demand his money back. Before Joshua had left the Wayfarers Inn the next morning, he'd grabbed her upper arm and squeezed until she'd whimpered. Then he whispered harshly that he knew what she'd done. When he released her, Margaret stumbled back and fell to the ground.

"Oh, Margaret, you're worried. I can tell."

"A little." She quickly wiped away the moisture. "I'm praying Joshua won't insist I pay him back the money I owe him."

"Let him ask for it," Carrie said through a clenched jaw. Her gaze narrowed. "I'll sock that rogue right in the mouth. He should have been protecting you, not taking advantage of you."

"I know." Margaret lifted her kid gloves and rubbed her fingertips against their softness. She'd like nothing better than to see Carrie give Joshua a taste of her fist, just like when they were children.

But they weren't youngsters anymore.

"I'd rather we forget the past, Carrie, than dream of getting even with Joshua."

"But the latter is ever so much more fun." She flashed a grin before momentarily disappearing beneath her black cap decorated with ivory silk roses and fat satin ribbons. Carrie fastened the long hatpin and announced she was ready to go.

With a lighter ambiance settled between them, Margaret strode toward the door. "Perhaps we'll find information about your husband today as we tour the hospitals with Cousin Mikey."

"I'm praying so, although I don't expect to learn anything until we're actually able to speak with Union detainees."

Margaret placed her hand on the ornate doorknob. "Ready?"

"As ready as I'll ever be."

Opening the door, Margaret led the way downstairs. Cousin Mikey paced the small receiving area. Seeing them, he pocketed his round, silver watch.

"Good heavens, girls, I nearly gave up and left without you!"

～ ❀ ❀ ～

After an exhausting morning of touring the Chimborazo, Camp Jackson, and Camp Winder hospitals, Carrie welcomed a quiet afternoon at home. Her only regret was that Cousin Mikey had refused to let them see the Libby Prison hospital, claiming the "enemy combatants" were too dangerous.

"Welcome back, girls." Cousin Eunice smiled. "How was your tour of Richmond?" She sat comfortably in an armchair in the parlor. An ivory cap covered her dusty-blond curls to keep away a chill. "Did you enjoy yourselves?"

"Oh, yes . . ." Margaret strode farther into the room, extracted the pins, and removed her hat.

Carrie did the same, setting both her hat and gloves on a tabletop near the entrance. Her cousins' slave, Betsy, would soon come to collect them.

Slavery. Carrie had read all about slave auctions, and she'd known people who owned slaves in Woodstock, but she'd never been so aware of the practice as she was here in Richmond, especially after their tour today. It was disheartening to actually see Lumpkin's Slave Prison, a horrid facility where men, women, and children were held against their will and then sold to the highest bidder. More distressing was when Cousin Mikey admitted his belief that Negroes were the evolutionary link between animals, particularly apes, and mankind. He cited Darwin's *Origin of Species* and English evolutionary biologist Thomas Henry Huxley's work. However, his educated, though flawed, opinion didn't sway Carrie. She presented the biblical argument that all men were created in the image of God. Cousin Mikey enjoyed a hearty laugh at her expense. Then he firmly warned that, while here in Richmond, she'd do well to forget those abolitionist notions that her Yankee employer put into her head.

Carrie quickly swallowed any further argument.

"Cousin Mikey took us through his jurisdictions," Margaret said, yanking Carrie's thoughts back to the present. The parlor had been tidied up from last night's reception and the furniture returned to its proper places. "He explained that the hospitals had been newly whitewashed and enemy combatants moved to Georgia and North Carolina."

Carrie caught her sister's mournful stare . What hope was there of finding Peyton now? She couldn't very well traipse all over the Confederacy.

"And you find the transfer of Yankee prisoners interesting?"

"Um . . ." Margaret's gaze darted around the room.

"Oh, we're not interested, Cousin Eunice," Carrie quickly put in. "It was merely part of the tour."

"Yes, that's what I meant to say." Margaret's features lost their frantic look.

"Ah, yes . . . well, the general is dedicated to his work."

"He has plenty of it." Carrie sat and met Margaret's concerned expression. This afternoon they'd overheard an enlisted man inform Cousin Mikey of the recent shipment of Confederate wounded who, again, occupied the hospitals. However, their severe wounds could not be properly treated because of the lack of basic medical supplies. And to make things worse, the men were freezing as there was no wood for fuel.

But a fire burned brightly in her cousins' home. While Carrie was grateful, she felt a tad guilty enjoying a warm hearth when so many others were dying from exposure to the unkind elements.

She moved closer to the fireplace and remembered the conversation that had taken place in the comfort of Cousin Mikey's carriage. After Carrie inquired about supplies, or lack thereof, he'd blamed the quartermaster general for the problems. So enraged was Cousin Mikey by the situation that he convinced several congressmen to garner public support for this cause by holding a reception in the Richmond capitol on Friday evening. Cousin Eunice would, of course, attend and she'd invited Margaret and Carrie to accompany her.

Was it wrong to look forward to the event? Peyton would have said it was Carrie's journalistic nature rising to the surface.

Cousin Eunice clucked her tongue. "I've never known women so interested in medical work."

"Margaret and I enjoy caring for the troops," Carrie explained. "That's why our tour made such an impression."

"We find it distressing to see so many men suffering," Margaret admitted, smoothing down the skirt of her tweed traveling outfit. "At least whiskey is plentiful in the north to ease men's pain. The South doesn't even have that."

"Well, I think it's despicable that we Southerners are suffering when our northern counterparts are not!" Cousin Eunice wagged her head as if trying to dislodge more than her cap. "Richmond is a prime example." She lifted her brows. "I don't suppose the general came home with you girls, did he?"

"No, he sent us home in the carriage from the Libby Prison hospital," Margaret said. "He had patients to attend there."

Oh, how Carrie wished he would have allowed them to assist.

"On a positive note," Margaret added, "Cousin Mikey said he'll try to get home in time for dinner."

"*Hmmph!* That means he won't be home until late, if at all." A look of what could only be disappointment filled the older woman's blue eyes. But, seconds later, she smiled. "How blessed I am to have you darlings to keep me company on a cold winter's afternoon."

"We're happy to do so." Margaret studied the dark gray yarn on Aunt Eunice's lap. "What are you knitting?"

"Socks for the boys in the Petersburg trenches. I'm told some have no shoes. She held up her knitting needles. "At least they shall have thick socks to wear." A sad smile curved her thin lips. "I unraveled one of my shawls. I really didn't need it, even though it was a gift from my dearly departed sister in North Carolina."

"That's quite a sacrifice," Carrie said. It seemed everyone in Richmond was sacrificing for The Cause.

"Our boys are worth it." Her features brightened. "Perhaps you girls would like to knit socks too."

"We're happy to help." Margaret sent a questioning expression Carrie's way.

"Yes, of course we are." She lowered herself into a chair and shivered. She hadn't realized how cold she'd gotten in the damp, wintery air this morning. She thought of the men freezing in the trenches. Aiding and abetting the enemy could hardly describe their willingness to help. It was a humanitarian need. Like nursing!

Now, if she could only convince Cousin Mikey to allow Margaret and her to nurse the troops in Libby Prison's hospital. She was certain to find answers to her many questions.

And then, of course, there were such things as miracles—and it would certainly be one if Carrie found Peyton.

Chapter 27

February 17, 1865

"I apologize, Pat, but I can't attend. I have an engagement tonight."

Only three days and already a scheduling conflict. Eli had hoped to lead a dual life while Carrie was in town—for her protection.

"Can't you reschedule, Eli? This political event is important. The entire Confederate Congress will be in attendance. I'd like you to meet these men." Pat puffed his fat cigar while seated comfortably in Eli's rented apartment above the apothecary. "They may be our future competition, you know, and their statements on Friday night could be held against them during my campaign." Half his mouth lifted in a wry smile.

His godfather made a good point, and Carrie would understand—at least he hoped she'd understand.

"Fine. I'll change my plans. You're right. This is an important event."

"Good fellow. And you'll escort Averly, of course."

Eli held up his hand. "No, Pat. We talked about this—"

"And I relayed your feelings to Averly. However, I can't allow her to attend a political function alone. Besides, your mother and Laurabeth will be in attendance. It's not as if it's an intimate dinner affair."

"All right. However, you must hire another associate who can act as Averly's escort in the future."

"I will. As soon as the right man comes along." He drew on his cigar. "I can't hire just anyone."

Another good point. "Very well. I shall be happy to escort Averly—as well as Mother and Laurabeth."

Pat stood. "I knew you'd be reasonable, Eli. You're going to make a fine political aide."

Cigar in hand, he crossed the room and collected his coat off the peg near the doorway. "This is a cozy little place, isn't it?"

"Not to mention I'm out of Mother's hair."

"And she's out of yours." Pat chuckled. "At least we're less than a mile away if anything urgent arises. However, the man you hired makes us all feel quite safe."

"Good." Eli had a hunch that Jim would do a good job for his family. Best of all, Mother was pleased with her new cook.

"The carriage will come for you at five o'clock sharp."

Eli crossed the room and saw Pat out. "I'll be ready."

—෬ ෬—

Carrie gave her appearance one last glance in the front hall mirror. Her dark brown gown hung loosely from her shoulders and she hoped no one would notice her too-thin frame. She'd promised Peyton she wouldn't wear black, should he not return from battle. Even so, Carrie couldn't bring herself to wear fashionable, brightly colored frocks. But it was just as well. According to Cousin Eunice, Richmond society shunned those who wore expensive clothes. One unfortunate man had his finely woven frock coat ripped off his back as he strolled down the street. Margaret, however, wore a gold, brown, and emerald plaid. One of her favorites. Aunt Ruth said it brought out the green in Margaret's eyes, and she was correct.

Dear Aunt Ruth. Only a few days here in Richmond, and already Carrie missed the woman. And why not? She hadn't been able to do much of anything else except knit socks for troops in the trenches. The task lent itself to deep thinking and soul searching. However, she and Margaret made Cousin Eunice proud. Each had parted with a shawl, unraveled it, and repurposed the yarn. The act seemed to permanently endear them to the older woman, which of course did not hurt their cause.

"You ladies look lovely tonight." Joshua's compliment was meant for all, but his smile seemed reserved for Margaret alone—and it appeared quite genuine.

Margaret looked anywhere but at Joshua, leaving Cousin Eunice to thank him for the compliment. As he helped Cousin Eunice with her cloak, Carrie accepted her wool wrap from Betsy and put it on without waiting for Joshua's gentlemanly assistance. He'd showed up rather unexpectedly earlier, in his best gray uniform, although even it showed signs of wear. He explained that he asked to call on Margaret and Cousin Mikey not only approved, but invited him to the lecture.

Margaret wasn't pleased in the least, and Carrie wondered over his intentions. Were they simply part of the ruse or did he have feelings for Margaret? Was Joshua worming his way into Cousin Mikey's good graces?

Deciding that it must be the latter, Carrie tied the ribbon on her wrap then followed the Bell ladies and Joshua out to the awaiting carriage. Funny how she no longer considered herself a Bell, even though she masqueraded as one here in Richmond.

Joshua politely assisted them into the coach before climbing inside. She'd keep her eye on him tonight. She wouldn't allow Joshua to harm Margaret in word or deed. With a mild jerk of the carriage, they were on their way.

"The general promised to meet us at the Capitol Building," Joshua announced.

Carrie occupied herself with the scenery of the City of the Seven Hills, as Richmond was often called. The entire city seemed built along a bend in the James River. Smokestacks belonging to Tredgar Iron Works reached heavenward and belched black smoke as it produced weaponry for the Confederate army. But tobacco was still king of the city.

After a series of uphill streets, slippery from the freezing temperatures, the conveyance halted at the side of the Capitol. They disembarked, and then walked up a steep flight of stairs. An attendant politely opened the door for them.

"This building can't hold a candle to the Executive Mansion." Margaret's whispered words tickled Carrie's ear. "And from what I saw as we passed the Confederate counterpart, where President Davis resides, that's not very impressive either."

Carrie smiled in reply, not wanting to be overheard.

A neatly attired black man collected their wraps and then directed them to the reception hall. Inside the spacious room with towering marble pillars, women wearing drab-colored frippery milled about, some escorted by gentlemen in stiff black suits or gray frock coats. Carrie spotted Cousin Mikey near the platform amidst rows upon rows of chairs. He spoke with two very distinguished-looking men.

"Well, well . . ." Joshua nudged Carrie. "It seems Colonel Kent has a new love interest."

Carrie glanced across the room and spotted Eli. On his arm was a flaxen-haired beauty. Envy nipped as she took in the woman's shimmering gray gown with a bodice that did little to conceal her womanly curves.

"I reckon the courtship is over, Carrie Ann."

"Yes, well, as a bard once wrote, all good things must come to an end." Carrie giggled at Joshua's bemused expression.

Across the room, the buxom blond prowled like a graceful lioness as she chatted with other guests. How confident of her abilities she seemed as she clung to Eli.

Jealousy pinched her again. But perhaps it was only that she missed Peyton and wished to be on his arm in another place and time—one in which there was no more war.

Peyton. Carrie's eyelids fluttered closed. Each day her husband's visage faded a little more. How grateful she was for his photograph. She'd left it safely on her dressing table at Piccadilly Place.

Carrie opened her eyes to find Eli's dark eyes appraising her, and her sorrow multiplied.

Joshua nudged her and Carrie forced herself to pay attention to Cousin Eunice. She was midway through introducing an elderly couple and it was Carrie's turn to acknowledge them. After exchanging polite greetings, the pair moved on and a young woman dressed in black silk and lace approached Cousin Eunice. They exchanged pleasantries.

"Hetty, dear, allow me to introduce my cousins by marriage, Miss Carrie Ann Bell and Miss Margaret Bell. And this distinguished officer is Margaret's beau, Major Joshua Blevens." Cousin Eunice turned to them. "Hetty is here tonight with her sister, Jennie Cary, and their cousin, Constance Cary."

"Pleased to meet you all." The woman's voice was feather soft and her face was classically beautiful, complete with flawless complexion. But a haughty self-awareness of her beauty was nowhere to be found in her demeanor. Only a certain sadness shone in the depths of her eyes that Carrie thought she recognized. "I'm eagerly awaiting General Bell's talk," Hetty said. "I've often wondered if my husband would have survived if medical supplies had been available on the field when he fell."

"I'm sorry for your loss," Carrie said. "And, forgive me, but I didn't hear your last name."

"Pegram. Mrs. John Pegram. If you've read anything in the newspapers, then you're aware that my husband and I were married all of eighteen days. I buried him only weeks ago."

Carrie had read all about it, although she hadn't realized Mrs. Pegram's ill-fated marriage was only a day shorter than her own. And for once in Carrie's life, words escaped her. She took Mrs. Pegram's hand as tears momentarily blinded her.

"You have lost someone too?"

Carrie replied with a subtle nod.

"Then we will have to work harder, won't we? Our troops need medicine, food, not to mention the basic necessities like socks and boots."

"You are right. We will have to work harder. We must bring an end to this war."

Mrs. Pegram's expression brightened. "Ah, so you see the bigger picture." Her auburn hair shone a magnificent red-gold beneath the lamps. "I commend you for your vision, Miss Bell. Indeed, I share it. If you have any suggestions, your cousin, Mrs. Bell, knows where to find me. Perhaps we can meet and discuss a plan to help make our vision a reality."

"Perhaps." Carrie suddenly wished she was a secesh girl, as the Confederate women in Winchester called themselves. She could use a good friend. Since Meredith moved into the Repairers of the Breach Orphanage, Carrie hadn't been able to have a good heart-to-heart conversation with another young married woman.

Mrs. Pegram gave her hand an affectionate squeeze and moved on to other attendees and guests waiting to speak with her. Carrie recalled reading somewhere about Hetty Cary Pegram and her smuggling operations. She brought much-needed supplies into the Confederacy from the North. Her beauty often allowed her to pass enemy lines without question, and now Carrie knew why. The pickets were likely mesmerized by her. Mrs. Pegram was also credited with making the Southern Cross battlefield flag for the Army of Northern Virginia. How proud she had once been of those brave ladies. After all, Carrie had grown up in Woodstock. She was a Virginian. She'd done her share of cheering for General Lee's men.

Glancing at Joshua she found a heavy frown creasing his forehead as he stared in Mrs. Pegram's wake.

"I served with John Pegram." His blue eyes slid to Carrie. "Seeing you and his wife standing side by side, one could swear you're related. And you certainly match Mrs. Pegram's daring and determination."

Carrie was tempted to smile. "Is that a . . . *compliment*?"

Joshua's gaze hardened. "Mrs. Pegram lacks your sarcasm. A pity she can't instruct you on grace and delicacy."

A quip on her tongue, she quickly swallowed it, sensing a presence to her left. She turned and found Eli standing beside her.

"Miss Bell." He gave a polite bow. "I would like to explain my circumstances, although not here."

"No need, Colonel Kent." Carrie forced her emotions to dissolve. "I plan to speak with my cousin tonight and put an end to the nonsense."

"No. I beg you to wait until we discuss the matter first."

Carrie bristled at the terse tone. Eli moved to Joshua, shaking his hand. He stepped to Margaret and bid her a good evening and then offered his arm to escort Eunice across the way so she could say hello to his mother and meet his family's guests.

Carrie stiffened. So he wouldn't introduce Margaret and her to his mother and the blond who quickly reattached herself to Eli's side once he returned. The woman glanced over her shoulder and met Carrie's gaze. Stubbornness alone forced Carrie to hold it unabashed. The woman's unnaturally red lips curved upward, but not maliciously. She appeared . . . friendly. Her left gloved hand lifted in a subtle greeting before she turned away.

"I have arms for both you ladies." Joshua's voice pulled Carrie back. "The Yankees haven't taken them from me yet."

"Oh, Joshua." Carrie wouldn't wish such disfigurement on her worst enemy. "I hope they never will either."

"Yes, and I pray your good fortune continues." Margaret placed her hand in the crook of his left elbow.

Carrie took his right.

"And now, ladies." Joshua smiled at Margaret, then at Carrie. "Shall we go find the refreshment table?"

CHAPTER 28

February 19, 1865

Eli didn't find time to visit Carrie Ann until Sunday afternoon. With every skirmish outside Petersburg, Federal prisoners were apprehended and brought to Libby Prison. Some arrived on stretchers, severely wounded. The conditions were deplorable and, except for having more food and supplies, Eli doubted things were better in northern prisons. He thanked God each and every day that he hadn't been sent to one of them.

Walking stick in one hand, he knocked on the Bells' front door with his other. The clouds had parted and the sun made a rare February appearance.

Betsy pulled open the door. "Colonel Kent. We wasn't expectin' you today."

"I realize that, but I must speak with Miss Carrie."

The black woman opened the door wider and Eli stepped into the house. Betsy announced his visit, took his overcoat, and led him into the empty parlor to wait for Carrie.

He heard the surprise in her tone then the rustling of her skirts as she made her way to the parlor.

"Hello, Eli. This is a surprise." She stepped forward to greet him.

He took her proffered hand. "I apologize for not sending a message asking to call beforehand. Life has a way of getting busy."

"I'm sure." She politely removed her fingers from his grasp. "You have many ladies in your life who demand your attention." Her smile appeared forced. "Please, sit down."

Wondering over her remark, he sat in an armchair. Carrie took a seat on the settee. She spread out her wide ebony skirt. If ever a woman looked enticing even in black, it was Carrie Ann Collier . . .

"I trust you're feeling well."

Eli still wondered over her "many ladies in his life" remark, but gave a nod in reply. "And you and the Bell household? All are healthy these days?"

"Yes, thank you."

Eli sensed her displeasure. He hoped not to add to it. "Carrie, I'm here to discuss a matter of great importance."

"Our . . . courtship?" She stared past him and toward the bank of windows.

"Yes." Pushing to his feet, Eli left his walking stick and crossed the room. Reaching the door, he closed it.

"Carrie . . ." He strode to the settee and took the seat beside her. "Forgive my forwardness, but no one must hear what I have to say."

"All right." That familiar dimple above her right eyebrow appeared.

"As much as I want to, I cannot introduce you to my family." He whispered each word. "My mother would not understand why Peyton's widow is here in the Confederate capital. She would not keep it to herself. She might even turn you in."

"I see." Carrie's slender fingers toyed with one of her gown's many folds.

"Presently, my mother has guests. Sir Patrick Winslow, a diplomat from the Barbados, and his daughter Miss Averly Winslow. I trust Averly even less with our secret than my mother. On the other hand, Pat is aware of the situation. I confided in him late Friday night, after the general's speech."

Carrie's eyes widened.

"I had to, Carrie. He's an observant man and noticed I didn't introduce you, Margaret, and Joshua last Friday evening. But don't worry. Pat is trustworthy. He'll help us if there's trouble. He is personally acquainted with President Davis and is friendly with the president's staff and the Congress. He is also acquainted with President Lincoln from years before the war when he brokered a deal in Springfield. Lincoln represented Pat's client on the legal front, and by Pat's accounts, they got along well."

"Then I suppose it's all right." Carrie's blue eyes darkened. "Besides, the thing is done."

"Don't be angry. I'm asking you to understand."

"Yes . . . and I understand." Her gaze sank into her gown. "Are you courting Miss Averly? She's beautiful. You two make a handsome match."

"No. I am not courting her."

Carrie lifted her chin and regarded him again. Her eyes reminded Eli of an azure autumn sky. Her neatly coiffed red-gold curls rivaled the turning leaves on the oaks and maples he'd seen last October in the Shenandoah Valley—a wasteland now that Phil Sheridan and his troops had their way with it.

"Eli?" She tilted her chin. "Is something wrong?"

"No." He shook himself. "About Averly . . ."

"Is she . . . your fiancé?"

"No!" He finger-combed back locks of his hair. "She's nothing to me other than a good friend of my family's. Pat is my godfather, so I've known the Winslows since . . . well, all of my life."

Carrie stood and walked toward the hearth. No fire burned this afternoon, most likely to conserve firewood. Everything was at a premium these days.

"You seemed quite attentive to her last Friday evening. It was awkward for me because my cousins observed it and wondered." She turned and faced him. "I wasn't sure what to say because you ordered me to wait until we spoke."

"I didn't order you."

"You did—and in your military officer's voice, no less."

Eli stood. "I meant no insult, Carrie. The truth is I agreed to escort Averly to political functions and dinner parties that she's required to attend with her father."

"Then I believe it's best to call off this courtship farce between us."

"Please don't. It makes a good excuse for me to check on you and make sure you're all right here in Richmond."

"I'm not a child. I don't need you to *check on me*. And you are not obligated. You're executor of Peyton's estate—"

"Shh . . ." Eli glanced at the door, hoping no one listened behind the panels.

"We won't be bothered. The general is away and Margaret will occupy Cousin Eunice so we can discuss the situation. I doubt Betsy will say a word."

"Very good." Eli clasped his hands behind his back. "Now, as you were saying?"

"You're not the executor of me, Eli, so you may stop behaving as my governess. It's most unattractive."

"Is it?" Eli narrowed his gaze.

"Yes." Carrie inhaled as if she could muster confidence with her next breath. "As for Miss Winslow, if you're seen around town together, people will assume you are a couple. How will I explain to my cousins? I will be made to look like a fool if you're supposed to be my beau and another woman is seen hanging on your arm in public."

A smile pulled at the corners of his mouth. She sounded jealous . . . and it pleased him.

He worked the mirth from his lips. "Carrie, I would never cause you to look like a fool. Never. My mother and sister have, so far, accompanied the Winslows. They are my mother's guests. It's nothing so unusual."

She folded her arms and gave him that same obstinate glare that he'd encountered on the first day she'd arrived in Winchester. "I want to tell Cousin Mikey that we're ill-suited and forget this game."

Eli wouldn't argue with her. He wouldn't win. She'd fight him with everything in her. However, he might still persuade her to see things his way.

"You're a lady's man, Eli. Don't forget that I witnessed you charming Miss Lavinia Monteague while you and your troops occupied Piccadilly Place."

"That meant nothing, Carrie."

"Miss Lavinia meant nothing and you charmed her, but Miss Averly means something and you're not tempted by her in the least?" She shook her head. "That makes no sense."

"Carrie, I see your point, but I had a lot of time to think while recovering from my injury. Things that I took for granted before, I am grateful for now. Ideas that never appealed to me, have somehow captivated me, motivated me."

"Like what?"

"My future, for instance. I had intended to remain in the army until I died. I planned to work my way up the ranks and make the military my profession. Now, however, I'm looking beyond it. Pat has offered me a good position once the war is over. I've accepted it."

"What will you do?"

"He has political aspirations." Eli would keep it very vague, even though Pat considered her a potential donor to his campaign in the future. "Pat has many ingenious ideas and doesn't favor the Confederate States over the United States. If things develop as he hopes, I will become head of his staff."

Carrie pursed her pretty pink mouth, obviously mulling over the matter. "I enjoy keeping up with politics, although I personally wouldn't want to function in the political realm."

Eli hadn't given her viewpoint on his future much thought, although he'd like very much for her to be a part of his plans. "Once Pat wins his desired position, I hope to settle down and pick up where my father left off in horse breeding. I'd like to win back my family's notoriety as renowned horse-breeders here in Virginia."

Carrie's eyes sparkled and a smile played across her mouth. "I like that idea."

"I hoped you might." Eli had learned months ago that she'd grown up on a farm in Woodstock.

"Not that it's up to me, of course."

"Of course." Little did Carrie realize how much of Eli's future depended on her opinion. For the present, Eli would keep it that way.

"All right." Carrie rolled her eyes. "We'll continue with our charade."

Smiling, Eli gave her a short bow.

"For now."

He chuckled.

She pointed her forefinger into the chest of his frock coat. "But if I read about you and Miss Averly in the newspapers, it's over."

"Yes, ma'am." He couldn't stop smiling. And she accused him of *giving orders*.

Her steely expression softened. "I will forewarn you, I'm not accustomed to courtships. If I do something wrong, please tell me. Advise me."

"I will." Except Eli found her statement difficult to comprehend. "Peyton didn't court you? Shame on him."

"We were in camp with thousands of troops, primarily cavalrymen. Peyton protected me, and we had daily visits—well, almost daily."

"An army camp is quite the romantic atmosphere."

Carrie finally let go of a laugh. "Indeed."

Eli listened as she talked of her time with Peyton, before and after their marriage. It was more limited than Eli imagined. Practically nothing.

"You weren't married in August when you and I first met?"

"No. Peyton and I married on October first."

Which meant Eli could have tried to win her hand while residing at Pic-cadilly Place. Then again, no. Carrie had room in her heart for Peyton alone. Eli had seen it in her smiles, in her eyes, whenever she spoke of him.

Still, Eli would have enjoyed the competition.

"So you see, Mrs. Pegram and I have much in common."

"Yes, I reckon you do at that." Eli's heart ached for her—and for Hetty Pegram. He had respected her husband very much, called him a friend. The loss of General John Pegram was a devastating blow for the Confederate army.

Carrie stepped closer. "Eli, I need your help."

How could he resist when she peered up at him with her heart in her eyes? "What can I do?"

"Would you, for me, be sure Peyton isn't . . . wasn't in Libby Prison or its hospital? Cousin Mikey won't allow Margaret and me near the facility. But perhaps you can find out for sure what happened to Peyton . . ." Carrie's voice trailed off.

"You realize that you may never find out what happened to his body. There are mass graves all over Virginia."

She nodded. "But perhaps one of the prisoners in Libby will know where I might find this mass grave—if, as you say, Peyton is dead? It's not that I don't believe you, Eli. I merely need *something*. A tangible tidbit." Her blue eyes pleaded with him as her hands clamped onto his fingers.

With a turn of his wrists, Eli captured her hands. "All right. I will do my best." He lifted the backs of her fingers to his lips. "Your wish, madam, is my command."

CHAPTER 29

February 27, 1865

Margaret gazed across the parlor table at her well-groomed dominoes opponent, Joshua Blevens. He'd visited a barbershop today as evidenced by slicked back, nut-brown hair and a freshly shaved jaw. She supposed he was a likeable fellow when he put his mind to it. Months ago, she'd hated him for trying to buy her innocence, but now that she'd gotten to know him better, she could at least stand to be in the room with him. Even so, Joshua hadn't won her respect—and never would.

He bent his head and deliberated over his next move while Carrie Ann and Colonel Kent played a lively game of checkers in the corner of the room. Margaret enjoyed hearing Carrie giggle. She'd always been the serious-minded, older sister—except when she was playacting, of course. And now, since Colonel Kent had searched the records at Libby Prison and turned up nothing about her husband, she'd begun to be at peace with her widow's status. Margaret only wanted her sister to be happy, and Colonel Kent seemed to be the one to accomplish that.

"King me," the colonel said.

"Oh, you rascal!" Carrie huffed and set the checker on his. "You and that military mind are too much for little ol' me."

"Don't take the bait, Colonel." Joshua glanced over his shoulder, making eye contact with him. "She's hardly the delicate magnolia that she'd have you believe."

"Words of wisdom, Major. Thank you."

Margaret laughed softly when Carrie batted her lashes at Joshua in a theatrical manner.

"Oh, but I am a delicate flower, sir."

Joshua gave an amused snort, the smile lingering on his lips.

Carrie's playacting tickled Margaret too. However, she disliked this courtship pretense. While Carrie and Colonel Kent seemed to enjoy a comfortable and mutual friendship, Margaret would never feel completely at ease in Joshua's company. A blessing they'd be leaving Richmond soon. They'd tapped all resources available to them. Now it was time to go home and Margaret looked forward to it. This feigned courtship taught her that marriage wasn't in her future. Instead, she'd become a woman like Rebekah Kercheval, a spinster taking care of orphaned children. But she'd be happy for Carrie if her sister chose to remarry.

What would Aunt Ruth have to say about the notion? She seemed to enjoy a house full of her new family members.

A glance at Cousin Eunice assured Margaret that the older woman enjoyed her guests' banter. She sat by a low-burning fire in the hearth. Here in the parlor, the war and crumbling Confederacy seemed very far away. However, it wouldn't have been cozy tonight if Carrie Ann hadn't purchased firewood today in town. With Confederate currency, a stick of firewood cost five dollars, but Carrie's gold coins held great power of persuasion.

So not only were they warm tonight, but they had dined earlier on Carrie's delicious specialty—snapping turtle in a pot, otherwise known as French stew. A rare cuisine, which made it palatable for Cousin Eunice.

"You won again, Colonel Kent!"

"I'm surprised at you, sister." Margaret leaned slightly to her right and peered around Joshua. Carrie and the colonel were clearing the checkerboard. "You usually win at checkers."

"Seems I'm a mite distracted tonight."

By her handsome opponent. Margaret swallowed a laugh. She caught Joshua's stare and shrugged.

"It's your turn." Joshua planted his arms on the small square table. "Are we playing a game of dominoes or are you going to sit there daydreaming?"

Seemed Margaret was a mite distracted herself. "My apologies."

"Tread lightly, Major Blevens." Cousin Eunice spoke up, reminding them of her presence. "Margaret and Carrie Ann walked to town this afternoon. I'm sure they're exhausted."

"I've marched over twenty miles in a day, Mrs. Bell." Joshua skipped Margaret's turn and made his next move with a selected domino.

"But my young cousins are not men, sir."

"So I've noticed, ma'am." Joshua's charm had won Cousin Eunice over many visits ago, but it failed to convince Margaret.

Cousin Eunice smiled over her needlework. "I'm happy to learn the war hasn't blinded you to the finer things in life, Major Blevens."

"Never!" He winked at Margaret.

She shifted in her chair. This was the part of courtship that gnawed at her insides. The romantic part. She wanted to stay clear of it. The idea of Joshua touching her had caused her many sleepless nights. He failed to make her feel like she could relax in his company. She was forever on guard.

Spinsterhood, on the other hand, was safe. She could be herself and her past didn't continually rise up and haunt her.

Tonight it would end. She and Carrie discussed the matter and they agreed. Margaret would tell Joshua that she no longer wanted his company—and why. She'd be polite, and if he requested a return of funds, Margaret would refer him to Carrie, who promised she'd give him no reason to turn on them and alert the authorities.

"I'd like a breath of fresh air." That was their cue. Standing, Carrie moved gracefully across the parlor and her shadow followed. They did without extra tapers or lamplight, more scarce commodities in the South these days. "Colonel Kent, will you join me outside on the porch for a few minutes—that is, if you have no objections, Cousin Eunice."

"No, of course I don't. The colonel has shown himself to be a true gentleman. Go ahead."

"I'd be happy to accompany you." Colonel Kent's low, smooth voice bespoke of his good upbringing. He impressed Margaret as the sort of man who'd rather fall on his sword than set foot in the Wayfarers Inn.

Now if *she* were playacting courtship with him, she'd be likely to fall head over heels in love with the man. Little wonder that Carrie was succumbing to the colonel's charm. He was respectable, gallant, and a gentleman . . .

Unlike Joshua.

Margaret lowered her chin and peered across the table at him. His blue eyes followed Carrie and the colonel out of the parlor. "Joshua, you said you had to leave early. Allow me to walk you to the door."

Cousin Eunice glanced up from her needlework. "Come again soon, Major."

"Thank you, Mrs. Bell." His brows cinched. Suspicion glowed in his gaze. Yet, he pushed to his feet.

In the receiving area, Margaret found his gray woolen cape and handed it to him.

"What's this all about?" he whispered.

"Our pretend courtship is over."

He pursed his lips and his gaze darted to the door before coming to rest on her face. "Is your sister aware of it?"

"She's aware of it all. Everything."

His gaze darkened, evidence that he grasped her meaning. "So she knows you cheated me?"

"Yes," Margaret croaked. "She instructed me to tell you that if it's a refund you want, you should speak with her."

He chuckled loudly and Margaret hoped it wouldn't bring Cousin Eunice from the parlor. "How nice to be taken care of by a wealthy widow."

She heard the sarcasm in his tone. "Yes, I'm blessed."

"Hmm . . . well, I remember a time when you weren't *holier than Thou*."

"I remember that time too." She lowered her gaze. "I'll never forget it. Sometimes I dream that Mr. Veyschmidt is pulling my hair, laughing, and pushing me toward a man who has nothing short of maltreatment on his mind. I awake trembling." She forced herself to meet Joshua's gaze. "I needed you to be my friend, Joshua, not a tormenter, but you were the latter."

"You're the one who flaunted her charms."

"For that I was extremely foolish. Without Carrie at the inn to protect me, I faced the consequences of my behavior, along with Mama's death, all alone."

"I was a little busy killing Yankees." He sounded proud of it.

Margaret thought of the sadness surrounding Colonel Collier's death and shrank away from him.

After several agonizingly long moments, he stepped forward. "Tell Carrie Ann your secrets are safe with me."

"Even though you lied to her after you'd made a pact never to lie to each other?" Margaret ought not press the prickly matter. If he accused them, she and Carrie would be locked up—or worse.

"What happened last summer is between Carrie Ann and me." He stared at Margaret hard, then pushed past her, purposely bumping her shoulder. "I thought Christians were supposed to forgive others their trespasses. Guess you've got more to learn before you can claim to be a woman of faith."

"I don't deny it." She held herself stiffly.

The door opened and a blast of wintery air blew in and encircled her. Margaret shivered. Only when the door slammed shut did she turn around. To her relief, Joshua was gone.

—☙ ❧—

"I have a surprise for you, Eli."

"For me?"

"Yes. Close your eyes and hold out your hand."

"Seems I've heard that line before—before us boys put frog brains in our teacher's palm."

"Tsk, tsk . . . well, I promise you no frog brains."

Smiling beneath the silvery moonlight, Eli did as she'd asked. Carrie dipped her hand into the pocket of her hooded cloak and extracted the pouch of tobacco that she'd procured for him. She set it in his hand.

"You may open your eyes."

Eli stared at it, then her. "What's this? Tobacco?" He brought it to his nose.

"It's quality Virginia tobacco no less."

"Carrie . . ."

"I know you enjoy smoking a pipe on occasion, so I thought you should have some fine tobacco to put in its bowl."

"Thank you." He inspected the pouch in his palm.

"Don't tell me you can't accept it because it's more for me than you." She leaned against the back-porch railing. "My papa smoked a pipe all my growing-up years so I learned to enjoy the smell of burning tobacco. It reminds me of happier times—of being home on the farm when my sisters and I would gather around Papa's knees and listen to his stories. He'd smoke his pipe and I idolized him. To me, he was the most wonderful, smartest man in the world." She smiled at the memory. "Then I discovered Papa is as human as the rest of us."

"What a disappointment when we mature and find that our parents don't possess superhuman powers."

"Indeed."

"Well, thank you for this gift. I will enjoy it, to be sure."

Bending slightly forward, Eli placed a kiss on her cheek. He lingered near the corner of her mouth. She felt his warm breath on her cheek. All Carrie would have to do is turn her head ever so slightly and their lips would meet.

She closed her eyes. Delicious shivers trickled down her neck and spine. Was it wrong of her to want Eli's affection?

When he straightened, disappointment assaulted her. "A-are you going to try the tobacco and make sure it's as fine as it smells through the burlap pouch?" Carrie couldn't get herself to meet his dark gaze.

"If you insist." The smile in Eli's voice was unmistakable. He removed his pipe from the inside pocket of his gray woolen cloak.

Carrie enjoyed the way his strong fingers scooped tobacco from its pouch and packed it into the pipe's bowl before taking a match to it. She closed her eyes as the smell of cozy home fires and Papa's stories wafted over to her.

"Fine tobacco indeed. I'm almost afraid to ask where you got it. However, I won't sleep tonight unless I know."

"A man named Mr. Jones escorted Margaret and me here to Richmond. We were assured of his reliability, but he's a puzzle. He didn't talk much, other than to advise us as to what we required for traveling, and we parted company once we reached Richmond. However, Mr. Jones said that if we needed anything we could leave a message for him at the Spotswood Hotel."

"Fine lodgings." Eli puffed on his pipe. "So you left Mr. Jones a message requesting tobacco?"

"Yes. I sent it yesterday and the pouch was waiting for me at the front desk today."

Eli neared. "Woman, you scare the liver out of me. Have you no sense of fear? By your own words this man, Mr. Jones, is a puzzle. He sounds quite shady to me."

"I can sense danger . . . when it's present. But Mr. Jones means no harm to Margaret and me." She paused, taking in his stern expression. "I see I've displeased you."

"No." His hand enveloped hers. "I meant no offense. You have pleased me greatly with your gift. I worry about you, that's all." Releasing her hand, he cupped her chin and urged her gaze into his. "Don't be cross with me."

"I'm not miffed with you in the least." She smiled easily and her face heated with her attraction to this man. He'd proven himself an ally. He made her laugh and caused her to dream of a happy future again.

But how did it happen? When had it happened? Eli Kent had somehow seamlessly woven himself into her heart.

"I'm flattered that you care about my welfare."

"I care very much." His hand fell slowly away. "But surely you can understand how your independence might worry a man. My father taught me to esteem women as the weaker vessel, and to cherish and protect them. Like fine and fragile crystal, he said, they are to be handled with the utmost of care. My mother would accept nothing less."

"Oh, Eli . . ." A self-deprecating laugh escaped her. "I'm much too hearty and capable to be considered a delicate Southern lady."

"You are a lady on every level, albeit, I will admit, a spirited one."

A frown weighed heavily on her brow. "And that's a problem, isn't it?"

"On the contrary." Again that amused tone. "It's part of your charm. But I would urge you to be very cautious. You'll save me from having heart failure."

Carrie smiled at his jest.

Setting his pipe on the porch rail, Eli placed his hands on her shoulders. He turned her away from the house so his voice would waft over the yard.

"Seriously . . . with each of Sherman's victories," he whispered close to her face, "the Confederacy crumbles a little bit more. Southerners everywhere, not only here in Richmond, are on edge. Women are arrested daily and brought to Libby Prison on the mere charge of suspicious behavior. Sometimes the crime is simply looking at a neighbor the wrong way, and despite having young children at home and a husband on the battlefield, they are locked up and kept behind bars for days. Weeks. I don't want to see that—or worse—happen to you."

Carrie didn't want it either. "I'll be more careful. I promise."

"That's all I ask."

His nearness made her dizzy. She toyed with the brass buttons on the front of his frock coat before peering up at him. His dark eyes searched her face. How she wished he would kiss her. Would he think her wonton if she initiated it?

Slowly, he moved closer, but then only lightly pressed the tip of his nose to hers. Stepping back, he picked up his pipe.

Carrie was tempted to pout.

"I'm sorry to say that I won't be able to visit you tomorrow. I hope you'll forgive me, but I must escort Averly to a dinner party."

At the mention of the other woman's name, Carrie wanted to scowl.

"Actually, it's not dinner, but a starvation party." He sounded amused. "There will be music, but no food, although we'll sit around the dining room table with good china in front of us."

"Sounds dreadful. Why would you escort Miss Winslow to such an event?"

"Because in attendance will be men whom Pat hopes to persuade politically."

"I understand." Carrie ran her forefinger along the top of the wooden porch rail so he wouldn't see her wounded expression. Peyton told her that she wore her heart on her sleeve.

Peyton. Carrie focused on the darkened yard. She'd had to share her husband with the Union army and now she was forced to share Eli with Miss Averly Winslow.

Except she had no right to feel the way she did. Besides, she wasn't the crystalline Southern woman he'd described.

But she knew who fit that mold—Miss Averly Winslow.

Carrie spoke her mind. "It's obvious to me, and others too, I'm sure, that Miss Winslow is the sort of fine and fragile lady you spoke of. She's perfect for you."

"Appearances can be deceiving."

"Perhaps, but it's I who will be brokenhearted when our feigned courtship ends." She swallowed hard. Baring her soul wasn't easy, but she was determined to speak from her heart. "Eli, I don't want to lose at this courtship game, although I have no right to my feelings."

Eli stared out into the night for several long moments before giving her a side-glance. "Do I dare hope these feelings, to which you have no right, are amorous in nature?"

"They are indeed amorous—and I'm ashamed to even admit it. I'm envious of Miss Winslow. And yet, I know without a doubt that I love—loved—Peyton. I miss him. I mourn him." She plunged her hands into her cloak's deep pockets. "So how, then, can I hold such affections for you?"

Eli set aside his pipe again and pulled her into his arms. Extracting her hands from her pockets, she hugged him around his midsection and placed her head on his chest. How safe she felt.

"You have no cause to be jealous, Carrie." A hint of amusement rimmed his response. "Tomorrow night's event is business, that's all."

She closed her eyes when lips brushed her forehead.

"The Cause is lost," he whispered close to her ear. "The Confederacy will soon be swallowed into the Union, but that won't keep her sons and daughters from suffering the effects of this war for years to come. Much effort will need to be spent on restoration of our towns and cities—and our souls. The healing process will be painstaking and will require time, but it also needs the right people in office to see the process through."

"And Mr. Winslow is one of those people?"

"Yes. Politicians must be able to see beyond their careers and their fat billfolds, and look into the hearts of Southerners. Pat is a man who can do that. With a dual citizenship and expertise in shipping and negotiating, he could potentially bargain with world leaders and convince them to invest in the South."

She pulled back slightly so she could see his face. "It's nice to hear of someone who can appeal to the *better angels of his nature*." She didn't remind Eli that those words were spoken by a certain Union president.

"Pat can . . . and will." Eli tilted his head. "Do you understand now why I must escort Averly tomorrow night?"

"I suppose so." She arched a brow, feeling stubborn. "I have no say in the matter anyway. Although fragile, crystal-like ladies might do well to stay home and let the men attend a *starvation party*."

Laughter rumbled in Eli's chest.

Carrie grew serious. "Can Mr. Winslow's ideas bring a swift end to the war?"

"No. I'm afraid Generals Grant and Sherman are doing that job." Eli's hold on Carrie tightened. "It won't be long and the Union will break through Confederate lines. There are too many for our half-starved and freezing troops. If that happens, we won't be able to protect Richmond and the city will fall into Union hands like Atlanta, Columbia, Charleston, and now Wilmington too."

Carrie rested her head against him once more. The idea of Eli returning to the battlefield suddenly terrified her. "You were wrong. I do have a sense of danger." She locked her arms around him. "I'm feeling it right now."

"What do you mean?"

"Eli, please don't return to battle." She heard the groaned reply. "Please. Seeing you wounded was horrible enough for me. Besides, I lost Peyton—" Had she ever spoken those words aloud?

"Carrie, I promise you"—he cupped her face and his palms felt warm on her cheeks—"you won't lose me."

"How can you be so certain?"

"Because"—amusement caused a subtle lilt in his voice—"there are things going on behind the scenes that you aren't aware of."

"What things?"

"Ah, but I can't tell you. At least not yet." Eli slipped his arms around her waist. "I can only ask you to trust me." His warm breath caressed her cheek.

"I do." She whispered the words. "I trust you with my life."

Carrie recognized the spark of desire in Eli's gaze. Lord help her, but she longed for him to kiss her. He pulled her close to him and she allowed it. She met his stare. When he lowered his mouth to hers, she closed her eyes with sweet expectation pumping through her veins.

But her next thought caused her to tense.

"I am a widow, aren't I, Eli?" She murmured the question against his lips.

"You are, indeed, my darling Carrie Ann."

Eli's mouth claimed hers and awakened pangs of desire. She responded to his kiss. Her hand found the back of his head, and she drew him closer, deeper.

"I love you, Carrie." Eli trailed kisses across her cheek. "Marry me," he whispered in her ear.

"Yes . . ." Oh, how she wanted this man—all of him. "It would be my privilege to become your wife."

Eli kissed her again, holding her as tightly against him as her voluminous skirts allowed. "Promise me, Carrie. You'll be my wife."

"I promise."

"You can't change your mind tomorrow when your reason returns."

She laughed softly. "I won't change my mind."

After one last kiss, Eli took a half step back, enveloping her hands in his large palms. "Neither of us is in any position to announce our engagement. You're in mourning, and Peyton deserves to be reverenced, so I suggest we wait until Thanksgiving next to share our news."

"Agreed." She tipped her head. "You sound as though you've planned this for some time."

"I have. I've considered all angles, including living off Peyton's money. I want to support my family with my own income, and I'm working toward that end right now. However, I shall warn you: there will be some bumps along the way because I've promised to escort Averly to various political affairs. But, please rest assured that it's you I'd rather keep company with, not Averly."

"And you can't get out of it?"

Eli shook his head. "Pat is offering me," he whispered close to her face, "a way to avoid returning to the battlefield. Between my feelings for you and my own troubled conscience over fighting and killing for The *Lost* Cause, I can't return to duty."

Carrie hugged him, her head against his chest. "I'm so proud of you . . . and, thank you. Thank you for not taking part in this bloodbath any longer. It has to stop."

"It will. Soon." Eli ran his hand over her hair and kissed her forehead. "You mustn't tell a soul what I've said."

"I won't. On my honor, I will keep your secrets." She enjoyed the feeling of being held in his embrace and taken into his confidence.

"That's one of the reasons I love you, Carrie. I know I can trust you to keep my secrets the way you trust me to keep yours."

Richmond Dispatch
Friday Morning, March 3, 1865

NEGROS FOR HIRE AND SALE.

FOR SALE, PRIVATELY, one likely Negro man, raised in Petersburg, and sold to raise money; he is a No. 1 dining-room servant, good cook, and, in fact, can do most anything. If not sold before Friday next, we will sell him at public auction at N. M. Lee's auction store, on Franklin street, by order of the owner. BURTON & WALLACE.

FOR SALE, PRIVATELY, a likely GIRL, a good NURSE for her age—say ten years old.

Also, a WASHER and IRONER, twenty years old. BURTON & WALLACE.

Chapter 30

March 3, 1865

Carrie slapped the newspaper down on the dining room table. "I cannot abide these offensive classifieds. They announce the sale of human beings as if they were nothing more than the thirty condemned horses and mules being auctioned by Major and Quartermaster Archer . . . whoever that is."

"Why, he's the major and quartermaster, dear." Cousin Eunice sipped her bitter brew. Her creased brow registered confusion as to Carrie's outrage.

"That makes perfect sense, Cousin Eunice." Margaret sent a wide-eyed warning across the table.

Carrie swallowed her opposition, lest she be arrested for "suspicious behavior" as Eli called it.

Betsy entered the dining room and ducked her head. Her dark eyes bore into Carrie as if she'd overheard the complaints. Did the woman object, or was she too warning Carrie to keep quiet?

"Mail come, Missus." Betsy set all but two envelopes in front of Cousin Eunice. "And two letters for you, Miss." With her dark eyes fixed on Carrie, the maid rounded the table. "One come on packet boat, the other got delivered by Colonel Kent's man, Jim."

"Thank you, Betsy."

The black woman bent slightly at the waist. "Yes'm."

"Well, we've learned one missive is from Colonel Kent, but who is the

267

other from? You must read them to us." Cousin Eunice craned her neck. "I'm sure it will be so much more interesting than the newspaper."

"You told me not to read about the war, so I read the classifieds this morning." Carrie tamped down the urge to giggle.

"And I found them quite depressing, as I have no money to spend." The older woman sighed dramatically. "But it's only a matter of time before General Lee beats back those dreadful *invaders*."

Carrie ignored the ignorant remarks. Clearly, Cousin Eunice turned a blind eye to the war, despite remnants of suffering that poured into her city on a daily basis. Confederate citizens came with hopes of their government helping them. But it did not—could not. With nowhere to go, weary women with children in tattered clothing, maimed veterans, old men and women, and crooks of every size and color crowded Richmond's streets.

Carrie opened and read Eli's note first.

"What does he say?"

Hearing the enthusiasm in her sister's voice, Carrie peeked over the piece of brown paper. Stationary was at a premium like everything else. "Eli invited me on an outing tomorrow. He'll pick me up mid morning."

"Only you and the colonel, dear?" Cousin Eunice's brow furrowed. "Unchaperoned?"

"He wrote that his younger sister will join us, so we'll be properly chaperoned, Cousin Eunice." Across the table, Margaret spooned a bite of porridge into her mouth and grimaced the way Carrie had at its tasteless flavor. "Otherwise, Margaret is welcome to come."

"Then who will stay with me?"

Carrie hadn't been aware that anyone needed to stay with her.

"Don't fret." Margaret set her hand on Cousin Eunice's forearm. "I will remain at home with you."

"Bless you, child."

Carrie caught Margaret's wink as she folded Eli's note.

"You didn't tell us who the second letter is from." Curiosity shone in Margaret's teal eyes. "Anyone else we know?"

Carrie inspected the envelope. It was postmarked Washington City. The handwriting was unmistakable. "It's from Au—our employer." She excused herself and went to the parlor. She had no intention of reading this letter aloud.

Dearest Carrie Ann,

Your absence is sorely missed in our household. You belong here with us. If you need anything, anything at all, contact Mr. L. S. Cameron. He did some brokering for me many years ago, as I refused to use our neighbor's business.

Carrie recalled that a former neighbor, Miss Lavinia Monteague's eldest brother, made his living in slave trading before it was outlawed and prior to the Union initiating their strategic Anaconda Plan.

Mr. Cameron still resides in Richmond. We correspond occasionally.

As for returning, my dear girl, please do make it soon. Tabitha and I are quite concerned for your welfare.

Ever Faithful,

RC

Carrie folded the letter and slipped it back into its envelope. She missed Aunt Ruth terribly and hated to worry her. But the thought of leaving Eli weighed heavily on her. Was it really so terrible to want to be with the man she loved?

She pocketed the letter and slowly made her way back to the dining room where Betsy cleared the table.

"Aren't you going to read your letter to us, dear?" Eunice ate a spoonful of jam. She'd hoarded her precious preserves along with other sweet treats on a shelf in her wardrobe. Margaret reported seeing them when she'd helped the older woman into bed one afternoon. Carrie couldn't have cared less that the woman didn't share. The delectables were hers, after all. However, Cousin Eunice's actions defined her character and did nothing to endear her to Carrie or Margaret.

Carrie reclaimed her seat at the table. "My letter contained nothing of importance. Our employer wants us to return as soon as possible." She placed her napkin on her lap. She eyed the now-cold porridge in front of her. Without butter, milk, sugar, or molasses, the mushy meal held little appeal.

Oh, for one of Tabitha's hot biscuits slathered with butter. Now that would taste divine. Carrie could practically taste its flaky goodness melting in her mouth.

Perhaps she'd splurge on another bag of flour—that is, if she could arrive at the mill without being attacked. Deprivations caused many citizens to revolt. The authorities struggled to control the city. However, Cousin Mikey lived in the vicinity of the Confederate President's House, as did Mrs. Robert E. Lee who resided up the block. They hadn't seen much trouble, and when Carrie did venture into town to post a letter or purchase groceries, she didn't venture near the docks. Cousin Mikey warned her and Margaret on their first day in Richmond to stay clear of the area.

"Oh, but you can't leave now, dear ones." Cousin Eunice's spoon was poised above the jam jar's opening. "Why, it's too risky to travel."

"Not really. People come and go from Richmond every day."

The sad pout on Cousin Eunice's face was surely intended to foster guilt and pity. However, Carrie wouldn't be persuaded. When it was time to leave, she and Margaret would go.

But for the time being, she would cast aside her cares and look forward to spending the day with Eli tomorrow.

—◦ ◦—

"How could Averly do such a thing?" Eli growled each word while staring out the windows of his small apartment at the busy street below. "How did she discover Carrie's true identity?"

"My daughter is an astute young lady."

And obviously jealous of my time with Carrie.

"Between hearing your mother's tale of how you came by your, um, *inheritance*, and asking some probing questions of General Bell at the starvation party the other night, Averly figured out that Miss Carrie Ann Bell is really Mrs. Peyton Collier."

Eli turned to face Pat. "Yes, but why didn't she come to you—or me—with the information?"

"That, I don't know." Comfortably seated in one of the two upholstered armchairs that Mother generously left behind, Pat examined his cigar.

"What possessed her to voice her suspicions to Hetty Pegram who, of course, will now alert the authorities?"

"I'm not so sure Mrs. Pegram will do that. She had only good things to say about Mrs. Collier. I believe we have some time, albeit not much." Pat puffed his cigar. "I think you'll agree that Mrs. Collier and her sister must leave Richmond immediately."

"Yes, I agree." Eli churned out a sigh and eyed his godfather. "Do you have any suggestions?"

"Yes, as a matter of fact."

"I'm listening." Eli lowered himself into the second armchair.

Pat released a cloud of smoke. "In the hours following my daughter's confession, I've come up with a plan. However, it involves your making a big decision."

"What sort of decision?" Eli leaned forward, his forearms on his knees.

"After the fight at Waynesborough yesterday, in which Custer's army proved victorious over Jubal Early's yet once more, General Lee sent a message to Grant, asking if they could resolve their differences. Grant refused. He reiterated that he will accept nothing short of the South's unconditional surrender."

"I'm not surprised."

"But wouldn't you agree that such a surrender is inevitable?"

"I would agree." Eli had agreed for some time that the Southern Cause was lost.

"So why not begin the process with yourself?"

"I don't follow."

"Packets are making fewer trips to Richmond from City Point. I predict that within a week, riverboats will be prohibited from making the trip between cities. It's yet another way to increase Confederates' hardship. I suggest that you, your loved ones, and Averly and I ride the mail packet boat to City Point tomorrow. One is docked at the harbor now, and I'm told it will set sail from Richmond at eleven thirty tomorrow morning. We will be gone before any investigation can even be launched against Mrs. Collier."

Eli gave the idea some thought and agreed. "But it will take some doing to convince Mother to leave Richmond."

"Then we have our work cut out for us this afternoon, don't we?"

Eli narrowed his gaze. "What does this have to do with me beginning the surrender process?"

"When we reach City Point, you will surrender to Grant."

Eli tipped his head back and laughed. "That is unacceptable."

Pat appeared anything but amused. "Eli, if you surrender now, you'll probably be jailed for a short time. A week, perhaps. I'll see to it that you're not abused. As a tradeoff, you will tell the officer in charge everything you know about Lee's positions."

"I should become a traitor?" Eli stood and walked to the front window again. "I will not!"

"You should become a hero. The sooner this war is over, the sooner the suffering will stop. Every officer will ultimately be forced to surrender and take the Union's oath of allegiance. You will simply do so ahead of time. Should the vice president of the United States make good on his threats, your actions will likely result in a full pardon."

"What good is a pardon from the United States if I'm considered a deserter and a traitor in my homeland?"

"You and thousands of others, Eli." Pat stood and crossed the room. "When the time is appropriate and I announce my candidacy for the Senate, I will allow you to explain your actions and describe how they bettered the South."

"And how do you think such actions will better anyone?"

"For instance, you are working for my election and I am a constitutionalist. I uphold states' rights and advocate limited federal government. I will present the argument that, had the issue of slavery been brought to Virginians for a vote, it may have been abolished without a bloody war. As you're aware, most Virginians do not own slaves. But alas, most Southern politicians are governed by their own prejudices and by wealthy slave owners who pay for their favor. You don't see members of Congress on the battlefield, do you?"

"I have seen their sons in battle."

Pat gave a nod in deferment. "By and large, congressmen sit around all day, acting important, chewing their tobacco, and eating peanuts."

Eli couldn't argue that point. He'd been working security detail for Pat the day General Lee came up to meet with the Confederate Congress. They behaved in the exact manner that Pat just stated despite the fact that General Lee had pleaded for supplies for his men. While many were moved by Lee's petitions, they had themselves to consider. The treasury would continue sitting on thousands of dollars in gold while Lee's army, barefoot and starving, was forced to continue the Congress's fight for rich cotton and tobacco grow-ers, shippers, and the like. Most of all, their fight was with President Lincoln and his administration. The Rebellion would continue.

"Meanwhile, politicians have scared their constituencies by convincing them that the United States government's sole purpose is to steal their land and confiscate their property. Farmers think of their homes and their crops. Plantation owners, on the other hand, think of their slaves. You understand the social divide, don't you, son?"

"I do, of course."

"Good. Because when the right time presents itself, a time that will come shortly, we will show Virginians that we hear their voices and will fight for them on the Senate floor, but not with weapons, nor more of our sons' blood. But with the United States Constitution."

Eli considered Pat's idea. It made sense, and it would get Carrie quickly out of Richmond—but was it practical? It seemed a gamble, and Eli disliked taking such costly risks.

"You don't have much time to think about it, son." Pat ground out the stub of his cigar in an ashtray. "We need to get a message to Mrs. Collier—"

"I planned an outing with her tomorrow . . ."

"Good. That will serve as a ruse for the Bells."

Disappointment coursed through him. He'd been looking forward to spending time with Carrie, perhaps kissing her again.

"Send Jim with a message to Mrs. Collier."

Eli forced aside the pleasant daydream. Carrie was in danger—thanks to Averly.

"She and her sister must pack and perhaps stash their bags somewhere that Jim can find them tonight. Tomorrow, Mrs. Collier and her sister can bid their cousins farewell."

"Instead of an outing," Eli finished, "they will board the packet and, along with Mother, Laurabeth, Averly, and the two of us, will be safely delivered to City Point."

"Exactly." Pat pushed to his feet.

"Just one problem. I'm on duty tonight at Libby Prison. If I don't show up, it will spark an investigation."

"Then you must show up for duty."

Eli ran his knuckles over his scratchy jaw. "How do you propose I board the steamer? Incognito?"

"No, no. You're my security detail. Remember?" Pat smiled then fetched his overcoat from the hook near the door. "I have sent a message to President Grant requesting passage to Washington via City Point. I have every confidence that he will afford me and my entourage passage on, perhaps, one of the last packet boats to and from Richmond."

"Then it appears I have no choice but to make the trip with you." Eli thought of Carrie. He wouldn't be able to bear it if authorities jailed her in Libby Prison. Not all Confederate soldiers were Southern gentlemen. Far from it, and at Libby, their bitter hatred of loyalist spies—or those they suspected as spies—was often evidenced by their abuse and neglect of prisoners.

"Do we have a deal, Eli?"

"Yes, we have a deal." He crossed the apartment and plucked his own overcoat from the row of pegs.

"We must hurry," Pat said. "There's much work to be done."

CHAPTER 31

"Miss, you'd best come out of that bath afore you shrivel up like a prune."

"Yes, I suppose you're right." But the hot water felt so wonderfully relaxing that Carrie hated to leave it.

She'd volunteered to go last, taking her bath after Eunice and Margaret. Betsy had been kind enough to keep water heating on the stove so she didn't have to wash in a lukewarm tub. With no one rushing her, she'd closed her eyes and allowed her thoughts to wander over this afternoon's puzzling events.

Shortly after lunch, Betsy brought her another message from Eli, only this one wasn't penned on brown paper. It was relayed to her by Eli's hired man, Jim, who told her she was "found out" and that she and Margaret needed to pack their belongings. They were to leave their bags near the shrubs by the back porch. Jim would collect them after dark.

A thousand questions swirled around Carrie's mind. How had she been discovered—and what, exactly, was found out? That she was a Collier and a Union officer's widow? It had to be that, but who knew?

Anxiousness fluttered deep inside of her. Jim said she wouldn't see Eli until tomorrow morning because of his duties at Libby Prison tonight.

Patience was never one of Carrie's attributes and she had half a mind to hire a conveyance and go to the prison complex and insist on speaking with Eli about the matter. But, of course, that was much too dangerous—even for Carrie Ann.

"Here's your wrapper, Miss. You'd best get into it before the fire dies away."

Grudgingly, Carrie pried herself from the now tepid bath. Betsy handed her a towel and Carrie wrapped it around her wet hair before stepping out of the tub. She then dried off her body, becoming more aware of Betsy's stare. The weight of it was unnerving.

Carrie turned her back. She didn't like being gawked at. She knew she was too thin, but weren't most Southerners in Richmond? "Is something wrong?"

"No, Miss. Just wondering when your baby's due is all."

"Baby? What baby?" Carrie pulled on her wrapper and tied the sash at her waist.

"I might be an ignorant slave, Miss, but I know what's inside that little lump you got."

Carrie's hands flew to her belly, and there it was. The small, but firm protrusion. Why had she not noticed it before?

"Perhaps I ate too many biscuits tonight."

"We all ate too many, but they shore did taste good."

"Yes, they did." Carrie gave a little laugh as she rubbed her palm over the lower part of her abdomen. Her reason kicked in; too many biscuits would hardly make her chubby within a few hours. Her gowns hung loosely and the rest of her belly was flat—apart from the small, low bump.

Carrie felt glued to the wooden kitchen floor. A baby. It couldn't be. It was too much to hope for.

She counted back the months. She'd had *the curse* shortly after September's battle at Winchester. She married Peyton the first of October, and . . . no curse ever since. But the sickness she'd experienced should have been a telltale sign.

"Mercy me!" Willing her legs to move, Carrie stumbled to the wooden chair nearby and sat. "I must be in my fifth month."

"I'd guess that'd be about right." Betsy busied herself in the kitchen. "Do your cousins know you're expecting?"

"No. I wasn't even aware of it myself . . . until now." Carrie's palm continued to rest on top of her belly. "I was so consumed with other matters." Like Peyton's disappearance, her father's appearance in Washington, her travels to Richmond, and now Eli.

"Us women wear lots of clothes, and I heard of some ladies who didn't know they were expectin' till the pains came and the babe come out." Betsy emptied the tub and stole another glance at Carrie. "Colonel Kent the papa?"

"No! . . . No. He's not the father." How would Eli react to this new development? She remembered his sweet kisses and how strong his arms felt around her waist. But would he want her now that she was expecting another man's child?

Carrie eyed the older black woman, wondering about spilling the truth. Would Betsy keep her confidence? What did it matter at this point?

"Please don't tell another soul about this." Carrie stood and neared the slave. "No one must know."

The woman gave a nod.

"I'm a widow. I married a Union officer." She whispered each word. "He was killed last October nineteenth. I was devastated, but I agreed to make the trip to Richmond with my sister Margaret because it forced me to think about things." That's the best explanation she could give, considering Eli's last message about being "discovered."

"You and the other miss is spies?"

"Oh, no." Carrie glimpsed disappointment in the slave's dark eyes. "We're truly only visiting our cousins and Colonel Kent is . . . well, he is a long-time family friend. He and my husband were roommates at the school they attended before the war."

"Reckon it's a good thing you's leaving soon," Betsy whispered.

"Yes." Carrie slid her palms across her little lump of love. Peyton's child. What a joy to be carrying him . . . or her.

"You best go comb out that hair o' yours. It's going in all directions."

Carrie took to the stairs. She felt like she walked on clouds and as blessed as the angels . . .

She was going to have a baby!

—⁀ ⁀—

Eli leaned on his musket and tried to dodge the frigid wind off the James that brought with it a stench so vile it wilted everything in its path—Eli included. Tonight's outdoor assignment held little appeal. Then again, indoors the stench was equally bad, although he'd be out of the elements.

He gazed at the building opposite Castle Thunder. All was quiet. When the wind abated, he marched the length of the wall to seek better shelter.

But when had a little cold, damp wind bothered him? He and his regiment had often braved inclement weather. They'd set their tents up in mud numerous times. They'd slept on frozen ground many more.

Being back in Richmond and suddenly caring about his health and appearance—mostly to impress a certain widow—had somehow softened his constitution.

"Colonel Kent!"

Eli looked toward the door where he saw another sentry waving his arm.

"Come quickly. There's trouble."

Eli hurried into the prison. He followed the jogging guard, although his bum leg prevented him from keeping up.

"Yankees are causing an uprising in one of the upper cells," the guard said as they took to the stairwell. Eli could hear the shouts and curses before he walked onto the floor.

"You're the ranking officer," a corporal shouted at Eli. "Order us to shoot some of these Yanks, and we will."

The noise inside the cell grew to an eardrum-splitting volume.

"All right, that's enough!"

Eli had to yell the order at the top of his lungs before the prisoners heard him.

The man who seemed to be the chief instigator was able to quiet the rest of the enemy combatants.

Eli walked closer to the cell.

"Careful now, Colonel."

Eli sized up the situation. He and his men were armed; the prisoners were not. But there were more than two hundred fifty of them, and if somehow they got freed, they could easily overtake Eli and the enlisted men on duty.

"What's the problem here?" he asked the Yankee who seemed in charge.

"Orderlies brought in a man who doesn't belong here. He's sick, and it ain't right that he's been brung in here to die."

Shouts to the affirmative followed until the prisoner-leader silenced the others.

"Where's the man?"

"Over there." The Yankee pointed toward a far corner of the cell. Men moved aside to make away for Eli to see him. From his vantage point, the man looked dead already. Besides, this could be a trick. Once the cell doors were opened, the Yankees could charge.

"So what would you have me do?"

The Union man wrapped his hands around the iron bars. "Get him outa here."

Eli narrowed his gaze. "And you expect me to open the cell doors and do as you ask and give you the chance to escape?" He smirked. "I'm not quite that stupid, Yank."

"What if I give you my word, sir?" Bearded and as thin as the rest of Richmond, perhaps thinner, the prisoner nodded toward the back of the cell. "We're demanding humane treatment for our sick comrade, that's all."

"Very well. Bring the man to the cell door. Lay him as near to it as you can. Then, you and the rest of the prisoners will back up as far away as possible."

One of the pickets came up behind Eli. "You can't be serious, sir. You're giving in to the wishes of the enemy."

Eli turned and faced the young private. "Human decency applies to all, whether Yankee or Confederate."

"Finally!" one of the prisoners cried. "There's a Reb with some common sense!"

Ignoring the enemy's praise, such as it was, Eli sent for two orderlies from the hospital to retrieve the lifeless-looking prisoner.

An enlisted man left for the hospital to relay the order.

In the meantime, the prisoners carried the skinny man to the cell door. They laid him on the scuffed wooden floor. His hair had been shaved and only stubble darkened the man's otherwise pale complexion. He was naked except for a silver chain around his neck and a loincloth.

The infirm man moaned and moved his head, plucking a familiar chord inside of Eli. Did he know this man from another incident of unrest? If he did, then it was likely that the prisoner had been a troublemaker.

Now, however, the fellow couldn't stand, walk, or talk, let alone cause problems.

A guard summoned the orderlies. Eli leaned against the far wall, taking some weight off his injured leg. He commanded one of the lower ranks to find a blanket, and the sergeant didn't disappoint. He passed it through the iron bars and another prisoner covered the unconscious man.

Eli stared at him, hoping for another hint as to his identity. Nothing came to mind.

At last the orderlies arrived. They gave Eli some guff as they had only just recently brought the man to the cell from the hospital. Eli outranked them, however, so he got his way.

"General Bell will have something to say about this."

"Then I shall answer to General Bell for my decision." He waved the prisoners away from the cell door, warning that if anyone took even a half step forward, he would be shot. Eli and his men readied their guns.

The orderlies made quick work of collecting the man, and then slamming the iron cell door back in place. Only then did the other prisoners come forward.

"His name's Pete Collins," one of the Yankees called. "Colonel Pete Collins. It says so on that metal around his neck."

"Fine." Eli knelt by Collins to check for a breath or a heartbeat. He'd guess the man was dead already. He could count each rib over which his skin seemed stretched. One of his boney legs had an unnatural bend to it, indicating a break that had never been addressed.

With his ear to the man's mouth, he felt just a hint of a breath. He set his ear on the man's chest, and heard a faint heartbeat. As he drew back, the man's eyes fluttered open. One was colorless and cloudy and most likely blind, but the other was clear and golden brown.

His lips moved but only a guttural sound emanated from them. Next Eli could have sworn the man smiled.

"What are you trying to say, man? Tell me." He put his ear to the man's mouth.

His words were barely audible and he had to repeat them. Eli, however, deciphered the message. *Surrender, Reb!*

The irony wasn't lost on Eli. This shadow of a man was in no position, physically or otherwise, to make such a demand. Chuckling inwardly, he waved the orderlies forward. But when the Yankee lost consciousness again, an eerie chill passed through Eli, a shiver that was not born of the bitter, winter cold that found its way into the prison.

It was one of familiarity.

Eli took hold of the man's silver chain and read the engravings on the cross-shaped medallion. It was bent and badly scarred. Even so, there was no doubt in Eli's mind as to the name printed there. It was not Pete Collins, as another Yankee claimed. It was Peyton Collier, United States Cavalry, Middle Military Division.

CHAPTER 32

Eli paced General Bell's hospital office. He was now certain the pathetic, nearly starved creature was Peyton. He couldn't shake the horror that gripped him, having seen his former roommate's appearance. And if Eli secured his parole, would Peyton survive the voyage to City Point?

Carrie, of course, would be dismayed and beside herself with worry. Should he tell her? Peyton still could die, leaving her a widow. Then her mourning would begin anew.

Eli placed his hands on the edge of a sturdy bookshelf and stared down at his scuffed leather boots. He had no right to dream of making Carrie his wife—not while Peyton still lived and breathed. To hope otherwise was unconscionable. And Eli couldn't shake the feeling that he'd been on duty tonight and responded to the prisoners' uprising for a specific purpose. God's purpose.

To try to save Peyton's life.

In doing so, however, something in Eli had to die: his dreams of marrying Carrie. She'd been the reason he had entered into the executor promise in the first place. And she was the reason he planned to turn himself in to Yankee authorities tomorrow. Working for Pat . . . yes, certainly that was a part of it. Eli wanted to support himself and his family with his own money, not Peyton's. But now things seemed as hazy as the fog of war.

General Bell entered his office. Eli straightened and stood at attention.

"I understand you disobeyed my orders, Colonel Kent." He crossed the room and sat behind his desk. "I am both surprised and disappointed. I had hoped to finish my rounds and be at home, sleeping in my warm bed, at this hour."

"My apologies, sir." Eli stepped closer. "With all due respect, I didn't intentionally disregard your command. I simply acted on gut instinct. Clearly the prisoner doesn't belong in a cold jail cell. He requires medical help—clothes at the very least."

"We have no clothes to give him. Richmond citizens walk around town in rags, or haven't you noticed?"

"I've noticed, sir." Although the elite were not wearing rags.

"As for medical attention, we have no elixirs or nurses. Confederate wounded take priority."

"I realize that, sir, more so now than ever." Eli took a step forward. "If I may be so bold as to ask, what's wrong with the fellow, General?"

"He's a Yankee for starters." The man's usually jovial demeanor crumbled. In its stead, hatred stared back at Eli. "God only knows the rest. He was admitted to the hospital before I took command in December." The general peered at Peyt's medical record. "It states here that he was admitted on November 30. He comes in and out of consciousness, which could indicate some sort of brain defect. He is blind in his left eye and his right leg was broken, although never set, as he wasn't expected to survive long enough to even get here."

Eli hid his cringe. He recalled a similar ride so painful that unconsciousness was a welcomed blessing.

"By the time doctors examined him here at Libby, there seemed no point in trying to save him. But obviously, he's one stubborn Yankee. Refuses to die."

"So he's been allowed to starve?"

"No, of course not. The man's record clearly indicates that he wakes periodically throughout any given day and takes some sustenance."

"Not to appear insolent, sir, but what sort of sustenance does he consume?"

"Cornmeal mush, I presume. Same as all the prisoners." The general slapped the record on his desk and leaned back in his chair. "We barely have food enough for our men in the trenches and the citizens of Richmond. Enemy combatants receive whatever cornmeal, bacon, and flour is left—which is practically nothing."

Eli saw the stark evidence of that. If he hadn't used some of the funds that Peyton left him, he and his family would be among those who vied for scraps on the streets of Richmond.

"Sir, allow me to beg your indulgence. This man, Colonel Peyton Collier, happens to be a personal friend of mine." Eli would not, of course, tell the general the entire truth. "We were roommates at West Point Military Academy. It is his aunt, for whom Carrie and Margaret work, who fed and clothed me while I was a prisoner in her home in Winchester before we escaped."

"I see." General Bell steepled his fingers.

"I would consider it a personal favor to me, sir, if you would parole the man into my custody."

Pursing his lips, the general gave it several moments' thought. "And what will you do with him?"

"I will secure his passage on the mail packet tomorrow and send him to a hospital in City Point. They will accept one of their own, I have no doubt."

"Hmm . . . I reckon they will. Meanwhile, our troops starve."

"Sir, I have a bit of money." Eli took care that it didn't come off as a bribe. "Perhaps I can . . . donate it to the hospital so the funds might be used to aid our soldiers, both the wounded and the boys in the trenches."

"Oh?" The general arched his brows and a light of interest flickered in his blue eyes.

"I believe you're acquainted with Mrs. Hetty Pegram."

"Why, yes . . ."

"She will help you get the supplies you need and any funds you can provide her will help."

"Hmm . . ." The general kneaded his jaw. "And I would manage these . . . funds?"

"Yes, sir."

"I refuse to be bribed. You will donate them regardless of my decision about your Yankee friend?"

"No question, sir. Yes, I will donate regardless." Eli sent up a prayer that the general would grant his request. "Well, then, I accept your donation on behalf of the hospitals in Richmond."

Eli bowed slightly. "Thank you, General."

"As for this particular patient"—again he lifted Peyton's record and scanned it before tossing it back on his desk—"I don't see why he can't be paroled. One less Yankee to feed will ease some of the Confederacy's burden. In fact, there are others I will parole also. You can be in charge of getting them on the boat tomorrow too. Let it not be said by the Yankees that we Secessionists are heartless creatures."

"Yes, sir." Eli headed for the office door. His next step was to enlist Pat's help to get Peyton aboard the steamer tomorrow.

His thoughts turned to Carrie and his footfalls down the empty hallway seemed to keep time with the beat of his heavy heart. Once she found out her beloved was alive, she'd move heaven and earth to be by Peyton's side.

And far be it from Eli to stand in her way.

$$\sim \! \! \! \! \! \infty \; \infty \! \! \! \! \! \sim$$

"Please? I must speak with you." Carrie accepted Eli's hand and he assisted her into the awaiting carriage. She placed her small quilted bag and reticule beside her on the leather-covered bench. "Couldn't I have just a few minutes of your time?"

"I'm afraid not, Carrie. We've got to be on that steamer and we're running late as it is."

"But—"

Before Carrie uttered another syllable, Eli strode to where Margaret said her farewells to Cousins Mikey and Eunice.

Little did the cousins know this was good-bye.

Carrie dipped her head and watched the goings-on near the house from beneath her wide-brimmed hat. It hadn't been difficult to convince Eunice that Margaret needed to attend this "outing," as Carrie and Eli wouldn't be properly chaperoned otherwise. With Cousin Mikey lingering over his scant breakfast and bitter coffee, he heartily agreed: Margaret must go with them on their country outing.

The tension lifted slightly from Carrie's shoulders as Eli and Margaret neared the conveyance.

So far so good.

Except, she had hoped to tell Eli her news before the voyage.

He assisted Margaret into the conveyance and called a signal to the driver, his freed man, Jim. Then Eli sat on the padded bench across from Carrie and Margaret.

"I trust our bags were collected last night without incident," Carrie said.

Eli merely inclined his head and looked out the window.

What on earth was wrong with him this morning?

Margaret adjusted her skirts and gave Carrie a nudge. Turning, she saw the questions in her younger sister's eyes. Carrie could guess what she wanted to know: had Carrie told Eli the news?

Carrie gave the slightest wag of her head. She peered across the carriage at Eli, who continued his preoccupation with whatever was outside. He didn't even attempt to make polite conversation. It would seem he had much on his mind—namely their safety and escape from Richmond.

Noticing his whiskered jaw, the shadows beneath his eyes, Carrie couldn't help remarking. "I'm concerned, Eli. You look a bit rough this morning. Didn't you sleep well last night?"

"I didn't sleep at all." His dark gaze shifted to Carrie in a way that made her want to sink into her cloak. She suddenly recalled the trepidation she'd experienced after they'd first met. She'd usually run for the safety of her bedroom at Piccadilly Place after receiving one of his sardonic scowls.

Too bad she couldn't run and hide now.

"I'm sorry that I put you and your family in this precarious position."

"No need to apologize. It's nothing you've done, Mrs. Collier."

Mrs. Collier. The formality successfully subdued her. Carrie sat back in her seat and folded her gloved hands. But though her mouth said nothing more, her mind refused to be silenced. It asked a thousand questions. Had Eli changed his mind about her—about them? By using her formal married name was he telling her they had no future?

"It's quite cool this morning," Margaret ventured. "But Cousin Mikey said he expects the weather to warm now that the sun has made an appearance."

When neither Carrie nor Eli responded, Margaret seemed to give up and they listened to the carriage wheels roll down the bumpy macadamized road. Within minutes they rode into a seedy part of Richmond. Gambling dens and brothels were plentiful and advertised in plain sight. Closer to the river's edge, carriages blocked the street, so Jim parked a block away.

Eli disembarked from the carriage and helped Margaret and Carrie alight.

Jim jumped from the driver's seat and the two unbuckled the luggage and handed it off to Negro attendants, who promised to transport it to the river-boat. Eli pressed a coin in each man's palm to better ensure that it happened.

A light breeze blew a putrid smell off the James and Carrie's stomach roiled. She held her delicately scented hankie to her nose.

"I'll see you in Washington City," Jim muttered to the colonel, although loud enough that Carrie heard it. He pumped Eli's hand and then gave Carrie and Margaret a polite bow before climbing back onto the conveyance.

"Godspeed, Jim," Eli called to him.

"Likewise, suh." Jim picked up the reins and slapped the team of horses into motion.

Carrie tugged on Eli's sleeve. "What did Jim mean just now?"

"Never mind."

Eli's harsh reply set her back a step. He was angry with her, no doubt about it. But why wouldn't he be? He and his family had been uprooted from their new home on account of her.

He offered his arms. Carrie and Margaret both threaded their hands around his elbows.

"We must not get separated, understand?" He peered at Carrie through dark, slatted eyes and then turned to Margaret, who nodded vigorously.

As they hastened down the street, Carrie had to jog to keep up with him. Margaret stumbled on a rise in the walk and he finally slowed. Carrie freed her hand and finally Eli halted. She was tempted to slap him for his mistreat-ment of them.

"What is wrong with you today?" Her breath came in quick successions despite her loosened corset. Standing on Eli's right side, Margaret gulped for air. "My sister and I cannot run to keep up with you, Colonel Kent. We'll have no breath left in our lungs and we'll faint dead away." Carrie tipped her head. "Or is that your diabolical intent?"

Whatever bothered Eli drained away and his expression lightened. "I'm sorry, ladies, and if you'll forgive me, I promise to escort you properly the rest of the way to the steamer."

What choice did they have?

Still miffed, Carrie threaded her gloved hand around his proffered elbow. Margaret did the same. They proceeded at a comfortable but lively pace.

As they neared the river, a long, narrow stern-wheeler and the sight of black men in ragged clothing filled Carrie's view. They tossed bulging bags of what appeared to be mail to one another all the way up one of the two gang-planks and onto the vessel. Sudden shouts from behind her made Carrie whirl around, although she clung to Eli so the throng of humanity didn't swallow her up. A small company of men in blue were herded like goats toward the other gangplank, although those severely injured rode in a wagon.

"Make way for prisoners." The Confederate in charge snapped a whip over the Union men's heads. "Make way."

Horrified gasps rose up from the crowd. Whispers about the dangerous Yankees wafted to her ears. But one glimpse at the soldiers' pale faces made Carrie's heart sink. Dark shadows underlined most men's sunken eyes. Some sported black eyes from recent beatings.

"Where are they taking those poor souls?" Margaret looked like she might cry.

"They've been paroled, deemed unfit to ever fight against the Confederacy again."

Carrie scanned each man's face as he shuffled or rode past. Against logic, she realized that she was still searching for Peyton among them.

Alas, none looked even remotely familiar.

She caught Eli's peculiar stare and stepped closer to him. "Have I done something to offend you?" she asked softly. "Please tell me if I have. I swear it was unintentional because I'd never purpose to hurt you or make you angry."

He pulled his gaze away from hers and shook his head. "You've done nothing to offend me, but your expression just now told me that you'll always love Peyton. No one else will ever fill his boots, will he?"

A heavy frown settled on Carrie's brow. What was that supposed to mean?

The "enemy combatants" boarded the boat, and people began to get turned away. Murmurs that there wasn't room enough on board for more passengers reached Carrie's ears. Cries of outrage and moans of disappointment rose up from the crowd.

She lifted her gaze to Eli. "What do we do now?"

"Mr. Winslow has our tickets." He nodded, indicating the well-dressed man across the street. Carrie recognized him at once. Mr. Winslow waved to them and they trotted over the mucky road.

"Ah, my security detail arrives at last." His hawkish gaze studied Eli's scowl. "Did you have trouble? I expected you and the ladies an hour ago."

"It's our fault," Carrie said, trying to be heard above the steamboat's shrill whistle. "Our cousin decided to linger at the breakfast table."

"Ah, well"—Mr. Winslow clapped his palms together and held them fast—"all that matters is you're here now." Lifting his arm, he drew their attention to the packet boat. "Shall we board?"

Mr. Winslow handed over their tickets and then led the way up the gangplank. Eli showed Carrie and Margaret into the stern-wheeler's saloon. He made the introductions, and, at last, Carrie met Eli's mother, sister, and the lovely Miss Averly Winslow. However, when the seats were claimed, Mr. Winslow sat beside Mrs. Kent, and Margaret next to Laurabeth. Eli stood with his back against one of the saloon's walls where he could spot trouble if it arose. But this left Carrie no other option than to sit alongside Miss Winslow.

Her gaze met Eli's and he seemed to look right through her.

"Eli and Daddy didn't get home until dawn," Miss Winslow said with a giggle from behind her white gloved hand. "Daddy doesn't appear any worse for wear, but poor Eli looks like he consumed far too much brandy last night."

Carrie lifted her quilted handbag and retrieved the novel she'd been reading. She had no intention of keeping company with Miss Winslow.

Another blast of the steamboat's whistle cut right through Carrie. After a few rapid jerks the weather-beaten vessel chugged away from the dock. The twin stacks belched clouds of black smoke that lingered in their wake. On their way to Richmond, Carrie hadn't minded the view of the meandering James or the many stops to refuel. Margaret had made good company. Together they had tried to figure out their mysterious escort, Mr. Jones.

As she opened her book, Carrie wondered if the man was aware that she and Margaret left Richmond. She supposed if he was a noteworthy spy, he'd most likely know. But perhaps it didn't matter anyway.

She looked at the seats up ahead. Margaret and Eli's sister seemed to be getting along well. Mrs. Kent and Mr. Winslow conversed amicably while Eli stood guard with his shoulders pulled back and chin held high, ever the proud Southerner. His expression was stony and his gaze seemed to miss none of the goings-on in the saloon. A card game between a few men. The male passengers who went out on the narrow deck for a smoke and then returned. Several ladies in the front crouched together in conversation. But Eli's gaze snapped away from hers whenever Carrie caught his eye.

Sadness knotted in her chest. Clearly it was over between them for reasons Carrie hadn't had time to uncover. But given Miss Averly Winslow's proverbial cat-that-swallowed-the-canary smirk, Carrie had no choice but to conclude that the woman had succeeded in snagging Eli's heart.

CHAPTER 33

Finally they neared City Point with its extensive wharf. Carrie slipped her book into her bag. She'd been reading Thoreau's *Walden* for a second time and enjoyed the idea of simplistic living surrounded by nature. She missed the good days on the farm, few as they had been.

After the packet boat docked, the wounded soldiers were allowed to disembark first. Carrie felt heartsick, watching from the window as the poor souls stumbled down the gangplank. Others were so injured they had to be carried off on stretchers. The word buzzing throughout the saloon was that the men would likely be taken to Depot Field Hospital, a large medical facility here at City Point. It would thankfully have the medical supplies and personnel that Cousin Mikey lacked in Richmond—that is assuming her cousin, like any good physician, was genuinely concerned about the welfare of his patients.

"You rich Northern women think you're too good to speak to the rest of us, don't you?"

Carrie turned to Miss Winslow. "Are you speaking to me?"

"Yes. In Richmond, you were too dignified to attend social functions with Southerners but you practically threw yourself at Eli Kent."

"I don't think I'm better than anyone else." Although Carrie had ignored Miss Winslow's prattle practically the entire voyage. "And I certainly didn't behave inappropriately with Colonel Kent."

"No?" Miss Winslow's green eyes sparked in a way that said otherwise.

"Then how grateful you must be that Eli found your husband alive in that terrible prison he guarded."

Carrie suddenly couldn't suck enough air into her lungs. "I beg your pardon?"

"Your husband." Miss Winslow inspected her perfectly coiffed blond hair in a small hand mirror. "I overheard Eli and Daddy talking this morning. Eli found your husband, half-dead though he is." She sighed and put away her mirror. "You'll likely be a widow before long anyway, so you may as well keep your dark clothing handy."

"You don't know what you're talking about." But just in case, Carrie turned to watch the last of the parolees leave the ship. None resembled Peyton.

But would she recognize him if she saw him after he'd spent more than four months in prison?

As if in answer to her own question, the repulsive photographs that she'd seen printed in several Northern newspapers came to mind. Pictures of skeleton-like creatures who were not only starved but demoralized by their captors who took photographs of them in such conditions. She'd read printed accounts from those lucky enough to escape, describing the gross injustices they'd suffered in prisons like Libby and Andersonville.

If Miss Winslow was indeed telling the truth, Carrie had given up too soon. Why hadn't she tried harder to find Peyton in that despicable place? Was this why Eli refused to speak to her?

Her hands began to tremble. She looked at Eli through the crowd. His expression seemed to reflect her own despair.

People in the saloon stood, gathered their belongings, and headed for the door. Carrie sprang to her feet, collected her bag, and pressed the crowd onward, but everyone seemed intent on blocking her passage. When Carrie finally reached Eli, he pulled her aside as the other passengers disembarked.

"Eli, is it true . . ." Her voice shook and her knees threatened to give way. Did she dare hope? But what exactly did she hope?

"Please listen to me . . . When I step off this packet, I will be apprehended by Union authorities. In their eyes, I'm an escaped prisoner. I promised you I wouldn't return to battle and I won't. By my own conscience, I cannot. So I'm turning myself in."

"But—"

"I don't want you to worry. I have every hope that I will be released before long."

Carrie shook her head. Why hadn't she anticipated this? How foolish she'd been to assume Eli could step off the boat and be welcomed by enemy forces.

She placed her hand on his arm. "Please, tell me if it's true—"

Before another word rolled off her tongue, Mr. Winslow stepped between them. "Come, Mrs. Collier, I will see you and your sister safely to the hotel."

"No, wait—"

"It's no trouble at all. I'm escorting my daughter and the Kents." His hand firmly around Carrie's elbow, he guided her to the doorway. She looked back and briefly caught Eli's gaze. Misery weighed down his every feature.

Once they'd cleared the gangplank, Mr. Winslow led her in the direction of the carriage, presently being loaded with their luggage.

"I have to know if what I've heard is true." She pulled her arm free.

Mr. Winslow pursed his lips. "What have you heard, my dear?"

Eli had descended the gangway now and two Union soldiers were approaching him. If Carrie didn't inquire now, she might never know if what Miss Winslow said was true or a lie as she suspected.

Lifting her skirts slightly, Carrie tossed aside all propriety and began to jog toward the soldiers. "Eli!" She reached him as one guard tied his hands behind his back. The other tried to forestall Carrie. But, as if sensing her determination, he retreated slightly.

"Eli, please tell me that Miss Winslow was lying when she said that Peyton is alive and among those poor suffering souls onboard with us today."

He rocked to and fro while one of the Union men secured his hands. Eli's expression of regret said more than words.

"So, it's true?"

"Quickly. Reach into my left inside pocket."

Carrie slipped her hand inside his gray frock coat. The warmth from his body penetrated her glove. Her fingers located something hard—a chain of some sort—and she pulled it out. She gulped in a breath, realizing the treasure she held in her palm.

"Peyton's silver chain and pendent." She choked on the words. Her vision swam with both happiness and remorse.

"I found him last night. He's very ill."

"You should have told me immediately."

"And what would you have done? Dismantled Libby Prison brick by brick?"

The soldiers chuckled at the quip.

Eli's demeanor remained somber.

"There's a chance Peyton didn't survive today's voyage, but it was a risk I felt worth taking."

Carrie turned the metal trinket in her palm. "And you're certain it's Peyton? Any soldier might have found this on the battlefield and put it around his neck."

The irony slapped her like a gust off the confluence of the James and Appomattox Rivers. Hadn't she been the one arguing for Peyton's life when all others believed him dead? Now she defied her own reasoning.

"I'm sure it's Peyt."

Carrie covered her mouth, hoping to forestall a sob. He was alive. Praise be to God! But, oh—what a faithless wife she'd been. Why hadn't she trusted Him more?

The guards grew impatient and turned, leading Eli toward a cold and gloomy brick building with iron bars on its few windows.

"Pat Winslow knows all the details regarding Peyton," Eli called over his shoulder. "He will help you and answer your questions."

"But . . ." Stepping forward, Carrie wetted her lips. She had questions to which Mr. Winslow couldn't possibly have the answers. What about them, Eli and her? Did he still love her? And she never got the chance to tell Eli that she was expecting a baby.

Except all of that didn't matter now.

Carrie stared at the identifying jewelry in her hand. Her husband was still alive. She should be rejoicing. Instead she felt inexplicably empty.

But didn't Papa tell her that a good journalist must always act, not react? Carrie tamped down her emotion. Peyton would need her by his side, and wasn't that what she had longed for all these months?

The reality of her situation began to gel. Married to one man, but in love with two.

"Carrie?" Margaret put an arm around her shoulders. "Mr. Winslow just told me that Peyton's alive. Eli found him last night!"

"Yes. I'm thrilled." And now she could tell him how much she loved him. God had blessed her with a second chance.

She glanced back one last time to see Eli entering the prison building.

"Let's get settled at the hotel and eat something." Margaret steered Carrie toward the waiting carriage. "After that, we'll check on your husband's condition. The medical personnel will have him settled comfortably by then. Mr. Winslow said we'd be wise to stay out of their way for an hour or so. There are many parolees being admitted."

Carrie walked numbly beside her.

"And, of course, we'll send a telegram to Aunt Ruth and Tabitha. Won't they be ecstatic with all our good news? The colonel's alive and you're in the family way!"

"Yes." Carrie eked out the word through her tears. Whether from elation or sorrow, she couldn't tell.

A smile spread across Margaret's face. She linked arms with Carrie and continued walking toward the conveyance. "You were right. You knew it all along."

"Did I?" Shame enveloped her, replacing the sense of shock. She'd had no right to carry on with Eli as she did. She'd been ready to give up mourning in order to be at Eli's side, in his arms. Excitement about Peyton's baby had already turned into dreams of life with Eli as the child's father, her husband. She chastised her wayward imaginings and gave in to self-recriminations.

They reached the carriage. Mr. Winslow assisted Margaret inside, but Carrie drew back when it came to her turn to board.

"No. Thank you. My place is with my husband."

"But, my dear, it will take time for him to be admitted."

She acknowledged Mr. Winslow's remark with a nod. "Thank you, sir. I shall find my way to the hospital."

Carrie turned toward the mucky road, intending to walk, but Mr. Winslow caught her elbow.

"Allow us at least to see you there safely."

After internal debate, she agreed, and climbed into the coach. She inhaled musty air made stronger by the dank smell of river water. In the seat across from her, victory seemed to glimmer in Miss Winslow's eyes while Mrs. Kent's glare could only be described as raw animosity. Only sweet Laurabeth offered a sympathetic smile, and faithful Margaret captured her hand.

Carrie stared at her bag resting neatly on her lap.

At last, an eternity later, it seemed, the conveyance jerked to a halt.

Ever the gentleman, Mr. Winslow disembarked and assisted Carrie's descent. "I shall come for you later and take you to the hotel."

His words had a hollow, wooden sound to them. Carrie recognized the man's fatigue and how it emphasized the lines around his eyes. In essence, it matched her own.

"Thank you, sir." She'd need a hot meal and a soft bed at some point.

As the carriage pulled away, Carrie stared up at the tent whose entryway flapped in a gust off the river. Much like the medical facility in Washington City, Depot Field Hospital wasn't brick and mortar, but a collection of massive canvas structures.

Defeat pressed in on her. How would she ever find Peyton among the rows and rows of sick and dying men lying on cots or the amputees sitting in wheelchairs with bandaged stumps in place of legs? The task seemed as daunting as the proverbial needle in a haystack.

Still, she had to try.

After two hours of searching, Carrie was finally directed to the tent where new arrivals had been taken. She hoped the officer in charge hadn't steered her in another wrong direction. Each disfigured face she looked upon, each broken body she glimpsed, caused Carrie to prepare herself for the worst.

"Excuse me, sir." She touched the sleeve of a passing orderly, a fresh-faced youth whose eyes seemed dull, as if they had seen more than someone of his age should be allowed. Yet his lanky bearing conveyed purpose. "I'm looking for my husband. Colonel Peyton Collier. He was brought here today from Libby Prison."

"Might try over there where the doctors are standing, ma'am."

Carrie nodded her thanks and made her way to the cot on which a poor skinny soul lay, unconscious. The sight filled her with anger at Cousin Mikey as well as at the entire United States government. It was General Halleck who ordered the stoppage of prisoner exchanges, thus preventing Southern troops from reentering battle once released from Union prisons. But at what cost? The lives of Union men—like this poor half-starved soul?

Carrie slowly approached the conferring physicians. "Sirs, forgive my interruption, but I'm searching for my husband. Colonel Peyton Collier."

"You have found him, madam." One of the doctors fingered the tips of his brown mustache.

"This man here?" She inched closer for a better view. With razored hair, sunken cheeks, and sallow skin, the man looked nothing like Peyton. "I fear you are mistaken."

"There's always that chance," a plump doctor stated while scratching his jaw, "although this man's identity was confirmed by a Reb who worked at the prison."

Eli.

Horror's icy fingers threatened to strangle her, but she stepped up to the cot. "As his w-wife, I know some identifying markings. May I have a look beneath his shirt?"

"Help yourself."

Ignoring the putrid smell emanating from the man's body, Carrie found the edge of his threadbare shirt and lifted the hem on its right side. There. A thick scar snaked from the center of his abdomen around toward his back, remnants of the injury Peyton sustained at Gettysburg.

"Well?" The stout doctor arched his brows.

"It's him." Carrie began to tremble. Not a single other feature she recognized. Her strapping husband had been reduced to a mere shadow of himself.

"His right eye must be removed." The mustached physician folded his arms. "It's infected."

Nods from the other doctors silently confirmed the decision.

"Then remove it at once. My husband can live with one eye."

"And his left leg . . ." The shortest of the three men removed the thin sheet covering Peyton's lower half. "It was broken and never correctly set. We must rebreak and reset it."

"Fine." Carrie failed to see their hesitation. "Do what you must."

"He may not survive the surgeries."

Carrie couldn't bear to look at Peyton's face. It resembled some Poe-like specter that threatened to haunt her dreams forevermore.

"But he will not survive," the mustached doctor added, "if the infection in his eye spreads to his brain and throughout his body."

"Then you must operate." Carrie would never forgive herself if she didn't try anything and everything to save Peyton's life.

"Very well." The mustached physician obviously outranked the other two. "As soon as a nurse becomes available, we'll take this man into surgery."

"You have chloroform, I presume."

"Yes, ma'am." The shortest of the three paused in conversing long enough to reply. "We just need a nurse to assist."

"I will assist." Carrie set down her bag on a nearby wooden chair before removing her hat and shawl. "I have experience and served under Major Paul-Henri LaFont when I, um, *volunteered*"—under Peyton's orders and supervision—"in the cavalry camp of the Army of the Shenandoah."

The men looked at each other, then at Carrie.

The mustached doctor gave a nod. "Then you are most welcome to volunteer. You will assist me."

"You won't faint just because this is your husband, now will you?" the shortest of the three grumbled.

"I assure you, I will not." Carrie hoped she didn't just fib. Truth be told, her face was aflame and her stomach threatened to pitch its meager contents.

She rolled up her sleeves and noticed Peyton's eyes had opened and now stared at her. His right eye seeped with green puss, which explained part of the odor rising up from him.

Carrie willed herself to smile. "Peyton." She lifted his hand and sat gingerly on the edge of the cot. "You are safe now. The doctors will make you better. And you'll be fed. Within no time you'll come home." Again, Carrie prayed she didn't lie. However, a heavenly home awaited all believers and Peyton possessed a strong faith—or used to. Did he still?

He stared at her hard and Carrie wondered if he recognized her. His lips moved as if he wanted to speak.

She leaned closer, then closer still, until her ear practically touched his mouth. She held her breath against the stench. A faint whisper tickled her, but then she made out the words, *"My sweet."*

Tears sprang to her eyes and she swallowed a sob. He knew her and yet he was but a half-dead stranger to her.

Even so, she owed him words of undying love. Words she should have said on that fateful October morning. "I love you, Peyton." A tear spilled onto his gaunt face. She wiped it away with her gloved hand. Again, she forced a smile. "You must get well. We're going to have a baby."

Did he understand? He only stared at her as if closing his eyes would make her vanish.

"Ma'am, it's time to get him into surgery."

Carrie stood, gave the orderly a nod, and reluctantly released Peyton's hand. She shed her gloves and tossed them on her other belongings. "I'm ready." She looked at Peyton. "And I shall stay at your side."

Orderlies lifted the cot and carried Peyton toward another part of the hospital. His left eye never strayed from her face. Carrie put on her bravest expression for his benefit as she followed. She could well imagine the horror of what was to come. Removing an eye. Rebreaking a leg. A long journey of recovery would follow and Carrie vowed that Peyton would have the best possible care.

Entering yet another tent, one designated for surgeries, Carrie took in the familiar equipment, the scalpels, knives, bone saws of various sizes and shapes, bone and artery forceps, artery needles, tourniquet screws, scissors, chisels, mallets, drills, retractors, and the like. She prayed for wisdom and strength as she pinned an apron to the bodice of her gown and then tied it around her waist.

As she held the chloroform over Peyton's nose and mouth, she whispered that all would be made right soon and they'd go home to Piccadilly Place where their baby would be born. "A boy, I hope," she added. "With your—."

She'd been about to say "eyes." His beautiful brandy-colored eyes. She tried to swallow away the lump in her throat. But surely Peyton could live normally with one eye. At least he was alive.

Alive!

And suddenly God's peace that passed all understanding soothed Carrie's taut nerves. She calmed, and her shaky hand stilled. In that moment, she knew she was right where she was supposed to be—

In the center of God's will, and by her husband's side.